God of Magic Child of Light

Book Two: Merlin in Moab

For Melissa
Best Wishes
Caryl Say

CARYL SAY

Contact the author via e-mail at carylsay.author@gmail.com

Editing and interior design by Richard Mahler
Relham LLC
P.O. Box 1055
Silver City, NM 88062
www.relham.com
575.534.4841

ISBN-13: 978-1535316682
ISBN-10: 1535316683

ACKNOWLEDGMENTS

There are many people who I would like to thank for their unwavering support of my literary efforts.

First of all, Lisa Albert, Jean Carson and Amy DiMauro deserve a huge thank you for reading through the manuscript, making corrections and providing constructive criticism. Publishing this book would not have been possible without them.

Thanks to Carol Martin, fellow rockhound and voracious reader, for pointing out that Merlin needed to finish Derek's sorcerer's staff.

Thanks to my friend Nancy Williams of the Celtic Nook and Mrs Morrison's Shortbread, for allowing me to sign my books in her booth at numerous Celtic Festivals.

Thanks to Ann Welshko and the Moab Library for inviting me to participate in the 2016 Comic Con.

Thanks to Ann Perri for creating my Facebook author page.

Also, I want to thank Ginger Aaron for the fabulous front cover design and author photo, and for helping me manage my Facebook author page.

And, of course, a big "Thank You" to everyone for buying my books! I'm so glad that you enjoy my stories.

Last, but not least, thanks to Peggy Dimauro, my sister and intrepid traveling companion, for our wonderful adventures in Scotland, Ireland and Wales in the past year.

Caryl Say's MERLIN IN MOAB series

The Heart of Magic
God of Magic, Child of Light

CHAPTER 1

January 27   Late Afternoon

I AM MERLIN AMBROSIUS, *the immortal Sorcerer of King Arthur's Court, also known as Myrddin Emrys, the Welsh god of magic and healing.* I grinned as I imagined introducing myself to my wife's parents.

"Merlin, I hope you're not serious. You can't tell them any of that!" Emily exclaimed aloud from the kitchen, appalled that I would even think of revealing myself to her mother and father. She certainly had improved over the past six months in hearing my thoughts, even when I wasn't projecting them.

"No, of course I wouldn't do such a thing," I reassured her. "But..."

...it's fun to think about what their reaction would be, Derek finished for me silently, and smirked.

Childish, is what it is, Emily thought.

I smiled and didn't respond as the good-natured bickering continued telepathically between the two of them. I loved them both dearly, but there were times when I wished they would stay out of my thoughts; privacy was a rare commodity in our family. I knew that I could easily block their thoughts, but I did enjoy feeling so connected to them.

I stood in the living room of our new home with my week-old daughter in my arms, looking out the living room window at the light dusting of snow in the front yard. There wasn't much in the way of landscaping, so the snow rested on bare dirt and rocks, and I knew that Em and I would have to continue our recent discussion about what we would plant in the spring. I favored native plants, and she had her heart set on a lawn and a shade tree, so currently we were at an impasse. It didn't make sense to me to plant something that wouldn't normally grow in this area, which was considered high desert. But I loved my wife and would probably acquiesce to her desires. I just wanted her to be happy.

Across the street in the house next to Derek's, a man started to close the drapes in his front room, but stopped long enough to give me a wave. I raised my hand briefly in acknowledgement, and I saw him nod and finish his task. He had been kind enough to help out when we moved in, and I searched my memory for his name. Rich? No, it was Rod. One of these days, I would have to invite him over for coffee.

I decided to close our drapes as well, as the large front window was transmitting the cold winter air into the room despite the fact that it was supposed to be double-paned. As the soft heather-colored fabric slid across the expanse, I could already feel a difference in the room temperature.

Behind me, Derek finished hanging the framed, enlarged wedding photo he had promised us almost seven months ago, then hurried out through the kitchen to the attached garage to put away the tools. He wasn't the only one who had procrastinated on fulfilling a promise. I had intended to create his sorcerer's staff out of a special oak branch we'd found on the trip back from Las Vegas the previous summer, but had yet to do so.

As I turned to inspect the portrait, my mind drifted to more immediate matters. I was feeling increasingly nervous about the arrival of my in-laws, which was most ironic. I could face an irate griffon or a fire-breathing dragon, yet I had qualms about meeting Emily's parents.

Just then, Lumina cooed and sighed and I looked down at her angelic little face. My heart skipped a beat as I felt a gentle nudge in my mind, and a sense of innocence, and I knew my child was already trying to communicate with me. Was I as precocious as this at one week old? Only my mother knew the earliest details of my childhood, but she had perished in the year AD 435, so I wouldn't be able to ask her. I had only recently recalled that her name was Lilith Ambrosius, the daughter of a

Welsh princess and a Roman centurion, and that she'd had glossy black hair and eyes as blue as the summer sky. While I hoped that additional memories would surface in time, this most recent one finally made sense of my last name, which certainly wasn't Welsh, and of my above-average height—my Roman grandfather Flavius Ambrosius had been even taller than I at six feet four.

Hearing my wife moving around in the kitchen, I came back to the present from my musings of the ancient past and considered the more recent events that had led up to this day. At my urging, Emily had reluctantly contacted her parents in December to let them know she had married and was pregnant. They had immediately informed us that they would be arriving soon after the baby's birth to stay for a week or two. I hoped I wasn't going to regret that decision.

"I knew I shouldn't have contacted them," Emily muttered as she bustled around the kitchen in her snug jeans and a pink sweater that strained across her full breasts.

I smiled, thoroughly in love with my wife no matter what mood she was in. We had known one another since April of the previous year and she had never once confided in me about the reason she and her parents were estranged, and no hint of family discord had been revealed through our bond. She had briefly mentioned that she didn't meet their expectations, but I couldn't believe that was the only thing that was amiss. I wondered if they felt slighted that we had not invited them to our simple wedding ceremony in Las Vegas the preceding July.

Traveling by car from northern California, Jack and Rae Crandall were scheduled to arrive at any moment. Emily was frantically trying to prove that she was the perfect wife and mother by putting the finishing touches on an already immaculate house, and on a sumptuous feast that she had been preparing for hours: honey-glazed baked ham, scalloped potatoes, steamed broccoli, salad and homemade bread, not to mention apple pie for dessert. My mouth watered as the delectable scents wafted through the house.

Fortunately, Lumina's birth had been easy, uncomplicated and thoroughly magical. She had teleported directly into my arms from her mother's womb. Since Emily had virtually no delivery trauma from which to recover, she thought nothing of plunging determinedly into cleaning and cooking for her parents' visit. I would have been more than happy to help her, but she'd insisted on doing it all herself.

Derek sauntered back into the living room just as a car pulled up in front of the house, and he unobtrusively pulled the drape aside so he could peek out the window. He intoned, "They're he-re," then looked at me with his warm brown eyes and quick smile and winked. "Good luck," he whispered.

"I heard that! Damn it, I'm not ready!" Emily fumed and growled.

"Would you be ready for them in an hour? Or two hours?" I asked, reasonably.

"No, I guess not," she agreed reluctantly, but stayed where she was.

"So, come in here and let's greet your parents," I insisted. As she walked hesitantly out of the kitchen and approached me, I kissed her cheek, handed her the baby and went to open the front door, switching on the porch light as I did so. It was nearly five o'clock, and the winter sun had already set behind the Rim. This seemingly sheer wall of red rock was only a few hundred feet from our house, and stretched for miles north to south on the westerly edge of Moab, Utah.

I hoped I appeared more confident than I felt. I glanced down at my attire and realized I probably should have worn slacks and a dress shirt instead of the everyday jeans and T-shirt that I had on, but it was too late to change now. I quickly reviewed my own personal tally sheet in my mind: *god of magic—check; ancient sorcerer—check; husband and father—check;*

son-in-law—oh, bollocks!

As the door swung inward and revealed the older couple standing on the porch, I wondered why she was so afraid of them. The gray-haired man was about six feet in height and very thin, his shoulders were rounded and he seemed to have a permanent frown. He had probably been at least my height and over two hundred pounds before he had allowed the cares of the world to drag him down. The woman was perhaps an inch shorter than Emily's own five feet nine inches tall. She seemed tired, distracted and nervous, her tinted reddish-blonde hair limp and lifeless, her face sagging with unhappiness. I decided to go into their thoughts later and find out more about them. Despite the fact that it was rude to enter someone's mind without permission, I felt that I was justified in doing so. After all, I was protecting our family.

No, Merlin, please don't. I'll tell you about them later, okay? I promise, Emily pleaded silently.

We'll see, Em; I may not be able to wait that long.

I greeted Emily's parents with a welcoming smile. I offered my hand to Mr. Crandall, who shook it half-heartedly. He then spoke to me in a rough voice that told me he was now, or had been at one time, a smoker.

"Call me Jack. No need to be so formal."

He extricated his hand from mine so quickly that I had no time to form an impression of him, other than the fact that he was quite unhappy.

Em's mother gave me a quick, unseeing glance and said flatly, "Nice to meet you," before heading straight for Emily and the baby.

"Hi Mom, hi Dad, it's, uh, great to see you," said Emily brightly, sounding anything but pleased to see them.

"Oh, let me see that darling child," Mrs. Crandall gushed, reaching for the tiny baby held so carefully, and possessively, in her mother's arms.

"Her name is Lumina, Mom," Em said. "And she's only a week old, so *please* be careful of her." I could hear the fear in her voice and I felt her incipient panic as she reluctantly handed our child to the older woman.

Em, you don't have to let her hold the baby if you feel it's not safe.

She's so little and fragile—I would probably freak out no matter who held her. It's just that there are so many things...oh, maybe I'm being paranoid.I haven't seen my parents for at least ten years. I'd like to think that things have changed, but I just don't know...

Whatever you decide, sweetheart.

Then, I overheard Derek introducing himself to Jack as Em's best friend and my distant cousin. He and I exchanged a wry look—obviously he couldn't say that he was my son. For one thing, he didn't really look like me. Although Derek's face was shaped very much like mine, rather narrow with high cheek-bones, his coloring, features and build reflected his mother's side of the family: Light, sandy-brown hair and brown eyes, aquiline nose, tall, muscular and, according to the young ladies in town, very handsome. And, of course, the main reason Derek could not claim me as his father was that we appeared to be about the same age. But appearances can be deceiving. I looked like I was in my early thirties, but I was actually approaching 1,600 years old.

I returned my attention to Em's mom and decided I'd have to keep an eye on her. Something about her was definitely off, and I was ready to stop time and take my daughter out of her arms if necessary. I hoped I wouldn't have to do that, however, as the consequences for using my god powers could be severe.

"Oh, she's just the sweetest wittle creature that ever lived," Rae baby-talked, and held Lumina so tight that she was starting to fuss.

I couldn't wait any longer to rescue the poor child.

"Why don't I put her down for a nap," I suggested, "and we can all have a glass of wine before dinner and get to know each other?"

I gently retrieved the baby from my mother-in-law's desperate grasp and settled her against my chest.

Emily relaxed somewhat and gave me a grateful look as she steered her parents to comfortable chairs. She then rushed out to the kitchen for the plate of cream crackers and gouda cheese she had assembled earlier. Emily also opened and began serving the chilled Pinot Grigio.

She had gone to so much trouble to please them that I hoped that her parents would appreciate her efforts. I smiled encouragingly as she offered the appetizers, and couldn't help but notice that her own smile looked a bit tremulous.

As I turned away and walked down the hallway to our bedroom, I spoke quietly to my daughter and thanked her for being patient with Rae. I sensed a slight, gentle response from the drowsy baby and lightly kissed her cheek as I carefully placed her in the cradle, covering her with a soft blanket. Suddenly, I remembered putting Derek down in a much rougher cradle with a coarse-textured blanket, many centuries ago. Of course, his birth name was actually Emrys; the change to "Derek" came later. I treasured every one of the infrequent memories I had of that time with my son. I hadn't even known we were that closely related until the previous July when my father, the Welsh god Llyr, had finally revealed the truth. In the fifth century, he had blocked my memories of my son and his mother, and had brought baby Emrys to the year 1985 from AD 442, knowing that to fulfill destiny's plan, Derek would have to grow up here, and we would have to meet as adults. I sighed, still regretting that I had missed his childhood.

I stared at my baby girl, vowing that I would not miss a single day of her life if I could help it. I started to create the dim light orb I always used as a night-light, but with mortals in the house, I decided a regular mundane light might be more prudent. I conjured one and plugged it in, then backed out of the bedroom and closed the door quietly.

As I started down the hallway towards the living room, I paused to listen to the conversation for a time before rejoining the family. Because of our bond, I was able to See everything through Emily's eyes, and to a lesser extent through Derek's. As it turned out, there was little interaction between Emily and her parents. Derek was valiantly trying to cover the awkwardness with tales of incidents that had occurred at Arches National Park, where he worked as a law enforcement ranger.

"And then there was the time when someone was so engrossed in the scenery that he drove right off the park road and got hung up on some blackbrush," Derek chuckled, as he remembered the incident, and then paused, as there was no reaction to his humorous narrative.

Dad, please get in here—I know you're there! This get-together is a big disaster.

I'll be there in a few minutes, I responded silently, hoping to sense something, anything, from these people. I concluded that the best way to determine what was going on was to find an excuse to touch each of them for longer than a simple handshake.

Finally, Emily stood up, admitting defeat at least temporarily, and said to her parents with a forced smile, "Well, let's get you settled in and then I'll put dinner on the table. How does that sound?" She tried to be cheerful as they continued to sit and stare at her, barely nodding in agreement to her suggestions.

I had heard enough and strode into the living room, rousing Jack to go outside with me to his car and retrieve their luggage. As he unlocked the big Chrysler, and we proceeded to unload the items he wanted to bring in, I attempted to engage him in conversation.

"I hope that you had a pleasant trip, Jack. Did you experience any delays due to inclement weather?" I asked.

"Well, we made it, although we got caught in a blizzard driving over Donner Pass, and I-80 was icy coming into Salt Lake City," he grumbled. "If it had been up to me, we would have flown and be done with it, but oh, no, Rae wanted to drive so she could see the scenery. Of course, I did all the driving, and she slept most of the way." Then, he fell silent as we brought the suitcases in and deposited them in the guest bedroom, which was tastefully decorated in restful shades of blue and boasted a queen-sized bed, a large dresser and a cozy sitting area. He grunted as I clapped my hand on his shoulder companionably. I deliberately left it there for several seconds and used my powers to quickly reach into his mind. I discovered a weak and weary human being who desperately wanted to reconnect with his child, but who had no idea how to break through the barriers erected over a lifetime of misunderstandings and mistakes. No enchantments there, just human frailty. And I sensed no connection to the Fae in his background, so Rae must be the one descended from the Elves.

I escorted my father-in-law back out to the living room and assured him that I would get him something stronger than wine if he desired it. He glanced at me for a moment and nodded, grateful for the consideration, and then he looked away quickly as if he was afraid to see what was really in my eyes. Little did he know. And in not-so-blissful ignorance, he sat down to await his drink. As I turned away, I saw him glance with distaste at my T-shirt. As many people were inclined to do, he judged me by my attire.

I walked into the kitchen in search of liquor, wondering if Em and her mother had had a chance to talk yet. Apparently they hadn't, as they were studiously ignoring each other. I searched through the liquor cabinet, selected a bottle and a glass, and poured a scotch, neat.

"Jack is having a whiskey; can I get either of you something else to drink?"

"No thanks, Mer…Michael, I'll stick with my wine, and I think Mom still has some left in her glass, so she's okay too." *Shit, I almost called you Merlin!*

Relax, love, this situation isn't as desperate as you seem to think. Let me take your mom into the living room and talk to her while you finish up in here. Is that alright?

Emily sighed and then nodded her head, knowing what I was going to do and apparently resigned to it.

"Come, Rae," I said. "Let's go in and join Jack and Derek, shall we?"

As I calmly guided my mother-in-law into the living room with one hand splayed against her back, I suddenly felt a rush of unfocused Fae energy emanating from her, which was keeping her unsteady and confused. I wondered how long she had been experiencing this energy surge. It was intense and, I would imagine, disturbing. No wonder she was acting erratically.

"Here we go, just have a seat and relax—dinner will be served momentarily." I guided the woman to one of our plush armchairs then handed Jack his drink. As I looked at Rae, I realized that even though she was centuries younger than I, she seemed much older.

Can you sense the Fae energy in her? It's causing a great deal of pain and confusion in her mind. Don't you feel it? I asked my wife, curious why she hadn't mentioned it.

Feel what? Emily asked distractedly as she continued to bustle industriously around the kitchen. Finally, she let her guard down and opened her senses to her mother's thoughts and emotions. *Oh, my God! I…I had no idea. Oh, poor Mom…no wonder she's been acting so weird.* Emily immediately stopped what she was doing, walked into the living room and stood next to me, staring helplessly at her mother, who looked up at her with a puzzled frown. *Merlin, what can we do? Can you help her?*

I will try, my love, but she is your mother and you share the Fae ancestry. You might be able to help her better than I can.

At least put both Mom and Dad in some kind of suspended state so that they're not aware of what we're doing, Emily beseeched me silently, her expressive hazel eyes looking directly into my own. She still wasn't entirely comfortable with her own powers.

Honey, I can do that for your dad, but your mom may need to be conscious for us to help her. Besides, being Fae, I don't think she'd react too well to my enchantment.

My wife pursed her lips, and then finally nodded her agreement, so I went ahead and placed a spell on Jack, assuring that he would be unaware of the proceedings. I retrieved the drink from his unresponsive hands and set it down carefully on the table.

Derek, who had been quietly observing the drama and listening to our silent conversation, got up from his chair and gently put his arms around his friend. *We'll be right here with you, Em. You can't let her go on sufferin', can you? You may not get along, but she's your mom. I never knew my birth mother, and I wish I'd had the chance to know her. So you're lucky yours is still around. Am I right, Stepmom?* Derek said to her telepathically.

Emily grinned weakly and nodded, appreciating the irony. Derek really didn't like the fact that, although they were the same age, he was her stepson and she usually teased him about it unmercifully. She took a deep breath and pulled away from him.

Okay, here goes...

"Mom, I love you and I just want to help you. Please tell me the truth," Emily said, looking deeply into her mother's eyes. "Do you remember that we're Fae, that we have Elven blood in our family?"

Rae looked blankly at Emily and said defiantly, "I don't know what the *hell* you're talking about! I'm just *fine*... Why is your father staring into space like that? Jack? Jack!" She became increasingly agitated and Em seemed to lose control of the situation.

"Mom, I'm just—Mom, you need to listen to me. Oh, crap," she said, frustrated.

Do you want me to take over?

Yes, please, Emily sighed. *I just have too many hang-ups about her to be objective—or patient, for that matter.*

I grabbed a stool and sat down in front of the woman, gently grasping her forearms. "Rae, look at me," I commanded in my Voice, exerting control over her psyche.

Unable to resist the compulsion, she looked reluctantly into my eyes and then gasped as she sensed the power I wielded.

"Rae, how came you to be under the influence of this Fae magic?"

"I… do…not…remember." Her face flushed with the effort it took to answer me. I realized that I might have to utilize my god powers in order to help her, but I hesitated to do so after the problems I had caused last summer. I had essentially flaunted my godhood in front of mortals, and according to the one God, I had caused an imbalance in the universe. But since then, I had learned well how to control that part of myself. I did *not* want to be exiled to the realm of the gods for eternity, leaving my body and my family behind; my quest for restoring the Once and Future King abandoned.

I decided first of all to go deep within my own being, and then initiate the journey that would reveal Rae's true self. I had done this with both Ryan and Gary the previous year when they had not remembered who they were: Sir Lancelot and Sir Gawain, formerly in King Arthur's service. In the past, the other person involved in the inner exploration had also learned *my* secrets, but I now knew how to keep my own true nature well hidden.

I expected to encounter a blank, impenetrable wall in

Rae's being, but that did not happen. I realized what the problem was as I traveled through her inner self. Over the years, my mother-in-law had subconsciously denied her heritage time after time. When her powers demanded to be recognized, she would push them away and try to cover them up. She had created her own blockage by continually denying and refusing to use her magic. Thankfully, I would not have to resort to drastic measures to resolve this situation.

I sent soothing thoughts to Rae as I prepared to unblock her powers and return her awareness of them. I positioned my hands so that my fingers spanned her cranium, making sure that there was adequate contact at her temples. And then, I used my magic to break through her self-imposed prison and neutralize the excess energy.

Emily had been present in my mind the entire time that I had been exploring her mother's being, and it was a revelation for her—she had never suspected the reason for Rae's disturbing behavior.

Finally, Rae opened her eyes, and they were clear and aware. She smiled at me, looking years younger.

"Thank you for helping me, Michael," said Rae. "I never could have freed myself."

She glanced at her daughter. "Emily, you should have told me you married a man with magic."

"Mom, you weren't yourself, and it's been more than ten years since I felt comfortable confiding in you. Besides, you'd never mentioned that we were anything other than human. I certainly didn't remember. It was such a shock when Merlin told me that I was part Elf that I had a hard time accepting it. Oh, Mama, I've missed you so much!" Emily cried and hugged her.

Oh, bollocks, she just called me by my real name. I hoped that Rae hadn't noticed. I got to my feet and glanced at Derek. His eyes were huge as he looked back at me and thought, *Aw, shit!* Jack was still under the spell I had cast, so I didn't have to worry about him. But it would have been easier to fix this if he'd been the one witnessing Emily's faux pas, as I could have just used my forgetting spell. Unfortunately, my spells that worked well on humans weren't compatible with Fae physiology, so making Rae forget wasn't an option. I'd had months to work on Fae-compatible spells, but had been too busy living a normal life as an expectant dad to complete them. I should have made the time.

"I've missed you too, darling, more than I can say," my mother-in-law said as she enfolded Em in her arms. My hopes that she had not heard my name were dashed as she looked over Emily's shoulder at me. I saw shock, recognition, and amazement in her reddish-brown eyes.

"Okay, I need to get dinner on the table," Emily said happily. She slipped out of Rae's grasp and went out to the kitchen, so wrapped up in the joy of reconnecting with her mother that she did not feel my unease. My wife was totally oblivious to the blunder she had made. Derek followed her and gave me a questioning look as he walked by.

"You are he…you are the Merlin of legend, aren't you? The Sorcerer of Camelot? How is this possible?" Rae asked, gazing at me in wonder while Emily set the table in the dining area.

It seemed that my earlier fantasy had just become reality, and I debated on the correct course of action. For some reason, it felt right that I should take a chance and tell her everything. I could sense Derek's surprise at my decision. *Sometimes, Derek, you just have to take a leap of faith.*

I took a deep breath and told her the truth. "Yes, Rae, I am indeed King Arthur's Merlin, and I'm the son of a god, and thus immortal. That is the reason I'm still alive after all these centuries. But please, don't share this information with anyone, Mom—is it alright if I call you that?"

Rae was stunned as I revealed the truth about myself, but

recovered enough to answer my question. Yes, of course, you may call me 'Mom,' Merlin, but perhaps 'Rae' would be more appropriate. After all, you must be considerably older than I am."

I smiled. "Yes, considerably. You're right, of course; it could be a bit awkward. Do you mind telling me how you recognized me?"

"My powers may be a bit rusty, but as soon as Emily said your name, I saw the truth of it in your eyes. My God, my daughter is married to the greatest sorcerer who ever lived," she said, shaking her head in disbelief. "Please don't worry, Merlin—I will guard your secret well."

We looked at each other silently for a few moments and I glanced away before it could become something more.

"When I met Emily last year, I had no intention of revealing myself to her, but she and I developed an attraction that could not be denied. And then she guessed my true name. Perhaps I had subconsciously given her clues to my identity, because I now know that it was my destiny to fall in love with her." I stopped and reflected a moment on how much my life had changed because of her love. "Perhaps having you know me was predestined as well."

"You would know that better than I. But I consider myself incredibly fortunate to have met you. Does Emily's friend Derek know who you really are?" Rae asked, and then realized her error. "Oh, but of course he would, he's a relative of yours. I believe he said that the two of you are cousins?"

I laughed. "Actually, he's my son, so yes, he knows who I am."

The look on her face was priceless; that knowledge seemed to shock her more than knowing who *I* was.

"But you two look so close to the same age. How…? I don't understand," she exclaimed, confused.

"I know, but remember, I am much older than I look,

and Derek was actually born in the fifth cent—"

I was interrupted suddenly by a loud clatter as Emily dropped the silverware and groaned, "I did *what*?" Derek apparently had informed her that she'd unwittingly revealed my name to her mother a few minutes ago.

Then, I thought of something else and turned back to Rae. "Does your husband know that you and Emily have Elven ancestry?"

She nodded. "Yes, I told him years ago when Emily was just a little girl. She'd started humming, as children do, and she made one of her toys float in the air. Jack went berserk and demanded that I tell him everything. But once I had told him, he insisted that I never use my powers again, and that I discourage Emily from using hers. He said it was unnatural, an abomination—which was ridiculous, of course; how could something I was born with be unnatural? I should have left him then, but I loved him and I was so afraid of being a single parent. Over the years, Emily forgot about what she could do and felt more and more resentful of both of us. Once she left home she never looked back. And I had denied my own gifts for so long that, well, you saw how bad it was." She frowned and her eyes filled with tears. "And I couldn't *fix* it." She excused herself, hurrying down the hall and into the bathroom.

I felt sorry for her, but I knew that I couldn't help her come to terms with her feelings—she would have to do that herself. I got up and went into the kitchen, whereupon Emily threw herself into my arms.

"I'm so sorry; I didn't mean to tell her your name," she whispered.

I held her against me and smoothed her hair. "It's alright, Em, your family has kept its own secrets for a long time. I don't think we have to worry about your mom keeping mine. Even though your dad didn't hear what was said, I'm going to have a little chat with him anyway. Since he's human, I can always make him forget, if necessary."

She nodded and reached up to caress my face. "I love you, magic man."

"I love you too, wife," I whispered as I kissed her sweet lips, and then I left the room to confront Jack Crandall.

CHAPTER 2

January 27 Early Evening

I STRODE INTO THE LIVING ROOM, a man on a mission, wishing just for a moment that I was back in my peaceful, solitary cave. I removed the spell that I had placed on my father-in-law and announced abruptly, as he blinked and reached for his scotch, "Jack, we need to talk. Let's go into the den for a moment to give us some privacy." I was trying hard to be patient and understanding, but I was upset with this ignorant man for hurting my wife and her mother, just because they were different.

He tossed the whiskey down his throat in one swallow and frowned in confusion. Then, as he registered my peremptory tone of voice, he slammed his glass down on the table. "Excuse me? What the *fuck* is going on here?" He looked around and noticed that the two of us were alone in the living room and he charged out of his seat like an angry bull. "Where is my wife? And who the hell do you think you are, ordering me around?" he blustered, straightening up to his full height.

"Be very careful, Mr. Crandall. Greater men than you have regretted speaking to me so disrespectfully," I said, keeping my voice low and even, holding onto my own temper with difficulty. Quickly, I stepped behind him and took hold of his shirt collar in one hand and his belt in the other. When he realized what I'd done, he bellowed in fury and tried to pull away; unsuccessfully, as I had initiated a restraining spell. As I guided the combative man down the hallway and into the room we used as a combination office, den and library, I was grateful that we had decided on a larger house so that we had this extra space. I shut the door behind us as my father-in-law continued to struggle against the spell, thinking that I was physically restraining him.

He grumbled and muttered under his breath, and I was tempted to muzzle him with yet another spell. I was tired of his grousing.

"What is the meaning of this, young man? You may be my son-in-law, but I warn you not to mess with me—you will be very sorry if you do," Jack growled.

I took a deep breath and tried to remember that this person was covering up his fear and insecurity with anger and resentment, and it would not help the situation for me to respond in kind unless I absolutely had to. But I was certainly tempted.

"Making threats will not help your case, believe me. Sit down a moment, as we need to discuss something that you will probably not be very happy about," I said, noticing that instead of sitting, he stood defiantly in front of the chair with his arms crossed over his chest and a scowl upon his face. "When I first met Emily she never mentioned her parents, and while I thought it most odd, I left it up to her to tell me about you in her own time. Then, after we got married and several…events…occurred, she indicated that there were hard feelings between the three of you. Only today have I learned the truth of your estrangement from each other. My wife has been so traumatized by her early life that she still hasn't told me everything. A few minutes ago, Rae revealed to me that she has, shall we say, a special gift, just as your daughter has. And she told me that, years ago, you had forced both of them to deny their heritage—to deny their magic and their Fae ancestry—causing anguish, resentment and strife in your family."

"That Fae stuff is *bullshit*. There's no such thing as magic—it's the work of the devil! And how is this any of your damn business, Mr. Reese?"

I raised my eyebrows. "It's my business because I'm married to your daughter, whom I love very much, and we just had a baby together. Your daughter and granddaughter are magical beings, Jack, and denying it isn't going to make it go away.

So I suggest that you try to open your mind and heart and allow yourself to accept the truth."

"And what would you know about this magical crap anyway?" he snarled.

I burst out laughing, throwing him totally off guard. "Oh, Jack, it's funny that you should ask that." I glanced at the light switch, throwing the room into darkness, and then I raised my arms and whispered: "*Caeruleum igne.*" This caused a bright blue fire to arc over my head between my outstretched hands. I silently conjured the traditional garb of a sorcerer to create a more intense effect, and with my face partly shadowed and my hair moving in ebony waves as if under water, the magical energy surged powerfully around me.

Jack's indrawn breath sounded harsh as he faced this manifestation of his fear. "No!" He backed up and fell into the chair behind him.

I must have appeared to him as the epitome of evil, and I had to smile to myself. But I could not bring myself to torture this pathetic individual any longer, so I released the fire, dampened the energy, and allowed the overhead light to come back on. I sat down on the corner of the desk, still in my sorcerer's robe, then crossed my arms over my chest and looked at him expressionlessly, waiting to see what he would do.

His voice quavered as he asked, "Wha…what are you?"

"Isn't it obvious? I'm a sorcerer, Jack, a person who has magical powers." I'd almost said human being, which wasn't entirely true. "Your wife and daughter have Elven blood, so their magic is a little different than mine. They're powerful, Jack, but they won't hurt you." I paused a moment before I said gently, "They love you."

"You're a *demon*!" He spat at me, practically frothing at the mouth.

"Actually, I thought that was true at one time, but in reality, I am a humble servant of the one God," I said, stretching the truth a bit and hoping that I wouldn't pay dearly for that statement. I could almost hear Llyr groaning in exasperation.

Jack just sat there gaping at me, at a loss for words.

Emily, bring your mother in here, please. And Derek, you might as well come too. We'll have a little family bonding time. I smiled grimly at my father-in-law, which made him even more nervous.

I could Hear the three of them coming down the hall, whispering softly, wondering what I was up to. *Merlin is helping Dad, I'm sure of it*, I heard Emily communicate silently to Derek.

A moment later, the door opened and in walked my wife, my son and my mother-in-law. I noticed Derek staring at my clothing. *Nice robe*, he said silently, trying not to smile.

Jack leaped out of his chair, sputtering and defensive as if by their very presence he was being accused of something heinous. By this time, it was obvious that Jack was exhausted with the effort of being angry and self-righteous, and I almost felt sorry for him. Almost.

I pulled up a few chairs and indicated that everyone, including Jack, should sit down, while I returned to my perch on the desk. "I'm having a difficult time convincing Jack that it would be in his best interest to accept that his family has magical abilities. If everyone gave a little demonstration, perhaps he would realize that there is nothing to fear. He's already seen an example of my magic, so perhaps each of you would show him something you can do. We are all part of one family now, and the cat is out of the bag, so to speak."

Rae smiled determinedly. "I'll go first. It has been years since I exercised my God-given powers, and it's time." She nodded to me and I dimmed the overhead lights with a glance. Then, she closed her eyes and started humming an odd little tune, in a slightly different way than Emily used her magic. But it worked. A stream of flickering lights began to twist and turn, floating around the room. As it passed by each of us it grew in size, color and brilliance until her humming reached a high note, and then the lights twinkled as they fell around us, eventually disappearing as the sound of humming tapered off. It was beautiful. I brought the room lights up slowly and left them at half the usual intensity.

"Oh, Mom, that was wonderful!" Emily was effusive in her praise, wiping the tears from her eyes.

I stole a glance at my father-in-law to see how he was reacting. His pale blue eyes were wide, and he stared at his wife as if he didn't recognize her. It was very likely that he had never before witnessed her magic.

"Would you like to participate, Derek?" I suggested. "You're part of this family."

"Ah, sure, I can do that," he said slowly, looking around the room for ideas. There were candles scattered about for the times we meditated in here, so he darkened the room with a flick of his wrist, and then glanced deliberately at the candles, causing each one to light and burn brightly, one after the other. Then, he motioned with one hand and all of the candle flames lifted off the candles. The effect was eerily beautiful as the flames danced and moved over our heads.

"*Extinguo,*" he said softly, extinguishing all the flames at once. He brought the lights up with another gesture, then grinned and said, "How's that? I can do somethin' a bit flashier if you'd like me to."

"No, that's fine, Derek, thank you." I noticed that Jack was now extremely nervous and perspiring heavily, and I could sense his heart pounding wildly.

"My turn," said Emily, glancing at me with a smile. I saw in her mind what she planned to do, and I dimmed the lights accordingly. She closed her eyes and started humming her tune, and her long, golden brown hair began to float around her face. Tiny sparks began emanating from her body as power filled her.

Her hair blew back as a sudden breeze danced through the room, and her body glowed. She then spread her arms out and raised them slowly, and pencils, papers, and books—everything loose on the desk—began to sparkle, moving in an intricate dance as they rose towards the ceiling. Her beautiful face alight with pleasure, the humming became a haunting song that rose to a crescendo and then gradually faded away. All the items that had risen into the air settled silently back onto the desktop. When she finally opened her eyes they were shining silver, and she sighed with satisfaction.

"Oh, Emily, that was lovely," Rae whispered in appreciation.

That was great, sweetheart. I was moved almost to tears by the love I felt for her at that moment.

"Daddy, magic is a wonderful gift; it's not inherently evil," she said gently, searching Jack's face.

For the first time I could glimpse a crack in the barrier he had erected within himself so many years ago. I sensed that he was impressed and awed by what his daughter and his wife had just done, but his fear wouldn't allow him to let go and accept the inevitable. And it was also obvious that he felt extremely intimidated by me.

"Jack, dear, it's alright." Rae stood up and held her hand out to her husband.

He slowly arose from his chair and walked over to his wife, embracing her gently. "I do love you, Rae."

Emily smiled and sent me a secret look. All of a sudden, she gasped as Lumina teleported into her arms and started whimpering.

Everyone turned and stared at the tiny baby she held against her breast, and I knew that one more family secret was definitely out in the open now.

"Oh, my God, how…?" Rae whispered.

Without answering, Emily merely said, "Please excuse us, it's time to change Lumina's diaper and feed her." She got up and calmly walked out of the room with the baby in her arms.

"How'd she do that?" Jack asked harshly, fear etched deeply into his face.

"She has magic, Jack, I told you that a few minutes ago. She has inherited my ability to move through space, and we have yet to discover what she has inherited from her mother," I said.

"Dad, I'm gonna go help Emily." And Derek appeared to wink out of existence.

I sighed, as I noticed the startled looks on my in-laws' faces. *Derek, you're not helping.*

CHAPTER 3

January 27 Evening

RAE ABRUPTLY TURNED and left the room, apparently following Emily and Lumina. Jack didn't even notice her departure as he stared at the seat my son had vacated. "Derek just called you 'Dad.' And he disappeared into thin air…" Jack said hoarsely.

Inwardly, I grimaced. My initial reaction was that this visit by my in-laws was an absolute fiasco. I was sorely tempted to wipe his memory of everything he had witnessed, and yet, I had the feeling that the gods had choreographed the entire scenario. Alright, so be it.

"Jack, please listen carefully to what I'm about to tell you, and understand that you must never reveal this information to anyone. Too many people know my secret already." And I began to tell him about myself, about Camelot and King Arthur, about the quest and about Derek's story.

Emily's father looked confused and skeptical as he sought to understand and absorb what I told him. "Okay, let me get this straight: You're really Merlin, King Arthur's sorcerer from Camelot, and you were born in the year AD 420. Derek, the nice young man I met earlier who claimed to be your cousin, is actually your *son,* and he was also born in the fifth century. He was brought to this time by one of the Welsh gods, who happens to be your *father*...You seriously expect me to believe this crock of horseshit?" he roared in frustration.

"I've been very patient with you, Jack, and while I understand that everything I've told you must seem like a fairy tale, it's all true. And I'm most disturbed by your persistent narrow-mindedness," I said grimly. "I will do my best to help you understand, but if you still refuse to accept the truth, I will have to take drastic measures. So, first of all, I am going to show you the reality of this story, and secondly, I am going to help you let go of this unacceptable attitude." I approached Jack purposefully and he tried to cringe away from me. I dispensed with the robe, as I realized that it wasn't helping matters. Then, I stood directly in front of him, positioned my hands firmly on his temples, Looked into his terrified eyes, and began to impart to this exasperating human being an abbreviated version of my story. Only Derek and Emily were aware that I was really the god of magic and healing, and I had no intention of giving Jack that sensitive information. I had learned my lesson the previous summer about broadcasting personal details indiscriminately. And while I was in Jack's mind, I made a much-needed adjustment to his attitude.

When I was finished with him, I dropped my hands and stepped back, hoping that now he would be more accepting of the situation.

Jack slowly lifted his head and met my gaze briefly then glanced away, cringing as he acknowledged that what he had just experienced was the truth. "My God, you *are* real. It's all real. I understand now. You, Derek, Rae and Emily, even Lumina—you're all supernatural, magical. I'm the only one in the family that's totally human. Strangely enough, I almost feel left out." He sat looking down at his lap for a moment, and then glanced up at me with pain in his eyes. "And how in the world can I ever make up for all the suffering I've caused?" His regret and desire to repent seemed sincere; apparently I had succeeded.

"What's past cannot be undone, Jack. Well, actually it can, but not without the direst of consequences. So, the only course of action for you is to do the right thing from now on." I held out my hand and he clasped it like a lifeline. "I'll help you all I can, but you need to talk to Rae and Emily and apologize to them—assure them that you intend to make amends."

Just as I finished speaking, the door opened and Rae, Emily and Derek came back into the room, Lumina swaddled in a blue and yellow blanket and held securely in her brother's arms. The three of them looked at Jack warily, but the expression on his face seemed to reassure them that all was well.

Emily gave a sigh of relief and went to him, hugging him affectionately. "Oh, Daddy, I'm so glad to see that you're feeling better."

"Thanks to your husband, my dear. How in the world did you end up married to a sorcerer?" Jack Crandall said in disbelief, glancing over at me with a grudging respect.

"It was ordained by the gods, Dad."

"Emily, there are no 'gods,' that's just myth and folklore; there's only the one true God," Jack said tightly.

"The gods certainly *do* exist!" she exclaimed indignantly. "My father-in-law Llyr is a god, and since I've met him, I know that he's real. In fact, my husband—"

I decided to interrupt at this point before my wife gave away the secret of my godhood. "Em, I think perhaps we should try to salvage dinner and then afterwards let your folks rest, love." I could see that there was a great deal of strain showing on Jack's face as he felt more and more challenged to accept what he perceived as religious differences. If he only knew that the God he worshipped reigned supreme over the gods as well.

Emily agreed that we needed to eat, and we all traipsed into the kitchen. Derek placed Lumina in the small crib we kept in the dining area, and we carried the food to the table in serving bowls. I then heated or cooled the various dishes to their appropriate temperatures using magic; it was way too late in the evening to adjust the temperature of the food in the conventional way. If the Crandalls noticed what I did, they made no mention of it. I think their capacity for adapting to new circumstances had been surpassed some time ago.

Dinner conversation was conspicuously absent as we were all too busy eating. The food was delicious, and both

Derek and I had a second helping of the pie. After we had finished the meal and Jack and Rae had retired to the living room with their choice of liqueur, Emily, Derek and I employed our magical abilities to put the food away and clean up the dishes in record time. Afterward, Lumina started to fuss, and Emily picked her up to comfort her. "Merlin, could you…?" Knowing exactly what she wanted, I put my arm around my wife and daughter and teleported the three of us into the bedroom, while Derek retreated to the living room with a cold beer.

"God, that was exhausting," Emily sighed as she turned on the lamp, sat down in the rocking chair near the bed, and quickly bared a breast so that the baby could nurse.

"I know, but you were brilliant, sweetheart," I praised her distractedly as I stared at the taught, blue-veined globe, and the nipple upon which Lumina was sucking lustily. It had been more than six weeks since Emily had felt comfortable making love, and I wasn't sure when she would be able to do so again. I could feel the pressure of my arousal building to an uncomfortable degree, and I knew that my wife could sense my desire.

"Soon, magic man," she whispered. "When Mom and Dad go to bed, maybe between us we can make sure my body is healed and back to normal. I really miss having you inside me."

My mouth felt dry and I could hardly speak as her words stoked the sexual inferno in me. "Yes, love. I miss that very much also."

As the baby drifted into sleep and released the distended nipple, Emily adjusted her bra, then quickly changed Lumina's diaper at the changing table and slipped a clean onesie on her relaxed little body. She gently placed her in the cradle and covered her with a warm blanket. After watching her sleep for a few moments, Em kissed Lumina's velvety cheek lovingly and caressed her dark hair. The baby had emerged from the womb with a cap of thick, dark brown hair, more than most babies had, I would wager, but then, she was a child born of immortal parents, so I expected her to be special in all ways. The little night-light I had conjured earlier in the evening was still illuminated, and as we walked out of the room, I flicked my wrist and magically extinguished the bedside lamp.

We stood in the hallway for a moment and Emily stared at my crotch.

"Uh, it isn't going to get any smaller if you keep staring at it like that, wife," I said, clearing my throat. I ached, I wanted her so badly.

Emily grinned. "Okay, I'll just go out and chat with my folks and I'll see you in a minute, big guy." She winked at me as she turned and walked seductively down the hall and into the living room.

I immediately started thinking about a cold shower. I heard Derek in my mind speculating on my absence, and then I could sense his amusement, as he realized why I had not yet joined them. That portion of my anatomy certainly had a mind of its own, and I finally had to employ a bit of magic to get my erection to subside. Eventually, I conjured a snifter of brandy and walked into the living room, ready to engage in desultory conversation.

Around ten fifteen, Derek yawned and declared that he wanted to make it an early night, departing immediately thereafter. And by the time Emily's parents were settled in, and we had locked up for the night, it was just after eleven o'clock. At this point, we were so anxious to touch each other that we didn't care what time it was. We left a trail of clothing from our bedroom into the master bathroom, and just for a moment we paused, gazing in fascination at each other's naked bodies. Em's soft hands traveled hungrily across my chest, stroking the dark hair around my nipples that arrowed smoothly down to my waist, and as she continued down to my groin and firmly gripped the object of her desire, I sucked in a breath as my arousal grew exponentially.

Then, it was my turn to explore her womanly curves, recently enhanced by her pregnancy. She was a little self-conscious of the weight she had gained, but to me she couldn't be more desirable; she was perfect.

As we entered the extra-large shower, kissing and stroking each other with some urgency, we felt our bond drawing us even closer together until our beings merged. We stood under the pulsing hot water with our arms wrapped tightly around each other, and together we explored Em's inner body. We found organs, glands and tissues that still needed to heal after nurturing the baby for all those months, and I used the white Light of the gods to make the necessary healing adjustments.

"Oh, honey, that feels so much better, thank you," Emily sighed in relief.

"My dear wife, you are most welcome," I said softly, intensely aroused again, my erection pressing insistently against her abdomen. We kissed deeply, inhaling each other's scent, and I was aware of her firm, taut breasts pressed against me. She had always been generously endowed, but with nursing the baby her breasts were even larger, the nipples huge and dark. I dipped my head and took each one into my mouth in turn, sucking gently. Emily moaned as the stimulation of her breasts created a tugging sensation within her womb. Our inner connection was so complete that I felt that sensation as soon as she did. My testicles tightened, my erection throbbed and my breathing became ragged, the pleasure was so intense. Then, as she looked into my eyes, she got down on her knees in front of me and took me into her warm mouth, causing me to inhale sharply and groan with anticipation. Knowing I would not last long if she continued on her present course, I finally pulled her up against me and caressed her intimately. She gasped with pleasure and I knew that she was more than ready for me to take her.

The urge to bury myself inside of her, to connect our bodies, was overwhelming. "Oh, gods, Emily, I need you," I whispered urgently, gently squeezing the rounded swell of her buttocks.

"Yes, my love, now, please," she breathed, and threw her arms around my neck as I lifted her up, braced her against the wall of the shower and slid into her. She gasped and cried out my name as I pulled out and thrust into her again. Her tight, wet heat surrounded me and I groaned at the intense pleasure of it. Her full breasts pressed against me, and with my hardness buried deep inside of her, I felt as if I was receiving that intimate invasion of my own body. I was Merlin and I was Emily at the same time; we merged and separated, giving and receiving. It was a profoundly unique experience and I treasured every moment of it.

Our orgasms happened simultaneously, and we tried to muffle our shouts of completion.

"Oh, my God, that was just amazing! I feel so content and relaxed I don't think I can even get out and dry off," Emily said softly, clinging to me, our bodies still connected as the water cascaded over us.

"I can take care of that." I teleported us out of the shower enclosure and onto the bathmat, turning the water off with a glance, then manifested a giant towel that magically wrapped itself around us.

"Em, that was one of the most exquisite experiences I've ever had," I confessed as I pulled out of her and gently set her down, using the towel to dry us both off. I thought about what I had just experienced and compared it to the way I felt when I used my magic. When I accessed the magical energy inside me and manipulated my power, it created an almost sexual intensity, and there was always a feeling of pleasure and satisfaction involved. But what I shared with my wife was not only about the physical connection between us, the animalistic coupling of bodies, it was about the mingling of our essences, and the feelings we shared through our marital bond. When I had died in the battle with Nimue the previous summer and returned to the realm of the gods, I had been at peace, no longer encumbered with a physical body. However, the lingering emotions and remembrance of the loving bond I had shared with Emily were among the reasons I had returned to the human realm.

"Uh, Merlin, honey…" Emily was trying to get my attention and I realized that I had been standing still, staring into space, with the towel hanging from my left hand.

"I'm sorry, sweetness, I was remembering being in the realm of the gods and longing to come back to you," I said with a smile that gradually became a frown as I noticed her consternation. "Is something wrong?"

"I hope I didn't just get pregnant again," she said in a small, worried voice. "I've heard that a woman is extremely fertile right after giving birth, but I totally forgot about using protection. I do want more kids with you, but not yet!"

The palm of my right hand glowed as I gently placed it on her rounded abdomen, knowing that I would feel the spark of a new life already starting to grow inside her if she was truly pregnant. I would have been happy to welcome another child in a few months, but I could understand her point of view—she wasn't ready.

"You're not pregnant, Emily. And we do not have to use 'protection,' as you call it. Remember, the pills you were using last year had not prevented Lumina's conception, because the gods determined that it was her time to come to this realm. Well, *this* god will make that decision next time. I will not impregnate you again until you tell me you're ready," I said resolutely. "What?"

Emily stood absolutely still, in shock, staring up into my face as she remembered once again who I was, what I was. I was not only her husband Merlin, but also Myrddin Emrys, the god of magic and healing.

Oh, no. "Em, please don't kiss my…ah, gods," I sighed as she sank down to her knees before me and planted several gentle kisses on my feet before resting her forehead on them. "Come on, please get up, Emily." I should have known better than to mention my god status. Recently, she had been so involved with carrying, birthing and taking care of our baby that she saw me only as her "magic man," her husband who happened to be a sorcerer; not as the ancient god that I truly was. And now I had unintentionally reminded her of the truth. I knew she had no control over her response—the strength of her devotion to my god self drew her to my feet any time she recognized me. But it still felt strange to have my wife humbling herself to me.

She finally stood up, her face reflecting an inner light. She threw her arms around me and laughed with joy. "I'm so happy to be married to my very own god, back in your body where you belong. It was the worst two hours of my entire life when you died, Merlin. God, I love you so much…" Her lovely hazel eyes shone with the strength of her emotion as she gazed into mine.

"And I love you more than you'll ever know, Emily," I said gently. "Let's finish up in here and go to bed." I steered her to the sink.

"Okay, magic man," she said affectionately. I marveled at her beauty as she applied night cream to her face, and then dried her luxurious golden brown tresses.

A comb through my own mop of raven-dark hair sufficed, as I had already used a simple drying spell. Finally, we both brushed our teeth and were ready for bed. I chuckled as I remembered the sparseness of bedtime ablutions during my many years in Camelot.

"What's so funny?" Em asked curiously, her eyes roaming admiringly over my naked body. Despite the fact that I was quite sated, I felt the intensity of her gaze on my skin.

"I was remembering the lack of hygiene in the fifth century. I bathed of course, and I know Arthur did, but not every day, and cleaning one's teeth wasn't really a priority for most people."

"I notice that you still have all of yours," Em said, parting my lips with her fingers to examine my dentition.

"Yes, well, you can thank my magic for that." And I walked out of the bathroom, followed by my wife, who swatted my buttocks playfully.

Back in the bedroom, we checked on our sleeping daughter, switched off the lamps, and climbed into bed. I turned over to look at Em in the semidarkness, stroked the silky hair back from her face and looked searchingly into her eyes. "Seriously, Em, I know that it must be difficult to live with me sometimes, knowing who—and what—I really am, but I am so grateful that you love me." I knew that I must sound rather pathetic, but I loved her so much that I truly felt I would rather give up my soul than to ever be parted from her.

Emily's eyes glistened with unshed tears as she sensed my heartfelt but silent declaration, and replied softly, "It *can* be very disconcerting sometimes, knowing that you're so much more than you appear to be, but I do love you, Merlin, so much that sometimes I think I'll die of happiness."

"Well, go ahead if you must," I said facetiously. "After all, you'll just come back to life again." I gently kissed her mouth, and then looked into her eyes questioningly. "Em, why didn't you ask me to heal you right after Lumina was born? Obviously, you must have felt a certain amount of discomfort, even though the birth itself wasn't difficult for you. And we could have made love sooner."

She didn't answer for a moment, apparently gathering her thoughts. "I think that I was so focused on the baby, that the discomfort wasn't important to me. And to be perfectly honest, making love was about the last thing on my mind." She reached out and ran her fingers through my hair, then cupped my cheek. "Don't take it personally, magic man."

I chuckled quietly. "My dear, I was celibate for hundreds of years before I met you, so a few weeks of abstinence really weren't a problem." I kissed her cheek. "Good night, wife. I'll see you in the morning."

Long after Em had gone to sleep, I was still awake, reliving the evening, and then I remembered that Jack had never bothered to apologize to either my wife or her mother. I hoped that he wasn't going to be a problem after all.

A few minutes later, as sleep continued to elude me, I realized that the artificial glare of the night-light annoyed me. I flicked my hand impatiently, turning it off, and then murmured the spell for the soft glow of the night-light orb: "*Mollis lux.*" Ah, much better…

CHAPTER 4

January 28 Morning

SINCE LUMINA HAD AWAKENED us only a few times during the night, we were rested and ready to get up when we heard Emily's parents stirring around eight o'clock the following morning. I had closed up The Moab Herbalist just before Christmas and wasn't intending to re-open the shop until early February, so our days weren't quite as structured as they had been, but Lumina had her own schedule that didn't always coincide with ours.

We both dressed casually in jeans, T-shirts and athletic shoes, and while Emily bathed our daughter, I sauntered out to the kitchen to start the coffee. Ever since my introduction to this tantalizing beverage the previous year, I usually drank six to eight cups per day. Emily and Derek also appreciated a good cup of coffee in the morning, so we had invested in a restaurant-sized coffee machine. If I was a normal man, I would probably have had major stomach issues by now from the excess caffeine and acidity, but since I was anything but normal, I could eat and drink anything I liked without consequences.

As I watched the rich brown liquid begin to fill the glass carafe, I recalled my experiences since April of the previous year: I had awakened in the Crystal Cave after a three hundred-year slumber, traveled to Utah searching (in vain, so far) for the new portal to Avalon, and attempted to discover the identity of the practitioner of dark magic. I had met and married Emily Crandall, been reunited with my son Derek, and had remembered that I was not just a sorcerer; I was actually an ancient god. And finally, I had defeated my nemesis Nimue and then died, returning to the realm of the gods, where I had decided my place was here in the mortal realm with my expectant Elven wife and my son, a sorcerer-in-training. I shook my head and smiled, then took a sip of the fragrant brew that I had just poured into a coffee mug with the name of my shop, The Moab Herbalist, on it. I'd had quite a few of them made, but they had been extremely popular, and I had barely grabbed one for myself before they sold out. I needed to order more, I thought, as I opened the drapes in the living room to let the sun in. As I admired the view of the Rim, I noticed Derek coming out of his house and greeted him silently.

Good morning, Son, I thought you had to work today.

Mornin', Dad. Nope, not 'til tomorrow, so I have a slight reprieve.

Derek paused in the midst of crossing the street and for just a moment his thoughts and feelings were unguarded and I saw myself through his eyes. As he glimpsed me through the window, he saw me as if for the first time, tall and mysterious, my body glowing with the light of the gods. And I felt it as he thrilled once again to the knowledge that I was really his father and that he himself had the gift of magic. But as he remembered the horror of my death after the battle with Nimue, he put away those painful memories that would plague him forever, shaking off his brief moment of melancholy. Then, that introspective moment was over and he continued across the street and started up our concrete walkway.

As he approached the front door I saw him gesture slightly, and the door swung open for him just as my in-laws came down the hallway.

"Good mornin'!" Derek announced as he walked into the house, leaving the door standing open, cold winter air entering with him.

I sighed in exasperation and flicked my wrist at the door, causing it to shut firmly behind my oblivious son.

Jack and Rae echoed, "Good morning," as they watched the magical interaction between Derek and me and the front door.

As Derek and Jack sat down in the living room and started conversing, Rae followed me into the kitchen. She seemed perturbed about something and I sensed that she had somehow overheard us the night before. Her Fae connection with her daughter could have enabled her to hear our postcoital conversation through the guest bathroom wall. Oh, bollocks, now I *would* be getting a visit from Llyr. I just stared at her solemnly as I waited for her to confront me.

"I'm afraid I have a confession to make, Merlin." She paused for a moment, as if trying to find the appropriate words. "I heard you and Emily last night saying some remarkable things, and although I realize it's none of my business, I have to know. Are you truly a god? Was I dreaming that I heard you say that?" Rae asked as she looked intently into my eyes. I glanced away before the Seeing could be triggered. Now that she was feeling better, the woman was not at all shy.

Troubled, I took a deep breath and let it out slowly. I was now in the dubious position of trusting Em's mother with the most important of my secrets.

"You were not dreaming, Rae. My name in this human realm is Merlin Ambrosius, but my true name in the realm of the gods is Myrddin Emrys. I had mentioned that Llyr, my father, is the Welsh god of magic and healing. While temporarily in human form, he impregnated my human mother, so I could be born in this realm in a human body. In truth, *I* am the god of magic and healing, not Llyr. He enjoys standing in for me while I am here on Earth. Perhaps, when the human race is ready, things can be different, but for now…

"In any case, Rae, we never intended for you to hear what we said, and it is obviously information of an extremely sensitive nature, so you must not share it with anyone," I said forcefully.

"Merlin, you are in no danger from me; I will *gladly* keep your secrets. And I won't tell my husband about you being a god—that news would definitely not go over well. Please believe that I didn't mean to eavesdrop, but my newly reinstated relationship with Emily has heightened my senses. I'm truly in awe that you are married to my daughter, and that you have allowed me to know who you are.

"And by the way, I noticed that you're wearing my Fae grandfather's ring as your wedding ring. It seems to fit you perfectly, so it's obvious that you have been accepted by the Elves. The ring has apparently been waiting for you—no one in our family could ever wear it." She looked at me speculatively. "I hope that Em won't be too upset that I know the truth about you...And speaking of my daughter, here she comes with my precious grandbaby."

On that note, having overhead the last few sentences, Emily walked into the kitchen with Lumina in her arms. She smiled widely. "Mom, if my husband trusts you with his secrets, I can do no less. Would you like to hold this little girl while I get breakfast ready? I just fed her so she should be good for a while." She handed the baby to her mom and settled a cloth on her shoulder in case Lumina spit up.

"I'm thrilled to hold her, and I promise that I won't squeeze her so tightly this time," Rae said happily, as she sat down with the baby in her arms, relaxed and competent as only a grandmother could be.

Oh, my God, did I understand correctly? She actually overheard what we said in the bathroom last night? Emily looked at me and grimaced.

The two of us assembled food and cooking utensils and started preparing breakfast as we communicated mentally.

Unfortunately, yes, but we haven't yet had a time-altering visit from Llyr, so apparently this was foretold. Perhaps she needs to know all of my secrets for some reason. She promised she would not share with anyone, not even your father, that

I am a god. I can only imagine how Jack would react to that pronouncement.

At that moment, I sensed that we were about to be visited by all three knights, Lancelot, Percival and Gawain, and I groaned inwardly. Could things get any more complicated? A knock sounded hollowly at the front door.

"Hey, Dad, guess who's here?" Derek called out from the living room. *Do we have enough food to invite the guys for breakfast?*

Emily and I just looked at each other and sighed. They were a regular addition to our family most days, as they came to pay homage to Lumina—and to me.

Sure, Derek, why not? I responded, as I put more bacon on to cook and grabbed another dozen eggs out of the refrigerator, resigned to the ensuing chaos.

"What's going on?" Rae asked curiously, still holding the baby, who seemed to be waiting for the visitors. Emily swore that she was too young to recognize people, but I think she knew her "uncles'" voices.

"We apparently have company," I said.

All three men strode into the kitchen heading straight for the baby, who immediately starting waving her tiny arms and making happy, welcoming sounds.

"Rae, meet our friends Ryan Jones, Gary Gardner, and Percival." I hoped as I introduced them that they wouldn't reveal their true identities until I allowed it.

"It's nice to meet you, gentlemen. Are you all from Moab?" Em's mom asked politely.

Percival immediately spoke up and said in his archaic accent, "I have shared an abode with Gawain here since summer last, but in olden times I lived in Camelot, my lady, serving the king."

"Ca…Camelot? Serving the…king?" Rae said faintly, her eyes wide as she looked to me for confirmation of Percival's outrageous claim. It was one thing to hear me talk about my history, but to have Arthur's knights suddenly make an appearance in the current time, dressed in modern clothing, was quite another.

"Gentleman, meet Emily's mother, Rae Crandall," I said, practically gritting my teeth as the morning continued to slide into madness.

"Damn," muttered Ryan, also known as Sir Lancelot, as he realized what Percival had inadvertently done. "Uh, it's nice to meet you, ma'am. My name is Ryan."

"And I'm Gary, Mrs. Crandall. We're sorry to barge in like this, but we usually stop to see Lumina in the morning. And of course we always check in with Lord Merlin every day in case he has some knightly duty for us to perform," Sir Gawain continued with a grin, offering yet more information that I hadn't planned on sharing just yet.

I took a deep breath and turned to my mother-in-law, whose mouth was now open in a "oh" of surprise. "Well, Rae, I wasn't ready to add this information to what you already know, but it seems that decision has been taken out of my hands. Meet Sir Lancelot, Sir Gawain and Sir Percival, once Knights of King Arthur's Round Table. Lancelot and Gawain were reincarnated into their current bodies in this century, and Percival was brought directly here last summer from the fifth century by Llyr."

"Gentlemen, it is truly an honor to meet all of you," Rae said solemnly to the three men. "But, I don't understand—why are you here in this time?"

Before they could respond to her, I said quietly, "To serve me." All three men reacted spontaneously by going down on one knee, heads bowed. I looked at each one with affection. "Thank you my friends, you may rise." As the knights got to their feet I glanced at Rae, wondering what she thought of this spectacle.

Just then, as if she sensed what her mother planned to do, Emily walked over and took the baby out of her arms as Rae gracefully got down on her knees in front of me and touched her forehead to my feet.

I looked at my mother-in-law in horror, and immediately reached down to gently draw her up in front of me.

"Mom—*Rae*—you don't need to do that! Why would you bow to *me*? You worship the one God and I'm not sure he would appreciate me upstaging him," I exclaimed, again worried that a visit from my "father" Llyr was nigh. Then, I realized that Jack was standing in the doorway, a look of outrage on his face as he witnessed his wife prostrating herself at my feet. I immediately turned to the older man, looked into his eyes, and held him motionless while I intoned a spell designed to make him forget what he had seen, and would keep him dozing until we called him for breakfast. As soon as I released him, Jack immediately retreated to the living room and went to sleep on the couch.

I turned around and saw that the knights were hovering around Emily and Lumina, and I could hear my daughter's funny little sounds of appreciation. Rae was still standing in front of me, the formerly nervous, sad and anxious woman now beaming with love and confidence, her face glowing, her hair full and lustrous. It was truly amazing to see the change in her, and I was touched by her sincerity, but I felt conflicted about her gesture until she spoke again, and then I knew without a doubt that I was in trouble.

"Merlin, when the knights bowed to you, my life's purpose became clear to me, and I understood what I must do. From now on, I am devoted to serving you, my lord," Rae proclaimed. "And I will assist you in your quest to bring back the Once and Future King."

CHAPTER 5

January 28

THERE WAS COMPLETE SILENCE as her words reverberated through the room, and everyone turned as one to gape at Emily's mother. Derek had walked into the kitchen just before she bowed before me and he stood frozen in place, as stunned as the rest of us. I don't know why I hadn't foreseen this happening, but I groaned silently as I realized the consequences of her proffered devotion.

Finally, Emily smiled sincerely. "Mom, I'm *so* proud of you." She stepped towards her and hugged her with one arm while cradling Lumina in the other. The knights started talking softly amongst themselves while Derek and I just stared at each other.

I cleared my throat. "Alright, let's get breakfast served. Derek, start some toast please, and Ryan, could you set the table? Gary, you can pour coffee and juice. Emily, could you join me in the bedroom for a moment?"

She nodded and released her mom from her embrace. I touched Emily's arm and transported us to the bedroom where she took the opportunity to change the baby's diaper.

"Gods, I should have seen that coming, but it took me by surprise," I confessed as I paced around the room.

"I know it did, my love, but personally I'm thrilled to see my mom so happy and committed. She's always needed to feel a part of something greater than herself, and now she is part of our quest for Arthur's return."

"But how is your father going to understand? He doesn't know who I really am, and now his wife has proclaimed her devotion not only to Lord Merlin, but also to the god of magic." I ran my hand through my hair anxiously.

Emily looked at me questioningly. "Are you sure? It sounded as if she was pledging her service, just as the knights had, to Lord Merlin alone."

"I could feel her devotion, just as I feel yours. Of course, our bond is different since we're married, but now I have a bond with your mother also. When a life is sincerely offered in devotion and service to a god, that god must accept what is offered—I must accept what Rae has offered to me," I said unequivocally.

"So, in other words, the knights are devoted to Merlin, but not to Myrddin Emrys, the god, because they don't know the truth. However, because my mom does know, her devotion is complete—and she has just chosen to worship *you* over the one God."

"Yes, exactly," I said.

"Oh, crap, we are in so much trouble," Emily breathed.

"Indeed."

CHAPTER 6

January 28

WE DECIDED TO PUT the baby down for an early nap and then teleported back to the kitchen. We had been gone only a few minutes, but everything was ready: the food and beverages were on the table, the knights already seated. Derek had remembered that Jack was unconscious in the living room, and was in the process of removing my spell. Only a blood relative of a sorcerer, with an intimate knowledge of that sorcerer's magic, can remove a spell without permission. Derek's magic was a part of him and he was a part of me, so he had no trouble doing so.

Jack and Derek walked into the kitchen and took their places at the table, chatting amiably. The spell seemed to be successful, as Jack gave no indication that he recalled what had occurred earlier. I was rather surprised that Derek would feel comfortable with the older man since he was so recently intolerant of our kind, but they truly seemed to like each other. Besides, it was obvious that Jack was trying to change his ways, so perhaps the unlikely friendship would have a positive effect.

The meal was consumed amid friendly jesting and lively conversations, the topics of which I don't remember—I was focused on the fact that I now had two devotees for whom I was directly responsible. And I wondered if Rae truly could guide us through the Other World to the Fae realm, and to Arthur. Most importantly, if she did succeed in such a venture, was this truly the time to bring about the long-awaited time of Albion?

"Merlin? My lord?" Percival was insistently trying to get my attention.

I came back to full awareness, realizing that everyone was quietly awaiting my response to the big knight. "I'm sorry, I was lost in thought for a few moments. What was your question, Percival?"

"I was trying to determine if you have need of our services today. As always, we await your command," Percival stated, bowing his head and keeping a subservient tone in his voice. We had been at odds last summer and since then he had always been overly respectful.

"I don't believe I have need of your services today, gentlemen, but I thank you for asking. However, keep your cell phones on," I said, hoping that this would be another peaceful day. I stood as the knights prepared to leave.

"Yes, Lord Merlin. And we thank you for your hospitality, Lady Emily," Ryan said formally, and the three knights headed out the front door.

Jack watched them go and then turned to me. "Ah, those men, they are your… what, servants? Bodyguards?" He was still trying to make sense of his experience in our magical household.

"They serve me, but not in the manner of household servants. Bodyguards? No, not really. I am more powerful than they are. However, I do also consider them to be my friends. They were Arthur's knights, serving him until they died at the Battle of Camlann. At least Lancelot and Gawain died and have since been reincarnated. Percival survived the battle and was brought here from the past, to assist me," I explained, knowing that this was going to be a touchy subject. "And all three serve me now as a gesture of respect. As Court Physician and Sorcerer of the Realm, I was an esteemed member of the Royal Household even after Arthur's death." I could understand the skeptical look on my father-in-law's face. After all, I looked like a modern man in twenty-first-century clothing. I sighed quietly and resigned myself to yet another demonstration.

Derek knew what I was thinking and volunteered to assist me by changing his appearance as well. So we stood and moved away from the table, and we both whispered the familiar spell, *"Mutabo meam apparentia."* Derek, having never lived in the fifth century as an adult, had to depend on the memories I had shared with him, so he chose to appear wearing a brick red tunic with vest and neck scarf, leather belt and loose brown pants tucked into calf-length leather boots. I appeared as I normally dressed around the castle, in a blue robe, which I preferred over the Roman style toga or tunic, and with my long black hair held in place by a narrow silver band. My dark beard cascaded down the front of my robe to the middle of my chest.

I smiled thinly and said first in the long-dead British language and then in modern English, "Lord Merlin Ambrosius and Derek Emrys Ambrosius Colburn at your service. Perhaps this transformation will help you to believe."

"Oh, my *God*!" I heard Rae and Jack say simultaneously, in shocked voices.

Emily grinned widely, enjoying the show. *Good job—you two look great!*

Silently, I released the spell and returned to my jeans and gray T-shirt. Derek followed suit, clad once again in similar attire. We both nonchalantly helped ourselves to more coffee, then turned back to see how my in-laws were faring.

They seemed overwhelmed as they stared at us in disbelief. Rae recovered the soonest as she saw our actions as divinely inspired, and her devotion shone brightly in her eyes as she gazed at me.

I looked back at her enigmatically. *I need to visit the realm of the gods and confer with Llyr about these recent developments,* I thought, communicating with Derek through our mental connection. *Despite the fact that the past few months have been free of attacks by our enemies, I'm starting to feel uneasy—perhaps it has been* ***too*** *quiet.*

I know what you mean, Dad, and I've been thinkin' the same thing. Maybe we've become complacent, Derek replied.

I'm going to the shop to meditate as soon as I say goodbye to my girls. I got up from the table and put my empty mug in the sink, then turned and clapped him good-naturedly on the shoulder. *Join me in a couple of hours and we'll discuss my findings.*

Derek nodded his assent and thanked us for breakfast. He then took his leave of the Crandalls and walked out the front door, closing it firmly behind him.

I looked at Emily and confirmed with a meaningful glance that she had heard my silent conversation with Derek; then I addressed my in-laws. "Please forgive me, but I must abandon you for a couple of hours. I need to take care of something at my place of business downtown. I'll be back later this afternoon."

"Take your time, Merlin, my husband and I have a lot to discuss," said Rae with a determined look on her face. Jack looked first at Rae and then at me and sighed, seemingly resigned to his fate.

"Would you care to join me in our bedroom for a moment, wife?" I murmured.

"After you, husband," Emily replied agreeably, and followed me out of the kitchen. We had decided simultaneously to walk mundanely through the living room instead of teleporting, having noticed the slightly glazed look in her parents' eyes.

We entered the bedroom and stood for a moment, gazing at our child as she slept peacefully in her cradle. Then, we turned and reached for each other at the same time, holding each other close, breathing in our combined scents and reveling in our bond. I pulled away slowly and looked at her precious face, knowing that I might have to leave her, and wondering how in the world I would ever survive it.

CHAPTER 7

January 28 Noon

I DECIDED TO WALK downtown instead of driving, feeling the need to breathe fresh air and to stretch my legs. It was quite cold outside, so I grabbed a jacket and slipped it on before I left the house—I didn't really need it as I was able to regulate my body temperature, but I didn't want to draw undue attention to myself.

As I strode along the sidewalk, enjoying the cold, crispness of winter, yet anticipating spring's warmth, I recalled with nostalgia the exhilaration of running along the paths through the forests adjacent to Camelot. The absolute quiet of a non-technological world would be broken only by the crack of an occasional twig beneath my feet, or by the call of birds high in the trees overhead. Although I loved the current time and wouldn't want to live in the fifth century again, I missed the wild, open countryside, the deep forests, and the unpolluted air, lakes and streams. I missed being able to use my magic openly, as I had been able to do as the official Sorcerer of the Realm. Here in Moab, having so many people aware of my powers seemed to be a disaster waiting to happen. So far, I had been fortunate. My son and my wife, having magical abilities themselves, would never willingly reveal my true identity to anyone without my permission. After all, they had almost as much to lose as I if it became known what they could do. Similarly, the wizards who had taken part in the battle against Nimue would never expose me as they would also expose themselves. The knights, well, it was obvious why they would never discuss my situation; in lieu of King Arthur, their devotion to Lord Merlin was absolute.

Now, not only did Derek's adoptive mother Lisa Colburn know the truth about me through a conversation we'd had the previous summer, but so did Emily's parents. I wasn't overly concerned about Lisa, as she was a wizard herself, nor was I worried about my mother-in-law since she was Fae and had declared her devotion to my god self, but Jack Crandall was a different story. He was human, mortal, and distinctly uncomfortable with the magical world he was suddenly a part of. I suspected that, although he would not admit it, he would always regard me with a certain amount of suspicion, resentment and fear. I hoped that he would continue with the new mindset, but that remained to be seen.

The fact that Llyr had not yet made an appearance allayed my fears somewhat. As my "watchdog" in the realm of the gods, he was always quick to inform me when I had foolishly or inadvertently revealed myself to mortals.

The longer I was in this human body with the awareness that I was the god of magic and healing, the more I realized how much the human part of me affected the god part. My spirit, being bound to this human form, could not fully access the vast knowledge, or experience the heights of bliss, available to an unencumbered spirit. But I was unwilling to give up this human existence to again become pure spirit, as transcendent as that state of being was.

As I strode along past the bank, the hardware store and the Mexican restaurant towards the heart of the downtown area, I glanced up at the hills east of town, which shone with brilliant hues in the winter sunlight. I was only partially cognizant of the people I passed, who turned and stared at me, puzzled, wondering if they should know me. This happened every time I was out in public and I was used to it; I knew they were sensing something different about me, but couldn't put a finger on what it was.

My musings were interrupted as I arrived at my destination. I stood at the rear entrance to my shop and decided to teleport inside, leaving the locks and protective wards in place. I didn't want to be disturbed, and Derek could teleport inside also when he arrived. He had not been able to navigate through my original warding spell so I had altered it somewhat to recognize his unique energy pattern. Being my son, his essence was similar to mine, though not identical. I made sure I wasn't being observed, and vanished into the shop.

I immediately realized that I should have left the heat on the last time I was here—the shop was frigid. Derek didn't have the ability to adjust his body temperature, so I decided to turn on the furnace, setting the thermostat to seventy degrees. I made coffee, and then moved efficiently around the room dusting the shelves and mopping the floor. I could have enchanted the mop and the dust cloth to do the work, but I needed the mindless activity to smooth out the wrinkles of the past eighteen hours. And I felt content to be alone and able to ponder those recent events. As soon as I had finished cleaning, I sat in one of the comfortable chairs in the reading area, calmed my racing thoughts and sank into a deep meditation, entering that all-encompassing Light.

An hour later, feeling refreshed, I opened my eyes and contemplated having my mother-in-law as my newest devotee. I really didn't want *any* devotees, but that was the risk I had taken coming to earth as a god in human form. When I didn't recall who I was, my real nature was not evident to mortals. But once I had remembered and accepted that I was actually a god, any truly humble, sincere, spiritually-oriented mortal might sense my true nature and offer his or her devotion, which was exceedingly rare, thankfully. And I would have no choice but to accept that devotion and extend my protection and guidance. It made sense that my wife had been the first to offer her heart and soul to me. She and I were connected, bonded, on so many levels that in reality she had declared her devotion long before our wedding day. Obviously, I didn't have the same kind of relationship with her mother, but the devotion had been offered and accepted; it was done and could not be undone.

I needed to talk to Llyr, as I had not connected with him during my recent sojourn in the Light, and I wondered if it might not be a good idea for him to come to me. Ever since I had killed Beli's daughter, Nimue, in our battle the previous summer, the Welsh god had been fomenting rebellion in the spirit realm, causing the balance of power to shift. I wasn't at all sure I wanted to be anywhere near that situation. Why the one God, who ruled over all realms, allowed it, I couldn't imagine. It was only recently that I had realized that Nimue's father was not just any demon, he was the god of death himself.

As I thought about the possibility of this war of the gods spilling over into the mortal realm, I shuddered. Derek was right, we had become complacent and I hoped that we weren't too late to address the situation.

I got up out of the chair and grabbed the mop and bucket, intending to clean them and put them away. Abruptly, with a flash of light, Llyr appeared in front of me, his six-feet-eight-inch frame dressed in jeans, hiking boots and a heavy parka. Although his garb indicated that his sense of humor was intact, his expression was grim.

"Merlin, you wanted me to come to you, so here I am. You are in great danger, my friend. Beli has finally revealed that he is seeking retribution against the one who killed his daughter: The true god of magic and healing, Myrddin Emrys. You. He did not believe me when I insisted that it was my idea. The gods are not supposed to become involved in their children's disputes on this plane of existence, but Beli seems to be ignoring—or circumventing—that restriction set by the one God long ago."

"It makes no sense that the gods, who are of spirit only, should be involved to this extent in the affairs of *men*," I said insistently.

He looked at me incredulously. "Seriously, Merlin? Are you telling me that you did not spend thousands of years scheming and involving many of us in your grandiose plans to come here…" Llyr spread his arms, indicating not only the inside of my shop but the whole of the human realm, "…as a man? I admit I have enjoyed taking on the form of a human male on occasion, especially when I had the pleasure of copulating with the mortal woman who bore you. And it has been strangely rewarding being your father. But you should recall that there is a certain amount of mind, of ego, present in our realm as well, or you might not have been so anxious to leave again once you were finally home."

"You're right, *Father*," I admitted, deliberately emphasizing the term. I put the cleaning equipment aside and poured myself more coffee. "Would you like some?" I pointed to my mug.

"No, thank you, I can't stay any longer. Tensions are rising throughout the realm and I have a feeling that the god of death is planning something unexpected, so please take great care, my son. As usual, I will intervene on your behalf when I can, but I have been under much scrutiny of late." And with a worried look, Llyr was gone.

As I stood in the middle of the room drinking my coffee and mulling over the implications of Llyr's statement, I experienced that sinking sensation of dread that always preceded a vision, and I stiffened as a shocking scene blasted into my mind. I dropped my coffee mug and it shattered on the tile floor, dark brown liquid splashing everywhere. A few seconds later I came out of it, weak and shaken.

Suddenly, Derek teleported into the shop, and with a frightened look on his face, tackled me to the floor.

We crashed to the damp, leaf-strewn ground, and I felt rather than saw a bolt from a crossbow hiss through the air directly above our prone bodies. We were no longer in the shop, and the immense trees around us told me that we were no longer in twenty-first-century Utah. We were in a different time and place altogether. Finally, Derek stirred and rolled off of me, and I was able to draw in a deep breath of moist, cool air laden with the familiar scents of a forest that had disappeared a thousand years ago.

Then, I heard a voice say, in Old British, "Merlin, what in all the kingdoms are you doing?" I knew now where we were—and when.

I slowly sat up and turned to look at my old friend, Arthur Pendragon, King of Camelot.

CHAPTER 8

AD 460   Day 1

DEREK SAT UP next to me and gasped as he saw a group of strangely dressed men surrounding us, crossbows at the ready, commanded by a haughty, sandy-haired young man with a thick band of gold encircling his head.

Derek, do not speak. I must find a way to explain this situation to Arthur, and you do not know the language or the customs of this time.

My God, we're in the fifth century, aren't we? And that's really....Arthur? Derek stared silently at the king, his eyes wide.

Yes, we seem to have been transported into the past, and that young man is indeed Arthur Pendragon, I responded. And my heart sang at the sight of the man whom I had loved, served and striven to protect so long ago, alive and well once more.

He looks different than he did in the memory you showed us last year.

He is much younger now. In the memory I shared with you, he looked as he had just before he died, a battle-weary man in his midthirties.

I could tell Arthur was becoming impatient, and responded to the query I knew was coming.

"My lord, I would beg your indulgence and request sanctuary for the two of us, and I will gladly answer your questions in private, once we have returned to Camelot," I said humbly to Arthur in the old language that now seemed so foreign to me.

He gave me a long suspicious look before he nodded and had one of his men relinquish his horse for my use. As the man came close enough to hand me the reins, I noticed the reek of old sweat, unwashed body and tooth decay. Carefully hiding my reaction to the noisome odors, I nodded my thanks. When the man nodded back and seemed surprised that I had acknowledged him,

I realized that the young Merlin wouldn't have done so. I had not considered myself to be particularly egotistical or condescending, but I had accepted that my position in the Royal Household put me in a higher class than someone of this man's rank. I would have taken his gesture as my due, rather than acknowledge the sacrifice it actually was.

After I had mounted, I motioned to Derek to come closer, and I reached down and grasped his forearm, assisting him to climb up behind me. I could feel his apprehension as he exclaimed silently, *But Merlin, I don't know how to ride!*

Hold onto my waist and grip the horse with your inner thighs, and you'll be fine, I assured him. I just hoped the animal wouldn't collapse under our combined weights. Contrary to the legends, the horses of Camelot were not the heavy, draft-sized beasts that were bred to carry the fully-armoured knights of the Middle Ages. These animals were of an average size, barely larger than the Welsh ponies I remembered from my childhood. Holding the reins in my left hand, I rested my right hand on the black horse's sweat-lathered neck and whispered, "*Vires.*" I sensed the horse's physical strength multiply tenfold, and I smiled as the animal snorted and pranced with his newfound energy. *Hold on, Derek*, I said silently.

I had no idea what excuse the king gave to his men, if any, for the unexpected change in plans, but we traveled quickly back to the castle from the forest in which the group had been hunting wild boar. I'm sure returning without the game they had anticipated would not endear me to these men, but I needed to discuss the situation with Arthur as soon as possible. I was most grateful that our relationship had always been one of trust and affection. I had already decided to tell him everything, but I knew that I would have to place a forgetting spell on him prior to our departure, whenever that would be.

Within several hours of our sudden arrival in the fifth century, we approached the bridge crossing to the main entrance of the castle, and I heard Derek inhale sharply in awe. After all, this was Camelot, but as unlike the twenty-first-century concept as it could be. Bright red pennants and flags bearing a dark red dragon outlined in black flew from many different levels of the structure. While certainly large and imposing, the castle was not constructed entirely of stone blocks as legend would proclaim; many sections were built of wood, with massive beams supporting roofs of thatch. Much of the castle itself had been constructed on the ruins of an old Roman fortress, which had been built originally on the mound of an Iron Age hillfort. Of course, when I had lived here long ago, I had not known the term for that era. However, Derek had made sure that I was educated regarding the accuracy of certain historical details.

I was thinking with amusement about the stark contrast between this true Camelot and the television version, when Arthur turned in the saddle and indicated that he wished to speak with me.

I reined in my horse to get closer to his. "Yes, my lord?"

"I will not press you for an answer at this moment, Merlin, but I find it most odd that you should leave this very morn for your annual visit to Gaius, and then be in the forest later in the day with a man unknown to us." Arthur paused as he eyed my clothing, my hair and my clean-shaven face. "Once you have refreshed yourselves, I expect both of you to make haste to my chambers, and to provide a satisfactory explanation for this… occurrence."

"As you wish, Sire," I said submissively, bowing my head slightly in acknowledgement of his command.

The king dismounted at the bottom of the steps to the main entrance, handed his reins to one of the knights who had been flanking him, and entered the castle, while we continued on with the rest of the entourage to the stables. After we had dismounted, I thanked the man whose horse we had borrowed, and as he led the animal away, I noticed the look of disbelief on his face as it pranced spiritedly.

As we traversed the stable yard and proceeded through the training area, Derek swung his head back and forth, trying to take in everything at once—from the servants bustling about their chores, to the young knights engaging in mock combat under the tutelage of older, more experienced men. Eventually, we reached one of the back entrances and, with a nod to the guards, we entered the castle itself.

I guided Derek up to my room using the servants' passages. We received many confused stares, especially from the old retainers whom I had known for many years. This was probably due to the fact that my beard was gone, and my hair was much shorter than they had seen it just this morning. Of course, they knew better than to question me; none of them had magical abilities and all were in awe of the king's sorcerer.

"I don't understand. Why were you so submissive with Arthur? I thought you two were friends," said Derek, as we climbed many steep, rough-hewn gray stone steps that finally ended at a landing several floors above the servants' quarters.

"Shh! Keep your voice down—we'll talk once we are inside my chambers," I said quietly, as we walked up to a large wooden door with rough, black iron hinges and door handle. The old-fashioned lock required a large key—which I did not have. I extended my hand and whispered, "*Aperitur ostium.*" The simple spell unlocked the door, and another disengaged the wards that I had always set when away from my rooms. We entered and I repeated the process in reverse, only then relaxing and taking a deep breath. I was "home." A home I had not seen in over 1,500 years. I closed the door and turned to my son.

"The politics involved in a royal household demand subtlety. Although Arthur and I have been friends all of his life, he is still the king and great care must be taken in front of others to observe the traditional hierarchy that exists between the Royal

Family and everyone else." Apparently my explanation satisfied him, but immediately he revealed his most urgent concern—and mine.

"How the hell did we get here? And how are we gonna get home?" Both excitement and fear were evident in the pitch of Derek's voice, and I threw an arm across his shoulders and pulled him into a quick embrace. My son had only been aware of his magic for a short time, around six months, and he was already a powerful, talented sorcerer, but at this moment he was just a scared young man.

"I don't know, Derek," I answered simply, "but I will find out." I released him and we both leaned against my workbench. "And now I wish to know how *you* knew to push me down in the twenty-first century to avoid being shot in the fifth. A vision?"

"No, it was more like an impulse, a feelin' of urgency to get you down to the ground. It felt weird, as if someone gave me a not-so-subtle push in your direction. I wasn't thinkin'—I just teleported from home directly into the shop and tackled you. I wanted to protect you, even though you're immortal and you could have come back to life. You died twice last year and I wasn't anxious for either of us to go through that again."

I smiled. "Well, I'm grateful, however it happened."

I noticed that while we were talking, Derek had calmed down and was looking curiously around my chambers. I looked around as well, relearning the attributes of my old quarters. We were standing in a spacious main room with a desk and workbench and shelves for books. An alcove contained a canopied bed alongside a tall cabinet containing my garments. There were numerous jars of herbs, equipment for creating potions, and several large crystals on my workbench. My earlier, younger self had left everything neat and well-organized. Brightly-colored woven tapestries covered most of the walls and helped to keep the drafts out. It felt homey and familiar to me and I found myself immersed in memories of long ago.

These rooms had been my home for nearly forty years before I left to occupy the Crystal Cave. When I had first moved into the castle to serve Arthur's father at the age of sixteen, I had shared a small room with several serving boys. When it became obvious that I was a favorite of King Uther and had been awarded the positions of both Court Physician and Court Magician, later changed to Sorcerer of the Realm, I was given my own separate quarters: these very rooms, as a matter of fact.

Gods, how I had missed being here in Camelot with Arthur.

As soon as the thought surfaced I felt guilty. How could I wish to be any place but with my wife and newborn child in the twenty-first century? I sighed and managed to let go of those conflicting emotions. They would only serve as a distraction, and right now I needed my wits about me.

While I was deep in thought, the sun had set, and the room had become dim and full of shadows. I heard Derek murmur, "*Adolebit,*" and every candle came to life, flames burning strong and clean. I realized that he had stopped talking and was patiently waiting while I reacquainted myself with my old life.

"So this is where you lived." Derek glanced at the candles, the glow from which didn't quite reach the rafters, and he created a light orb, directing it to float above us so that he could better see the huge exposed beams. He seemed puzzled and somewhat disappointed. "I thought the castle would be all of stone, but there are wooden beams, and part of the roof is thatch. And you actually have glass windows! I didn't know you even *had* glass in the fifth century."

I chuckled at the look on his face. "Twenty-first-century notions of this time are grossly inaccurate. The Romans were extremely advanced in some ways and we learned a lot from them. The term, The Dark Ages, comes not from the lack of sophistication and technological advancements, but from the lack of surviving documentation; much knowledge was lost in the centuries after the Romans left." I thought about all the things that had been lost, and gained, when the Romans left Britain early in the fifth century, before I was born. Our land had been returned to us, enhanced by Roman culture and accomplishments, but without the strict guidance required to make that culture a permanent part of our ongoing civilization, the Roman influence declined and became instead a part of our history.

Derek watched me as I lectured, grinning as my accent broadened and I easily dropped back into my old language patterns. Forgetting his fear temporarily, he laughed and shook his head. "I really love you, Dad."

I gazed directly into Derek's warm brown eyes and smiled. "I am most pleased that you do, Son, and I love you as well."

"Sometimes I'm still amazed that you're my father, ya know?" He wandered around the room examining my things. "By the way, where are you supposed to be right now? God, I hope that Merlin doesn't come back for a while; I mean you, the one who lives here in this time," Derek said, confused.

"I left this morning, on horseback, to visit Gaius in a village about a day's journey from here, and I remember that I had planned to stay about a month. This is the year 460, and I am forty years old. Arthur is twenty-two and Gaius is around seventy-three, I believe. We should have plenty of time to resolve this dilemma before my younger self returns." I became lost in thought for a moment, and then remembered that Arthur was waiting for us. "Let us wash up and change our clothing so that we do not stand out overmuch," I said as I opened the elegantly carved wooden cabinet doors and drew out a robe for myself and clothing for Derek.

"Yeah, I definitely need it," he said with disgust as he felt the seat of his pants, wet with sweat from riding behind me on the lathered horse. Then, I noticed that he was looking around surreptitiously.

"If you're looking for a toilet you won't find one—at least the kind you're used to. There are latrines of a sort in most private chambers, as well as several on each floor, in the corner towers." I pointed out the door to mine in the opposite corner of the room, behind a decorative screen. "It will be hundreds of years before the term 'garderobe' will be used for the latrines we have now, but that is exactly what they are. The servants come in every morning with buckets of hot water laced with sage and juniper and clean them as best they can, and then they strew sweet-smelling herbs to help mask the odor. I had also implemented an on-going spell to funnel odors out the latrine windows and away from the castle."

As Derek proceeded to use the primitive toilet, I reacquainted myself with my things. I discovered that there was still a small amount of water in the bottom of the pitcher and poured it into a shallow bowl so that I could rinse my face and hands. As I used a thin linen cloth to dry myself, I realized that I was smiling. I was inordinately pleased to be here, despite my concern for Emily and Lumina. Whoever had engineered this scenario to send me to the past had not counted on my enjoyment of the experience, nor had he, or she, realized that Derek would be here with me. However, someone had provided Derek with the urgent feeling that I needed help, and I wondered who it could have been. And then I had a disturbing thought: Nimue was alive in this time and could be here in Camelot. I heard Derek close the latrine door and decided to put aside these dark thoughts for the moment, blocking them from him.

As Derek rejoined me, I watched my son's face as he acknowledged one of the main drawbacks of fifth-century life: the lack of indoor plumbing. I was not particularly thrilled about it either, but I had lived with it for so many years that I was accustomed to it.

Derek looked at the water in the bowl and frowned. "Can you please conjure some clean water for me?" Although he had done well learning his spells and utilizing his magical abilities in many other ways, conjuring anything other than light orbs seemed to be impossible for him. Personally, I felt that he had some sort of mental block—perhaps he just needed to apply himself more diligently to practicing his conjuring skills.

I passed my right hand over the bowl in a circular motion. "*Aqua pura,*" I murmured, and the bowl was suddenly full of pure, clean water. "There you go, Derek." And I realized that I could have done the same for myself, instead of making do with the small amount left in the pitcher; this was Camelot, after all, where using magic was as natural as breathing.

As he washed his hands and face, I pondered our situation. I knew that he and I would need to spend some time later discussing what we should do. I hoped I would not have to use my god powers to get us home, since the consequences of such an action could be severe. And perhaps that was just what the perpetrator wanted—me to be banished from the earth forever, leaving the human realm wide open for the conquering. That had been Nimue's plan, and now it could very well be Adrestia's or Beli's intention to get me out of the way. As I handed Derek a clean cloth with which to dry himself, I couldn't help but compare it to the large, thick twenty-first-century towels to which I had become accustomed.

Then, all other thoughts vanished as my memories of what had actually occurred here during my absence flashed through my mind: the Saxons had attacked Camelot.

CHAPTER 9

AD 460 Day 1

MY HEART POUNDING, I remembered the death and destruction that had occurred in the surrounding villages as the Saxons had caught us at a vulnerable time. Scores of men, women and children had been killed, and dozens of knights and soldiers of Camelot had been wounded in the fighting. Arthur had directed the physician's assistants that I had trained to take care of the wounded in my stead, and had sent a messenger to ensure my immediate return.

And I knew without a doubt that this was the vision I had experienced back in my shop in Moab, before Derek and I had been transported to the past. No, not a vision but a memory, dredged up from deep within my subconscious mind, perhaps by my reminiscing about Camelot on the way to the shop.

Having this foreknowledge, I could prevent the bloodshed and misery and the loss of many citizens of Camelot. But I knew I could not do anything that would change history—I would have to allow things to unfold as they had done before. I blinked as my mind came back to the present.

Derek was watching me with a horrified look on his face, and I knew he had seen what I had. "The Saxons are gonna attack while we're here?"

I nodded. "Yes, but we will talk about it later. Right now, we need to get going."

We changed quickly, and I was amused at Derek's exclamation of displeasure as he donned my fifth-century clothing. He hadn't expected the cloth to be wool, and while it was relatively fine and soft, it was still a different texture and weight than he was used to. The pants were rather tight on him, the cut unlike his twenty-first-century clothing. I had well-developed muscles, but I was slender and a few inches taller than he. Derek was bulkier than I, and more muscular from working out regularly; my clothes did not fit him properly.

"Not what you expected?" I asked, as I used magic to clean the sweat and horsehair off of Derek's jeans.

"Knowin' intellectually what somethin' might have been like, isn't the same as experiencin' the reality," Derek said, dismayed that the clothing felt so strange.

I reached for a pair of stockings and my old boots and handed them to him. "At least our feet are of a similar size and shape. Hurry now, we must attend the king. To keep him waiting is most unacceptable." I was mixing language patterns and my accent came and went. Derek was grinning again and I was glad I had made him smile.

"Uh, I can't get these socks to stay up—there's no elastic."

"Pull them up over the tops of your boots, or just use magic to make them stay up; that is what I have always done." I demonstrated and he followed suit.

As we left my rooms, I realized that I should have brought a torch. I had forgotten how dark it was in the corridors that had no access to outside light, and at this time of day there was no sunlight in any case. I created a light orb that was adequate to light our way through the many passages within the castle proper and had it float above us. The older servants we passed were not alarmed, nor were they particularly impressed, having seen far greater examples of my powers over the years. Yet, the use of magic was enough of a novelty with the younger ones that they stared intently at the orb and then at me, whispering amongst themselves.

When we arrived at the entrance to the king's chambers the torches were all lit, and the guards glanced disinterestedly at me as I dispensed with the orb. I noticed Derek tugging at the crotch of his pants, trying to ease the fit, and he glanced at me self-consciously. I returned the look with a twitch of my lips, and then spoke to him telepathically.

I intend to tell Arthur everything now, even though I will have to make him forget that information prior to our departure. Please say nothing unless, or until, I give you leave to speak. We wouldn't want to inadvertently change history; you are not even supposed to be here in this time. Alright, let's go.

I knocked, and from within Arthur bade us enter and turned towards us with a questioning look.

I strode purposefully towards the king and we embraced, both of us grinning widely. It mattered not that from his perspective we had seen each other recently; we had always been demonstrative with each other in private. Derek just stood back and marveled at being in King Arthur's presence.

"Arthur, I am going to tell you the truth and hope that our love for each other will be enough to persuade you to believe my story." I gazed into Arthur's glittering brown eyes and saw an unwavering trust and a regal nod of assent.

"I am not the same man who departed this morning for Gaius' village; I am a much older Merlin who has traveled here from almost 1,600 years in the future." I looked into Arthur's eyes and tried to gauge his understanding and acceptance of my outrageous statement.

The King of Camelot gazed back at me with a wry smile on his aristocratic face. "Somehow, I am not overly surprised, Merlin. I have never told you this, but I have long suspected that you must be immortal. I have known you my entire life, and you are far more to me than a mere servant, or even the trusted advisor that you are. You are my friend. I noticed years ago that you were no longer ageing. You are unique, Merlin, and although you have always appeared to be human, there is something so different about you that I think you must be the offspring of one of the gods."

Arthur had always been astute, but I had not realized that he had guessed that part of my nature before I had. Of course, he did not know that I was actually a god, and I did not think it necessary to reveal that piece of information.

"You are correct, Sire; I am the son of Llyr, the Welsh god of magic and healing."

At that moment, Derek, who had been staring intently at the king, turned to look at me with an inscrutable look on his face. I was struck by a similar expression on Arthur's face, and I glanced back and forth between Derek and the king. There was a definite resemblance between Arthur and Derek: they were nearly the same height, their noses both aquiline with a slightly prominent bridge, their lips full, and both men had warm brown eyes. Derek's hair was a sandy-brown color, and Arthur's was a lighter shade, almost blond, but both men wore their straight hair in a rather shaggy style. Derek's face was a little narrower, more like mine, but it was obvious to me that the two men were related. Suddenly, one additional memory surfaced of my time with Derek's mother, Cara—she was Uther's bastard daughter, the result of an illicit assignation with a serving wench.

Gods, Derek, I just remembered something. Your mother, Cara, was Arthur's half sister. He is your uncle.

What? Oh, my God. Does that mean I'm...the heir to the throne of Camelot? Derek blinked and sat down hard on the chair closest to him. His question went unanswered as the king reacted to Derek's collapse and dazed look.

"Merlin, what has happened? Who is this man?" Arthur demanded.

"Sire, he is my son, and as it turns out, he is also your nephew."

As the three of us sat at the ornate table in Arthur's chambers, drinking wine out of silver goblets, he stared at me, and then at Derek, and shook his head. "This tale you tell is quite unbelievable. You have brought your son with you from the future, yet he was actually born here in Camelot—in Old Town to be precise. He looks to be within a few years of your own age, and he—who is older than I by a good six years—is my nephew. Well, he *must* be my nephew if his mother was my half sister," King Arthur reasoned. All of a sudden, he made up his mind and reached over to grip Derek's hand.

"I can see the resemblance to my father in you, and as I trust Merlin implicitly, I hereby accept your claim. You are most welcome here, Derek, my kin. And as this unexpected occurrence has linked me further to Merlin, I am grateful, for I love him well." Arthur spoke to directly to Derek, in Old British, of course, not realizing that he could not comprehend what was being said. I had been mentally translating Arthur's words for Derek when he suddenly interrupted me. *Dad, I would like to speak with him directly. Please, give me the old language through our bond,* he begged silently.

I considered the ramifications of such an action, and decided that he deserved this chance to converse with Arthur, whom he idolized.

Alright, Son, Look deeply into my eyes—you know the drill. He complied, and in mere seconds I had shared with him the knowledge he'd requested.

As the link faded, he smiled and thanked me silently, then turned to Arthur, who waited impatiently for one of us to speak. "My liege, I have dreamed of this day for my entire life, never realizing that it would actually come to pass. Tales of your adventures have survived into the twenty-first century and I have always striven to be your champion. When I found out that my friend Michael was actually Merlin, the Sorcerer of Camelot, I was elated. And later, when I discovered that he was actually my father, I was ecstatic. But the fact that I am also related to *you* makes my life complete; I could not ask for more. I am forever at your service, Sire." And with that pronouncement, my son got up from his chair and down on one knee in front of Arthur, pledging his loyalty to the King of Camelot. I smiled and felt a surge of fatherly pride in my offspring.

Arthur gazed at him for a moment and then gave him a regal nod, accepting his fealty. "Nephew, you are the son of a powerful sorcerer and the grandson of a god, so therefore I presume that you also have magic, is that not so?"

Derek looked up, startled for a moment, then glanced at me as he replied, "Yes, Sire, that is indeed true."

"Then wield that magic in my service as your father has always done and I will be well pleased."

CHAPTER 10

AD 460 Day 1

WE HAD RETURNED to my chambers shortly thereafter, as Arthur was scheduled to preside over a particularly important council with his senior knights before the evening meal. This, of course, caused Derek much excitement, since he assumed that all of the legendary knights he had read about would be present.

"I hate to disappoint you, Son, but Sir Leon is the only knight you would recognize from the stories who will be at the meeting. He served Uther for a short time as a new recruit, and has been at Arthur's side for many years now. Our friends, Lancelot, Gawain and Percival will not arrive for at least another year. Remember that Arthur has not even met Guinevere, and the creation of the Round Table has not yet occurred," I said kindly, wishing that I had news for him of a more exciting nature.

"Tomorrow, why don't we walk through Old Town and I'll show you the shops. Perhaps we can even stop in at the tavern and have a pint of ale with our midday meal while we discuss our strategy for getting home. But for now, let us go to the kitchens and see if we can persuade Cook to feed us our dinner."

"Sounds good, I'm actually pretty hungry. And I really need a shower." As soon as he said it, Derek remembered where we were. "Oh, crap, I forgot, there's no indoor plumbin'," he groaned.

He looked so disappointed, I finally admitted that I had a wooden tub in my room, and I would instruct the servants to bring hot water when he was ready to bathe.

Several hours later, after our simple meal of chicken, bread and ale, and a walk through the castle corridors, we were back in my chambers watching one servant lay a fire to warm the room, while several others poured bucket after bucket of steaming water into my tub. Knowing that they would have to come back and remove all that water in the same manner after Derek had finished cleaning up, I decided to reuse the water for my own bath. However, having become accustomed to twenty-first-century plumbing and an abundance of hot water, the thought of getting into someone else's used bathwater, even if it was my son's, did not appeal to me. *Welcome back to the fifth century*, I thought wryly. Most families in the village had no tub at all, and if they were fortunate enough to have one, the whole family would use the same water until it was dark and filthy.

No, I thought, why should I do that when I can just use magic to purify the water? As soon as Derek had finished bathing, I muttered a spell to clean and reheat the water, then took my own bath.

Later, after the servants had removed the bath water, Derek and I finally stretched out on my bed, our feet hanging over the end of the mattress, which was a large, flat sack stuffed with down and feathers. We had thrown the covers off, as the fire had warmed the room to an almost sauna-like temperature. I tried to still my racing thoughts to prepare for sleep, and then sighed as I realized how much I missed my wife and daughter.

"It'll be okay, I'm sure of it," Derek said softly. "I miss 'em, too. But at least we're here together, right? And meetin' King Arthur, discoverin' that he's my uncle, well, it's been worth it to me, whatever happens." He turned to face me and patted my shoulder. "Remember that I love you, Dad."

I could faintly see his features in the dim glow of the night-light orb I had conjured, and suddenly it seemed so incongruous that my twenty-eight-year-old son was comforting *me*, an ancient sorcerer. I laughed out loud at the absurdity.

"What's so damn funny?" he asked, at once insulted and hurt that I would respond that way to his heartfelt declaration.

"Oh, Derek, I wasn't laughing at you, I was laughing at myself," I confessed as I invited him to look into my mind.

He chuckled as he understood. "Yeah, that is pretty ridiculous." He yawned widely and turned over, pulling a light blanket up around his sleek, muscular shoulders. "I think I can sleep now. See you in the mornin'."

"Sleep well, my son," I whispered, grateful that this young man, whom I had sired so long ago, was a part of my life. I pulled my half of the blanket up until it settled around my waist, then closed my eyes and began breathing deeply and rhythmically, relaxing as my mind finally drifted into sleep.

"Daddy, don't worry, Mommy and I will be fine until you get home." The voice paused for a moment, and then continued, *"We love you."*

I heard the child's voice clearly, as if she was standing right next to the bed, and I gasped and sat up.

Derek's sleep-slurred voice mumbled. "Is there a kid in here?"

"You heard that? I thought I was dreaming," I said, my heart racing. "I think it was Lumina, contacting me from the future."

"You can't be serious—she's a newborn baby! How can she be talkin'?" Derek sat up and flicked his hand at the candle on the bedside table, which flared obediently. He blinked in the light and looked at me askance.

"Derek, she is a unique being, and for all we know time is flowing faster there than here and she is already old enough to talk in complete sentences," I conjectured, my heart aching as I thought of all the things I may have already missed in her life.

Derek swallowed hard and looked worried. "We've gotta find a way to get home—soon."

"I know," I said quietly as I lay back down. Derek took my cue and magically extinguished the candle, both of us settling back against our pillows and allowing sleep to take us once more.

And I dreamed of holding my wife in my arms.

CHAPTER 11

AD 460 Day 2

THE FOLLOWING MORNING when we arose we did not discuss the voice we had heard, and we were both lost in our own thoughts as we performed our ablutions. Derek wore the same garments as the previous day and I settled on pants and tunic as well—I did not want to attract undue attention to myself as we traveled about, and Merlin's distinctive robes would be all too recognizable. It was odd how I had started to think of my earlier self as a different person.

As we headed to the kitchens I reminded Derek to call me "Dad" only in our private conversations while we were out and about; in this time it was known that Merlin had no children. He nodded in agreement. I was relieved, as he loved to call me that, and did so as often as possible.

We each begged a sausage and some fresh-baked bread from Cook for breakfast and left the castle, heading for the village that everyone in Camelot had always referred to as Old Town. It was situated just outside of the main enclosure but still defensible within the outer ditch. The mound upon which Camelot had been built was constructed hundreds of years ago, before the Romans came to Britain, and was virtually impregnable. The deep, steep-sided ditches surrounding the entire mound, as well as another ditch around the inner citadel, had successfully deterred invasions since the Iron Age.

"I've seen construction like this before, the last time I was in England. I visited Old Sarum, on the outskirts of Salisbury, and it was a lot like this, except there were extensive castle ruins," Derek said as he wrapped the bread around the sausage. He took a large bite of the resultant sandwich and glanced in my direction, chewing assiduously as he waited for my response.

"Yes, I am aware of that. I was present in 1070 when William the Conqueror began to build the royal castle within the old earthworks. The original timber castle was replaced by stone structures during the reigns of Henry I and King Stephen, and then the New Hall was built during King John's reign. Most of the ruins you saw were most likely from John's time." I knew that in their day-to-day interaction with me, both Derek and Emily would sometimes forget that I had been alive for more than a thousand years, experiencing what I now thought of as "living history" during the times when I was not in a state of suspended animation.

He laughed. "Sorry, sometimes I forget how old you are, and everythin' you've seen in your life."

I smiled. "No need to apologize. You'll see incredible things yourself, since you are also immortal. And you will look exactly as you do now a thousand years hence."

"Yeah, and that's really hard for me to relate to," Derek said with a wry grin. He was eyeing the remaining half a sausage in my hand so avidly that I held it out to him, convinced that I had just saved my son from imminent starvation.

We continued on into the town on narrow, cobbled streets, passing shop owners and stall vendors preparing their wares for the day's sales.

I stopped to chat with an old acquaintance of mine, and when I looked for Derek some twenty minutes later he was nowhere in sight. I felt a brief twinge of concern when I sent out a brief mental call and he did not answer right away, especially knowing that Nimue could be here, possibly shielded from my sorcerer's senses. But when I felt no evidence of her presence after an intense probe, I decided to give Derek the benefit of the doubt and just casually looked for him on foot; I had wanted to see the town again anyway. I could sense his presence here but he, or someone, was apparently blocking me to the extent that I could not pinpoint his exact location. I was immediately suspicious of magical interference of some kind, as this behavior was most unlike him.

After having scoured the entire area thoroughly without finding him, I finally gave in to my unease and sent out a more urgent summons. *By the gods, Derek, I suggest you answer me immediately! I'm worried—where are you?*

Sorry, Dad, I'm here, my wayward son finally replied sheepishly. And he stepped out of a small, ramshackle building hand in hand with a striking young woman.

I felt from him a myriad of emotions and physical sensations having to do with the woman at his side: arousal, happiness, guilt and longing. I was so surprised that for a moment I was speechless.

"Derek, what were you doing? Who is this?" I asked carefully in Old British. I had never interfered in Derek's sex life; after all, my son was a fully-developed adult, not an adolescent, and it was none of my business with whom he shared his body. But this was Camelot, not Moab, and it would be most inappropriate for him to get involved with anyone here. And the speed at which this...liaison...had occurred was extremely suspicious.

I earned a black look from my son, as he obviously had heard every one of my thoughts and didn't approve of them in the slightest.

Dad, seriously? You think so little of me that you assume I just had sex with a total stranger? Jeez, thanks for the vote of confidence.

I had the feeling that he was protesting too much; he had obviously been thinking about having sex with her and knew that I was aware of his physical and emotional reactions. He made a conscious effort to calm himself, and then addressed me in the old tongue as well.

"My lord, may I introduce Lady Addie? We became acquainted during the time you conversed with the proprietor of the herb shop. She dwells here in Camelot, and she has magic." Derek was excited as he turned to the woman and smiled; that he was smitten with her was obvious. She seemed attracted to him also, but remained curiously aloof. I wondered why he hadn't noticed that. I hoped that he wasn't under some kind of subtle enchantment, which would certainly explain his uncharacteristic behavior.

He immediately responded to my thought. *No, Dad, I'm not under any spell; relax.*

I just looked at him, and then turned to his friend Addie. She curtsied to me, yet avoided my gaze by looking at Derek, seeming rather shy. Her reticence gave me an opportunity to take in the long shiny black hair, the flawless complexion, the vivid blue eyes and her above-average height—at five foot seven or eight she was much taller than other women of this century—and I felt a nagging sense of familiarity. This was ridiculous, of course, as I knew without a doubt that I had never before met her. But there was *something* about her…

"My lady, I am most pleased to make your acquaintance," I said as I nodded to her pleasantly. She had not given me her hand as was the custom here in Camelot, which in itself seemed odd. But I did not change my facial expression and I was careful to guard my own thoughts while trying to gain access to hers.

"And I you, Lord Merlin," Addie said softly, with such heartfelt sincerity that I tried to catch her eye again, unsuccessfully. Something was going on below the surface of this encounter and I wanted to know what it was, yet try as I might, her mind remained completely inaccessible to me. She did indeed have magic if she could sense and evade my subtle probing.

"I have lived in Camelot all my life, so of course I know who you are, but I have never had the honor of being in your presence, my lord," she said flatteringly, eyes lowered modestly.

Just as I was about to reply, a chorus of screams rang out from a few streets over, and Derek and I immediately cast our senses out to determine the cause of the fear and hysteria. Of course, we both were on edge, expecting the Saxons, but I knew that they would not be able to get this far without obtaining access to the entrance bridge—and that was highly unlikely unless one of the guards was a traitor.

"Dragons," I said, realizing what the hysteria signified. I searched the skies for the fire-breathing creatures.

"Yeah, but where are they?" Derek muttered, shading his eyes against the sun as he gazed up into the intense blue of the morning sky.

"My lords, they come," Addie whispered, her eyes closed and her head thrown back.

As I extended my sorcerer's senses outward to find the exact location of the dragons, I felt, for just a moment, the living presence of my daughter Adrestia. I closed my eyes and enhanced the sensation, hoping to locate her, but her essence was elusive and seemed to retreat from me. Without considering the consequences, I sent out a wave of love to her, hoping that she would receive it and recognize that I wasn't the monster her mother had portrayed me to be.

Immediately, I realized what I had done—I might have changed the future, for I wasn't supposed to be here in Camelot at this time, knowing of her existence. I groaned to myself and thought, *When will I learn not to be so impetuous?*

Dad, what was that, what did you just do? I heard Derek's query as he picked up on my distress, but not the cause of it. He was so besotted by this girl that his mental acuity was off.

I opened my eyes and looked into his worried countenance. I sighed. *I had sensed your sister and I sent her my love, not thinking that my action could change the future. I'm going to pray that I was meant to do that. My influence in the realm of the gods must surely count for something.*

There was no more time to discuss the issue as tongues of flame came out of the sky and screams of terror erupted from the marketplace. There were a number of the creatures suddenly flying low over Old Town, releasing bursts of fire that ignited the tinder-dry structures and practically laid waste to the open-air market. Shoppers ran in all directions to avoid being incinerated.

As Derek's friend Addie appeared to be unable or unwilling to wield her magic against the flying invaders, he and I protected her between us as we both threw bolts of magical energy. Derek had learned a great deal about battling dragons and other winged enemies during the invasion of Moab by Nimue's forces last year, but he still lacked my years of experience and he didn't quite have all the strength and finesse of my magical abilities. This was not surprising considering that mine were enhanced by my god powers. But despite his relative inexperience, Derek was powerful, and he had a big heart and strength of will that I truly admired. He always did his best, and I knew I could count on him.

We seemed to barely be keeping up with the onslaught of creatures, and I finally decided I had to utilize my powers and Voice as a dragonlord. There were too many of them to deal with individually with weapons, or with the bolts of energy we had been wielding, and these dragons were real, not just the magical constructs I had encountered in the twenty-first century. Their intelligent persistence was evidence of that.

I wrapped my powers around me like a cloak and leaped into the air, levitating above the destruction. I threw my arms wide and manifested a shield of energy over the entire town, the castle, and all of the outbuildings and courtyards that Camelot contained. At that point, I used my Voice to growl in Old British, "*Begone creatures of darkness and do not return,*" and I mentally projected a burst of powerful magic.

The dragons recoiled, and as one turned and quickly departed the area.

Still hovering in midair, I looked down upon the upturned faces of the Old Town inhabitants who had witnessed my actions, and I was relieved that here I did not have to hide my magic. Everyone was cheering at my success in averting disaster, and gazing curiously at Derek, since he had obviously been assisting me—and using magic. And what had our actions in defense of this village, and mine in sending my love to Adrestia, done to affect history?

I descended swiftly, noting that Derek was now holding Addie in his arms protectively. He didn't see what I did, that she was staring at me intently, almost knowingly, and I wondered again about her background. I tried to hold her gaze, but before a deeper connection could be made she quickly glanced away and refused me access to her thoughts. Short of forcing a connection with her, I was not going to be able to find out her story. It was quite obvious that she knew what I was doing and wanted no part of it. And neither did Derek, it would seem.

Dad, stop it, will ya? She doesn't want you delvin' into her mind, okay? How rude! Derek admonished me telepathically, a frown wrinkling his usually smooth brow.

For a moment, my temper flared, and I wanted to remind him just who he was scolding—not only his parent, but also his god. I could see his eyes widen as he felt my incipient rage, but he stood his ground. Addie glanced at me again, startled, and then hid her face against Derek's shoulder. I took a deep breath and reached for the serenity deep inside me; I always had to take care to contain my god self, as that part of me could be more than a little imperious. And I had to remind myself as well that Derek had never actually declared his devotion to my god self in the way that Emily and her mother had. If he worshiped anyone, it was the God of his childhood.

Derek reminded me of Emily in times like this—she always stepped up to fearlessly put me in my place when she felt I was wrong. I appreciated Derek's remonstrance to curb my innate response, for my fifth-century self would never have created such a scene.

I took a deep, calming breath and organized my thoughts. Since the dragons were well and truly gone and the danger had passed, I knew that Derek and I should head back to the castle and meet with Arthur. Belatedly, many knights and soldiers were finally showing up and the king would be anxious to hear the details of the encounter. I mentioned it to him.

"You go ahead, Merlin, and I shall find you in the king's chambers or in your own quarters," he said dispassionately in Old British, the cadences rolling off of his tongue as if he had been speaking the language all his life, and with no trace whatsoever of his southern accent.

I agreed, but then I pulled him aside and warned him telepathically to be cautious regarding his relationship with Addie. He was quite unhappy with me, as he took my warning to mean that I didn't trust him, but it wasn't that so much as the fact that I was aware of the intensity of a young man's sexual urges, which could overcome even the most honorable of intentions. Derek himself had been conceived under just such circumstances. I had become enamored of a tavern serving wench, misinterpreting my lust for love, and I had given in to my desire. I realized later that I did not love her. And after discovering that it was King Uther's bastard daughter whose virginity I had taken, my ardor had dwindled. Gaius had been horrified that I had risked my magic for a sexual liaison, and that effectively ended any sort of tie between us—until she came to me months later with a child growing in her belly and a tearful request for my assistance. Thank the gods Uther hadn't cared one way or the other, or my story might have been a different one altogether. Of course, I now knew that having sex did not take one's magic away; in fact, magic could vastly enhance the sexual experience, as my wife and I had discovered to our mutual delight.

I took my leave of Derek and Addie and slowly made my way back to the castle, being waylaid at every turn by the grateful residents of Old Town, and then by Arthur's soldiers, who demanded that I give them the details of the confrontation. However, I made it quite clear that I would only discuss the situation with Arthur himself. By this time, I was anxious to get back and decided to teleport, that is, if I could still utilize my ability to do so. I focused on my quarters within the castle and willed myself there. I rematerialized next to the bed, and I felt relieved that I still had that ability available to me should a real need arise. Of course, if a true emergency occurred, I could call upon my god powers, but at what cost, I shuddered to think. My god self was always anxious to unleash those powers, but I couldn't give in under normal circumstances.

I was startled out of my reverie by a staccato rap on the heavy wooden door leading out into the main hallway.

"Yes, what is it?" I called out in the old language.

"The king wishes to see you, Lord Merlin," a familiar voice responded

I grinned. "Is that Sir Leon outside my door?"

"Yes, my lord."

"Come in for a moment, if you please," I said, as I removed the wards and unlocked the door using magic. I could get used to this…again.

Sir Leon carefully opened the door and stepped gingerly into my quarters, his rugged, bearded face reflecting his caution—having been around my magic for many years, he knew that he shouldn't take anything for granted. "What can I do for you, my lord?"

The tall, lean knight looked puzzled as he stared at my clean-shaven face and much shorter hair. He had seen the younger Merlin the previous day, so except for the difference in appearance he thought nothing of our face-to-face discussion. But *I* had not seen *him* in many centuries, and thus it was with the utmost pleasure that I gazed upon him.

"I merely wanted to thank you for your many years of loyal service to the Pendragon family, and to me." Rarely had I complimented the staff or the knights in the early days, and it was only recently that I understood the value of expressing one's gratitude.

"Why, you are most welcome, my lord. You know that I would gladly forfeit my life in the service of my king, and for you as well, Lord Merlin. Arthur values your advice above all others and treats you as a member of the Royal Family; I could do no less. But now perhaps you would accompany me, as the king awaits you…"

"Most certainly," I responded, and as we exited my chambers and I closed the door, I silently intoned a warding spell of protection.

CHAPTER 12

AD 460   Day 2

AS I ENTERED THE ROYAL chambers, King Arthur asked sharply, "Merlin, what, by all the gods, happened this morning?" I gave him a brief description of our experience in Old Town. "I am most concerned that this dragon attack could herald further incursions into the kingdom." He paced over to the window and looked out at the lingering coil of smoke in the direction of Old Town. Deep in thought, he ran one hand negligently through his shaggy, light-colored hair, which was currently free of the confines of his crown.

He was correct—the Saxons would raid the countryside in a matter of days. But I hesitated to reveal my knowledge, as this battle had already occurred in my time frame and must happen in exactly the same way in order to keep time balanced. I dared not think what changes to the timeline our actions this morning had created.

"Sire, the dragons attacked without warning and without provocation. It was sheer good fortune—or the will of the gods—that Derek and I had ventured in that direction just prior to their appearance." Of course, at this point I could not help but wonder if they had been sent against us by Nimue's father, Beli, the god of death, who had not taken into account my ability to command dragons. I remembered Beli from the time I had been in spirit form in the realm of the gods, before I was born as Merlin, and I knew that he could be impatient, unkind and deadly—and not overly bright. It was highly likely that he had been the cause of our transport to the past, unless he was in league with someone else.

Just then, I felt Derek seeking me out, and as he suddenly materialized at my side he went down on one knee to his uncle the king, and apologized for his abrupt entrance.

To say that Arthur was startled would be an understatement, and I realized that I had never teleported as an adult living in the fifth century, so Arthur was completely unaware of this singular ability.

"What did you just do, Nephew? How did you appear in such a manner?" Arthur asked, eyes narrowing as he looked expectantly between Derek and me.

I hurried to explain. "In the future, it is called teleportation, my liege, and it is an ability that both my son, and my daughter Lumina, have inherited from me. Simply stated, we can move from one place to another by an act of will."

"I have never witnessed you doing this, uh, tehl-leh-por-tay-shun." He stumbled over the unfamiliar English word that had no translation into Old British.

"Arthur, I apologize. I had not rediscovered this ability until I had been living in the twenty-first century for some months, and it is now so ingrained in my behavior that I utilize it without thought. Derek has been perfecting his ability to teleport since his powers were revealed to him and he is quite good at it."

"Well, mayhap this ability will serve us well should the Saxons allow their greed to overcome their common sense and attack us, eh?" Arthur's grim smile transformed his young face into a hardened mask.

"Uh, yes, Sire." I glanced at Derek, who nodded slightly. "It would be our pleasure to serve you in this way should the need arise." *Oh, bollocks*, I thought, *I was afraid of that—we would have to fight this battle, yet not save the people who were destined to die.* As I looked into Derek's frightened eyes we shared a moment of trepidation.

"Please excuse us, Your Highness. We have had a rather trying day and very little food, and we would like to retire to my chambers, with your permission," I said submissively, head bowed slightly as I backed towards the door.

"No, you are *not* excused yet, Merlin. What did you mean, your 'daughter' can also do this…teleportation? You never mentioned a daughter, or a wife for that matter. I wish you to tell me of them." Arthur stood tall with his hands clasped behind his back looking fierce, but his warm brown eyes were twinkling.

I gazed into Arthur's eyes, so much like Derek's, and smiled. "After all those centuries of being alone, it was the will of the gods and certainly my good fortune, to meet and marry the most wonderful woman on this earth. Her name is Emily, and being part Elf, she has her own magic, as does our baby daughter, Lumina. I love them both more than I can say, and I miss them terribly," I admitted, hoping that I had not revealed the depth of my emotions to my king.

Arthur looked at me compassionately. "Merlin, you have just become more human in my eyes and that is not something to be ashamed of. I hope that you and Derek will be able to travel home, and soon, for I suspect that it would not be beneficial for your younger self to find you here. Now, go, get something to eat, and rest. I will send Sir Leon for you, as I did earlier, should your services be required."

"Arthur, the truth is, all you have to do is call to me in your mind, and I will hear you, and come to you instantly," I said gently.

Arthur just stared at me wide-eyed, and then nodded regally, indicating that we were free to leave his chambers. We left by the door, rather than teleporting, as both of us were aware that the king had experienced enough shocks since we had arrived.

CHAPTER 13

AD 460 Day 2

DEREK AND I MADE our way to the kitchen and procured our dinners of sliced venison, roasted chicken, fresh bread, and wine. Despite the fact that it was only mid-afternoon, we had missed lunch and were starving, and the kitchen cooked food throughout the day. As soon as we were out of sight of the servants we teleported to my quarters, whereupon I conjured an assortment of fresh vegetables and fruits to supplement our diet.

"I don't know how my body functioned properly when I lived here before," I muttered in twenty-first-century English, although with my archaic accent, which had come back almost immediately since we had arrived here.

"Dad, your body may look human, and function in the human way, more or less, but I suspect your god self enables you to do just fine on whatever you eat. That's probably how you could survive all those centuries without eatin', durin' the times you were 'asleep.'"

"Oh, I know that now, but I didn't then," I said diffidently, crunching on a carrot.

"I really appreciate the fruit, though, 'cause otherwise my digestive tract wouldn't be workin' right. And conjurin' stuff just ain't my thang," Derek said casually, exaggerating his own accent as he munched on a chicken leg.

I looked over at him and grinned.

"What?" He stared at me as I chuckled softly.

"Could you have even remotely imagined this a year ago, Derek? You were practically worshiping Arthur and me; you didn't know you were my son and the grandson of a god, or that you and your mom had magic; you didn't know Emily was an Elf.... And now, you're in fifth-century Camelot, sitting in Merlin's chambers, having just talked to King Arthur, your *un-*

cle, and you're casually eating a piece of chicken joking about your magical abilities. Ah, what a difference a year makes." I was still grinning and shaking my head, when suddenly my mind made an important connection, and I gasped and choked, all mirth forgotten.

"What's wrong?" Derek grabbed my arm and looked into my eyes with concern.

My thoughts were in such turmoil that I could hardly get the words out, sensing that Derek had done the unthinkable. "*Please* tell me you didn't have sex with Addie after I left Old Town."

"Uh, well, I know you said not to, and I'd said I wouldn't, but I was so damned attracted to her, and she wanted me too, so…" Derek stammered and looked guilty.

"Oh, gods, Derek, she's your *sister*!" I groaned as I envisioned an incestuous relationship between the two of them.

"*What?* My God, Addie is *Adrestia*? How do you know?" Derek asked, horrified.

"I finally put it all together. She seemed so familiar to me, and yet I knew I'd never met her. But I just realized that she resembles my mother. All of her magic must be concentrated into her telepathic powers, because she was able to block me most effectively. She obviously realized I'm her father, but she might not have sensed that you are her brother. If she did recognize your relationship and proceeded anyway, that implies an even more insidious plan. We'd better pray that she's not pregnant."

"I took…precautions, so she shouldn't be pregnant," Derek insisted. "Oh, my God, I had sex with my *sister*—that's just gross! Please don't say 'I told you so.'"

"Gods, Derek, this is exactly what I was afraid of." I rubbed my forehead and sighed deeply. "I *would* say 'I told you so,' but since it won't change anything, I'll refrain."

Derek just stood silently, looking stricken, then said quietly, "Dad, what am I gonna do if she *is* pregnant?"

I grasped him by the shoulders and looked into his eyes. "Pray to the gods, to your God, that she isn't."

Both of us were silent for a moment, stunned.

"I can't believe I didn't sense her—*she was standing right next to me*!" I suddenly exclaimed in self-reproach.

"Dad, you may be the greatest sorcerer who ever lived, and you're a god and all, but while you're in your human body you're not perfect, so don't feel so bad. And I'm the one who screwed up, not you."

Derek was trying to make me feel better. It wasn't working.

Sometime later, I finally let go of my self-castigation regarding Adrestia, and Derek brought up the topic that had been on our minds since we had arrived here the previous day.

"How in hell are we gonna get home to Moab?" Derek asked, frustrated.

"I think that we must first ask ourselves how we came to be here. If we can determine that, we might be able to figure out a way to go home," I said. "Llyr had visited me at the shop just prior to your appearance and our subsequent transport to the fifth century, and he warned me that Beli had been spreading ill will throughout the realm of the gods recently, due to the fact that I had killed Nimue."

"But that happened more than six months ago—why is he just now retaliatin'?"

"Time moves at a different rate in that realm, Derek. Or, perhaps, he just realized that 'twas I who accomplished the deed and not Llyr; that *I* am the true god of magic and healing despite the fact that I am in a human body and living in the human realm. Beli has never been overly astute."

Derek looked puzzled. “But…I don’t understand how that can be. Wouldn’t all of the gods have the same level of intelligence, bein’ pure spirit?”

“If I was in my spirit form at this moment I might be able to answer that question. I agree with you though—there shouldn’t be any ignorant gods. However, despite the fact that my soul was present at the beginning of time, I don’t know everything; only the one God knows.”

Derek sighed. “Be that as it may, I think we should try to contact Llyr. I’m really not ready to leave Camelot yet—I’d like to get to know Arthur better—but we don’t belong here; our lives are waitin’ for us in the twenty-first century.”

“I’ve been trying since we arrived to contact the realm of the gods, to speak to Llyr, but I can’t seem to get through. And I can’t fathom how Beli, of all the gods, would have the strength to send the two of us here from the future without a blood offering. Oh, no…” I suddenly realized exactly how he had accomplished it. In my mind, I pictured the moment Emily and I had gotten out of her car and started walking towards her back door the day we’d arrived in Moab the previous April. I had carelessly tossed the blood-soaked towel from my injured shoulder into the rubbish bin. I had known at the time that it was a very bad idea to discard it, but I had been so disoriented by my recent arrival in twenty-first-century Utah—and so focused on the beautiful woman I was with—that I had ignored my inner warning of danger.

Derek followed every scene in my mind as my thoughts raced. “You mean the towel Emily gave you for the shoulder wound you got fightin’ the dragons out in the desert?”

“That’s the one,” I said tightly. “How could I have been so stupid? I knew better! Having my blood gave—and still gives—him control over me. And the only way he would have known about the discarded towel was if he’d been keeping track of me all along, starting with my awakening in the Crystal Cave.

But why didn't he use it against me before this?" At this point I was almost talking to myself, trying to deduce the whys and wherefores.

"Addie!" Both Derek and I shouted at the same time, as we came to the same conclusion simultaneously.

"Addie, not Beli, had obtained it originally, most likely at Nimue's request, to have something in reserve to use against me. But then, for whatever obscure reason, she did not use it during the battle."

"And then somehow Beli got a hold of it, and here we are..." Derek's voice tapered off as he realized we still had no way to get home.

We sat at my table, deep in thought, until finally I stood up and said, "Enough. This isn't accomplishing anything but giving us both a headache. Let's go out into the forest and take a walk. We could use the exercise, and maybe we'll come up with something later."

He stared at me for a moment as if I'd lost my mind, then a smile formed on his familiar face. "That sounds like a plan."

CHAPTER 14

AD 460   Day 2

THERE WAS STILL a good hour and a half of daylight left as we walked through the courtyard and out the main gate, being wary of the horse traffic constantly coming and going. Since no one expected me to be here, dressed uncharacteristically in the pants and tunic associated with the lower classes, and with my hair shorter and face shaven, I was essentially invisible. I liked it.

We initially headed out the main road, but I steered us off onto a narrow track commonly used as a shortcut by those traveling on foot to the outlying villages.

Once we were deep in the woods the sunlight could not penetrate the dense foliage, and we continued in the gloom.

"Derek, how are your levitating skills?" I asked.

"Uh, okay, I guess. I don't really use them much at home since I don't want anyone to see me usin' magic. Once in a while, I go out to the park durin' a full moon and hop up on top of Landscape Arch or Balanced Rock, just because I can." He grinned. "Why?"

We had reached a small glade ringed with tall oak trees interspersed with alder and ash—all trees that were sacred to the Druids—and instead of answering, I just leaped into the air and levitated to the top of the highest oak and proceeded to sit on a fairly sturdy branch, which swayed slightly under my weight.

I heard an excited cry from Derek on the ground below me, and then he appeared, moving a little more cautiously, until he was sitting on another branch across from me. We looked at each other and laughed joyously from the sheer pleasure of using our magic freely and openly. Up here we were in the late afternoon sunlight, which was warm upon our upturned faces, and the air was crystal clear and fresh, having no unwelcome pollutants to spoil our experience. I breathed deeply, and the familiar scents of vegetation and warm earth stirred memories of my early years here. We weren't really that far from the castle, perhaps two or three miles, but it seemed we were truly alone in a primitive world. Well, we were—it was the fifth century, after all.

I glanced at Derek, enjoying his expression of excitement and awe as he drank in the sights and sounds of a world totally alien to him—a world without modern technology. Despite the fact that he had been born here in 442, he had been taken away to the year 1985 at such a young age that he truly was a child of the future, and not of this century.

He knew I was looking at him. "What is it, Dad?" he said with a smile, gazing into the distance towards the towers of Camelot.

"I was just marveling that we are together, here where it all began; where you would still be if Llyr hadn't taken you ahead in time—to your destiny."

He chuckled. "My destiny, indeed, my lord," he said in the old language, with a touch of irony, picturing in his mind the night when I revealed myself to him.

We rode the branches in the breeze that swept up from the forest floor, and I couldn't help but remember the thrill of flying as a bird last summer. Despite the fact that my avian adventure had ended in a deadly fashion, I still remembered that giddy feeling of gliding above the Colorado River.

"There's no reason you can't do it again. After all, is flyin' all that different than levitatin'? Who says you aren't really Superman in disguise?" Derek said softly, his eyes twinkling as he easily shared my thoughts.

I considered his words, and although I was sorely tempted, I knew that now was not the time to be experimenting with my powers. "I suspect you're right, Derek, and be assured that I will think on it."

But as I sat there in the top of the tree I pictured myself soaring—in my own body—up in the air and looking down on the towers of Camelot. This feat need not involve my god powers; it would take utilizing my sorcery to an extent I had yet to experience. However, I knew that it was possible. I was the most powerful sorcerer ever to walk the earth—surely I could do this.

Derek just glanced over at me with a knowing smile, which very much reminded me of his uncle. "You know, Leonardo da Vinci once said, or will say, 'Once you have tasted flight, you will forever walk the earth with your eyes turned skyward, for there you have been, and there you will always long to return.'"

I had never met da Vinci, but I knew that he had been a brilliant man, perhaps even a time traveler, since he had known things someone born in his time shouldn't have been aware of. And he was correct—I longed to return to the sky.

We finally descended in a leisurely fashion to the forest floor, and headed back to Camelot through the darkening woods. We were both perfectly comfortable, knowing that we could easily see our way with a light orb or two if necessary. Having magic could be both a blessing and a curse at times, but at the moment we were both content to be what we were—wielders of an incredible gift.

By the time we had reached the edge of the forest, Derek decided he preferred to walk the rest of the way by orblight and started to call it forth, when I heard something ominous and put out a restraining hand. He looked at me questioningly.

I heard something, Derek. It sounds like troops coming through the underbrush, which our soldiers wouldn't do; these could be Saxons. His eyes widened in fear. I invoked an invisibility spell that I had used many times in the past, and we disappeared.

Not too far away, in the Saxon language, the men began to discuss setting up camp without fires, and the directive was also given to not speak, under pain of death.

So it begins. I cannot bear the thought that we must allow so many to die.

But like you said before, it has to happen this way, whether we like it or not, 'cause for us it's already happened.

That is correct. We need to get back to my chambers right away. I lightly touched his arm and seconds later we were standing next to my workbench, in the dark.

"Adolebit." The candles all flamed brightly as I uttered the spell that in English meant simply "burn."

"We have to figure out a way to get home—now. We promised Arthur that we would fight, but we cannot. If by some chance our participation changes the battle, and people who were meant to die end up living, we truly will have changed the future—to the extent that we may have nothing left to go back to." I was absolutely certain that we could not take part in this conflict—the feeling was growing ever stronger in me.

I decided there was nothing for it but to use my god powers to take us home. There was no other choice—and we had to go as soon as possible. I just prayed that I would be forgiven and still be allowed to remain in the human realm.

A light tapping sounded at my chamber door. We looked at each other and frowned as we both sensed who it was: Adrestia.

Block your thoughts, Derek, we must not give anything away, I thought as I went to the door and opened it.

The young woman who was my daughter and Derek's half sister stood in the doorway, an expression of uncertainty on her lovely face, and for a moment my heart ached with the desire to hold her. But I immediately shut away that dangerous thought and courteously asked her what I could do for her.

"My lords, please forgive the intrusion," she said softly, glancing back and forth between the two of us, her gaze coming to rest upon my son's face with scarcely concealed longing and an undeniable sexuality. "I have had a premonition that you will be making a long journey soon, and I beg of you to take care. Although I cannot see any details, there is something, or some-one, of unknown power and intent awaiting you at your destina-tion." She frowned in confusion. "I do not understand it, but somehow I may be there also…I…I am so sorry, I must go." And she fled as if demons were chasing her.

"Good-bye, Addie," Derek whispered, in English. He watched her go with such regret on his young face that I ached for him.

CHAPTER 15

AD 460   Day 2

AFTER I SHUT and warded the door, I hurried to the wardrobe and drew out our twenty-first-century garments and footwear, throwing Derek's to him and quickly stripping off my fifth-century clothing. I donned my jeans and T-shirt, and then put my shoes on. Something didn't seem right…and I realized that I still had on the woolen stockings. I switched them as fast as I could and noted that Derek was now ready also.

I began to hear distant screams, and cries of battle, and the warning bell sounded. Derek and I exchanged a worried glance. Then, the mental call came from Arthur and I knew that we were out of time.

"We have to do an enchantment over the entire area to make everyone here forget us, similar to the one we used over Moab prior to the battle with Nimue—we don't have time to visit each individual with whom we have interacted."

"Dad, we can't go without seein' Arthur one more time—if we don't show up he'll think we betrayed him, even if it's only for a few minutes, until we get the enchantment in place. And I couldn't stand that."

"I know. I never intended to leave without saying goodbye to him; I love him too dearly to hurt him that way." With one last glance around my quarters, and with a brief apology to my younger self for leaving them less than pristine, I touched Derek's arm and teleported the two of us to the king's chambers.

Arthur was in the midst of donning his armour and strapping on his sword when he saw us materialize. He whirled towards us, and his manservant faded unobtrusively into the background as he saw who it was. "Merlin, Derek, we must stop this invasion before—"

"Arthur, my liege and my dear friend," I gently interrupted him. "We're so sorry to leave you like this, but it is imperative that we go now. We have realized that it would be a grave error to be involved in this battle at all; the future would be altered irreparably. From our perspective, this battle was fought many centuries ago, and we know that even without our help, you *will* win the day…but unfortunately not until there is a terrible loss of life here and in the villages. It is the way it must be, but we are devastated to leave you at this crucial time."

Not best pleased to be interrupted nor to be gainsaid, Arthur struggled to remain calm. "I am…most disappointed and dismayed at this news, Merlin, but I also trust you not to lie to me—you never have—and I will just have to accept that you know best in this matter." He stood tense and battle-ready, yet he gave us the opportunity to explain our actions.

"My lord, I will never forget that you welcomed me as your kin, despite the fact that you knew me not. I shall always treasure the memory of our meeting," Derek swore in Old British as he knelt before his uncle.

King Arthur pulled Derek to his feet. "Come, let us embrace and we shall celebrate our kinship in our hearts. And Merlin, my dear friend, I will never forget this meeting, no matter that you most assuredly intend to place some sort of enchantment of forgetting over the whole of Camelot," he said with a wry grin.

Derek and I each embraced the young king. I gazed into his eyes once more, my heart heavy with the knowledge of what was still to come. We then teleported directly from his chambers to the highest point of the castle, which was a lookout tower abandoned by the soldiers who had been called forth to take an active part in the fighting.

It was now fully dark, and the torches of the invading army cast a garish glow against the night sky as the Saxon warriors streamed through Old Town and fought to gain access to the main compound. We stood gazing in horror at the invasion.

"We don't have time to build our energy as we did previously, Derek, so I'm going to have to augment our magic with my god powers. Stand behind me, against my back, with your arms spread, and allow me to channel through you." He obeyed immediately, without questioning me, and I went inside myself to the part of me I normally kept in check, and allowed the power of my true self, Myrddin Emrys, to flow through my body. Effortlessly, it flowed out of me in all directions, including through Derek, and the two of us became a dual beacon of magic and light, the power of which spread over the castle, the village called Old Town, and at least a half mile beyond. My god power was intoxicating, and I felt myself become one with the universe. When I sensed that we had covered the area sufficiently, I spoke aloud the simple spell, infusing it with my intention for anyone whom we had encountered to forget that we had been here.

"*Oblitus*." My voice rang out as deep and resonant as the sound of thunder, echoing as if from the realm of the gods.

And then I focused all of my will across the centuries and used that infinite power of the gods to take us home.

CHAPTER 16

Moab Present Day

DAD? DAD! ARE YOU OKAY?" I slowly opened my eyes. Derek was standing in front of me, his hands on my shoulders and a concerned look on his face. It took a considerable effort to come back to this frame of reference, this mortal realm, after being immersed in my god self.

It finally dawned on me that we were standing in my living room, in twenty-first-century Moab. Everything seemed a little unreal and out of focus, but I attributed that to our lightning-fast trip through time.

"Emily? Emily!" I called out, frantic to see my wife and daughter. I cast out my senses and realized that they were not in the house. There was no residual power lingering from a magical intruder, so I surmised that Emily had simply taken the baby and gone out, running errands perhaps. But in the back of my mind, a seed of doubt was planted—why had I not sensed her through our bond? Normally, we felt each other's presence no matter where we were.

I breathed a sigh of relief as a key turned in the front door lock, and I heard Emily's voice as she talked to our daughter. The door swung open and she entered the house carrying Lumina and her canvas shopping bag.

"Merlin, oh my God, and Derek," Emily cried as she noticed us standing in the middle of the room. She dropped the bag and rushed over to us, the baby clutched in her arms as she sought my embrace. Derek put his arms around all three of us and we celebrated being reunited.

Some time later as we sat in the kitchen with a bottle of good Irish whiskey before us, our glasses having been filled and emptied twice, we told Emily our tale, of being transported back to fifth-century Camelot, of meeting with Arthur and discovering that he was Derek's uncle, and of journeying home by using my god powers. And we realized that time was indeed off, as we had been in Camelot for only a few days, but an entire week had gone by in the twenty-first century. It was now the beginning of February.

I held Lumina in one arm and had the other around my wife, ecstatic to be with them again. Emily related how her father had decided to leave earlier than they had originally intended, and Rae swore that she would return at my summons to assist me with the quest. Em then confessed how frightened she had been for our safety, until she'd had a dream that Lumina spoke to her, telling her that we were safe with King Arthur and not to worry.

Derek and I just looked at each other, recalling the night that Lumina's voice had awakened us. "That had to be a future version of our daughter communicating with all of us," I said. "Even a telepathically gifted, magical child would have to have rudimentary skills to communicate in full sentences; a newborn baby would not yet have those skills."

"Has she been communicatin' with you durin' the day, Em?" Derek asked.

"She's been learning to make her needs known, but all I get is an impression in my mind: She's hungry or tired or needs her diaper changed; there are no words."

"Speaking of needing to be changed..." I stood up, holding Lumina out in front of me.

"That's alright, I'll do it," Emily said, reaching for the baby. "You and Derek start dinner, if you would, please. There are hamburger patties in the 'fridge, along with potato salad and coleslaw. Just fry up the patties, heat the buns, get the condiments out and we'll be all set." She headed into the bedroom and my son and I exchanged glances—she apparently had sensed we'd be back today.

"I feel like we're in an episode of that old TV series, *The Twilight Zone*," Derek muttered, as he got the food out of the refrigerator and I plugged in the electric frying pan.

"I'm afraid our presence in Camelot did change history. I now have a memory that I don't recall having before. I remember returning from Gaius's and noticing that someone had been in my room, since it was messy and the bed hadn't been made. But I suspected that it was a future Merlin, since no one else would have had the knowledge of the spells and wards, nor the ability to deactivate them."

"Shit, I hope that's *all* that changed," Derek said, just as someone knocked on the front door.

"Would you guys get that, it's probably Addie—I invited her for dinner tonight. She's the one who sensed that you'd be home today." Emily's voice sounded hollow as she spoke from the bedroom.

"Oh, crap..." Derek whispered as I went to greet my oldest daughter.

My heart was pounding and my mouth was dry as I slowly opened the front door. And there she stood, grinning at me as if we had a normal father-daughter relationship. Her glossy black hair, so much like mine, was cut in a style I had never seen—one side longer than the other and swept forward so that she was continually flipping it back out of her eyes. She was wearing designer jeans, high-heeled boots, and a bright red sweater top that left her midriff bare, and she sported half a dozen earrings, at least in the ear that I could see, and one nostril of her elegant nose was pierced. Her eyes sparkled as she said, "Hello, Father," in modern English, of course.

What could I do? I opened my arms and she walked into them, hugging me tightly. I was overcome with the joy of holding my daughter in my arms. She reached up to kiss my cheek and then stiffened as she spied Derek behind me.

I released her and stepped back, wondering how they would greet each other. For Derek, it had only been a matter of hours since he and Addie had had a sexual encounter that, unbeknownst to them at the time, was incestuous. His feelings were still raw, but it was obvious that she had known his identity for centuries and had come to terms with their true relationship.

"Hi, Derek," she said hesitantly. "Welcome home."

"God, Addie, please believe me that I didn't know you were my sister, or I'd *never* have..uh…" He stopped and cleared his throat, his face red with embarrassment.

"Oh, Derek, it's okay, it was a long time ago, at least for me. Water under the bridge, right? I'm just grateful my mother didn't kill you last summer, thanks to Father," she said, looking at me appreciatively.

Emily appeared with Lumina in her arms, and her face lit up. "Hey, Addie, I'm glad you could make it."

"Hi, Em, thanks for inviting me. How's my little sister doing?" Addie reached out, and my wife handed her the baby as if she had known and trusted her for years.

Derek glanced at me. "As I said, it's like an episode of *The Twilight Zone*."

There was something terribly wrong with this whole scenario, but I could not figure out what it was. There was a throbbing in my temples and I could feel a massive headache coming on.

"After dinner, we need to talk, Adrestia," I said to the woman who had on several occasions conspired with Nimue to kill me.

We sat at the kitchen table long after we had finished eating, and as I gazed at my eldest daughter, I acknowledged the inner conflict that I was experiencing. I had suffered greatly the previous summer due to the actions she and her mother had taken against my family and me, and yet my recent experiences in the past had tempered my emotions to some extent. I looked at

Derek and he also seemed to be at a loss as to how to feel about her. It was obvious that he and I needed to talk to Addie privately and bring everything out into the open. I didn't know if I could ever trust her after what she had done, but that didn't prevent me from feeling a father's love for her.

And I was extremely curious—and suspicious—as to how she had insinuated herself so thoroughly into Em's and Lumina's lives in the short time we had been in the fifth century. She had to have shown up here shortly after we were transported from the shop, which led me to believe that she was aware of her grandfather Beli's actions—or that she was in fact his accomplice. If that was the case, everything she had said and done since she had arrived this evening was an award-winning performance.

I was just about to ask her how she had met Emily when a powerful burst of magical energy, originating outside of this mortal realm, surged into me. I had no control over my body as my arms flung wide and my head was thrown back. I stiffened and groaned, feeling as if I had been hit in the center of my being by a lightning bolt. The pain was excruciating. Through the sound of static in my head, I sensed Derek, Emily and Adrestia shouting and trying to figure out what was happening to me. Suddenly, I could feel a dark force pulling my spirit from my body—it could only be Beli, utilizing my blood in a ritual meant to destroy my connection with the mortal realm. Without thought, I responded in the only way I could: I took control and transformed into the god of magic and healing, to counter this attack on my higher self. I still looked like Merlin, but now I was like Llyr, a good six feet eight, a manifestation of spirit that only resembled my human body, my countenance glowing and my green eyes reflecting the light of the gods. Invincible. And the dark force backed off as if this had been its goal all along, to force me to reveal myself. And he had succeeded, I realized, as I saw my human body sprawled in the chair, an empty shell.

I heard gasps and sobs from my wife, and then Derek whispered reverently, "Oh, my God, Dad, or should I say, oh, Dad, my god." And he did something he'd never done before: he prostrated himself before my god form.

"My son, there is no need for you to do that," I said, my voice now deeper and more resonant.

Derek looked up at me in awe and said, "There's every need." And he bowed before me again, his head on my feet for one precious moment before he arose.

"Merlin, what *happened*?" Emily sobbed as she moved between my body and my god form. I heard her thoughts clearly, as she realized that this action could very well be irrevocable, and that our lives together had truly come to an end.

"Emily, I had not intended for this to happen now, but the choice was taken out of my hands. I don't know if I will be able to return to my body, love, I'm sorry," I said, reaching down to lightly caress her sweet face. I could feel the inevitable end to the story closing in on us, but at the same time, I still had a nagging sense that I was missing something; something wasn't right.

I heard harsh breathing and felt her terror as Adrestia realized who I was. I turned to her and met her gaze. She stared up at me incredulously then turned to flee.

Instantly, I flashed in front of her and said, "Where are you going, Daughter? Did you really not know that your father was a god? I believe your grandfather Beli sent you here to spy on my family, and I will not allow that."

"I'm sorry, Father, but he gave me no choice. And I truly didn't know you were Myrddin Emrys; Grandfather never told me." Her voice quavering, Addie cowered before me.

"I can read your thoughts clearly now, Adrestia, and surprisingly enough, it appears that you are telling me the truth. I believe that there is still some good in you, my daughter. However, you are forbidden to interact with this family again until I give you leave to do so. Is that understood?" I towered over her and exuded the threat of immediate retribution should she fail to heed my edict.

"Yes, Father," she whispered.

"You and I still need to have a discussion, but it must wait until I have dealt with your grandfather. Now, go," I commanded her.

"Yes, Father, I understand," she said, and quickly departed through the front door.

CHAPTER 17

Moab Present Day

I FLASHED MYSELF BACK to the kitchen, where Derek had gotten to his feet. Emily was standing still, holding Lumina, her face streaked with tears, her emotional turmoil clear to me through the bond that still existed between us. Both of them were silent as they waited for me to speak.

"Well, this is certainly not what I had anticipated happening tonight." Despite the disturbing fact that I was separated from my body, I felt amazing; I was free and my god powers had fully manifested. I knew that I had no need of spells or enchantments at this point: I could create or destroy with a thought. But with that knowledge came an understanding of the enormous responsibility I carried, and the part of me that was still Merlin whispered, *It's too soon, you're not ready for this*; *the world is not ready for you—are you sure this was supposed to happen?*

And another voice from behind me said, "You're right, Myrddin Emrys, about the world not being ready, but it certainly appears that *you* are. Looking good!"

"Llyr. How did you know?" I turned to face my friend—it seemed ridiculous to refer to him as my "father" at this point—and for the first time we stood eye-to-eye.

"Well, the backwash of power surging into the realm of the gods gave me a clue, dude. And remember what was said in that little family gathering you had in January when your in-laws were here? About the cat being out of the bag? Well, this cat is the size of your house and the bag is bigger than one of those hot-air balloons."

"Is God extremely angry? Am I being recalled to the realm of the gods?" I heard Emily moan and Lumina started crying as she sensed her mom's distress.

"Well, of course. What did you think would happen? The situation has certainly evolved past any instructions you had given me in how to deal with things in this realm. It's really a shame about your body, though, after all you went through to bring it back to life last summer. But I think it's time to confront the god of death, as it's obvious that he is the one who precipitated this fiasco. Come, Myrddin Emrys, time to rock and roll. Say your goodbyes and then join me," Llyr said as he disappeared.

I turned to look at my son, my wife and my daughter and felt a surge of regret.

"Oh, Emily, I don't know what to say, sweetness. This isn't what we'd planned, is it?" I leaned down to hold her and the baby against my god form. I knew that she was totally numb, facing a life without me in it, having to raise our child alone. Derek would help her, but it wouldn't be the same.

She suddenly twisted away from me and exploded, her Elf magic manifesting as bolts of blue lightning.

"You sanctimonious bastard, you *promised*!" she shrieked. "You came back from the dead for me, for us, and now you're going to leave again, just like that? You'd better try your damnedest to get your ass back here, into your body, or I swear I will hate you forever!" The numbness was gone and what was left was unadulterated fury and mental anguish. Her magical energy was uncontrolled and I feared for the baby's safety. Lumina wailed in fear as I took her from Emily, and I created a shield to protect her from the power Em was releasing. I could sense Derek shielding himself with his own magic as Em kept fueling her despair, anger and disappointment. The entire house was being demolished by her raging, uncontrolled magic.

Finally, I'd had enough. "Emily, stop this now! I am still your husband, and I am your god, and I command you to *cease*." My voice thundered through what was left of the house, shocking her out of her supernatural temper tantrum. She immediately subdued her magical outburst and sank down to her knees in front of me, a broken woman.

"Emily, I am so sorry," I said. The baby, who had quieted in my arms, stirred as I looked down into her sweet little face. In her innocence, she returned my gaze unreservedly, and I knew that our souls were connected, forever. Her being was pure and lovely, and through our connection I knew that she would take care of her mother in the future. Finally, I handed her to Emily, who had gotten back up on her feet, defeated, and I turned to Derek.

"I wish I could assure you that our relationship will be the same, but that won't be possible as I will be in the realm of the gods." I paused for a moment. "You have offered me your devotion, Derek, but I also feel a certain amount of hesitancy from you."

"I'm kinda shaken up by your transformation—it was so unexpected. I've always looked up to you, loved you; but now, I actually *worship* you, and that scares the hell out of me."

I looked deeply into his eyes and despite his protestations saw his devotion shining like a miniature sun, and I returned his love tenfold. He cried out with joy and fell to his knees.

And then the mortal realm dissolved into the brilliant white Light of the gods.

CHAPTER 18

Moab Present Day

I HEARD A STRIDENT voice summoning me and I dragged myself out of what felt like a bright, soft cocoon. I must be in the realm of the gods now, but it felt wrong. The Light was there, but I was alone and I ached all over.

I reluctantly opened my eyes and discovered that I was back in my body. I was lying on the carpeted floor of my living room in Moab, and the persistent voice was Derek's own, hoarse with shouting for me to wake up. The room was in shadow as the sun had already set behind the Rim.

"What happened?" I asked, confused and disoriented. I pulled myself to a sitting position with Derek's help, and I realized that he was vibrating with the power that he had been trying—unsuccessfully—to manifest into healing magic. The remnants of numerous failed spells remained as ribbons of energy in the air.

"God, I'm so sorry, Dad! I was tryin' to reach you inside, through our bond, to somehow heal what ailed you and I just couldn't." His face was drawn and pale with the effort he had expended on my behalf.

I stared at him, suddenly aware that he truly had saved me, but he didn't realize it. "Derek, you *did* bring me back. A tremendously powerful force was actually pulling my spirit out of my body and *you saved me*."

Derek looked into my eyes and blinked. "What?"

I smiled and gripped his shoulder. "You saved me. Thank you, Son."

"But, I don't know exactly what I did," he said, bewildered.

"I don't know either, but we'll figure that out later." I gingerly got to my feet, stumbled over to my favorite chair, and sank down into its plush comfort. "You know, just once I'd rather not have to worry about someone trying to kill me or throw me back in time." I was truly starting to get pissed off. I had never used that particular phrase before, but it was certainly apropos. I closed my eyes, remembering every detail of the past few hours I had experienced—in my mind, apparently: Adrestia being here as Emily's friend and confidant, having my spirit pulled out of my body by Beli, and manifesting in my god form. And worst of all, abandoning my family…again.

I breathed a sigh of relief to be back in the twenty-first century, and moreover, to still be in my body. That hallucination was one of the most disturbing things I had ever experienced, since the attempted murder of my human body and removal of my spirit self from the human realm had actually happened in the midst of it.

Suddenly, I felt Emily in my mind, her excitement contagious as she felt my presence through our bond. I bounded out of the chair, rushed to the door and threw it open so hard the knob almost made a hole in the living room wall, then ran outside.

My wife had just pulled her SUV into the driveway, and I barely gave her time to turn the key in the ignition before I yanked the driver's side door open, removed her seat belt and pulled her into my arms.

"Merlin, oh God, I've missed you so much," she cried, tears tracking down her cheeks. She held me tightly against her while I buried my face in her neck and breathed in her scent. A faint cry reminded me not to neglect my daughter. I opened the rear door, unbuckled the harness and lifted Lumina out of the infant car seat, holding her against my chest and feeling the comfort of her warm little body. The three of us entered the house and joined Derek, who greeted Emily and Lumina with open arms.

The next few hours were nothing like my hallucination, thank the gods. Emily did not have dinner ready, so we ordered pizza and salad and had it delivered. Addie did not show up, and Em scoffed at the notion that she would ever willingly befriend someone who had caused me so much anguish, even if she was my daughter. She was horrified and furious that a fellow god would behave as abominably towards me as Beli had done. And we all laughed at the idea that we would be drinking Irish whiskey, when we all preferred Scotch.

While Derek enthusiastically regaled Emily with the details of meeting his uncle, King Arthur, and of our experiences in Camelot, I paced the length of the living room, mulling over the hallucination or vision that I had experienced. It was obvious that Beli would have to be dealt with, which might be an interesting proposition, considering that he was the god of death and not a simple sorcerer. I truly did not want to confront him tonight—or at all, if truth be told—but I decided that I needed to at least contact Llyr for his advice.

"You called?" The tall god stood in our living room in designer sweats and I started chuckling. "I'm trying to fit in here, Myrddin Emrys. No need to be insulting," he sniffed.

"Grandfather!" Derek had seen Llyr materialize and quickly entered the living room and bowed before him.

"Grandson, it is good to see you, but right now it is essential that I talk privately with your father," Llyr said kindly, as he helped Derek to his feet and clasped his shoulder affectionately in his big hand.

"Yes, sir, I understand," Derek said reluctantly, but as he retreated obediently to the kitchen I stopped him.

I looked directly into Llyr's eyes and said assertively, "No, my son and my wife both have earned the right to participate in this discussion; they have been part of my journey, and they have also suffered at Beli's hands." I had already communicated silently with Emily, requesting that she join us. She checked on our daughter who was sleeping in the dining room crib, and then came to my side. Derek stood next to her.

Confronted with this evidence of solidarity, Llyr nodded his assent and indicated with a wave of his hand that I should proceed.

"How much of that hallucination I had did you catch?" I asked the big god.

"Since we're quite connected, Son, I experienced it as thoroughly as you did, and found it most disturbing. Especially since I knew the identity of the perpetrator. Beli has gone too far this time and you, as the victim of this assault, should report him! And you *must* retrieve that bloody towel from him. What possessed you to discard something that could be used against you in that way?"

"I was bewitched by my lovely Emily at the time, Father. I have no other excuse—it was a most unfortunate decision, I admit."

"Well, I am going to help you to retrieve the towel without leaving this house. As the god of magic and healing you should already be aware of this, but I suspect that you need a little refresher—residing in a human body seems to have dulled your higher senses somewhat. I shall probably find myself in trouble for assisting you, but so be it." And he put the palm of his hand on my forehead, transferring the information I needed to create the spell. I jerked as the rush of energy permeated my being.

I blinked. "Of course, how could I have forgotten about that? Thank you for reminding me."

"Why don't you do it now, while I am here, Myrddin Emrys? If Beli decides to show his face, we can confront him together. At this point, I am spoiling for a fight."

I closed my eyes and dove deep into my inner self, where the source of my magic as a sorcerer resided, then wove the spell Llyr had given me and whispered, "*Veniat ad me*." I held out my right hand, then suddenly made a fist and yanked it towards me. There was a flash of light and a feeling of compression, and I opened my eyes…to see that the blood-encrusted towel was in my clenched fist.

As I let out a sigh of relief, I realized that I had been holding my breath, perhaps in anticipation of resistance by the god of death.

And then there came the response I had expected, echoing through my inner connection with the realm of the gods: a wordless growl of anger, frustration, and a promise of retribution. I glanced at Llyr and he raised his eyebrows, acknowledging that he had also heard the unspoken challenge.

Both Emily and Derek, although they had not been privy to the message directly, had felt it through their bonds with me, and shared a look of concern.

"Well, it's definitely not over, but the towel has been retrieved," I said, brandishing the offending fabric, "and I will destroy it forthwith." I immediately teleported to the top of the Rim with the object in hand. Throwing it down in an open sandy area edged with snow, I directed to it a flash of energy so powerful that the towel incinerated instantly and completely, and all the snow within a fifty-foot radius evaporated. The inhabitants of Moab who happened to be looking in the right direction would undoubtedly have seen a brilliant light in the dark sky, but would probably have thought it to be lightning.

Then, I was home again. I thanked my father profusely for his assistance, and bowed before him.

He started to fade out, but halted his departure abruptly. "By the way, I strongly suggest that you as act as soon as possible to seek out an audience with the one God. Beli is a formidable foe, and as he has no conscience, your family may be in danger. Just saying." And then he was gone.

"What are you going to do?" Derek appeared pale and exhausted as he contemplated his grandfather's words.

"I don't know yet. Perhaps until this is resolved, the three of you need to take refuge in the Crystal Cave," I said, feeling almost as tired as Derek looked.

"Well, hopefully it won't come to that and we'll have time to make a definite plan. I think we need to sleep on it—I know I do. See you in the mornin'," Derek said through a wide yawn that made his eyes water. He disappeared.

And I was finally alone with my wife and child.

CHAPTER 19

February 4 Night

EMILY AND I SAT in the kitchen a while longer, our need to talk temporarily overshadowing our need to hold each other. After what seemed like hours, our discussion was finally winding down.

"I feel as if I've already talked to you about all of this, but it was in my hallucination," I said. "In Camelot, Derek and I heard a young child's voice assuring us that you both would be fine until we got home; it was our Lumina, I'm sure of it, but from what year I wasn't able to discern. Has a future Lumina attempted to contact you? Have you, at any time, felt any special mental connection with the baby?"

"I was understandably upset when I realized you were gone, Merlin, but not enough to mistake who contacted me. It wasn't a future version of our daughter who spoke to me. *You* did—don't you remember?" Emily looked into my eyes in confusion.

I was stunned. I had felt no active connection with her at all while I was in Camelot. But I suppose it was possible that my subconscious mind had reached out to her from the fifth century—after all, our bond was powerful and unique. I remembered that I had dreamed vividly about Emily, and the contact must have occurred at that time.

"Well, I'm glad that you heard a message that comforted you, wife," I said as I reached out and gently squeezed her hand. She returned the gesture, but still had a puzzled look on her face.

"To answer your other question, whether I experience a connection with Lumina: yes, of course I do. I'm her mother, and a mother has a bond with her child that is magical in its own right. As to whether she actually communicates with me mentally, I'm starting to feel little nudges from her mind when she's hungry or tired. But that's all." Emily was silent and contemplative for a moment, and then she raised her clear hazel eyes to gaze lovingly into mine and ran her hand slowly up my bare forearm, causing me to shiver with desire. "Enough talking. Come, with me, magic man." She plucked our sleeping daughter from the small crib, and as we headed down the hallway towards the bedroom, I magically secured the front door and turned the lights off.

While Emily put Lumina down for the night, I availed myself of the modern toilet and reveled in the knowledge that I could have a shower, with plenty of hot water, at the turn of a faucet. I had forgotten how truly primitive the fifth century was in regards to personal hygiene, despite the various spells I had added to make things more tolerable. I pushed the handle down and watched with renewed interest as the water swirled in the bowl before disappearing with a gurgle into the unseen sewer system. *I like this century*, I thought, as I padded barefoot to stand in front of the mirror.

I leaned over the sink and examined my face closely, rather hoping to see that something had changed, perhaps a blemish or two, a few wrinkles to reflect all of the years I had lived and things I had experienced. I sighed. No change—I looked the same as I had since AD 452, the year I stopped ageing, with a few lines around my mouth and at the corners of my eyes. Exactly the same. But what did I expect? It was in my immortal nature to be immune to ageing.

"Merlin, you already know how handsome you are, so quit staring at yourself in the mirror," Emily exclaimed from the other room.

I grinned as I grabbed my toothbrush and ran a strip of paste along the bristles, then applied it vigorously to teeth and tongue—I had neglected my oral hygiene for the days that I'd been gone. I finished by swishing with mouthwash, then rinsing thoroughly, and finally felt that my mouth was clean enough to kiss my wife properly.

Emily entered the bathroom and as I turned towards her, she walked directly into my arms. I had thrown off my clothing already, so I was naked, holding my still fully-clothed wife.

"I think you need to remove your clothing, wench," I whispered as I kissed her full lips that were now turned up in a grin. I stroked her hair and held her even more tightly against me.

"'Wench,' really? I think your mind is still in the past, perhaps in the tavern, admiring the local serving girls," she laughed, as she pulled away to unzip her jeans and shimmy out of them, tugging her sweater over her head. I reached to unhook her nursing bra, releasing her full breasts, and she slipped off her purple cotton bikini underwear.

After having been away, even for two days, wondering whether I would ever get home again, I was anxious to join with my wife. I barely allowed her the time to remove her socks before I gathered her into my arms once more. Gods, she felt so soft and welcoming against my body, which was already completely aroused. We kissed each other deeply, our tongues dueling as we sought to get closer yet.

"My love, let's shower first and take this to our bed, shall we?" Emily said softly, nipping at my earlobe.

"You're right, I'm not particularly clean," I said as I ran my hands down her back to her buttocks and gave a gentle squeeze.

In the shower, cleansing each other's bodies under the generous spray of hot water became an erotic prelude to our anticipated lovemaking, and afterward, we made short work of toweling each other off.

Finally, I grabbed Em's hand, tugging her into our bedroom as my arousal became most demanding.

I threw back the covers impatiently and we lay down, reaching for each other. I kissed her thoroughly and she responded with an equally thorough, almost savage exploration of my mouth and tongue. I began my journey towards the ultimate destination by kissing and stroking the delicate skin of her neck and the area just below her collarbone. As I stopped to enjoy her breasts, she gasped as her nipples puckered and hardened. I continued down to her navel and across her rounded abdomen to the apex of her thighs, whereupon I stroked her hips and encouraged her to open her legs so that I could use my tongue and long fingers to best advantage at her core. Emily whimpered and arched her back as I sought to increase the pleasure she felt by adding a touch of magic. Suddenly, she stiffened and cried out with the intensity of her climax. Even as she was sighing and breathing hard from that experience, I rose above her. I entered her slowly, feeling her still-pulsing inner muscles surrounding my hardness. My body deep within hers, I gazed into eyes ringed with long dark lashes and I felt our essences merge until, for just a moment, we were one being. That sweet moment seemed to last an eternity, and then it was over. As I came back to myself I immediately realized that I was looking up into the face I had just seen in the mirror; a masculine face with brilliant green eyes that widened in shock. Emily and I had switched bodies.

"Oh, my *God!*" I heard my own horrified voice say. "Merlin, I'm you…and you're me…how did this happen? Oh, *crap*!"

"Be calm, sweetness, we'll fix this, just relax," I heard myself say in Emily's voice. I became aware of the hardness inside of me, and noticed that my breasts were huge, the nipples so sensitive they were almost painful. And as I was discovering these sensations I could see by the look on that male face above me that Emily was experiencing the intense lust I always had for her, feeling that purely male urge to complete the sexual act. She moaned and kissed me frantically as she began to move within me, the pressure of arousal creating a frenzied drive to achieve fulfillment. And I responded to that frenzy by returning her passionate kisses and grabbing hold of her buttocks, trying to force that hardness deeper, the fullness and friction causing an amazing sensation, a pressure that built up until I thought I would go mad with longing for…something…*ohhh, gods*… I experienced a release so intense that I was powerless to keep from crying out, weeping with joy. Emily suddenly growled with lust as she thrust deeply once more and experienced her own climax.

We lay still for a few moments, Emily sprawled limp and very heavy on top of me, smashing my sensitive breasts and making breathing difficult.

"Emily, sweetheart, I love you, but you're going to have to get off of me," I gasped, not able to move as the almost two hundred pounds of male body still lay motionless. I tried to push her off but soon realized that this female body I temporarily inhabited was not very strong. I knew I would pass out soon if I wasn't able to take a deep breath, and then I remembered that, of course, I still had access to my powers—they were a part of my true self, my spirit, my soul. I immediately levitated Emily, in my body, over to the other side of the bed, and took a long, quavering breath—and started weeping again. Oh, gods, the hormones that were still raging through this body; how could she stand it?

"What happened?" Emily asked groggily, in my voice but with her intonations.

"Em, you almost crushed me until I remembered that I could still use my powers," I complained.

"Well, now you know how I feel, honey. You don't look it since you're so slender, but you're *heavy*—and strong—these muscles are just amazing. And Merlin, oh, my God, now I know what you feel when we have sex! Holy shit, that was so intense; it felt like your body just took over! It just wanted to *screw*, never mind making love. And knowing what you must go through just to control yourself when you're all aroused and I'm not—*whew*—I'll never tease you again or make you wait so long. This penis is quite an appendage; I kind of wish I had one." Emily was fondling her still semi-aroused male genitals with amused interest. "Oh, that feels so good, I'm sure I could get hard again and—" Then she glanced at me and realized that tears were making delicate tracks down my face.

"Are you crying? Oh, sweetheart…female hormones are a bitch, aren't they? Just so you know, they were much worse before you healed me a week ago. Hey, maybe we can stay in each other's bodies for a day or two," Emily said excitedly, as I frowned in disapproval.

"Wife, I know that this has been a good thing to experience each other's bodies, but quite frankly, I want mine back. I don't know how women do it," I exclaimed loudly, forgetting that I would wake the baby.

I heard a whimpering cry, which quickly escalated in volume.

"Merlin, she probably wants to nurse, and since you are currently the one with the breasts, I guess you'll have to do it," Emily said smugly. It was extremely disconcerting to watch her expressions flicker on *my* face.

I got out of bed, picked up our daughter and sat back down amidst the rumpled bedding, then looked at Emily questioningly.

"Just cradle her like this—," she positioned Lumina at one breast, "—and she'll do the rest. She's learned a lot in the last week."

Lumina grabbed hold of my nipple with her questing mouth and started to suckle. I gasped at the incredible tugging sensation that raced straight to my womb as the milk flowed. I gazed down at the tiny mouth working so industriously and I felt a loving tenderness I'd never known before. Lumina opened her eyes and looked at me as she nursed, and I experienced a connection to my baby daughter that I'd never felt while in my male body. At that moment I envied Emily for having had this child actually growing inside of her. I smiled and raised my eyes to look into those familiar green ones; then, in an instant of disorientation, I was back in my own body, watching my wife nurse our child. The pang of loss I felt was so unexpected that it startled me. I would never see Emily's role as wife and mother in the same way again.

CHAPTER 20

February 5 5:45 AM

RESTLESS, I AWOKE quite early the following morning, thoughts crowding in unbidden. Turning my head on the pillow, I watched my wife as she slept, oblivious to my wakefulness. I gazed at her face, her hair, her curves under the blankets, and I couldn't help but remember how it had felt to inhabit her body, to be a woman briefly, to nurse my child. What an exquisite sensation it had been when Lumina looked deeply, trustingly, into my eyes during that intimate moment at my breast.

I would never have been able to experience that precious time with my daughter if Derek hadn't intervened to prevent my spirit from being forcibly removed from my body. I could not begin to express my gratitude for his actions. Since he had never evinced any aptitude at all for the healing arts—whether by sorcery or through the knowledge and application of herbal remedies—I was especially amazed that my son had saved me from Beli. He and I would have to talk soon and experiment with his powers; he obviously had an ability with which I was unfamiliar.

I yawned widely and stretched, appreciating the fine, soft texture of the sheets against my bare skin and the firm, padded comfort of our bed supporting my six-feet-two-inch frame. It was a contrast indeed between the bedding in my old quarters in Camelot—however luxurious for the time—and the superior construction of a modern mattress. Many people in this century exceeded my height by as much as ten inches, which amazed me. I was much taller than most people in the fifth century and of course, the goose-down and feather bed I had slept on had been made for a shorter man, so my feet had always hung over the end, as had happened when Derek and I had shared my sleeping arrangements. Naturally, this observation led to other thoughts of our recent journey to the fifth century.

When we had first arrived in the past, I had been pleased to be there, and thrilled for Derek to experience the real Camelot. I was grateful, and deeply moved, to see the young King Arthur again and to discover Derek's kinship with him, but battling the dragons, worrying about Derek's uncharacteristic sexual adventure, and then witnessing the Saxons invade Old Town, had effectively soured my overall enjoyment. Then, returning to the twenty-first century, only to be immersed in a massive hallucination created by the blood-ritual black magic wielded by Beli—a very real threat to my existence in this human realm—I was more than ready to settle back into our normal life. However, I realized that while destroying the bloody towel the previous day had accorded me a certain triumph over the god of death, there would be no true resolution without a judgment against him by the one God who ruled us all.

I decided to get up and start the coffee, allowing Em to sleep as long as possible, or at least until the baby awoke. I managed to grab some clean clothes and creep silently out of the bedroom without disturbing either of them. I quickly washed and dressed in the guest bathroom and teleported into the kitchen to get the coffee going. It occurred to me that Derek and I were teleporting more and more frequently, and therefore we must be on guard against doing so in the presence of normal humans. I grinned as I remembered the shocked look on Arthur's face when Derek had appeared in his chambers without warning. The king had been more accepting of the situation than I would have given him credit for, and he had definitely surprised me by his perception of my real nature. I was grateful that I'd had the opportunity to be with the young Arthur again, but gods, I was glad to be home. The quest was once more foremost in my mind and heart, and I knew with a bone-deep certainty that the time was rapidly drawing near when we would have to attempt to bring Arthur back from his resting place with the Fae. The time of Albion beckoned.

I sensed Derek approaching the house, already dressed in his Park Service uniform, and I cautioned him telepathically to be silent. Suddenly, he was standing beside me in the kitchen with a big grin on his handsome face. I wondered how I had ever missed seeing his resemblance to Camelot's ruler.

"I just love bein' able to do that," he confessed. "Bein' a sorcerer is totally awesome!"

I chuckled at his enthusiasm. "Oh, I enjoy it also, but as I'm accustomed to it after all these centuries I tend to take it for granted."

"I'll never take my powers for granted," Derek swore vehemently.

"I hope that the experience does remain fresh and new for you, Son, over the years," I said, noticing that his eyes looked tired. "You're up early, did you have trouble sleeping last night?"

His expression sobered. "Yeah, I woke up and started thinkin', and then I couldn't go back to sleep. You?"

"Yes, the same," I admitted.

We just stared at one another, both of us remembering what had occurred the previous day, and how close I had come to leaving this realm permanently. And then, we found ourselves in each other's arms, my son sobbing uncontrollably. I just held him that way for a time, until I saw Emily over Derek's shoulder, standing in the doorway in her robe with a concerned look on her face, and I let her know silently that everything was okay. She nodded, blew me a kiss and went back to the bedroom.

I said reassuringly, "It's alright, Son, you succeeded! I'm still here, thanks to you." I rubbed his back as if he was a young child and he finally quieted.

"Derek, you will never really lose me, for even if I do have to leave this body permanently some day, my spirit, my essence—my consciousness—will still *be*. I existed in that form until I came to this realm to become Merlin, remember, and I will continue to exist until the end of time. You will always feel me in your heart, in your soul and in your mind, my son. We are a part of each other." I kissed his cheek.

"I know," he whispered, pulling away and self-consciously wiping the tears from his face, "but I can't bear the thought of losin' you, Merlin, the physical you. You're my father, but you're also my friend, my brother…my hero. And now, there's, uh, somethin' else..." He looked at me almost shyly. "In your hallucination yesterday, when you left your body and manifested in your god form—like Llyr appears to us—I…I actually worshiped you."

"I remember you saying that, but—wait, you experienced my hallucination? You were actually in it with me?" I was aghast.

"Yeah, and I felt your god power inside of me when you gave me your love."

"Gods, Derek, that's how you saved me—it has to be! You were able to hold onto my essence and keep me here because I was inside you. You embraced my essence. I…thank you, Son. I don't know what to say."

"You're welcome, Dad, and I'm glad it happened, even if I don't understand it. But, back to the, uh, worshipin' thing—God, this is really awkward—am I supposed to kiss your feet, or bow to you or somethin', like I did in your hallucination?" he asked, flustered.

"As I told Emily, I will never require my family to bow to me or to kiss my feet. However, you must do what you feel in your heart." I was touched by his sincerity and with the depth of his devotion to Myrddin Emrys; it had been just a matter of time before he expressed his true feelings. So, now I had three devotees, and my god powers seemed closer to the surface than ever.

Finally, we sat down to drink our coffee, content to enjoy each other's company in the early morning silence. Eventually, Emily entered the kitchen with a squirming baby in her arms, and Derek reached out to take his sister so that we could start breakfast. His obvious affinity for the child made me wonder how long it would be before he decided to start a family of his own.

The knights were conspicuously absent this morning, which was just as well, as I was much too preoccupied to deal with them. As I mixed pancake batter and preheated the grill, unresolved issues were like a maelstrom in my mind, particularly regarding Adrestia. What in all the kingdoms, in all the realms of reality, was I going to do about my eldest daughter? During my hallucination, I had sensed that there was still a core of goodness within her, but that could have been wishful thinking on my part. I suspected that she had been controlled and conditioned for so long by her mother that evil had consumed her very soul. I hoped that I was wrong, but I feared the worst—she was most likely beyond redemption.

I had to drag my thoughts away from her or I would be immersed in misery all day. Instead, I chose to focus on the many positive, joyful aspects of my life, and when I looked at my lovely wife next to me as we prepared breakfast, and at my grown son holding his baby sister gently in his arms, I felt that here was the true magic in my life.

Forty-five minutes later, we had eaten and cleaned up the kitchen, and Emily excused herself to start a load of laundry and clean the bedrooms.

I frowned. "Em, you can do that later, or I can just take care of it using magic."

"I appreciate the gesture, my love, but I know how much you want to talk to Derek right now…Besides, I've got a few magic tricks up my sleeve. Did you really think I was doing all that work the hard way?" She smiled and winked at me, then turned and walked out of the kitchen, her hips swaying provocatively. I grinned and shook my head, feeling my body start to respond to her sassy invitation. Reluctantly, I turned away and started another pot of coffee.

As I waited for it to brew, all the issues I had been pondering since I woke up this morning came rushing back to the forefront of my mind, and rather than allowing myself to feel overwhelmed, I decided to deal with one thing at a time. Coffee ready, Derek and I had one last cup before he left for work.

"What the hell am I gonna tell them? I've been gone for a week without permission. What if I've lost my job?" He was getting himself all worked up, so I suggested that he use his magic to influence his supervisor's mind.

"Convince him that you were very ill and you had stayed home under a doctor's care."

"But that's cheatin'!" My son looked horrified that I had suggested such a thing.

I sighed. "Society would say that it is, Derek, but we have to live by different rules than mortals do. Do you really think any of this—your job, your supervisor, your co-workers—will really matter in fifty or a hundred years? A thousand years? Try to put things in perspective. I normally wouldn't condone dishonesty, but you had no control over the force that swept us back in time, and you can't tell your supervisor the truth, now can you? 'Hey, sorry, but I'm actually a sorcerer, and black magic transported me and my dad Merlin back in time to Camelot, where I met my uncle King Arthur and battled dragons and Saxons.'" I ended my statement with a disingenuous look.

Derek laughed as much at the look on my face as at the obviously ridiculous statement I had just made. But his expressive features reflected the conflict he was feeling about this situation, and I could see it as he finally resigned himself to a different course of action than he would have preferred to take. "No, I guess I can't. I mean, I can always find another job, but I like this one, and an unexcused absence would sure have a negative effect on my record."

He finally departed, with the intention of doing what I'd suggested, and I decided to go ahead and open up my shop. It was a day for taking a step forward. It wasn't until I arrived at The Moab Herbalist and turned the sign around to "Open" that I realized that he and I had never discussed what to do about Beli.

CHAPTER 21

February 5 8:30 AM–4:00 PM

IT FELT GOOD, AND RIGHT, to be back at work at The Moab Herbalist, creating potions and interacting with my clients, after having been gone for several months. When I'd first arrived this morning, I had opened up the windows and doors briefly and allowed the fresh, cold air in to dispel the stale, closed-up feeling. Invigorated, the oxygenated blood flowing to my brain stimulating my awareness, my sense of purpose returned. I smiled as I marveled anew at the intricacy and sensitivity of this human body.

The chimes on the door tinkled continuously throughout the morning as my customers dropped in to make purchases large and small, and to express their pleasure in seeing me again. I was pleased to see them as well, having forged a connection of sorts during our many interactions over the past year.

Several clients suggested that a reading or story-telling session take place the following week, and I agreed, promising to notify them when I had finalized the details. As I noted possible days and times on my new calendar, I paused for a moment to admire the artwork adorning it: stylized views of "red rock country," in vivid colors and bold brushstrokes, captured the beautiful starkness of our unique landscape. The local artist who had created these scenes was extremely talented; I could almost feel the heat on the sun-drenched sandstone cliffs in one picture and the coolness of a shadowed arch in another. Derek had given me the calendar for Christmas, a holiday that I normally didn't celebrate as I was not a Christian. I had decided to participate to please my family, and then found that I quite enjoyed the aspects of the holiday that were of ancient pagan origin.

Around eleven o'clock, business was so brisk that I admitted to myself the necessity of hiring someone part-time, or at least of having Emily come and help out a few hours a day. It was during this hectic time that I realized my stock of herbs was low. I had yet to place an order this season and would need to do so soon, as several clients had inquired about specific herbs. One person in particular asked about a few that I had never carried or used, at least in this century: Catmint, Hog's Fennel and Hound's Tongue or Ribwort. All three were ancient herbs intended for treating snakebite, which could be useful here in the high desert, but I was not convinced that the average hiker would be carrying the other items necessary to complete the tonics. For instance, betony, deer bone marrow and vinegar would be needed along with the Hog's Fennel, to actually treat the wound. I was surprised that anyone would even be familiar with these herbs unless they had read an old herb book. But the most interesting thing about this encounter was that the man had used the Old English words for those herbs: Nepte, Cammoc and Ribbe. I hoped he would come in again once I had ordered them. Unfortunately, in the rush to wait on other customers, I had neglected to get the man's phone number or email address. I hadn't even asked him for his name, nor had he mentioned it.

Finally, in the early afternoon, the flow of customers trickled to a halt. Although I had initially intended to remain open until five o'clock, I took the cessation of business as a sign that I was done for the day, and locked the door. I sat down for a few minutes with a mug of coffee and thought about Derek's confession early this morning. Remembering the look on my proud, stubborn son's face as he asked me if he should bow to me or kiss my feet, I felt…humbled. I stood up and put the mug on the counter. I decided that this was the perfect time to work on Derek's staff, the oak branch that had been stored in the shop for many months, awaiting my attention. I found the branch leaning against the wall in the back room and spent several minutes contemplating the ideal sorcerer's tool, taking into account my knowledge of Derek's powers.

Originally, I had planned to shape the staff and carve the runes the old-fashioned way, with a special woodcarving knife, but as that was a long, involved procedure by hand, I decided just to use magic for the entire process. I held the branch up in front of me, parallel to the floor, visualized the finished length of it complete with the appropriate symbols, and channeled the magic through my arms and hands into the wood. For a moment, the oak branch glowed with an incandescent yellow light as my magic changed and shaped it to its new purpose. Abruptly, the light was gone, and I was holding a finished staff that Derek would surely be able to wield as easily as I did my own. Covered by runes and sigils, it almost vibrated with power as I ran my hands over it. Yes, it was ready.

I was pleased with my endeavors and put the staff aside to be given to Derek at an opportune time. I used a shielding spell to hide it, as he was a frequent visitor to the shop and spent a good deal of time in the back room with me as I prepared my tonics and other herbal concoctions.

His birthday was coming up in March, but I hoped to give it to him before that, as I had been procrastinating long enough, and he needed to practice using it.

After I'd spent some time straightening the shop and making lists for purchases I would have to make in the near future, I felt the restlessness of this morning return. A residue of magical tension from creating the staff threatened to break free and override my common sense—and inhibitions—and I had a burning desire to be outside and up in the air. I decided to come back later to prepare my deposit and do any remaining chores, and stepped out into the alley, my mind already on what I was about to undertake. I locked the back door and set the wards to protect the shop, then glanced around to make sure no one would witness my disappearance. Fortunately, I was alone.

I teleported to the top of the Rim, to the spot where the defunct chairlift had terminated, and pondered my decision to fly—not just levitate—but to really fly. Ever since Derek had mentioned it while we were in the fifth century, I had been considering the possibility. I had no intention of becoming a bird this time, and I had powerful magic to call upon to accomplish this feat without shapeshifting. I thought back on the battle of the previous summer, and how I had effortlessly kept myself in midair while utilizing my other powers to fight the invasion of supernatural creatures, and realized that I had not been merely levitating, I'd been flying.

According to the story of Superman, which I had read recently, he had been sent to this planet by his father to escape the destruction of his home world, Krypton, and Earth's yellow sun had given him his powers. I might be as different from normal humans as Clark Kent was from the citizens of Smallville, but I was not an alien—I had been born on this planet. And my spirit self was a part of the essence of this world, so therefore I should be able to easily manipulate that essence, bypassing the restraints of gravity that kept mere mortals earthbound.

I closed my eyes and sensed no one within miles of my location. Good, I didn't need, nor did I desire, a human audience. However, I did perceive a gaze upon me and noticed a collared lizard—turquoise body and gold head glittering like jewels in a sudden shaft of sunlight—looking up at me intently. It seemed unlikely for this creature to be sunning itself during the chill of winter, and I wondered for a protracted moment if it was a shapeshifter—a man in another form. Then, I dismissed my suspicions as I realized that my desire to fly far outweighed my concern that I was being observed, and my heart began pounding with excitement and anticipation. The lizard, apparently coming to its senses, scuttled under a rock, and I scoffed at my folly; sometimes a lizard was just a lizard.

I took a cleansing breath, focused carefully inside myself and recognized the part of my being from which I normally accessed my levitating abilities, and went even deeper into that well of magic. I leaped into the air and imagined the limitless expanse of sky above me, and the fact that I was truly one with it—and kept going. Wind buffeted me and made my eyes water as I streaked through an occasional cloud and felt ice particles on my face, neck and hands. The air was considerably colder and thinner at such an altitude, and I had to make adjustments to my body temperature to keep from freezing and to my lungs in order to obtain enough oxygen. I sensed the planet below me, and the blanket of stars above me, and for a moment felt my unique isolation.

When I finally paused to look down, I was much higher than I had intended to fly for my first attempt. The clouds below parted and I saw a satellite's view of the world, and was just barely able to identify the Four Corners area of the United States in the giant planetary "map" below me. I looked for Wales and hardly recognized the small shape that was my homeland. Several months ago, Emily and I had found an old globe at a thrift store, and we had marveled at the way the countries had looked, as if one was gazing down from an immeasurable distance away.

Now, I was actually viewing the multicolored land masses of the Earth, the swirl of clouds and the deep colors of the oceans, and knew that I was seeing the ebb and flow of life on this planet. My god self seemed to expand and encompass everything I witnessed below me. The feeling of being at the heart of the universe became a pulsating joy which urged me to return to the source of all things, and I had to make a concerted effort to stop myself from leaving my body behind.

As I succeeded in acquiescing to the limitations of the flesh, I felt the tug of gravity reminding me that I was still in my human body, a body that needed to feel solid ground beneath its feet. I could feel my heart pumping and the blood rushing through my veins and arteries, yet I felt the tingle of magic arcing through me, reminding me that I was much more than human—obviously. For here I was, suspended above the planet upon which human beings fiercely clung to their mundane existences, my body surviving despite the fact that there was little or no air to breathe.

Finally, I decided to reverse direction and fly back the way I had come, arrowing sleekly through the thickening atmosphere until I glimpsed the details below me, of the City of Moab, the Colorado River and the top of the Rim. I reveled in the strength of my inner connection with the air and the sky, realizing now that the arbitrary line I had drawn between my sorcerer's powers and my god powers was faint indeed. The ease with which had I utilized my powers in overcoming the limitations of gravity convinced me that there was no appreciable difference in the two at all.

But I was still human enough to want to share this incredible experience with my family, so I sent a telepathic message to my wife.

Emily, get your binoculars, go outside and look up, perhaps 1000 feet above the place on the Rim where the old chair lift used to terminate.

As soon as she did what I'd asked, I heard my wife in my mind, exclaiming wildly as she became totally immersed in our special bond. It felt now as if she accompanied me on my return flight. I reached out to Derek as well.

Derek, are you feeling this? I'm flying!

Congratulations, Dad; I knew you could do it. Derek was thrilled at my accomplishment. He'd heard my query, felt the intensity of my experience through our bond, and had "tuned in" as I flew. I could sense him at the National Park Service office on Resource Boulevard, so he'd apparently been able to retain his employment status.

My mind seemed suddenly crowded with both my son and my wife clamoring for my attention. *My God, Merlin, how did you know you could actually fly? Are you using your god powers?* Emily's thoughts echoed clearly in my mind, interrupted by Derek's cheers of *Yahoo, you go Dad!* And, *Can you fly upside down?* Then, *We need to get you a cape!*

I answered Em's query first. *I'm not sure—perhaps. I believe I've always had the ability to fly, I just didn't recognize how to access it. In the past, when I levitated, I was barely tapping into that power. The desire to fly has always been mine—perhaps I knew instinctively that the potential was there.* Then, *Yes, Derek, I can fly upside down,* and *No, I don't want a cape.*

Suddenly, my elation knew no bounds, and I threw my head back and my arms out and laughed aloud in joyful abandon. As the cold wind blew through my hair, I relaxed and allowed myself to fall free, the earth appearing to rush up to meet me. I heard my wife nervously calling to me in my mind, and I tried to allay her fear by sharing with her, and with Derek, my joy and excitement. As I came closer to the place from which I had started my flight, I took hold of my power and slowed my descent, so that I touched down as gently and safely as getting out of bed in the morning. Em was relieved that I was no longer airborne, but I assured her there had never been a point at which I was in danger.

Back on the ground, the differences in altitude were quite obvious: The air was warmer and heavier here on the Rim—although in the low forties, it felt balmy compared to what I had experienced aloft. A sudden updraft from the valley floor brought the odors of civilization: roasting coffee, cooking, the exhaust from hundreds of vehicles and the scent of the winter-bound earth. I stood gazing out over the valley, noting the lazy plumes of smoke issuing from the chimneys of the homes using wood to keep their families warm, then sought out a view of my own house below on the right. I could see my wife standing in the front yard, holding the binoculars up to her face with her right hand and clutching our blanket-wrapped daughter against her body with her left. I smiled down at her and she waved the binoculars at me excitedly.

I wonder if I can fly? I heard my son ask wistfully. I could sense the yearning in him, but this was not really the time to discuss or explore his powers as he was still at work.

Go inside yourself, later, when you're home, and discover on your own whether or not you have that ability, I said kindly.

I know it sounds stupid, but I'm afraid to. I'll be home soon and maybe you can help me try to fly then.

Alright, we'll talk about it later. I had a feeling he already knew the answer but wasn't willing to accept the truth. I just hoped that he would be content with levitation if flying truly wasn't an option for him.

I sent a telepathic message to Emily to let her know I'd be home soon, but that I needed some time alone first.

No problem, my love. I need to take Lumina back inside anyway. I'll see you soon, Emily responded.

I breathed deeply of the cool, juniper-scented air and closed my eyes for a moment. I was content to stand on the precipice with the smooth red sandstone, coated with a light dusting of snow, under my feet, and the washed-out denim blue of the winter sky over my head. The music of the spheres sang through my being as I connected once again with my god self, and I embraced the Light.

Without warning, I was yanked back to full awareness as a tremendous force knocked me off of my feet and over the edge of the cliff. I fell like a lead weight, striking agonizingly against protruding boulders and stunted Utah junipers as I tumbled hundreds of feet, out of control. I reached for that power inside of myself that I had recently accessed, and attempted to stop my unplanned and decidedly painful descent. I intended to fly back to the ledge upon which I'd been standing a moment ago, healing myself almost instantaneously as I did so. I knew that Beli had done this, and that he would be waiting for me, huge and angry.

As a father, I could understand why this god wanted revenge. But as the victim of his daughter's cruelty for centuries, I had no patience left, and didn't feel any sympathy whatsoever for this vengeful god. I recognized that I had no choice but to destroy him, or at least destroy the part of him that had manifested in this realm.

These thoughts raced through my mind in the split second before I realized that I couldn't access my god powers, nor could I use any but the most basic of my sorcerer's abilities; I most assuredly couldn't fly back up to the top of the Rim. I was barely able to surround myself with a slight shield of energy that would hopefully keep the fall from tearing my body apart. I couldn't help but be reminded of a small bird spiraling down to its death the previous summer.

I heard a faint, deep, sinister laugh echo in my mind, and I lost consciousness.

CHAPTER 22

February 5 4:00-6:00 PM

THERE WAS ONLY DARKNESS, and excruciating pain. I drew in a short, ragged breath and slowly tried to open my eyes. I could barely see through the wet stickiness obscuring my vision. Puzzled, I reached up to wipe the unknown substance off of my face and even that slight movement caused my entire body to scream in protest. I looked at my hand and saw blood. Tentatively, I touched my face again, as well as my neck and scalp and realized that I had numerous gaping, painful wounds, all bleeding profusely. I carefully glanced down and noticed that my clothing was ripped and filthy, and I could feel the evidence of other injuries on the rest of my twisted and broken body. As I shivered in the cold air, wondering why I had no jacket on, I tried to draw a deep breath and agony lanced through me, causing me to flinch and gasp. It felt as if my ribs were broken, and even though one of my legs was bent at an unnatural angle, I couldn't feel it—I was numb below the waist. Was my back broken?

What the hell had happened to me? My thought processes sluggish, I couldn't seem to remember anything but that I had fallen from above. I was lying amongst sharp, snow-covered rocks in the shadows at the bottom of a rugged wall of sandstone, and I could just barely perceive the edge of the precipice almost a thousand feet above me. *Absolutely impossible*, I thought. If I had fallen from such a height I would not now be alive. I groaned feebly, the effort to move having exhausted me.

"Dad, my God, what happened? I got here as soon as I could. Are you alright?" I heard a male voice, high-pitched in fear, and someone scrabbling towards me through the loose rocks, but I couldn't answer. Somehow, it didn't seem relevant.

And besides, I wasn't anyone's dad…was I? I couldn't remember.

A calloused hand reached out tenderly and touched my face. I flinched and the hand withdrew.

"How could this have happened, Dad? Why didn't you just fly back up to the top? Or teleport? Shit, I've got to get you home, Emily is freakin' out. She had to stay with the baby or she'd be here with me now."

Huh? What in the world was he babbling about? Fly? Teleport? Baby? Was he serious? God, his chatter was driving me crazy. I roused myself enough to croak weakly, "I don't know who the hell you are, or what you're talking about. Just call for a damned ambulance, will you? I'm dying here!" I sensed the man's shock at my words, and then I felt him clasp my left arm firmly. There was a strange sensation of movement and I passed out.

As I slowly regained consciousness, I felt a soft, warm, wet cloth moving over my body, and a feminine voice said, "Welcome back, sweetheart—I think you're going to survive after all." I heard water splash and sensed someone moving next to me, rinsing a cloth and wringing it out.

I opened my eyes carefully and saw a pair of hazel ones gazing down into mine. Fully expecting the searing pain again, I was surprised to find that it was now at a manageable level. I realized that I was stark naked, lying on my back on a soft bed in a well-appointed bedroom, being given a sponge bath by a total stranger. While she was a very pretty woman, with her golden brown hair, delicate freckled nose and shapely figure, and under normal circumstances I would be attracted to her, I was disconcerted by the uninvited intimacy. Although my limbs were stiff and sore, and apparently not broken after all, I could move them, and I proceeded to try and cover at least the lower portion of my body with the sheet next to me. Especially since the lady's ministrations had caused a noticeable swelling in my groin area, completely against my will.

"I'm pretty sure I've seen your junk before, magic man, so there's really no need to cover yourself up," she said, obviously amused. She pulled the sheet out of my hands and began to gently wash my chest, my abdomen and the part of me that was the center of attention.

My face flamed in embarrassment at her casual treatment of my private bits. As I tried to concentrate on something other than the indignity I was suffering, I realized that she had just called me "magic man." What was that about? Then, I heard muted footsteps as if someone walked across a thick carpet, and the same male voice I'd heard before murmured, "What's he doin' Em?" A handsome man in his late twenties, with light brown hair and intelligent brown eyes, stood next to the bed so I was able to connect a face to the voice. He seemed to be wearing some kind of uniform.

"He's acting unusually modest, like he has no idea who I am. What the hell's the matter with him, Derek?" she asked in a worried tone, as she toweled the moisture off of my body.

I finally found my voice, shaky and hoarse. "Who *are* you people? Why didn't you take me to the damned hospital?"

The man and the woman looked first at me, and then at each other, in confusion, and the woman said, "What do you mean, who are we? And why would we take you to the hospital?"

"Because I'm injured, you idiots! What the *fuck*?" I shouted in frustration. I couldn't believe this was happening.

"I've never heard him use the F-word before, have you? He obviously doesn't remember who he is, Em. How weird is that?" the man said, as he reached out and examined my arm and other areas of my body where I knew I'd had severe injuries. I felt my skin crawl as I was handled without my permission, but I was still too weak to pull away.

"It looks like he's healin' himself anyway—automatically. Damn, I thought he had to consciously access the inner Light to do that." He scratched his head and stared at me in disbelief. "I don't know why I'm surprised, though, after everythin' I've seen him do."

"I'm right here!" I snapped, at the end of my patience, as they both talked about me as if I wasn't there.

The woman, Em—short for Emily?—sighed, ignoring my comment. "Well, that's just great—my husband, the god of magic, has amnesia. I was worried that something would happen up there, and he assured me that everything was okay. What do you want to bet Beli did this, the bastard!" Then she apparently heard something in another room and she turned and hurried out.

God of magic? Okay, this was seriously creeping me out. The pain had faded, my strength was returning and I was feeling almost normal—how was that possible? *I should be dead after a fall like that*, I thought, uncomprehendingly.

"You're immortal. Even if you had died, you would've come back to life. In this case, you healed yourself automatically. *That's* why we didn't take you to the hospital. Pretty cool, huh?" The man standing next to the bed smiled as he gazed down at me, arms folded over his chest.

I looked at him in shock. "You just read my mind!?"

"Yeah, I did," he said matter-of-factly.

I sat up carefully and stared at him, concerned that he wasn't entirely sane. "Where are my clothes? I really need to get out of here." I glanced around but didn't see them, and wondered if I would recognize them if they were here.

"The clothes you were wearin' were torn to shreds and we threw 'em out, but I'm sure you have plenty more. Let's see…" And he proceeded to dig into a chest of drawers, pulling out a green T-shirt, gray cotton briefs and a pair of jeans. "Here, put these on. But you don't *need* to go anywhere, Dad—you live here." The man whose name was apparently Derek tossed the clothes to me as I sat up, and I caught them awkwardly, still feeling weak.

I pulled the clothes on, surprised to find that they fit me perfectly, and grateful that my genitals were no longer on display. "Why do you keep calling me that? I'm not your damned father!" I gritted my teeth at his persistence.

He just sighed and said, "Yeah, you are, Merlin, trust me. Maybe if you see yourself in the mirror that will help jog your memory." He helped me to stand up and finish fastening my jeans, then he steered me over in front of a set of mirrored closet doors, and stood next to me as we gazed at our reflections.

I stared at myself intently—who was this stranger? I did not recognize myself. At least six feet two and slender, I had straight, medium-length, jet-black hair and bright green slanted eyes. Cat's eyes. I looked...mysterious. My skin tone was light, not swarthy, as might be associated with such dark hair, and I appeared to be Caucasian, but what nationality was I? There was a strange cadence, a trace of an accent, in my speech—could I be English? I shook my head in confusion, hoping, perhaps, to dislodge a memory or two. I took a closer look, at the long straight nose, the relatively unlined skin of my face, and the ripple of muscles in my arms. Although I appeared to be in my early thirties, some inner sense told me that I was far older than I looked; in fact, quite ancient, more than a thousand years old. I shook the feeling off and thought to myself, *What utter nonsense.*

I glanced surreptitiously at the man next to me who claimed to be my son. I did see a resemblance in the shape of his face, but that was all. I had no memories to draw from—perhaps we were cousins. And then it dawned on me that the man had called me Merlin. *The magician? Sidekick to the legendary King Arthur? Was he fucking kidding me? No way.* But how did he know so much about me unless he *was* a relative—or a friend?

"I'm your son, but I was your friend before you showed me who you really are, who *I* really am," he said, once again responding to my thoughts.

I gave him a black look. "You know, that's extremely annoying." Then, suddenly feeling a rush of confusion and uncertainty, I sat down gingerly on the bed, still expecting to feel at least some twinge of the pain I had been in such a short time ago. I couldn't believe that my injuries no longer bothered me.

Once again he responded to my thoughts. "That's because you're completely healed, Dad, and you did it yourself. You're a sorcerer and a god. I just don't understand how you can have amnesia, but Em's right; it must be Beli's doin'. He's the god of death and you killed his daughter last summer."

I was speechless. Either this guy was a certified nut case, or he was telling the truth. He had read my mind, and I seemed to be completely healed. But, he said I was a *god?* And I killed another god's daughter? What the *hell?*

"I…I don't understand." I was overwhelmed and started to shake with reaction—to the fall, to being in this house with two strangers who seemed to know all about me, to the very real possibility that I was losing my mind. *I can't be a sorcerer or a god, can I?* I thought in near panic.

"Yeah, you can. You *are*," Derek exclaimed, practically tearing out his hair in frustration. Abruptly, he commanded, "*Albus lux,*" and an orb of white light about the size of a softball appeared in the palm of his hand. Without warning, he tossed the glowing object to me, and without thinking, I caught it. I inhaled sharply as I felt a strong tingling throughout my body, and the orb not only remained in my hand but also brightened considerably.

"There, see? I told ya!" he chortled, brown eyes crinkling at the corners.

"Wha…what do I do with it *now*?" I stuttered nervously, my hand vibrating with energy.

"What do you want to do with it?"

"I just want it *gone*!" I said, frantically. And it was, as if it had never been there. I stared at my hand, my mouth open in shock. I raised my eyes slowly to gaze into Derek's, and he just grinned a little, then appeared to make up his mind about something.

"Okay, this is ridiculous, just let me hold onto your bare arm for a minute, and look into your eyes, and I'll try to fix this. We usually don't have to touch each other anymore to connect mentally, but you're not yourself right now. And I'm not very good at healin' either, but I'll do my best." He reached out to me and I cringed away from him.

"Don't touch me, you pervert!" I said fearfully, putting my arms behind my back.

Derek sighed and rubbed one hand over his face. Then, he looked directly at me, trying to connect with my eyes, and I glanced away nervously. He grabbed my face in his hands and made me look at him.

"Look at me, and just listen! You're the most powerful sorcerer who's ever lived, and you're almost 1,600 years old. You were King Arthur's advisor: Merlin, the Sorcerer of Camelot. You're also the Welsh god of magic and healin', and I'm your son. Emily is your wife and Lumina is your daughter," Derek recited harshly. There was no doubt in my mind that he believed it, but I couldn't relate to something so outlandish. It had to be pure fantasy—Merlin and King Arthur were shadowy figures of legend; they weren't real. I was Welsh? That would explain my accent. And the god part—seriously?

"Oh, my *God*! You're one stubborn son of a bitch, you know that? You'd think you'd want to remember!" Derek growled in disgust and disappeared into thin air.

"Where did he…? Shit, I'm out of here!" I muttered, thoroughly unnerved by this time. I decided to try and sneak out, although I didn't know where the front door was. I stood up and walked swiftly to the bedroom door and peered out into the hallway. I was barefoot but didn't intend to waste any time looking for shoes. I could hear two adult voices in another room along with the high-pitched sounds made by a very young child—the baby Derek had mentioned.

I realized that the hallway led to a living room, which I could just catch a glimpse of, and the way seemed clear for me to get the hell out of here. As I strode out through the living room, pulled the front door open and made my escape, I heard Derek cussing and the woman, Em, saying, "Well, just teleport—your bond will keep you linked to him."

Although the air was quite cold and I wore no jacket, it didn't seem to affect me as it had earlier, and as I began to run as fast as I could down the concrete sidewalk, I realized that I felt pretty good. In fact, I felt wonderful, powerful. All the pain was gone, and for a moment, I thought that I might be able to…fly. I gave into the feeling and actually lifted off the ground, startling me so much that I lost my concentration and dropped back to the sidewalk. *Oh, my God, I can fly! What if it's all tr—*

Before I had finished my thought, the man Derek appeared out of nowhere, right in front of me. He grabbed my arm in a vise-like grip, and suddenly, we were standing next to Emily in a warm, welcoming kitchen, fragrant with the smell of dinner cooking. I felt completely disoriented and faintly dizzy.

Derek peered at me rather desperately, finally letting go of my arm. "God, Merlin, this is insane. I'm gonna call Llyr—this has gone on long enough." He closed his eyes for a moment, and before he could open them again, a huge man, standing at least six feet eight appeared before him, clad in jeans and a flannel shirt. I gazed up at him in startled confusion—was he a lumberjack? He looked just like me, like the image I had seen in the mirror, only larger. I was terrified and just stood there, quaking.

Derek immediately got down on his hands and knees in front of the giant lumberjack and bowed, touching his forehead to the guy's feet. Then, he got up and started to relate what had happened, but before he had said more than two sentences, the man interrupted.

"I know, Derek, I can see the details in your mind. And it is obvious that Merlin has no idea who he is, or who I am. Don't worry, Grandson, I will take care of him," the huge man said in a deep but gentle voice that reverberated throughout the room.

Grandson? If Derek was telling the truth and he was actually my son, then this person that looked almost like my twin, only larger, must be my…father? Oh, *shit.*

The giant came closer to me and I cowered. "Oh, Merlin, what did Beli do to you, my son?" he murmured, as he gathered me against his muscular frame. I immediately felt soothed. I blinked and sighed, relaxing in his arms, knowing that I was safe. Then, as if a dark cloud had moved away from the sun, I was filled with a brilliant white light and I knew the truth. I remembered who I was, who held me lovingly in his arms, and who surrounded me with cries of relief and love.

CHAPTER 23

February 5 6:00-7:00 PM

I SAT AT THE KITCHEN TABLE with a mug of coffee warming my hands, gazing at my family as they laughed and talked with my father. I couldn't believe that Llyr had chosen to stay and chat. The big god leaned nonchalantly against the counter, sipping coffee out of a mug that had the saying "Live Long and Prosper" printed on it in bold letters. Emily glanced at me and squeezed my arm, and I smiled at her.

I love you, she said silently. Every so often she got up to baste the turkey she had in the oven, then sat back down and joined in the conversation again. She and Llyr had become friends of a sort, which I was happy to see, as she had always been awestruck and tongue-tied around him in the past. And it was obvious that he was completely captivated by his daughter-in-law. I chuckled to myself—I'd never seen him so relaxed.

I was infinitely relieved to be back to normal, for it had been a strange and uncomfortable experience to be totally unaware of my identity, ignorant of my magic. I remembered everything I had done—and said. I couldn't believe that I had used such foul language, but constantly being around Emily's and Derek's profanity, my subconscious mind must have picked up on it.

I was feeling introspective to say the least, and more than a little vindictive towards the one who had forced this situation upon me. I had believed that I'd removed the instrument of his control over me when I had retrieved and destroyed the bloody towel, but he must somehow have retained a small piece of it. Even a few threads, still encrusted with my dried blood, could produce the results he desired. Just a few threads were all it would take to undermine the very foundation of my existence in this mortal realm.

I'd been warned of the danger I was in having the god of death as my enemy, but I hadn't taken it seriously; after all, I was confident that my own god powers would keep me, and my loved ones, safe. Apparently not.

A deep, sinister voice in my mind interrupted my train of thought. *I am waiting, Myrddin Emrys.*

Llyr's head snapped to attention suddenly as he heard that voice of evil summoning me to a confrontation. He started to speak, then sighed and looked resigned, put his mug down, and disappeared from the kitchen.

"Recalled to the realm of the gods," I said in response to the inquiring looks I received from both Derek and Emily. Llyr had managed to give me this information an instant before he was pulled away. "This issue is between me and Beli, and God apparently feels that Llyr has become much too involved in my affairs on this plane. As much as I hate to do it, I must confront Beli—*alone*." I emphasized the last word as my son and my wife both reacted as if they intended to go with me.

I leaned down to kiss my fuming wife, walked over to the crib and touched my sleeping daughter, and gave my brooding son a bracing hug. And then, I teleported back to the spot from which I had been pushed only a few hours ago.

Beli was waiting for me, dark and menacing; as tall as Llyr but bulkier and considerably larger than my human form. I thought, ironically, that there must be some sort of predetermined size for gods manifesting on this plane. I myself had ended up the same size in my hallucination.

The god of death laughed, and the sound grated on my nerves like fingernails being drawn deliberately across a chalkboard. I felt a faint quiver down my spine as I realized that I had no choice. I hoped that the one God would understand, no matter what course of action I took, but I wasn't going to submit to any more abuse. Beli had attempted to murder me several times and I intended to stop him before he actually succeeded. While it was true that under normal circumstances I could overcome death, he had proven that he could employ methods that might prevent me from doing so.

I'm sorry, I said silently to the universe, to any and all beings that might feel that my actions warranted an apology. At that point, I accessed my powers and increased in size as I had done several times in the past, but this time the power within me seethed with the strength of my god self. I was still nowhere near Beli's six feet eight, but considerably more impressive than my normal size. My powers pulsed and sang, and my enhanced body glowed, as I considered how best to defeat this manifestation of evil. He just waited, seeming confident that nothing I could come up with would rival his destructive force.

Without warning, I leaped into the air towards him, ramming him in the gut headfirst with all of the power I could gather from these ancient rocks. He flew violently backwards and hit squarely on a rather large boulder a half mile away, bouncing off of it and landing in a wide patch of prickly pear cactus. He roared out his pain and displeasure, and his face twisted with hatred as he extricated himself from the spiny plants.

"Myrddin Emrys, you are nothing but a flea on the rump of a particularly annoying camel," he growled in a piercing tone that carried over the distance between us. "In this despicable human form you are weak and I intend to eliminate your worthless self from this and every other realm." And as he rose smoothly to his full height, he unleashed a wave of dark energy more powerful than anything I had encountered in the past, and I was swept over the precipice for the second time that day. But this time I was prepared.

As the god of death, he certainly had more experience in destruction than I, but in my spirit form, I had been present in the realm of the gods at least as long as he had—and I was the light to his darkness. Darkness had no way to perceive the light, for any amount of light completely banished the darkness.

"Sorry to disappoint you, Beli." Actually, I wasn't at all sorry, and instead of an uncontrolled fall, I flew back up and met him at the edge of the cliff. I unleashed a brilliant Light from within my god self, and enhancing it with blue fire, I directed it at him in a narrow beam through my hands. A powerful explosion ripped through the form he had assumed in this human realm, effectively forcing his spirit to retreat to the realm of the gods. The sound was surely heard for miles, and I hoped people would assume it was a sonic boom. A wordless cry of fury echoed powerfully across the valley, and then slowly dissipated.

I waited for several minutes for him to return, as I could not believe that banishing him was that simple. He did not reappear. As I returned to my normal size, I took a deep breath and then exhaled in one long sigh. Surely the all-knowing God was aware of every aspect of my situation, so there should be no repercussions. Besides, the spirit of the god himself still existed; only his form here in the human realm had been eliminated…for now.

I teleported back to the house and Emily was waiting for me with our daughter in her arms, a grim look on her face. Derek was on his feet, fists clenched, looking pale and angry on my behalf.

"He's gone?" he asked abruptly, having experienced the violent but short-lived confrontation through our bond, but still wanting verbal confirmation of Beli's banishment.

"Yes, but I have a feeling this is far from over. It looks like I'll have to make an official visit to the realm of the gods and request an audience with the one God, as Llyr suggested."

"An audience—with *God*?" Emily asked, her eyes widening in disbelief.

"Well, yes, why not? I am Myrddin Emrys, and I have the right to protest the actions that have been taken against me.

Llyr has already stated that he would back me up, having experienced Beli's behavior through his connection to me."

"I'm not questioning your right to do that, Merlin, it's just a little hard for me to relate to," she gulped.

I smiled and reached out for my wife and daughter, kissing both of them gently. "I know, but I suspect that God is more approachable than one might think; although I don't really remember being in his presence, I must have been when I was in spirit form." I reluctantly released the two of them. "I'm going to head back to the shop now, and finish a few things. It was extremely busy today."

Emily nodded, glanced at the clock and asked me to be home for dinner as soon as possible, then turned towards the bedroom intending to change Lumina's diaper. She paused for a moment and came back, giving me a scorching kiss to remind me of what to expect later in the evening when we were alone and the baby was asleep.

"I'll be here, sweetheart," I assured her, my eyes following her shapely form as she walked away. "Derek, would you like to join me at the shop?"

"Yeah, I'll be there in a few minutes—I just need to gas up my truck," he said, as he headed for the door.

"Alright, I'll see you there," I said, and teleported back to The Moab Herbalist.

I had finished my deposit and was thinking I'd just drop it off at the bank in the morning, when my son's vehicle pulled up to the curb and I unlocked the door with my mind. My magic was becoming increasingly subtler as I incorporated some of my god powers into my daily life. Occasionally, I still used spells and hand gestures out of habit, but my intention alone was enough to accomplish most tasks. When I was young, before I met Gaius, I used no spells, relying on my instincts alone to manipulate my magic. Perhaps there was no difference between my sorcerer's magic and my god powers, although at that time, I was unaware of my true nature. Now, of course, my god powers controlled and directed my magic in yet subtler ways.

"I can't believe everythin' that's happened today. You really didn't have any warnin' that Beli was comin', did ya?" Derek exclaimed as he strode into the room, leaving the door wide open in his excitement. This recent habit of his was beginning to annoy me and I would have to address it sooner or later.

"You know very well that I didn't," I said calmly as I closed the door behind him with my mind and locked it the same way.

"Yeah, well, it was pretty damned disconcertin' to be sittin' in a meetin' and suddenly feel you fall off a cliff—the woman in the seat next to me thought I was havin' some kind of a fit, especially when I felt you hittin' those boulders on the way down." He looked extremely upset by the memory.

"Sometimes being as connected as we are can have its disadvantages. I'm sorry that you had to experience that, Derek; I wasn't awfully fond of it myself." I decided to change the subject. "I sensed that you took my advice when you went back to work this morning. I knew you would be able to 'convince' your supervisor that your absence was a legitimate one."

He looked relieved to be diverted from his painful memories.

"It was actually easier than I thought it'd be, but I still felt kinda funny manipulatin' everyone," Derek admitted.

I nodded, understanding his reluctance, but knowing he hadn't had a choice. And he may not have a choice about flying either, I thought, as I remembered his request prior to my "accident."

"After I had returned from my flight, you indicated that you wanted me to help you to fly, but I think the best thing for me to do is Look into your being right now and check your powers."

He agreed, and since we no longer had to physically touch each other to connect to our innermost selves, we just Looked deep into each other's eyes. I immediately had a sense of sinking into a warm pool, a feeling of belonging, kinship, trust, love—and devotion. It was a journey through opened doors and revealed secrets, until I found the part of him that enabled him to rise into the air in defiance of gravity; the ability to levitate. Then, I sought the extra spark that indicated the possibility of true flight and...it wasn't there. I could feel his intense disappointment, but I didn't think there was anything I could do; one was born with certain abilities and not others, and that seemed to be immutable.

Derek had inherited many of my abilities, or powers, but one in particular was conspicuously absent: healing. On more than one occasion he had attempted to heal me, or himself, and had been unable to do so. It was certainly unfortunate—and ironic—that the son of the god of magic and healing lacked that important ability. Also, he seemed unable to conjure anything more than a light orb, and try as he might, a simple cup of coffee was beyond him. He was proficient and effective at using complicated spells, though, which led me to believe that he just hadn't yet found his own personal "trigger" that would unlock his conjuring ability. And now we knew that he utterly lacked the ability to fly. That seemed odd to me, though. If flying was the natural extension of levitating, why should he not be able to do so? I hated feeling his intense disappointment and wondered if there was something I could do about it.

But there was no question as to the strength of the powers he did possess. When he had prevented my essence, my spirit, from being torn from my body when we returned from Camelot, it was not by any healing effort on his part—it was due to his act of holding a part of my spirit within himself, thus anchoring it to this realm. And I knew that this was a unique ability all his own, one that I could never have imagined.

Derek continued to look devastated that he would not be able to fly with me, but I reminded him gently that he was still able to levitate—he would just not be able to go much higher than the top of the Rim.

"I guess I'm bein' ridiculous, since I have all these other powers that work fine, but I'm really disappointed that I won't be able to fly with you," he said sadly.

"I know you are; me too," I said quietly, clasping his shoulder. I changed the subject. "Oh, by the way, we're having a storytelling session next week, and I was wondering if you would like to participate?"

"Me? Uh, I don't know…why would you want *me* to tell a story? What would I say?" He gazed at me in bewilderment.

"Derek, you're my son, you should have inherited some of my 'legendary' ability to weave a tale. Haven't you had the most amazing experiences of your life in the past year? Surely you can adapt some of those experiences into a story that will interest the guests?" I just looked at him with my eyebrows raised.

He gulped. "I guess I could do that. What night is it?"

"I'll let you know—I'll make sure it's a night that you don't have to work late," I assured him, rather pleased that I had succeeded in distracting him. I glanced at the clock. "Why don't we go back to the house now and have dinner with Emily and Lumina? I believe we're having turkey, mashed potatoes and gravy, and green beans."

"Okay, I'll meet you there since I have to drive my truck back home."

"I'll see you soon," I said as Derek left and I locked the door behind him. I immediately teleported out of the shop—and into a stifling hot semidarkness.

CHAPTER 24

February 5 Early Evening

INSTEAD OF THE SANCTUARY of my kitchen, I had teleported into…Hell. At least that's what it appeared to be—the deep red sky overhead glistened like freshly-spilled blood, the rough ground where I stood burned hot through the soles of my shoes, and a horde of demons surrounded me in the thick gloom. It was the epitome of the biblical Hell, reeking of sulfurous fumes. All that was missing was the quintessential devil: Satan, with his leathery skin, his horns and cloven hoofs, and his forked tail. Or the grinning death mask of the god of death and destruction.

I couldn't believe it. "Not again!" I groaned, assuming that it had been Beli who transported me here. It felt as if my flesh was beginning to blister and melt off of my bones, and pain, anxiety and fear permeated my being. I instantly quelled my reaction, as I knew that those sensations were not originating within me. I used my powers to cool myself off, heal the imaginary blisters and burns, and to vanquish the fear. I was surprised that Beli had been able to manipulate me again so soon, but as I prepared to assert my god powers and leave this realm, I heard a familiar voice and suspected that I was about to face his accomplice.

"Well, look who's here," a taunting voice said in English. "The all-powerful god of magic…oh, and of *healing*, pardon me all to *Hell*. Get it? Hell? Never mind, you obviously have no sense of humor, do you, Father?" The demons backed away and bowed as Adrestia showed herself. She stalked out from behind a demolished building, draped in black strips of some silky fabric, her breasts and her crotch barely covered, and she came right up to me and began sinuously rubbing her body against mine. She was wearing shoes with extremely high heels, which brought the exposed parts of her body perilously close to the part of my body that a daughter should never touch.

I averted my eyes and wisely kept quiet, although I wanted to admonish Adrestia for her disgustingly inappropriate behavior. I was absolutely horrified that she had sunk to such depths of depravity, and I hoped this proved to be another detailed vision. Unfortunately, it felt all too real. I cringed inwardly and desperately wanted to pull away from her, but held my ground.

She pranced around me and began to laugh, the lovely voice I remembered from Camelot altered to a rough, uncouth mockery of the sweet tones I had heard not so long ago.

"How did you end up here, Daughter?" I finally asked in a quiet, neutral tone, careful not to imbue my own voice with any of the emotions I was experiencing.

She turned and gazed suspiciously at me for a moment before she shrugged and said, "Guess it can't hurt to tell you. When my mother was preparing to do battle with you last summer, Grandfather Beli put me here to keep me from joining her; guess he'd had a premonition that you were going to kill both of us and he wanted to save me. He obviously didn't give a shit about *her*.

"Unfortunately, he didn't plan ahead too well and I had to resort to some drastic measures to survive down here—the demons tend to be rather *physically* demanding." She cocked a hip and postured as she looked into my eyes challengingly. "If you understand what I'm saying?" And she reached between her legs and caressed herself in a manner that left no doubt as to what she meant.

Although I showed no outward sign of it, I was sickened to the depths of my soul that my daughter had given her body to demons in order to survive in this sweltering place of eternal suffering. Beli had so many things to answer for that I hardly knew where to begin.

"As the daughter of a god, and the granddaughter of the god of death, I find it hard to believe that any demon or demigod would have the audacity to assault you, Adrestia."

"Well, that certainly didn't stop them. What's more, I didn't notice *you* rushing to save me!" All of her anger, resentment and pain came pouring out as she shouted at me.

Despite the fact that my heart wept for her plight, I refused to allow her emotional outburst to weaken my resolve; she obviously felt no remorse for all the evil things she had done since the fifth century. She was a child of my body, but not a child of my heart or mind, like Derek—or Lumina for that matter.

As much as it pained me, I would have to leave her here. She obviously had established herself as the queen of this demonic place—with her grandfather's blessing. Let her rule here where she could do no more harm in the mortal realm.

I went deep inside myself to release my god powers, only to find that all but the most basic powers of sorcery had been blocked. Again. I was alarmed, especially after my recent experience with the loss of not only my powers but also my memory, and I wondered if this underworld realm, rather than Beli, could possibly be having some kind of effect on my abilities.

Adrestia had finally finished her tirade with a few choice insults aimed at Derek, and then seemed to sense that I was unable to depart. My decision to leave her here proved to be justified—as soon as she realized that I was powerless, she ordered her minions to attack.

Fortunately, at that moment, I felt Emily attempting to communicate with me. I focused on my wife's voice and on her energy, and then redoubled my efforts to transport myself back home, out of the clutches of the oncoming horde, and away from my evil offspring.

Suddenly, a powerful burst of magic blossomed in the center of my being, and as I channeled it through every cell in my body, I was able to unblock my god powers and to escape from Hell.

As I appeared in the kitchen next to Emily, I gasped at the temperature difference: the air was at least forty degrees cooler in my home then it had been in the Underworld.

I sighed in relief and reached out to draw my wife into my arms, touching my forehead to hers gratefully. "Thank you, my love. A force, whether it was Beli or Adrestia, or just the Hell realm itself, was keeping me from accessing my god powers. It seems that everyone has been saving me lately, except me! Your magic has definitely grown stronger to be able to assist me in that way." I gave her a relieved smile and we held each other tightly.

"Daddy, I helped." A child's voice interrupted me, and I looked down at a little girl staring trustingly up at me.

As she saw the startled expression on my face, Emily said, "Uh, Merlin, this is Lumina." Her voice shook with emotion. She released me to put her arm around the child, who appeared to be about three years old. Long dark brown hair and hazel eyes looked the same as in the vision I'd experienced the previous summer. Our daughter was wrapped in the blue and yellow blanket that normally covered her in her cradle, and she was naked beneath its warm folds.

I was speechless. I gazed at Emily in disbelief, and she shook her head helplessly. "I have no idea how this happened. I was finishing up dinner and I heard her fussing and crying, so I ran in to the bedroom and found her like this."

My baby daughter, whom I had seen just a short while ago, was now walking and talking, and evidently exercising some impressive magical abilities. I squatted down in front of her and gently brushed the hair back from her face.

"You've grown, Lumina, how is that possible?" I murmured.

"Daddy, I got bigger," she said, in a sweet innocent voice. "Are you mad?"

"No, sweetling, I'm not mad; you didn't do anything wrong. Thank you for helping me to come back home."

I reached out to her, and she literally flew into my arms, almost dropping her blanket. I gathered it around her delicate child's body, cuddling her against me as I stood up.

I glanced at Em. "I'm surprised that Derek isn't here by now. He had just left the shop when I teleported out, and he'd planned to stop by to have dinner with us."

"He texted me and said he was going to stop at the store," Em responded as she began to set the table. "He's probably still there—you weren't in that horrible place very long, magic man; a couple of minutes at most." *Derek, where are you?*

I just left the parking lot, Em. Dad, what happened to you? I couldn't hear your thoughts for a few minutes; are you okay? Derek sounded worried.

Yes, I'm alright. When will you be here?

I'm turnin' onto Doc Allen right now, so I'll be there in a minute.

We heard Derek's truck pull into his driveway, and seconds later he teleported into our living room. Seeing us standing in the kitchen, he walked in clutching a grocery bag and a six-pack of beer. I was still holding Lumina, and he looked at the two of us in confusion.

"Who's this?" he asked, a slight frown creasing his forehead.

"It's me!" Lumina exclaimed in her high-pitched voice, obviously insulted that he hadn't recognized her.

"Me who?" For a brief moment he looked puzzled, and then I could see his dawning realization of her identity. "Lumina?" he gasped in disbelief. *Dad, her voice sounds about the same as the kid we heard in Camelot.*

I hadn't yet thought about the implications of her present state, but Derek was correct; her voice had the same pitch, and it certainly could have been she who had contacted us that night.

You may be right, Derek. Although, the way she spoke seemed to indicate a child older than three. I had my doubts that she was the same child I saw before me now.

So are we gonna prompt her to communicate with our past selves?

But we're already back—why would she do that? Perhaps the message we heard was sent from an alternate universe.

Emily was listening to us mentally with a thoughtful look on her face. "I think that's the most logical explanation, but maybe we should have her do it anyway."

"Mommy?" Lumina piped up, her face tilted to one side questioningly.

"Just a second, sweetheart; Mommy's thinking." Em pursed her lips as she considered the possible scenarios.

"Now, wait a minute. We've been speakin' telepathically and Lumina hasn't given any indication she can hear us. How the hell could she contact us in the past if she doesn't have any telepathic ability?" Derek insisted.

"I'm sure that she has at least a rudimentary ability—she was already trying to communicate with me when we were waiting for Emily's parents to arrive. Right now, maybe she doesn't know enough to tell us so. Perhaps we just need to ask her." I looked into her eyes and said silently, *Can you hear me, Lumina?*

Yes, Daddy, the child's sweet, clear inner voice said. She grinned at me and kissed my cheek.

My heart ached with love for this child of light who had suddenly gone from a tiny baby to a three-year-old in one day. As I put her down and she ran to her mother, clutching her blanket around her, I shook my head in disbelief. The magic that had created her had its own schedule, it seemed. And a future Lumina, or a Lumina from an alternate universe interacting with us in this time, suddenly seemed possible.

CHAPTER 25

February 5 Early Evening

SUDDENLY FEELING EXHAUSTED and overwhelmed, I considered the ramifications of Lumina's involvement in my rescue, as well as her probable communication with us while we were in Camelot. Derek and Emily's discussion escalated in volume, Lumina's high-pitched little voice added to the confusion, and my head was pounding. I was dizzy and felt frantic with the need to escape.

"Enough!" I shouted, stopping time. I took a deep breath and gazed at my family, all of three of them now frozen in the midst of their frantic gesticulating. I pushed the hair back from my forehead in frustration. *What the hell was happening?*

I almost hoped that everything that had occurred since we returned from Camelot was a surrealistic vision, for if it was reality, my life had just dissolved into utter chaos. For a brief moment, I yearned for that peaceful eternity of spirit in which I had existed for millennia, before I had come to this realm, born as Merlin Ambrosius. But of course, since I had begged for the opportunity to have a human body—and a family—I couldn't very well wish it hadn't happened.

I reflected upon the events of the last couple of weeks. Lumina had been born the third week in January, and the following week Emily's parents had come to visit, with all the discoveries and commitments associated with that event. Then, Derek and I had been swept back in time to fifth-century Camelot, whereupon we had determined that the possession of my bloody towel had given Beli power over me, and I had utilized my god powers to bring us home, only to be thrust into a nightmare hallucination underlying which was the very real attempt on my life. Derek had saved me, I had flown, Beli had thrown me off a cliff and I had lost my memory, and I had been sent to Hell and confronted Adrestia, all of which culminated with me being rescued by my youngest daughter who had mysteriously grown into a three-year-old child overnight.

Bollocks. I sat in the kitchen with my head in my hands, my family still caught in the freeze frame of stopped time. I just wanted all of the chaos and confusion to cease, and I wanted most of all to resume my quest for Arthur. It suddenly felt like an unattainable dream, and I wanted to weep.

And then I was floating free of my body and bathed in Light, with the sensation of infinite Love surrounding me. And a Voice that wasn't a voice sounded like the sweetest of music, soothing my senses.

"Myrddin Emrys, your mission in the realm of man has only begun. Do not be discouraged by the trials and tribulations you have recently encountered, for they will make you stronger and will hone your purpose to its original focus. Remember that you are Mine, first and foremost, and I will never leave you. The being that you are has always been, and will always be. You are a spirit of light, My light, and a being of love, My love, on Earth at my behest. You are a force for good, and your intentions have always been pure and true. Henceforth, I am allowing you to manifest your god powers in the human realm, as events will soon unfold that will require you to use those powers. Your life, your family and every step you take have been foretold. Have faith in Me and in yourself, and all will be as ordained."

The words sounded so familiar—had someone spoken them to me before? As this thought drifted into my consciousness and then was carried just as quickly away, the Light and the all-encompassing Presence held me in a gentle embrace.

"Derek, do you think he's in the realm of the gods? He looks so…content. Should we just let him sit there, or carry him into the bedroom?" Emily sounded worried, and I considered coming out of my state of euphoria to assure her that everything was alright.

"I think he's listenin' to us, Em. Just let him sit there until *he* decides to come back."

CHAPTER 26

February 5   Around 9:30 PM

TIME WAS PASSING, and Merlin was still in his meditative state. Despite Derek's reassuring words to Emily, he was concerned about his father's unusual behavior. He'd seen Merlin meditate many times, but tonight he had actually stopped time in the middle of an important, though rather heated discussion. The magical intervention had worn off after a few minutes, and when Derek had become conscious again, he had quickly perceived what Merlin had done; he just didn't know why. He sighed in confusion as he voluntarily finished the kitchen cleanup while Emily got the kid ready for bed. He guessed that it wasn't really acceptable to question the actions of his god, who was also his father and his best friend, but then again, Merlin had always been open with him before. He didn't understand what was going on and felt left out—which was putting it mildly.

He dried the last plate and slid it onto the stack in the cupboard, then turned to look at his famous father as he sat completely motionless in a straight-backed kitchen chair. It appeared that he wasn't breathing, but Derek sensed the slowed beating of Merlin's heart and knew that he was close to the state in which he'd survived the centuries—suspended inside of his own being.

Derek finally decided to go home, as there didn't seem to be anything he could do, and Emily appeared to have everything under control regarding Lumina's surprising growth spurt. He felt a tickle as she reached into his mind.

Go ahead, Derek, we're doing okay, so you might as well take off. Thanks for helping with the dishes. He thought that the words he heard in his mind held a slight hint of desperation, but maybe he was wrong.

No problem, Em, just let me know if you need anythin'. He projected the thought to her as he donned his hooded sweat-shirt and walked slowly out into the frigid February night, closing and locking the door behind him The stars twinkled like diamonds embedded in the velvet darkness of space, reminding him that Merlin's spirit was undoubtedly mingling happily right now with his grandfather's in the realm of the gods. For some reason, that made him feel abandoned. He tried to shake off that feeling and only partially succeeded. He entered his own house and locked the door behind him with a flick of his wrist, then turned on the lights, adjusted the thermostat and started a movie, also using magic. He was alone, so he could do as he pleased, right? Grabbing a beer, he threw himself down in his recliner and leaned back, hoping the movie would distract him from his feelings of loss and confusion.

CHAPTER 27

February 5 Around 10:00 PM

FINALLY, I BEGAN to emerge from my timeless state, and wondered where everyone was. I extended my senses and found Derek, comfortably ensconced in his chair at home watching an old *Spiderman* movie, and for a moment, I was puzzled at the unexpected feeling of loneliness emanating from him. I then searched for my wife and discovered her in the extra bedroom, fixing a pallet for Lumina on the floor. I could sense her yearning for my loving presence and support; that had been a factor in drawing me back to the "real" world.

I slowly opened my eyes, and realized that I was still sitting motionless in the darkened kitchen, the clock indicating that I had been "gone" for over three hours. Apparently, I had missed dinner, as the food had been put away and the dishes were done, but I wasn't hungry. My body had shut down temporarily, as it had always done in the past when I had slept for hundreds of years. I noticed that I was emitting a glow, much brighter than the normal phenomenon that Derek always referred to as "leakin' god light," and I felt…changed.

I had been with the one God, in perfect peace, love and understanding, and I noticed that my doubts, concerns and feelings of being overwhelmed had disappeared. I stood up and stretched, refreshed, feeling younger than I had in centuries. And since I was a very old man, immortal or not, that was a welcome sensation.

I teleported into the extra bedroom, which had been intended for Lumina anyway when she had outgrown cradle and crib, and realized that we would have to furnish it as soon as possible. I wondered if she would continue to grow older at the same pace, in which case she might outgrow even the new furnishings. I hoped she would not grow again too soon—I couldn't bear to think that she might be an adult by the end of the year. Emotional considerations aside, how would we explain such a thing to our friends, neighbors and clients?

"Daddy!" Lumina yelled ecstatically and clapped her hands in childish enthusiasm. She was now wearing one of Emily's old T-shirts as a nightgown, and it was obvious from the flowery scent of soap and shampoo that she'd recently had a bath. I picked her up and kissed her, then twirled her around, and we both laughed joyously.

Emily turned from where she had been arranging Lumina's bedding. She smiled in obvious relief at my reappearance. "What happened, magic man? Where did you go?"

"I was in the presence of God," I said reverently, my spirit soaring and my aura flaring brightly around me as power surged through my being.

"*What*?" Em whispered, the look of awe and devotion on her face telling me that she was about to kiss my feet.

And I let her.

Later, after our child was put to bed amid a flurry of hugs, kisses, stories and murmurings of "I love you," Emily and I finally adjourned to our own bedroom, only to face the reality of an empty cradle. She sat in the chair next to the bed, tears welling in her lovely eyes as she touched her swollen breasts.

"Are you alright, my love?" I asked gently, kneeling on the floor in front of her and pulling her into my arms.

"No, I'm not," she sobbed. "Oh, God, our baby is gone! I'll never nurse her again. She's only a few weeks old, but now she's as big as a three-year-old, walking and talking already. How can the gods think that this is a good thing?"

"It's neither good nor bad, my love, it simply is. And we must accept it. You, Derek and I aren't like anyone else in this realm and neither is Lumina," I said serenely, still floating in that ocean of love. "Come, let's go to bed." I turned the covers down with a look, and then stood up with my wife in my arms and deposited her carefully on the soft sheets before climbing in beside her. I magically whisked our clothing away, and reached out to caress her. She moved suddenly against me, kissing my lips fervently, her warm hands reaching, stroking and teasing, seeking the solace that our physical and emotional joining would give her. I gasped as my body responded instantly to her touch, and the urgent need to come together erased everything else from our minds. We rolled over until I rested atop her soft body, kissing and stroking her until she parted her legs and said urgently, "Now, please, *now*." I reached down and positioned myself, and as I slid inside her, she sighed and tightened up around me. I thrust deeper and she welcomed me enthusiastically. We moved slowly, savoring every moment, using our magic for each other's pleasure. The result was a rising ecstasy. Time seemed to stand still as we focused entirely on the blending of our essences and on the sensation of our naked bodies sliding against each other.

"I love you, Em," I groaned as my climax claimed my senses.

After experiencing her own fulfillment, she whispered, "I love you, too, Merlin." She held onto me tightly, her face against my chest. Silent tears, whether from joy or from loss, or perhaps both, dampened my skin.

Later, as we curled up together, preparing for sleep, Emily said, "Could you please relieve the pressure in my breasts, otherwise I'll have to get up and use that damned breast pump."

Of course, sweetheart. I cupped my hands around her gently, the power of my magic effectively easing her discomfort.

"Thank you, love," she sighed, and immediately succumbed to her exhaustion.

I lay awake at her side for some time, thinking about the recent encounter with Beli and the unexpected experience with God. While Beli had been sent back to the realm of the gods, there was no guarantee that he wouldn't return and attack me once again, as evidenced by my quick trip to Hell and back. I still wasn't completely sure whether or not Adrestia had played a part in that scenario, but it was too much of a coincidence if she hadn't.

However, God had made it abundantly clear that he was aware of recent events, and had assured me of his love and support. He had gently admonished me to have faith not only in him but also in myself, and therefore I would try my best to do that. As I drifted towards sleep, I couldn't help but wonder at Lumina's destiny, and finally, the memory of Derek's loneliness brought my mind back to full awareness. I was concerned, as I had never felt that emotion from him before, and wondered what had caused it. I decided to talk to him about it the next day. Then, the realization of my own subtle metamorphosis wrapped itself around my consciousness as sleep finally claimed me.

I dreamed that I was looking down on two people sleeping, a man and a woman, from a vantage point perhaps eight feet over their heads. Formless, I drifted near the ceiling, noticing that they looked familiar; I should know them. The man had shoulder-length black hair, and I knew that his eyes were an intense shade of green, although at the moment those eyes were closed in sleep. The woman was lovely, her golden brown hair spread out on her pillow, and she had her arm around the unconscious man.

Suddenly, I realized that this was not a dream—I was gazing down upon the sleeping forms of my wife and myself. I willed my spirit back into my body, and lay there with my eyes open, contemplating this ability to spontaneously leave my body and just as easily return to it. And I understood that I could keep my body alive while my spirit traveled where it would. Interesting, I thought, as I grinned widely....

CHAPTER 28

February 6   4:45 PM

LATE THE FOLLOWING DAY, I was stocking the shelves with a new batch of potions when the door chime tinkled, and a familiar voice said in Old British, "Tis true then, you are a god."

I stiffened in shock as I turned and beheld a sight that chilled me to the bone: Arthur, King of Camelot, was standing in the doorway of my shop in twenty-first-century Moab.

"My lord, what are you doing here?" I exclaimed, also in Old British, which sounded so alien in this time and place.

"Ah, Merlin, my old friend, I am afraid I do not know; although, I suspect you would be able to answer that question far better than I," he said in a wry tone. His face was lined with exhaustion and he was filthy, covered with mud and blood. "The last thing I remember was battling the Saxons after you and your son had departed. And then, suddenly I am in another place, another time, in front of an herbalist's shop, and the gods are directing me to enter…and here you are." His voice trailed off and he looked as if he was about to collapse.

I quickly locked the door and lowered the blinds using magic, and put an arm around my king, providing support as I escorted him to the most comfortable chair I owned. I used my god powers to instantly cleanse his body and his garments and to provide him with wine and food in gold vessels appropriate to his station. Arthur was startled, as I had rarely engaged in such overt magical feats in his presence, and he stared at me, silent for a moment, obviously overwhelmed by his transition.

"Gods, Merlin, what have you done?" he whispered.

I couldn't answer, as my horror at this turn of events had made me mute.

It was obvious that the king had just arrived, as he wouldn't have been able to wander around town in his fifth-century accoutrements, bloodied as he had been, without attracting unwelcome attention. He must have been caught in the time vortex that had transported us back to Moab, but it was a mystery to me how that could have happened, as my magic had been very specific to Derek and me. And how had Arthur remembered that we had even been there? My forgetting spell was powerful, having been fueled by my god powers and channeled through not only me but also through Derek.

Suddenly, I realized that his first words to me when he entered the shop had been, *'Tis true then, you are a god.'* How had he known that? I glanced at him as he sighed and leaned back in his chair, fatigued. He lifted the golden goblet and took a sip of his wine and put it down, then looked around at the relatively small dimensions of my shop, as if comparing them to my spacious quarters in his castle.

"Arthur, I…" I took a deep breath and exhaled slowly. How does one apologize for ripping someone away from everything they had ever known? "I am so terribly sorry to have caused this upheaval in your life, for I fear that our precipitous departure from Camelot brought you here, to the twenty-first century."

"What? Do you speak truly?" His eyes widened, disbelief warring with his lifelong inclination to trust me.

"Yes, sire. But how did you happen to deduce that I myself am a god, and not merely the son of a god?" I asked, hearing a note of challenge and a touch of arrogance in my voice as my god self surfaced, catching me unawares and threatening to overwhelm my human personality. I closed my eyes for a moment, seeking to restrain the part of my true nature that was so close to complete manifestation in this realm.

Arthur gave a tired, half-hearted grin as he witnessed my struggle to retain control. "I may not have your magical powers, Merlin, but I have always had an uncanny intuition. Surely you had noticed that? I have seen the unmistakable look of ancient wisdom in your eyes, and I have sensed a powerful, otherworldly being within your human shell. And just now, the struggle you engaged in when that part of your being threatened to take over, well, 'tis obvious to me that you are a god."

I felt an overwhelming sense of sorrow, knowing that I had lost something precious as Arthur acknowledged that I truly wasn't human. And without further warning, my hard-fought battle to maintain my humanity was lost, and I gave in to my true nature, aloof and separate from the cares of men.

"You are correct, Arthur," I said flatly, with narrowed eyes, as the last vestiges of my compassion for, and understanding of, the human race left me. "I am the god of magic and healing, and I will no longer kneel before you, or any other earthly king. I have existed since the beginning of time itself, and shall exist long after this body and, in fact, all of humanity has gone to dust. What care I for your plight when I have more important things to do, such as to destroy my fellow god Beli, who has caused me so much aggravation. In fact, I no longer care to pursue the quest to return you from your moldering state in far-off Avalon. I shall bring about the time of Albion myself, as I no longer need you to perform that task."

And then I did the unthinkable: I manifested fully in my god form and directed a bolt of powerful energy at Arthur, whose look of terror and betrayal was the last thing I saw as he disappeared—forever.

I heard that tiny part of me that was all that was left of Merlin, cry out in anguish and—

I awoke in a cold sweat with a scream of horror tearing loose from my throat.

My wife was shaking me and yelling, "Merlin, wake up! My God, what's wrong?"

Tears streamed from my eyes and a sob broke loose as I cried, "Oh, gods, no, no, what have I done?"

"Merlin, wake up! You've done nothing wrong, my love, *WAKE UP*!"

Finally I heeded her urgent cry and sat up, quieting in her loving arms as she stroked my back and murmured what sounded like nonsense phrases. And then, I realized what she was actually saying and I froze in horror.

"It's about time you got over that stupid quest, lover. Let's get serious about taking over the world."

I scrambled backwards and was brought up short by the headboard, as it dawned on me whose voice I was hearing.

"*Lux*," I croaked, and the resultant light orb revealed Nimue in bed with me, grinning wickedly as she reached out to trace her long red fingernails along my naked body.

I gasped in outrage and disbelief as I beheld the woman whom I had killed the previous summer and—

I realized that I was still standing in the back room of The Moab Herbalist. I staggered and grabbed the edge of the work bench, breathing hard and feeling nauseated, a sensation that I rarely experienced. Recalling every moment of the multi-layered vision that had wracked my mind and body for—I glanced at the clock on the back wall—ten minutes, I seriously considered leaving this realm before I destroyed the very things, and people, that I had worked so hard to protect.

I collapsed in my desk chair and cradled my head in my hands. It was apparent that my own deep-seated fears, and my recent experiences with Beli and Adrestia, had precipitated the vision. I took a quavering breath and knew that I needed to pull myself together before Derek arrived. We had communicated telepathically earlier in the day, and agreed to meet at the shop shortly after closing time. I was surprised that he had not contacted me immediately after my vision ended—usually he experienced what I did through the close bond that we had. For that matter, Emily had just as close a bond with me, if not closer, and she had not contacted me either. I dragged myself up and went to prepare my deposit, calming myself as I remembered my time with God yesterday. But I was more determined than ever to end my unwanted connection with the god of death, no matter what I had to do to accomplish the task.

CHAPTER 29

February 6 After 5:00 PM

I WAS COUNTING the day's receipts as the chimes sounded and Derek came through the door and closed it, looking tired and confused. He paused for a moment and reached back to make sure the lock was engaged. The mere fact that he hadn't bothered to use magic indicated to me that something was wrong. I could have entered his mind easily to determine the problem, but I chose not to; if he had wanted to confide in me through our bond, he would have already done so. And if he hadn't felt my disturbing vision, I was certainly not going to mention it; it had obviously been a manifestation of my own fears.

"What's going on, Son?" I asked carefully, slipping the completed deposit ticket into the bank bag along with the currency and checks. I remained standing at the counter, watching him drift listlessly across the room.

"Hell, I don't know," Derek answered crossly, throwing himself down on the armchair in the reading area.

"I think you do. I could find out, with or without your permission. However, I'd prefer not to invade your privacy. I'm still your friend, I hope, and isn't that what friends do, confide in each other?" I was trying to remain calm, but I was worried; I had never seen him so depressed and irritable. He was normally a happy, well-adjusted young man still experiencing the thrill of his magical nature, so the fact that these emotions had come on so suddenly was disturbing to say the least.

Derek rubbed his forehead and frowned. "Yeah, you're right." He took a deep breath and looked up at me and grimaced. "I think part of the problem is that I'm lonesome, and on top of that, I'm damned horny. I haven't had a date in, hell, I don't know, *months*."

I was silent for a few moments, contemplating all the centuries I had been alone and without the comfort of a woman's body. "What happened to Maria, the woman that works at Moab Brews? Weren't the two of you seeing each other for a while?"

"Yeah, but I felt bad for leadin' her on, when I just didn't feel the same way. Especially after we started havin' sex pretty regularly and she told me she loved me," he confessed. "All I could think of was that she was gonna get old and die, and I wouldn't. And I couldn't tell her that I'm immortal; I still can hardly believe it myself. I cared about her, but she wanted more than that, so…we broke up." He sighed and ran his hand through his hair in such a way that it stood up in spikes, and I had to suppress a grin that would be inappropriate considering the gravity of the situation.

"Yes, there is that aspect to being with a mortal," I admitted. "Being an immortal sorcerer can be…interesting…when it comes to *any* kind of relationship. Remember how hard it was for me to tell you the truth about myself last July, when I wasn't aware that you were my son? But I had spent so many centuries alone that I couldn't stand the loneliness any longer. The difference in this case is that you're *not* alone; many people know what you are, and love and support you."

"I know that, and I appreciate it, but I really want a partner, someone I can trust with my secret. I want a relationship like you and Em have. And just so you know, I'm not jealous anymore, but I envy what you two have together."

What could I say that wouldn't sound trite? I knew that Derek was much more sociable than I had ever been; he liked to go out in the evenings, drink beer, play pool and flirt with the ladies. He and Ryan Jones, alias Lancelot, had established an ongoing friendship after their initial rocky start the past summer. After the battle with Nimue and her supernatural army, they had settled their differences and generally got together at least once a week. Since the ex-knight knew he was my son and that he had magical powers of his own, Derek could enjoy his company and be himself. And he was occasionally able to persuade the former member of the Round Table to share stories of old Camelot. But it was no more than a platonic friendship, of that I was absolutely certain.

I wish that I could reassure him that he would soon meet someone who would fulfill his personal dreams. But I had always refused to use my powers to predict the future, even though in the past my insight often was seen as prophecy. I knew that my god powers made it possible to know every detail of what was to come, but I did not want to assume that kind of responsibility, and therefore didn't normally use them in that way. But I might be able to at least give him a little hope.

I had taken so long to respond to Derek's statement that he was again wandering restlessly around the shop, his unhappiness almost tangible as a dark cloud surrounding his body.

"I'm sure that someone will be there for you when you need them the most, Son," I stated calmly.

Derek gave me a grim look. "If you say so, Dad."

"You don't believe me?" I said, eyebrows raised in mock outrage.

"I think you're full of shit," he said quite irreverently.

"Shame on you, Derek, for talking to your father that way, let alone your god," I said seriously. But I couldn't keep a straight face for long, and grinned at him. I was surprised that I could feel light-hearted after my earlier traumatic experience.

"Whatever. See ya, Merlin, I'm going to a meetin' tonight and want to get some dinner first." He flicked his wrist at the door, which swung open obediently, and he strode purposefully over the threshold, the door closing itself behind him. At least he was utilizing his magic again, and had actually remembered to close the door. Perhaps he had reconciled himself to his current situation. Right.

I shook my head and sighed, hoping that I had handled that correctly. Being a father was not easy, particularly when dealing with an adult son who was also a full-fledged sorcerer. I loved him to distraction but occasionally it was a challenge.

I groaned as I remembered that I also had a three-year-old daughter who needed special training to manage her unfolding powers—and I had neglected to purchase the furniture for Lumina's bedroom. By the gods, how could I have forgotten such an important task?

Don't worry, I took care of it, Merlin, and I bought her some clothes while I was out and about this afternoon, I heard Em's voice in my mind. *See you at home for dinner?*

I'll be there as soon as I stop at the bank, love. I went out the back way, warded the building and drove off in the old black Chevy pickup, still wondering how I could have had such a devastating vision about Arthur without either my son or my wife experiencing it.

CHAPTER 30

February 6   Evening

DEREK GROWLED in frustration as he left The Moab Herbalist and walked the half a block to where he had parked. Defiantly, despite the presence of a group of tourists, he used magic to unlock the driver side door of his year-old silver Chevy pickup, then yanked it open and slid behind the wheel. He was angry with himself. He understood that Merlin had only been trying to help him, and he was deeply ashamed of the way he had spoken to his father. After all, he owed his very existence to the man, and he loved him so much that sometimes he would ache with the joy of it. But he was being driven crazy by the feeling that he was missing something major in his life: he was almost thirty years old and had no family of his own. He started the vehicle and put it in gear, checked the lane next to him, then carefully pulled out into traffic. He headed south on Main Street, noting the number of tourists in town. He'd been here for almost ten years and it never failed to surprise him how many people came, even this early in the year, to enjoy the recreational opportunities in red rock country.

When his friend Ken joined him at Moab Brews twenty minutes later, Derek was already drinking his second beer in an attempt to alleviate his dissatisfaction. They didn't have time to linger in the bar or they would be late for their meeting, so they were pleased to be seated swiftly in a booth at the back of the dining room. He expected to see Maria waiting tables, but she apparently had the night off. Perhaps it was just as well; they hadn't parted on the best of terms. Both men ordered fish tacos and settled back to wait for their meals to be served. They had known each other so long that their silence was a comfortable one.

During dinner they discussed a recent movie they had both seen, and Derek finally relaxed enough to enjoy himself. He could always count on Ken, whose positive attitude and cheerful demeanor seemed to bolster his spirits. As he laughed in response to one of his friend's jokes, Derek was cognizant of the gleam in Ken's eyes and his wide white smile, and realized that he was quite a good-looking man. Suddenly aware that he was staring, he glanced away and beckoned to the server to bring their check.

They decided to drop off Ken's Jeep at Derek's place, and then headed out to Arches National Park in the Chevy for the monthly meeting of the sword and sorcery group they both belonged to. Derek finally decided to ask Ken what he really thought about magic and sorcery. He'd been tempted for months to show Ken what he could do, and Derek was ready to reveal himself in all of his sorcerer's glory. God, he was nervous about it, though—his palms were sweating on the steering wheel, and his armpits were wet, even though it was a cold evening.

They drove out the park road in companionable silence until finally, he said with a forced casualness, "Hey, Ken, I have a question for you. I've been thinking about this a lot lately. Do you think it's true that some people could actually be sorcerers, with magical powers?" He felt strange and deceitful asking such a question, since his own powers were tingling in readiness within him.

Ken turned to look at him questioningly and scratched his chin—he was letting his beard grow and it itched sometimes. He'd inherited his curly hair and beard from his African American father, but due to the influence of his Caucasian mother's side of the family, it was a soft curl rather than kinky. "Well, I don't know, Derek, I suppose magic could be real. Maybe sorcerers are among us and we just aren't aware of it. They would probably try to keep a low profile if they do exist. All I know is, I really wish *I* could work magic." It sounded like Ken was just humoring him, and Derek was feeling sensitive about the whole subject, but he really wanted to tell Ken about himself. He was afraid of what Merlin would say, but the urge to share his secret with someone was so strong that he blurted out, "*I'm* a sorcerer, Ken; *I* have magic!" *Oh, fuck*, he thought, *now I've done it*, instantly regretting his impetuous decision.

"Yeah, right, Derek, *you're* a sorcerer. Sure you are. Why in hell would you say that, anyway?" Ken scoffed in disbelief, and then made a rude noise.

They were approaching the entrance to the Balanced Rock parking lot and Derek abruptly turned in and parked. He sat for a moment considering what he was about to do.

"What are you doing, Der? We're already late!" Ken exclaimed.

"I need to show you somethin'." Derek stepped out of the truck and started walking towards the natural sandstone structure. It was fully dark at that point, and the wide sidewalk angled several times between the parking lot and the thick pillar of stone, but he knew his way—this was one of the formations he used when wanted to practice levitating.

"Wait! Where're you going?" Ken shouted as he followed his friend. He tripped over the curb and cussed under his breath.

Derek turned back towards him, stretched his right hand out and whispered, "*Lux,*" and the walkway was suddenly illuminated in front of Ken.

He could hear Ken's indrawn breath and feel his astonishment as he croaked, "What the *hell*?"

Derek stood still, waiting until the other man walked up to him, then he motioned with his hand and the light disappeared.

"Huh? Did *you* just do that?" Ken asked incredulously.

"Yeah, I did. Now I have somethin' else to show you. Stay here." He'd decided to do what Merlin had shown him when he'd first revealed himself last summer. He walked some distance away from Ken, up the incline towards the formation, then raised his arms above his head and voiced a spell that echoed against the rocks: "*Caeruleum igne.*" Iridescent blue fire immediately shot out of his fingers and arched above his head. He slowly levitated over one hundred feet into the air, until he was standing on top of Balanced Rock, blue fire surrounding his athletic body. Working this kind of magic made him feel so high, so powerful, that when the fire had erupted from his hands it had practically given him an orgasm.

"Oh…my…*God!*" Ken said slowly and reverently, his eyes wide with awe, as he watched his friend's display of magic.

Derek finally extinguished the fire, and just for a moment, before he leaped off of Balanced Rock, he felt a faint, familiar energy signature that could only belong to one person: Merlin. He was both shocked and puzzled, as he could think of no logical reason that it should be there. Ken was waiting for him, however, so he filed the mystery in the back of his mind to ponder later, and floated down to the ground. He stood silently in front of his friend, feeling a little nervous, wondering what his reaction would be.

Ken just stood there with his mouth hanging open and his eyes practically popping out of his head, and Derek was suddenly reminded of the last time he'd caught a fish. He immediately banished that unflattering image from his thoughts and returned his attention to Ken's state of mind.

"Uh, are you okay?" Derek asked uncertainly, hoping he hadn't shocked him into some kind of trance-state.

"Derek, how did you do that?" Ken's voice shook with suppressed excitement.

"I just told you, I'm a sorcerer."

"But I've known you for years! Have you kept that secret from me all along?" Ken asked incredulously.

"No, I've only known about my powers since last July when my dad showed me who—and what—I really am," he admitted.

"Wait a minute—your dad? I thought he died a few years ago," Ken said, forehead wrinkled in a frown.

Derek didn't answer the question, but said abruptly, "It's cold out here. Let's go back to the truck and turn the heater on, okay? *Albus Lux.*" He used the little orb of white light he'd created to illuminate the way back to the parking lot, and as he extinguished the orb, he thought he heard Ken mutter, "I want one of those."

"Okay, start talking, Der!" Ken insisted as soon as they were seated in the cab of Derek's vehicle, with the engine running and the heater cranked up high.

Oh, God, Derek thought, *Dad's gonna kill me!* He deferred answering until he had adjusted the heater vents.

Finally, he took a deep breath and decided to go for it. "First, you have to promise not to tell anyone. I'm not gonna be able to hide this from my dad 'cause we're both telepathic." Then, the magnitude of his actions suddenly hit him. "Oh *shit*, I'm in so much trouble," he groaned. What in the hell had he done?

"You're *telepathic*? Damn. Okay, I promise. Now what the fuck is going on? Who's your dad? How come you told me he was dead?"

"My dad—my adopted dad, that is—really *is* dead. He died in a car accident several years ago. I found out that I'd been adopted when I met my biological father last year. That's when I found out that I'm different...*really* different." Derek paused, and then continued when Ken motioned to him to keep talking. "My real dad is a sorcerer, and he lives in Moab; in fact, he lives across the street from me."

"I thought that Michael Reese, your friend that owns the herb shop, lived across the street from you. And he married Emily last summer," Ken said, confused.

"Yeah, that's him," Derek confirmed.

"But, he's your age, isn't he? Maybe a few years older, early thirties, like me?" Ken was thirty-three.

Derek chuckled and shook his head. "Nope. He was born in the year 420."

For a moment, there was dead silence from the passenger seat, and then Ken cleared his throat. Familiar with the legends, it didn't take him long to figure it out.

"That was the year King Arthur's sorcerer Merlin was supposedly born. Now, wait a minute. You're telling me *Michael Reese* is *Merlin*, and he's your *dad*? What've you been smoking, man?" Ken said in stunned disbelief.

Derek just stared at him with a knowing half-smile on his face.

"No way," Ken said in a skeptical tone of voice.

"Yep, Michael *is* Merlin and he's my dad. He's immortal, Ken…and so am I."

"Whoa. What?" Ken's face registered absolute shock

"I know, right?" Derek grinned. "So, does that mean you believe me?"

"Oh, man, after what I just saw you do, how can I doubt it? You just proved to me what you are. I won't tell anyone, Derek, this is just too important," Ken promised fervently.

He breathed a sign of relief. "Thanks, I appreciate that. Dad's gonna be upset with me as it is, and like I said, I can't hide anythin' from him." He glanced at his watch. "I guess we'd better get movin' if we're gonna make that meetin'. Isn't it out at Windows?"

"Yeah, but at this point I really don't care. It'll seem pretty anticlimactic after what you just revealed to me," Ken exclaimed.

"Well, let's just show up and then go back to my house for a beer, okay?" Derek suggested.

"Yeah, that'll work."

It took only a few minutes to drive from Balanced Rock to the Windows section of the park, and as Derek pulled up next to the other vehicles and turned the key, he was glad that he'd told Ken his secret. And he wondered why he kept pretending to enjoy this stupid club when he had the real thing at home—sword *and* sorcery.

"Why are we meetin' out here in the dark?"

"I'm not sure. Apparently someone thought it would be mystical and cool—and it *is* pretty amazing under the stars. Maybe there's a meteor shower tonight or something," Ken conjectured as they exited the truck, craning his neck as he looked up at the heavens.

"Cool isn't the word for it. It's fuckin' freezin' out here, and neither of us brought a heavy coat," Derek muttered, as he rummaged behind the seat, hoping to find something warmer to put on. He found an old Park Service vest that he put on over his hoody, then tossed a windbreaker to Ken—the lightweight outerwear wasn't enough to truly keep them warm, but it'd have to do.

He pressed the button on his truck key to lock the doors, and then realized that he could've used magic, since he didn't have to hide his abilities from Ken anymore.

People were gathered up on the path to the east of the parking lot talking and laughing, and the two of them turned on their flashlights and started walking up the sloped path. A few light sabers winked on ahead of them and someone gave a whoop of approval.

They could hear two individuals conjecturing that the strange blue glow they had just seen in the direction of Balanced Rock was actually aliens. Ken chuckled softly, pleased that he knew exactly what had caused that particular phenomenon.

One of the guys in the group noticed Ken and Derek traversing the rocky path and yelled out, "Where the hell have you two been, parked at Balanced Rock making out?" Everyone snickered at that and Derek thought, *How fuckin' juvenile.* But he was annoyed enough to do something equally childish—he quietly uttered a spell and the man who'd made the snide remark was abruptly knocked backwards onto the hard ground. Unfortunately, that caused everyone to laugh even harder, which made the guy angry.

"Hey, which one of you assholes pushed me?" he growled, looking around accusingly as he scrambled to get up off the cold rocky surface.

Ken whispered, "Derek, did you do that? Be careful, man, Bill's a jerk, and he's not worth outing yourself for."

Derek rubbed his forehead and said quietly, "You're right, that was pretty stupid, wasn't it? I shouldn't have taken offense—it's not like I'm gay."

But I am, Ken thought to himself. Derek's head came up with a jerk and he stared at his friend. He'd never intruded into the man's thoughts before, but Ken projected so much emotion that he'd heard him.

And he was taken aback. He never would have guessed that this guy he'd worked alongside of for years, someone he was close friends with, was gay. Not that Derek had a problem with Ken's, or anyone else's, sexual orientation, he was just surprised that his friend had never mentioned it. He must have had a telling look on his face in the glow from the flashlights, because it was apparent when Ken remembered that Derek was telepathic and had heard his admission: he suddenly looked sad and defeated, as if he assumed Derek would reject him.

It's okay, man, we both have a big secret to hide. We have each other's backs, right? Derek projected to Ken's mind.

"I guess you're right," he said quietly. "To hell with 'em, let's go."

They turned their backs on the sword and sorcery group and hurried back to the truck, to jeers and catcalls from Bill and his buddies.

"What did I ever see in those guys?" Derek muttered as he backed his vehicle out of the parking space.

As the two men rode back down the hill towards Park Avenue they were silent, thinking their own thoughts, each wondering what would result from the night's revelations. The stars winked silently in the blackness overhead, their own secrets hidden in the vastness of space and time.

Derek, what did you do? Merlin's voice in his head made him wince, because he knew that the question was rhetorical—his father had sensed the truth already through their unique bond.

"What's wrong?" Ken asked, noticing as Derek suddenly tensed up.

"Um, well, Merlin just asked me what I did. He's already aware that I told you our secret."

So, you told Ken about us, without discussing it with me first.

Yeah, I did. I'm sorry, Dad.

I truly hope you know what you're doing, Son, because your decision could have far-reaching consequences, jeopardizing everything we've worked for.

Dad, he won't tell anyone, he promised.

Alright. Both of you come to my house. Now. It was definitely not a request.

Yes, sir, we'll be there in twenty minutes or so; we're still out in the park. Derek was sure that his inner voice quavered a little as he responded to Merlin's instructions.

I'll see you soon, then.

Yes, sir.

"What's happening?" Ken asked insistently, looking worried as he noticed his friend's trepidation.

"Merlin wants us to stop at his house to talk to him," Derek said, swallowing a sizable lump in his throat. He normally wasn't afraid of his dad, but tonight he thought he might make an exception.

"Damn, this is epic, man!" Although he was feeling a bit anxious, Ken looked forward to meeting the legendary Merlin.

"I know; this is my life. So, I might as well tell you the rest."

"There's more?" Ken exclaimed.

"You know those three men who are always hangin' around 'Michael's' house?" Derek asked.

"Yeah?"

"They're Sir Lancelot, Sir Gawain and Sir Percival; Knights of the Round Table, reborn in this century, or in Percival's case, transported directly from Camelot, to serve Merlin."

"Fuck, are you *kidding* me?" Ken was stunned by Derek's latest confession.

"And when I was gone last week, we—"

Ken interrupted, "Yeah, you were really sick."

Derek shook his head and grinned. "Nope, I enchanted the boss into thinkin' I was. Actually, Merlin and I were transported back to the fifth century—to Camelot—and I met King Arthur."

"Now you're dreaming. I suppose next you'll be saying King Arthur is your brother or something," Ken said sarcastically.

"Uncle," Derek corrected him firmly.

"*What?*"

"King Arthur's my uncle, but we do look rather like brothers. My birth mother was Uther Pendragon's illegitimate daughter."

"You're talking about Arthur as if he's still alive," Ken said, confused.

"I know, it's weird, but in a way, he is. I'm beginnin' to wonder about the nature of time; instead of a river, flowin' from one place to another, maybe it's more like an infinite ocean, where every moment is like a separate drop of water in that ocean," Derek said quietly.

Ken just sat staring at Derek, then shook his head and groaned. "You're getting way too philosophical for me, dude."

Derek shrugged, and they continued on in silence, down the hill and past the entrance booth, until they finally stopped at the end of the park road. He looked both ways, then accelerated out onto sparsely trafficked Highway 191 and headed south back to Moab, the lights from the hotels on both sides of the river sparkling in the crisp night air.

Ken cleared his throat. "So, Merlin impregnated King Arthur's half-sister. God, I could have done without that particular visual just before meeting him. You know, I don't think I'm going to survive this. Are you sure you're not messing with me?"

"It's all true, I promise," Derek assured him with a quick glance.

Ken took a long, deep breath and let it out slowly. "Okay, let's go talk to your dad."

CHAPTER 31

February 6   Around 10:00 PM

AGAIN THEY WERE SILENT, lost in their own thoughts, as they traveled over the Colorado River Bridge, drove past hotels and campgrounds that were already full of tourists, then turned right onto 500 West and headed home—at least to Derek's home; Ken lived out in Spanish Valley south of town. A few minutes later they pulled into Derek's driveway and he turned the key and pocketed it, then set the emergency brake.

He glanced at Ken. "You ready?"

"I feel like I'm headed to a firing squad," Ken complained.

"Oh, it's not going to be that bad…I hope."

The two men got out of the truck and walked across the street to a brightly-lit house that seemed to pulse with energy. Merlin met them at the door looking stern and otherworldly, his slanted green eyes impassive. Ken was very nervous and had a hard time looking him in the eye when the man shook his hand. At six feet two and two hundred pounds, Merlin seemed to tower over Ken's own five feet nine and one hundred and fifty pounds. But then, as if he had passed a test, the sorcerer relented, smiling slightly as he said, "Welcome to our world."

They stepped into the warmth and comfort of a well-furnished living room, and Ken was surprised that it looked as if a normal twenty-first-century couple lived there. He jerked as Merlin answered his thoughts.

"Did you expect a witch's cauldron bubbling away in the corner, or an enchanted broom flying around?" Not really expecting an answer, Merlin paused to look appraisingly at Ken and then continued, "I suppose it wouldn't hurt to show you what I looked like in the fifth century." Instantly, his appearance changed. He was clothed in a long blue robe, the closely woven fabric richly embellished with gold and silver decorations that looked like arcane symbols of power. Circling his brow was a narrow band of silver, which indicated his elevated status within the Royal Household of Camelot and kept his thick black hair out of his eyes. The long beard and mustache accentuated the sharp planes of his handsome, deceptively young-looking face, upon which a mocking grin revealed mostly straight white teeth.

Ken gasped in shock, then recovered enough to return Merlin's smile. Suddenly, he was utterly thrilled to be in the presence of this legendary figure straight out of the Dark Ages. It was obvious, though, that he still felt somewhat anxious about the encounter, so Merlin finally returned to his jeans and T-shirt.

Derek left Ken at the mercy of his father and went into the kitchen to see Emily and Lumina, only to discover that his sister was already in bed; he hadn't realized it was so late. Emily asked him to help her with the refreshments and he seriously considered levitating the tray of chocolate chip cookies—but thought better of it as he remembered the fragile state of Ken's nerves—so he manually toted it and the coffee mugs out to the front room. Em followed with the pot of coffee. The hot coffee was welcome; it was a cold night and the warmth of the mugs felt good to their chilled hands.

Emily tried to draw Ken into a conversation, since they had known each other for many years, but it was an effort to keep him talking. Derek wasn't particularly voluble either as he still felt guilty for sharing their secret with a mortal, close friend or not.

Finally, after both cookies and coffee had been consumed and there was a lull in the limited conversation, Merlin impatiently cleared his throat. "Derek, let's give Ken a little demonstration, shall we?"

"I showed him the blue fire when I levitated to the top of Balanced Rock, Dad, so he's already convinced. And seein' you in your Camelot robe and long hair seemed to be pretty effective, too," Derek commented, directing a smile towards his friend, who nodded in agreement.

I thought we could teleport him up to the top of the Rim for a night view of the stars above and the city lights below.

Well, okay—hopefully that won't freak him out too much.

Oh, I think he'll survive. Merlin's eyes twinkled. *What do you think, Em?*

I think he may just enjoy it if the shock doesn't kill him. Just kidding, he'll be fine, I'm sure. She laughed aloud as she remembered the first time her husband had teleported her, stark naked, to the top of the Rim. She hadn't felt like laughing then, she was so angry, but now she could see the humor in it.

Ken was anxiously looking back and forth between the three of them as they sat staring intently at each other, apparently communicating telepathically. "Uh, what's going on?"

Neither Merlin nor Derek answered as they put their mugs down, stood up and stepped to either side of him, each one touching an arm of the shorter man—and teleported to the top of the Rim.

"Holy shit, what the—" Ken yelled as he had a moment of intense disorientation. Then, he looked down on the city of Moab, aglow a thousand feet below them.

"Oh, my God, this is so incredible! How did you do that?" He started to shiver violently in the cold air, both he and Derek having left their sweatshirts behind in Merlin's warm living room.

"We can teleport, Ken," Derek said. "And conjure jackets." He held a red one out to his friend, who immediately pulled it on gratefully, and then conjured one for himself in navy blue. He noticed that Merlin's eyebrows had risen in surprise, disappearing under the dark hair on his forehead, when the jackets appeared. He guessed it had just taken the right reason to break through his mental block about conjuring.

"Damn, I'm a little overwhelmed here. But this is...*awesome.*" Ken looked down at the bright lights of Moab, at the night sky above them, then around the shadowed sandstone ledge dusted with snow that the three of them occupied. And lastly, his gaze fell on the two tall sorcerers standing nonchalantly next to him. Unbelievable.

Derek knew that Merlin was watching him share this unique experience with his friend. Silently, he beseeched his father to allow Ken to retain his memory of the evening.

Yes, I'll allow it, Derek. I can see in his mind that he will never reveal our secret—he's much too impressed with the whole thing.

Thanks, Dad, I appreciate it. Ken's my buddy, and it's important to me that he knows who I really am.

I know. Believe me...I know.

Emily was clearing away the remnants of their snack as the three men reappeared in the center of the living room. "Well, how was it?" she asked Ken with a smile.

Derek watched as his friend's eyes lit up with wonder. "Amazing, just amazing." Ken returned his gaze then pointedly looked at Merlin and Emily, and said, "Really, thanks for everything. I'll never say a word to anyone, I promise."

"I know you won't, Ken," Merlin said kindly. "Good night." He put an arm around Em's shoulders, hugging her against him as the two men grabbed their now-superfluous sweatshirts, said their own "good nights," and left the house.

They traversed the short distance to Derek's front door, which he opened using magic, much to Ken's delight. Although they had just had coffee, beers seemed to be in order, and they took their drinks out to the patio. They sat quietly side by side in the folding chairs, bundled in their conjured down jackets, admiring the Rim, which looked ghostly in the reflected light from downtown, and taking a swig now and then.

Ken fingered the thickness of his new outerwear, and then turned to his friend with a laugh. "This has been one crazy, awe-inspiring night, and to top it off, I've got a magic jacket in my favorite color."

"Yeah, I'm just happy that it worked—conjurin' isn't easy for me. I've tried for months to conjure a cup of coffee and can't seem to do it." Derek gave a wry grin and finished off his beer, setting the empty bottle on the concrete next to his chair.

"Maybe conjuring is meant for more important things than a cup of coffee; ever think of that?" Ken murmured.

"You may be right," Derek chuckled.

The conversation bounced back and forth comfortably between them, and Ken talked excitedly about what a privilege it was to meet Merlin, and how lucky Derek was. Derek completely agreed with him: He was an immortal sorcerer and the son of the legendary Merlin—his life couldn't get any better than that. His earlier feelings of unhappiness and dissatisfaction were forgotten.

As he watched his friend's face while Ken expressed his gratitude for the evening's surprising events, Derek wondered why he had never mentioned that he was gay. It really wasn't any of his business, but for some reason he was feeling intrigued, and more than a little curious, about how it would feel to make love to a man. He felt weird even thinking such a thing and attributed the uncharacteristic thought to his current celibate state. But he was feeling oddly attracted to this man tonight.

Ken finally took a breath and realized that Derek was watching him with an unusual intensity, and correctly interpreted the questioning look on his face.

"You're curious about me, aren't you?"

Derek nodded, a little embarrassed as Ken started to talk about the experience of being...different...during his school years.

"You know, I realized when I was in high school that I wasn't like the other guys, who couldn't wait to see a girl naked, especially her tits. I wanted to see the guys naked in the locker room, and I could care less about a girl's tits. It was hard making friends then, and it still is. Even though I don't act like the limp-wristed, super-feminine gay guy, some men seem to sense what my sexual preference is and just steer clear of me; especially in a small town like Moab. So, I've really appreciated the fact that you wanted to be my friend, Derek." He paused as if considering the consequences of his next words. "But...now that you know the truth, I...have to tell you that I, uh, oh, Christ...I'm in love with you," Ken blurted out, then blushed, giving his brown cheeks a ruddy hue.

Derek just stared at him, shocked—but, surprisingly, not unhappy about Ken's declaration. But, *he* wasn't gay, was he? He enjoyed having sex with women. Admittedly, he'd had very few sexual encounters over the past few years, other than the short-term relationship with Maria, but that didn't mean he wanted to be with a man, did it? God, he was confused.

Making eye contact, Ken reached out slowly and caressed his cheek, then leaned over and tentatively pressed his lips against Derek's.

Rather shaken by his friend's sexual advances, but feeling an overwhelming desire to take the encounter further, Derek returned the kiss, pulling the smaller man closer.

Finally, he sat back, staring into Ken's eyes. He smiled widely as he made a decision, then stood up and put out his hand. "Come on, let's go inside where it's warm," he said softly.

Ken took his hand and rose to his feet, following Derek as he led him into the house.

CHAPTER 32

February 6 Late Night

IN THE SEMIDARKNESS of the master bedroom, Ken stood close to him and stroked his face, kissing him tenderly. Sensing Derek's slight hesitation, he asked gently, "Are you okay? We don't have to do this if you've changed your mind."

"I haven't changed my mind. I'm just a little nervous—I've never been with a man before."

"We can take it slow, babe, don't worry. God, I've wanted you for so long," Ken whispered as he reached out to unbutton Derek's long-sleeved shirt. He pushed it off his shoulders and ran a questing hand across the muscular chest revealed. Derek's breath caught and he shivered with desire as Ken's warm lips sought his own once again. They explored each other's mouths until they had to come up for air.

"My turn," Derek said hoarsely, as he pulled his friend's long-sleeved T-shirt off over his head. He placed his hand on Ken's bare chest and traced the soft, curly dark hair down across his stomach, and then reached to cup him intimately through his jeans. Derek realized that he was intensely aroused; it gave him so much pleasure just to touch this man, and the hardened ridge of flesh beneath his hand made it quite obvious that Ken felt the same way.

He swallowed nervously as he looked searchingly into the other man's eyes. He looked away before the Seeing could be triggered. "I want you."

"I've been hoping and praying for this moment for years. You don't know how difficult it's been to hide my feelings," Ken said simply.

Derek stammered, "I…I didn't realize that I *had* feelin's like this for you."

"I'm glad you do," Ken murmured, kissing him again and pulling him closer, until their bodies came together, electrifying them both as their bare torsos touched and their passion flared.

"Oh, God, you feel so good," Derek groaned as he stroked his hands down Ken's back, and then squeezed his ass through the denim of his jeans.

"I think we have too many clothes on," Ken said. Derek nodded his head in agreement, and they both hurriedly shucked their jeans and briefs. As the last sock dropped to the floor, the two men slid under the covers, straining to get closer, until they were pressed tightly against each other, legs entwined. They both gasped at the sensual contact of their naked bodies, and they began stroking each other, their passion mounting. Making love slowly, with exquisite care, they pleasured each other for hours, the rest of the world fading into the background.

Later, as they reclined on the bed, relaxed and satisfied both physically and emotionally, Ken ran his hand along Derek's thigh and sighed. "That was just ...incredible."

"My God, I had no idea it could be like that," Derek said softly, feeling content and well-loved. He turned his head on the pillow to look at his friend, then caressed the other man's cheek and leaned in for another slow kiss.

Ken smiled and gazed deeply into Derek's eyes. Before Derek could warn him that it wasn't a good idea, they had already started to See into each other's beings. Unlike Merlin, he had no experience in preventing the other person from seeing his own life, and he couldn't stop the process, but he found he was able to guide Ken's experiences to some extent.

Ken gasped as he Saw the details of Derek's magical heritage, and Derek Saw the entirety of Ken's life from birth to the present. Time had no meaning during their immersion in each other essences. Finally, after a certain amount of trial and error, Derek was somehow able to bring them back to their separate selves. Ken's eyes were glazed and he was breathing hard.

"Shit, Ken, I'm so sorry, I should have warned you that you can't look into a sorcerer's eyes like that. Are you okay?" Derek asked, worried that the experience had been too intense for his friend.

Tears coursed silently down Ken's cheeks, and he wiped his eyes, which were a surprising light blue. "That was the most beautiful thing I've ever experienced, besides making love with you," he gulped. "Did…did I actually see your *soul*?"

"Yeah, you did," Derek said gently. "That's why some practitioners of magic say never to look a sorcerer in the eye—it triggers an intense connection that may or may not be a good thing for either person."

"Is it like the 'Soul Gaze' in the Harry Dresden books?" Ken asked in disbelief.

"Something like that," Derek said evasively, not able to easily explain the unique connection created when two people Saw the secret depths of each other's inner selves, and not willing to compare it to some author's definition of the soul.

"How do you deal with all this? I mean, you were born in the winter of *442?* In Camelot? Seriously*?*"

"I know—it seems crazy when you think about it. Merlin was only 22 years old at the time, seven years younger than I am now."

"So he has to be…almost 1,600 years old. My God," Ken gulped.

"A little less than that, but, yeah, he's pretty old," Derek said.

"Jesus! But that means *you're* over 1,500 years old! I know I just saw the events of your life, but I have to confess, I was so blown away that some of it's just a blur in my mind."

"Actually, I was brought to 1985 by my grandfather Llyr when I was just a few months old, so I really am only twenty-nine; I never lived through all those centuries like my dad did. My adoptive parents always celebrated my birthday in March instead of December for some reason, so it's a little off. But who cares, right?"

"Wait a minute. Your grandfather *Llyr* brought you through time? How do I know that name?" Ken frowned as he searched his memory. He'd read some Welsh mythology a few summers earlier, and if he could just remember... It was obvious when he accessed the memory naming the ancient Welsh gods, as his eyebrows shot up and he gasped. "Your grandfather is the Welsh god of the sea? I…I'm feeling kind of out of my depth here," he confessed, his dark face exhibiting a surprising pallor.

"You want me to help you forget all this?" Derek asked sympathetically. "I can enchant you if it's too much to handle."

"You can do that?" Ken looked a bit worried.

"Well, it's not like I'm a vampire glamourin' you or somethin'," he said indignantly. "I'm still just Derek Colburn…although, come to think of it, that's not my real name."

"Then, what is?" Ken asked faintly.

"Emrys Ambrosius."

"Ah, I guess I should have Seen that also, but, like I said, my brain is overloaded. I…I'm pretty sure I can't handle any more tonight," he stated thickly, sounding like he was drunk.

"Oh, come on, there's somethin' else you need to know."

"Shit, what now?"

"Emily's part Elf and she's immortal, too, since she married my dad," Derek said matter-of-factly.

Ken's mind decided it had had enough, and he fainted.

He felt kinda bad for pushing him so hard, but Derek had really wanted Ken to know all of those additional details of his life. He lay on his side and just stared at the man he thought he'd known so well, and in reality hadn't known at all. This man he'd just had sex with—God, he could hardly believe that he'd done that—who claimed he was in love with him. He looked back through his memories to see if there had been signs and he'd overlooked them. He slowly began to remember all the times Ken had touched him, patted him, and draped his arm across his shoulders. Derek had just felt that he was being overly friendly and he hadn't really minded, because it made him feel good—wanted, needed.

In the heat of the moment tonight, and in the relief of knowing that he didn't have to hide his true self any longer, he had returned Ken's sentiments—but did he really feel that way? Did he honestly love him, or was he blinded by the intense sexual experience he'd just had? In some ways, this—whatever it was—would be no different from having a relationship with a mortal woman: he was still going to outlive his lover. Ken's lifespan in relation to his was a mere flash of light in the vastness of eternity. His friend would grow old and die right before his eyes, and now he could understand why Merlin had abstained from sexual relations—in fact from any close associations—for all those centuries after Arthur perished. Well, for most of that time anyway. Did he want to leave himself open to the certainty of heartache that would ensue if he pursued this affair?

Derek realized that Ken's blue eyes were open, and that he had been watching him ponder this dilemma. He reached out and ran his fingers through Ken's soft dark curls and shivered with the sensation of closeness he experienced. Ken's emotions were so clear and strong that he felt his love washing over him.

"You're worried about all this aren't you?" the man said softly, gazing at his lover in concern.

Derek glanced at him quickly, then pulled his hands back, feeling embarrassed. "Yeah, it took me by surprise. I'm kinda confused, 'cause I've always thought of myself as heterosexual."

"Well, I don't think you're gay, I think you're bisexual—you're capable of being aroused by either a male or a female," Ken said with a brief smile. "You know, I've been in love with you for years. Didn't you think it was strange that you never saw me with a woman?"

"No, not really, because I wasn't with anyone either for a long time."

"That's because you thought you were in love with Emily, at least until she married Michael Reese—oh!" It was easy to see the shock on Ken's face as it occurred to him, again, who Michael really was.

Derek grinned. "Yeah, I had a tough time dealin' with it until my dad basically told me to grow up. It was the best thing he coulda done. I respected his advice and knew he was right, even though it was hard on my ego. You know it's funny—before I met him, my entire life was so centered around the *legend* of King Arthur and Merlin and the knights that I never thought about anythin' else. Maybe some part of me sensed the truth. So when I found out that Merlin was real, and that I was his *son*, I thought I'd died and gone to heaven!" He saw a peculiar look flash across Ken's face.

"You know, there's something that's bothering me, something I Saw in you that I'm having a hard time with. Uh…" Ken stopped and cleared his throat.

Derek frowned for a moment then his face cleared. "Ah, I'll bet I know what that is, and I agree with you—it's pretty unbelievable. Merlin is actually a god; he's the Welsh god of magic and healin', Myrddin Emrys. And since the children of gods are considered demigods, well…"

"You're a demigod." Ken sat up abruptly, his eyes wide and his mouth open in shock.

"Yeah, but it's really not that big a deal, I—"

"It's a huge deal, Derek! Oh, my God, my lover is an immortal sorcerer and the son of a god!" Ken was grinning so hard that he thought his face would crack. He enthusiastically tackled Derek, and as they collapsed in a heap of tangled limbs, their heightened emotions and the sensation of skin on skin caused both of them to become aroused again.

As they made love once more, there was still a doubt in Derek's mind that he was doing the right thing. But he refused to acknowledge it, deciding to think about it much, much later.

CHAPTER 33

February 7-22

MY RENEWED SENSE of purpose and awareness of the increasing urgency of the quest continued throughout the month of February. However, I did not at any time forget the threat that Beli still represented. As I had temporarily sent him back to the realm of the gods, and thus he was no longer able to utilize the remaining threads of the bloody towel, I felt relatively safe, but suspected that this respite wouldn't—couldn't—last. All of my attempts to locate that last elusive piece of fabric had failed.

However, failure was definitely not a problem at The Moab Herbalist—the shop was proving to be extremely successful. Business had increased to an astonishing degree, as if the human population of Moab was drawn to the shop like metal shavings to a magnet. There was a point at which I could no longer do everything myself unless I used magic openly, and of course as Michael Reese, human proprietor, I couldn't do that. I wasn't quite ready to hire anyone, leery of bringing in an individual who might witness the unexplainable. Of course, the obvious solution was to find and hire someone who had the gift of magic, so I kept my senses tuned for that eventuality.

In the meantime, I seriously considered enlisting Emily's help for four or five hours a day, despite her necessary preoccupation with Lumina. After she had resigned her position with the National Park Service the previous summer, she had assisted me very ably, and had learned to make many of the simpler potions. Her knowledge of herbs had expanded over the months, as her belly had expanded during her pregnancy. As she grew more and more uncomfortable physically, and the holidays neared, we had decided to close the shop so that she was able to stay home and prepare for the birth of our child.

I finally persuaded her to become my assistant again in our family business. She insisted on bringing Lumina with her to work, as leaving the child with a babysitter was out of the question. I agreed. We had considered calling on the knights to act in that capacity, but as they had no magic, they would be at the mercy of our daughter's unpredictable behavior. Not only that, but if Beli should come for her, the knights could not truly protect her, or themselves. It was apparent that they felt slighted, however, so I invited them to stop by and visit her occasionally as they had done when we were at home all day. I found myself missing the presence of those special men who had been my friends and Arthur's loyal protectors, and happily welcomed them when they did stop by. I realized that they missed me as well, and that without an active assignment for the quest, they were at loose ends, in need of a purpose. I had allowed my focus to drift and I swore that I would do whatever was necessary to fix this lapse.

Lumina had experienced no recent growth spurts, but I sensed that it was just a matter of time before the next one occurred. Emily wondered why, with the unimaginable and seemingly unlimited powers at my disposal, I couldn't see every step in her unusual aging process, but it was apparent that my own daughter's destiny was beyond my control. After my communion with the one God, I had assumed that every step on my path, including the details regarding my family and home life, would suddenly be clear to me, but that was far from the truth. So, once again it was obvious that even a sorcerer with powers of a deity could not afford to make assumptions.

At the shop, we had to be extra vigilant, as my daughter's powers were developing to such an alarming degree that we were afraid she would suddenly teleport across the room, manifest a toy or conjure a light orb in the presence of customers. Thankfully, she was still a young child and needed a nap in the afternoons, and my former apartment upstairs came in handy for that purpose. The respite from our constant vigilance was most welcome.

Lumina was a happy little girl, a joy to have around, and we loved her to distraction, but both Emily and I experienced daily the loss of the sweet, innocent little baby she had been for such a short period of time.

We hadn't seen much of Derek since he and Ken had become lovers, although I sensed him daily through our bond. He was considerably less attentive to me than he had been, and the growing sense of distance between us truly disturbed me. Our first story-telling session of the season had been scheduled and my son had agreed to be there, but when the time came, he never showed up. I, of course, had plenty of stories to tell, and had chosen the tale of Arthur's conception and birth at Tintagel Castle, always a favorite with my customers. As usual, I had to downplay my own role, as I was not anxious to reveal my true name to those in attendance. However, I could feel my aura shining brighter than it normally did, so it was a good thing that no one present had the ability to see it. After the session had concluded and the last person had departed, I could admit to my disappointment that Derek had never even called to let me know he wasn't coming.

I was tempted to contact him telepathically on more than one occasion, but each time I sensed that he had blocked himself off from me, a sure sign that he and Ken were engaging in intimate activities and didn't wish to be disturbed. I missed him greatly, and although Emily assured me that it wasn't his intention to do so, my feelings were hurt.

At first, I had suspected that Derek's lack of interest was an extremely subtle ploy on the part of Beli to drive a wedge between us, just as I had thought was the case when Derek had become enamored of Adrestia in Camelot. Both instances exhibited atypical behavior on my son's part. But I didn't think it likely that Beli, still in the realm of the gods, had enough power to influence Derek here in the mortal realm.

Then, I thought perhaps Ken had somehow hidden the fact that he was actually a practitioner of magic, a Fae creature or a demon. However, I had to let go of that notion as I had seen very clearly into his being that night on the Rim, and he was what he seemed: a human male who had fallen in love with Derek, apparently satisfying my son's need for sex and companionship his own age.

I became more and more displeased with Derek's behavior as time passed, until I was convinced that I would have to intervene. This liaison with Ken was causing him to neglect his role in the continuing preparations for our quest. Derek's lover monopolized his time to the exclusion of all else except his work—and since they were partners on the job, Ken had a controlling influence on that part of Derek's life as well.

During the winter months, Derek and I had spent many hours discussing our renewed search for the Avalon Portal, but those plans had never been finalized, and the time was fast approaching when we would need to get out in the field again.

One day at my shop, he and I had had a rare moment alone. It had been necessary for Derek to sneak away, for his friend's possessive nature had surfaced with a vengeance.

I had been aware right from the start that the two men were lovers—I could hardly have missed the signs—and it was apparent that Derek was curious what I thought about it. In truth, previous to his affair with Ken, I had not been aware that Derek's sexual preferences were so flexible; I had never had any reason to suspect that either gender was acceptable to him as a sexual partner. But I had to let that go—it was none of my business. The only thing that did concern me was the knowledge that if Derek eventually wanted to carry on our magical and immortal heritage with his own children, he would need to be with a woman.

I felt bound to discuss this situation with him, but I considered my words carefully, as I did not want to make things any more uncomfortable between us than they already were.

"I hesitate to bring this up, Derek, but I feel strongly that I should do so. If you prefer a male as your life partner, that is, of course, your choice. However, make sure it's what you really want, because it's very difficult to let go once you have become emotionally attached to someone, and the obvious drawback to being with a man, is that you won't be able to have your own children with him."

"You're right, I never thought about that," Derek had confessed in dismay. "I've always wanted to have kids of my own some day. Ken and I could always adopt, but if they weren't genetically mine, they wouldn't have any chance of being immortal. God, what a quandary."

At that point, I had let the subject lapse in favor of making plans to continue our quest. He had promised to schedule time with me the following weekend, but I never heard from him.

The sense of urgency I had heretofore experienced paled in comparison with what drove me now, and I knew that, with or without Derek, I had to find the new portal to Avalon. It seemed that the location of the portal was being actively hidden from me—for what purpose I couldn't fathom—but I had no choice except to overcome my frustration and accomplish my sworn goal in any manner at my disposal. It was my destiny and this planet's only hope of a united future, to bring back Arthur Pendragon and assume my place at his side, utilizing my fully-manifested god powers to bring about the global Albion.

CHAPTER 34

February 23

THE WEEKEND AFTER I had vowed to pursue the quest without Derek's assistance, I drove my old black Chevy pickup truck south of town and took the La Sal Loop Road into the mountains, hoping to feel an energy pulse or other indication of the Avalon Portal. I had never pursued the possibility that the object of my search could be in this area, but if nothing else, I would be able to cross it off my list.

I had inserted a disc of Indian flute music into the CD player, and enjoyed the haunting melodies as I drove the winding road up out of the valley. I allowed my mind to drift and marveled at the similarities between the music of the Native American people and that of many other cultures, some separated by space and time.

I cast out my senses in a wide arc and perceived the ancient energy present in these mountains, an energy that called to the equally ancient god powers within me. I felt my consciousness expanding until I could easily have left my body behind, which would have been particularly inconvenient since I was driving.

As I passed the turnoff to Warner Lake, I realized that I had not yet been there, and made a mental note to do so as soon as the snow melted at the higher elevations. A customer had recently mentioned how much he enjoyed camping there every summer and it sounded very appealing.

A few miles further on, I pulled the vehicle onto a wide shelf of rock next to the road, and turned the key. The quietness was a stunning backdrop to my perception of the power deep within the earth. I would never lack for assistance here, should I need to augment my magic. Reaching out for it even slightly would result in a potent rush of support from the earth itself.

As I sat for a few moments with my eyes closed, I reveled in the glow of light and power, feeling it caress me and call to a very primitive part of my inner being. I slowed my breathing and continued to focus inside myself, and one by one, each individual portal in the vicinity was revealed. Any one of them was of sufficient size and strength to be the object of my search. I sensed each and every one of them within a mile of where I had parked.

I blinked my eyes and refocused on the physical world, then opened the truck door and stepped out. I felt a tug on my senses and turned to stare up the hill across the road; there was a portal not too far from where I stood. I no longer found it necessary to use spells to locate the openings—I actually observed the energy pouring forth from them. It was ironic that with all the powers at my command, I still hadn't found the portal that would reunite me with Arthur Pendragon. *Help me to find my way back to you, old friend...*

I was quite alone up here, so I launched myself into the air and flew up to the portal, hovering above it as I considered how to proceed. I felt a rush of optimism as I sensed a magical presence beyond the opening, and descended to take a closer look.

The portal itself seemed rather insubstantial, but I felt that it posed no danger of collapse. I was sufficiently intrigued by the power exuding from it that I knew I wanted to explore, but before I went through it, I contrived a way to pull myself back from the other side after a specific period of time.

I gingerly stepped through the slight resistance of the portal and found myself on what seemed to be the same hillside, the brush thick and about shoulder height. As I turned my head to gaze down the hill, I saw a truck very much like mine in age and style but it was white, not black. Then, I heard the sound of someone making his way through the vegetation and I sensed the man's identity. I swiveled slowly and faced...myself. We stared at one another for a moment in silence and I felt a shiver run down my spine.

"This must be an alternate reality, a different dimension from my own," I said to my other self.

"It must be. From whence do you come, and what call you the city in which you dwell? How came you here?" The other Merlin was as calm as I was which shouldn't have surprised me—we would presumably be of the same or similar temperament. I noticed that his speech was stilted, and his accent much more pronounced.

"I have come from the twenty-first century, and the city in the valley is called Moab, in the state of Utah. I left the Crystal Cave almost a year ago after having been summoned to find the new Avalon Portal, for which I am still searching. I had hoped that this portal could be the one," I replied.

My alter ego frowned. "I live in the same century, however I have only recently arrived in Moab. I cannot explain why my path has diverged from yours. I have failed to locate the portal to Avalon as well, but as it has been difficult to get away from my shop since I have no one to help me, my opportunities to search have been limited. The townsfolk are most suspicious of my activities; I was required to make myself known to the Society for the Protection of Non-Magical Beings, as sorcerers are considered a threat to normal humans here. Only by the grace of the gods am I able to conduct my business. Magic is a necessary evil to most people, so they do hire me, but I make little money."

"You are able to practice magic openly?" I was dumbfounded, and a bit envious. It seemed that this other Merlin was not as fortunate as I had been in other ways, however. It appeared that he had not married Emily, nor had he found his son Derek. I felt a rush of pity for him.

Suddenly, a sense of urgency stirred in my being, and I knew that the enchantment I had created would soon draw me back to my own reality. "I'm afraid I don't have much time left here, but please allow me to give you some advice before I depart: find a woman named Emily Crandall and a man named Derek Colburn. In my timeline, both of them work for the National Park Service. If you can find them here, in this Moab, I believe that things will change for the better for you, Myrddin Emrys," I said earnestly, thinking that if I acknowledged our god name if would make more of an impression on him.

He cocked his head in confusion. "By what name do you call me? My name is Merlin, not Myrddin, although some have indeed called me Emrys over the years."

I was stunned into silence. He didn't even know his true name.

He looked at me suspiciously. "And the two people you mentioned, how could they cause such an alteration in my circumstances?"

I was in a state of shock, but I forced myself to respond. Just before I was pulled back through the portal, I said urgently, "Find them! Emily is destined to be your wife and Derek is your son."

My sight blurred briefly and then I was standing on the hillside above the road, alone, and I could see my own black pickup parked below. I glanced at my watch and realized that I had only been away a matter of minutes. It seemed like hours, and a sense of strangeness clung to me like a damp cloak.

Shaken and depressed by my experience in the alternate timeline, I didn't have the heart to continue the search, so I hurried back to my vehicle and drove home as fast as I dared.

When I arrived back on Doc Allen Drive and parked hurriedly in the driveway, I leapt out of the truck and ran into the house, calling frantically for my wife.

"What's wrong, magic man?" Emily emerged from the kitchen wiping her hands on a dish towel.

I threw my arms around her and held her close to me, practically weeping with gratitude that she existed, that she was mine. I was devastated that my other self was alone, and that he might never find the love of his life, as I had. And it bothered me more than I cared to admit that he wasn't aware of his true self. Even before I realized that I was a god, I had known my true name and that there was a hidden significance to it.

"Where's Lumina?" I gasped, my need for my wife suddenly consuming me.

"In her room taking a nap, why?" Emily asked curiously.

"Because I'm going to make love to you, *right now*," I said, and picking her up, I teleported into our bedroom, locking the door with a thought.

Sometime later, as we lay in each other's arms, drowsy and satisfied, my thoughts kept returning to that meeting with myself. I wondered how many infinite versions of Merlin there were, and if it was possible for dimensions to overlap, allowing the inhabitants of alternate universes to interact with each other, without using the portals. I suppressed a shiver and pulled my wife closer, taking comfort, as any mortal would, in the warm reassurance of our bodies touching.

As she held her husband in her arms, his head tucked snugly in the crook of her neck, Emily blinked back a few tears.

He was afraid; she could sense it. This ancient god, the most powerful sorcerer who had ever lived, was afraid. And if Merlin was experiencing such an emotion, how should she feel? But it didn't really matter—she would give her life for him, this incredible, gorgeous man who had chosen her above all others. She shivered with apprehension as she sensed more dangerous days ahead for her family, but she would fight to her last breath to protect them all. She stroked Merlin's sleek, muscled back and swore that she would try and figure out where the last vestige of that damned bloody towel could be. That seemed to be the key—as long as Beli, or that bitch Adrestia, held any kind of power over him, one or both of them could still wreak havoc in their lives.

As I lay in my wife's loving arms, I felt her tears on my face and heard her thoughts. Gods, she was fierce. Was I afraid? I hadn't even considered it, but perhaps I was. It was interesting that the encounter in the alternate reality should stir my emotions so violently. Perhaps I saw myself as I might have been, if I hadn't come to Moab when I did, if I hadn't met Emily or Derek, if I hadn't recognized my true self...

I had to blink back my own tears as I came to the conclusion, once again, that being with my family meant more to me than the quest, more than my god powers. I wish I knew exactly what I needed to do.

CHAPTER 35

February 24-March 9

THE DAY AFTER my unsettling experience in the La Sal Mountains, I was opening The Moab Herbalist for yet another profitable day when my thoughts were once again consumed by the dilemma regarding my son and his lover. Unfortunately, that meant that the issue of locating the towel fragment was put on the backburner—again. I sighed as I started a pot of coffee, then turned the computer on and set up the till.

As much as I had liked Ken originally, I now felt resentful and impatient towards the man. I truly hoped that Derek's infatuation—for that was what Emily and I suspected it was—would eventually come to an end.

I felt increasingly frustrated that I had not had the opportunity to present Derek with his finished staff. He had ignored or refused all of our recent invitations to join us for a meal, or even for just a cup of coffee in the morning before work.

I knew that at some point, everything would work itself out and I would look back on my worries with the superior view of hindsight, but at the moment, I just had to concentrate on the present, and try to enjoy my day.

I wondered idly whether that fellow who had known the Old English names of the herbs would ever drop by to pick up his order. Although I had put the herbs into stasis, so that they would not lose potency, I would just as soon sell them if he did not intend to return.

On the first of March, Emily reminded me that her birthday was the following week, and that Derek's was only a few days after hers. She suggested that we invite both men to celebrate with us, using that time to present my son with his sorcerer's staff. She was quite proud of herself for thinking of it, and I had to agree that it could be an easy solution to our dilemma.

"We can have a barbecue and you can give him his staff then. Neither of them can possibly refuse to come to a birthday celebration, right?" She bounced excitedly from stove to table as she served breakfast that morning.

"But, Em, that's your special day; are you sure you want to share the spotlight?" I asked doubtfully as I handed Lumina a piece of toast and poured a glass of juice for myself. "I do want to spend time with Derek, of course, but I thought you'd want to go out for a romantic dinner."

"Yes, I'm absolutely sure. I do want to have a lovely evening out with you, but we can do that on a different day. I really miss him, Merlin, and Ken needs to learn to share Derek with his family," she said firmly as she sat down and started to eat her own breakfast. She paused with a forkful of egg halfway to her mouth and then set it back down, and a frown marred the perfection of her lovely face, "There's something really wrong with that relationship. He's monopolizing your son—my friend—to the point that Derek's losing his sense of who he is, and he's forgetting about the quest."

"I agree with you, my love, although I'm not sure what we can do about it. I could forbid him to see Ken, and as his god I would have every right to do so, but I know he would deeply resent such an action."

Em sighed, then picked up a sausage and took a bite out of it. "You're right. I just wish he could meet someone with magic."

"Don't worry, love, I think that is a definite possibility in the near future." I didn't want to get any more specific than that, but she sensed that I was hiding something from her and gave me a knowing look.

"Em, I truly don't know the exact details—it doesn't work that way."

"Uh-huh, right," she smirked. "Well, I'm going to contact Derek today, even if I have to call him at work, and make sure he knows he has to be here tomorrow to help plan our party."

The day after my conversation with Emily, the four of us made the effort to get together and discuss the details of the upcoming joint birthday celebration. We agreed that we would all enjoy a barbecue, and that it would be most appropriate to have it at Arches National Park. Emily, Derek and Ken had long-standing associations and fond memories relating to the park, and I had spent untold hours scouring its cliffs and canyons for the Avalon Portal.

"What about the knights? I think they should be invited. We haven't seen much of them lately and I know Lumina would like to see 'em." From the look on his face, it was apparent that Derek would benefit from their presence as well.

I was quiet for a few moments, considering what it would mean to have all three warriors present. Not only were they were good company, but in the case of an emergency they could assist in getting Emily, Lumina and Ken to safety. I was not anticipating such an occurrence, but it couldn't hurt to be prepared.

"I think you're right, Derek, and I'm glad you suggested it. I've been neglecting the knights lately, and I'm sure that including them in our plans would help them to feel useful. I'll give Ryan a call tomorrow and set it up." Ever since the battle with Nimue the previous summer, Ryan Jones, otherwise known as Sir Lancelot, had been the de facto leader of the men who had once been King Arthur's finest.

Normally, early March was a bit too cool to contemplate a picnic out at Devil's Garden, in fact, in past years there had still been snow on the ground at that time. Recent temperatures had been unseasonably warm, however, and we decided to chance it.

The day finally arrived and we were up early to begin preparations. We packed up the various salads—potato, fruit and green—that Em had made the previous day into one of the ice chests, along with the marinated ribeye steaks we had agreed upon, and carefully wedged the wrapped sheet cake into the back of the SUV. Utensils, plates and other related gear were also loaded, including our portable grill and charcoal.

"Have we forgotten anything?" Em glanced at me, then at Derek.

"I don't think so—we've got enough stuff to camp out for a friggin' week," he said impatiently, grabbing the ice chest of beverages and securing it to the roof rack. "Where are the knights?"

Emily had just gotten her cell phone out to call Ryan when his big Hummer pulled up to the curb, and Gary, better known as Sir Gawain, leaned out the window and waved.

"We were beginning to wonder if you guys were going to show up!" Em called out.

"We discovered we had a flat tire, so we fixed it right away, but of course that made us late getting here."

"Don't worry about it—at least you're here now!"

"Daddy!" Lumina tugged on my pant leg, her head tilted back as she stared intently up into my face, trying to get my attention.

"What, Daughter?"

"Can I bring Teddy?" she asked in her high-pitched little voice. She clutched the bear tightly against her.

Before I could answer, Emily turned from her spirited discussion with Gawain and interjected somewhat impatiently, "Lumi, I already told you that it would be best to leave him at home; he'll get all dirty taking him on a picnic. I've got other things for you to play with, as well as a book to look at."

"But, Mommy…" She whined and stamped her foot, sounding like she was working up to a good tantrum.

"Lumina, Mommy's right. Teddy is staying at home this time. But look who's coming with us." I pointed to the vehicle waiting at the curb, and succeeded in distracting her.

Her pout immediately changed to a grin of welcome and she waved to her adopted uncles, who responded with their own smiles and waves.

"Come on, let's get you into your car seat," I said firmly, picking her up and placing her in the seat, making sure she was buckled in. I carefully closed the car door then glanced at my wife's still-exasperated expression and smiled. "Take a few deep breaths, love, and relax."

She did as I suggested, and smiled back at me, mouthing the words, *Thank you.* She looked pointedly at my feet and pursed her lips as she pantomimed a big kiss.

I rolled my eyes and shook my head slightly. *No foot-kissing today, please, especially in front of Ken*, I said in a silent, private message.

She just grinned widely and climbed into the back seat of the yellow Xterra. She moved over next to Lumina's child seat and I got in beside her so I had the window. It was a tight squeeze, but I didn't mind having my wife's body pressed against mine. We were taking Em's vehicle today, since it was the only one that had room for all of us plus our gear, and Derek was driving. Ken rode shotgun. It was a luxury to be a passenger for a change, and I lowered the window as we headed out towards the park, pleased to feel the warm air blowing gently on my face and bare arms. The knights followed close behind us.

We all remarked on the fine weather, and as the conversation veered off into discussing park business, I enjoyed the scenery. I never took the beauty of this place for granted: the topaz blue of the sky and the intense reddish-brown color of the steep cliffs and tumbled boulders still fascinated me. The bright sunlight gleamed and I closed my eyes against the intense glare, smiling as I remembered how I had yearned to come here, to this planet, to live as a human being.

Suddenly, I had the urge to leave my body and did so. I hovered in spirit form above the vehicle as it moved down the highway, past the remains of the uranium tailings pile and the intersection with Potash Road, then into the right lane in preparation for turning into the park. I started to drift higher, to see a larger perspective…

"Merlin? Honey? Are you okay?" My wife's concerned voice instantly brought me back into my body and I opened my eyes. Turning towards her, I gazed into familiar hazel depths and smiled.

"I'm fine, Em, just recalling a time centuries before I was born, when I longed to come to this plane, to be a man." I heard a snort of disbelief from Ken—he still had trouble relating to the fact that I was not only a sorcerer, but also a god.

"Well, you're definitely that, and more," she said, reaching out to cup my cheek gently, and sending me a private mental image of how she would celebrate my manly attributes when we got home. I shivered, my body starting to respond as it always did to her touch.

How did I ever exist without your love? With my mind, I gave her an intimate caress in return that caused her to gasp.

"Okay, you two, cut it out," Derek demanded as he paused briefly at the fee booth, waving to the park employee who motioned us on through. "I know exactly what you're doin' back there. Your daughter can hear you, for God's sake!" He was only partly amused.

Ken murmured, "I may not be telepathic, but I can feel the vibes in here and they're definitely x-rated." He looked over his shoulder at me. "I can't believe I'm about to say this to you, Merlin, but, *get a room!*"

"Alright, we'll tone it down. Sorry to offend your tender sensibilities," I said wryly. I glanced at Em and winked, and she made sure neither man was watching when she pretended to give me a particularly erotic kiss. I laughed out loud and pulled her into an affectionate hug.

Derek and Ken looked at each other and just shook their heads.

We all arrived at Devil's Garden picnic area about thirty minutes later, and found a couple of empty tables sheltered by a massive rock formation at the edge of the picnic area. A Utah juniper and several good-sized boulders gave the spot a semblance of privacy and we were well satisfied with our choice. We began unloading the ice chests and other picnic gear, setting up the grill on one end of the first table and smoothing out the tablecloths on the remaining surfaces. The knights seemed inordinately pleased to have been included in our family gathering and pitched in to get our barbecue started. I couldn't help but remember a time in the distant past when all of Arthur's knights would come together for a celebration in the Great Hall, their exuberance exceeded only by their attentiveness to the king. With the ghostly echoes of good cheer still sounding in my mind, I roused myself and looked for my daughter. I didn't need to look far.

Lumina was so excited by her first excursion into the park that she was running around in circles screaming and laughing, until I finally reached out and swung her into my arms as she ran by. "Alright, sweetheart, please calm down now."

"NO, DADDY, IT'S FUN," she yelled at the top of her lungs and kicked me in the stomach with her little sneakers hard enough to leave a bruise. The couple at the table across from ours looked over and frowned disapprovingly, and my own group watched with amused interest as the drama unfolded.

Lumina, that's enough, I thought sharply, struggling to hold on to her squirming body. And then she became still.

"Put me down, please, Daddy," she said quietly. I set her back on her feet and she looked up at me. I stared back in surprise as her gaze revealed, for the first time, an ancient awareness.

I am merely acting like the child that I am, the presence within her stated calmly.

My eyes widened. Apparently, I was not the only deity in human form standing here today.

CHAPTER 36

March 9

I SUSPECTED THAT THE GODDESS might not know who, or what, she really was. After all, it had taken centuries for me to regain awareness of my true nature, so it was unlikely that she had that awareness this early in Lumina's development.

I directed a focused stream of thought towards her, revealing my own true self and status in that silent communication.

I beg your pardon, my lady. However, in this incarnation you are my daughter, and I will love and guide you as I deem appropriate. Do you understand?

For a moment, her child's face reflected the goddess's sudden realization that she had overstepped her bounds.

As you wish, my lord. She bowed her head briefly, then that ancient being seemed to disappear and my daughter's own personality was once again in place.

We grinned at each other and then I turned to help with the barbecue, while she obediently sat down at the table to look at her picture book.

Derek and Emily, having heard the telepathic exchange between Lumina and me, were staring at the two of us in shock. Ken looked completely confused.

"She's…a goddess?" Em's eyes were wide in her pale face.

"It appears so, but I believe that she doesn't yet remember who she is, or who I am. Although she did seem to recognize my status, so there is some awareness there. This certainly explains how she had the strength to assist you in bringing me back from Hell." I raised my eyes from my self-assigned task of getting the grill ready, and noticed that Ken was gaping at me. Apparently, Derek had not shared that bit of information with his lover. I continued to watch Ken silently, careful not to initiate the Seeing, until he grew uncomfortable and looked away.

The charcoal was perfect, nurtured to its current state of readiness by a simple enchantment created by my son specifically for grilling steaks. Although it was a mundane use for his magical talents, I couldn't dispute its usefulness. The rest of the food was set out on the table, along with the plates and utensils. As it turned out, we had neglected to bring the steak knives, but none of us were too concerned about it except Ken.

"It's no big deal, I'll just enchant the regular knives to cut through steak," Derek said nonchalantly to his lover as he bent to grab a few beers out of the ice chest. He and Ken had just returned from a quick walk around the campground to evaluate the possibilities—they intended to camp out here soon and had decided on a couple of promising sites. Clutching their brews, they wandered off discussing their future camping trip, Ken apparently mollified by Derek's resolution of the knife issue.

I got the steaks out of the cooler and tossed them on the grill, with the resultant scent of cooking meat making my mouth water. I recalled a recent discussion with one of my clients regarding her decision to stop eating meat. I was thankful that I was able to eat anything I desired, and although I could understand the rationale behind being a vegetarian, I was happy that was not one.

"The steaks will be ready in a few minutes, Em, so perhaps you ought to wake Lumina up now." Our little girl had fallen asleep with her head on her book, so we had put her down for a brief nap in the back seat of the Xterra while we relaxed and talked.

"In a minute, magic man, I want to finish my beer first."

"Sure," I said absently, remembering an event that had happened last year when I was still trying to understand my god powers. "Hey, Em, do you remember that time when we ended up in the Crystal Cave and Llyr had to rescue us..." My voice tapered off as I looked up and saw her face, and the love, pride and devotion reflected there literally took my breath away. We gazed raptly into each other's eyes and connected deeply through our bond, our wedding rings warming as they resonated with our love.

Suddenly, I remembered what I was supposed to be doing and grabbed the long-handed cooking fork to turn the steaks. When I looked back at my wife a moment later, she had her eyes closed and a secret smile on her face, and I knew she was remembering the last time we had made love. She opened her eyes with a satisfied sigh, stood up and stretched, and then sauntered over to the vehicle to get Lumina up from her nap. I was breathing hard just watching her. I shook my head to clear it of the distinctly adult thoughts, which were clearly not appropriate for a family outing, and returned to my cooking duties.

"Okay, everything's done. Let's eat!" I announced soon after that and stacked the medium-rare steaks on a platter. Derek and Ken hurried back to the table and each grabbed a plate, Derek muttering a quick spell to serrate the knives. The knights left off the conversation they had been having and came to the table, more than ready to devour their meals.

Sir Percival nodded to me and to Emily, and then grinned companionably at Gawain and Lancelot, obviously pleased to be included in our family event. Quiet prevailed for a time as we all heaped food on our plates and then sat down to enjoy the feast. Lumina was calm and quiet as well, her augmented consciousness evidently trying to process our earlier confrontation.

After we had eaten our fill of the delicious meal and the few leftovers had been cleared away, I retrieved the birthday cake from the back of the SUV. I had ordered the sheet cake from the Town Market bakery, and had asked that it be decorated with a caricature of the traditional sorcerer and a pointy-eared little female Elf beside him who seemed to be admonishing him for his magical activities. I decided to enhance its entertainment value prior to cutting it. As everyone stared at me, wondering what I was planning, I whispered, "Live," and waved my right hand above the surface of the cake. The figures started moving. Delighted, Lumina clapped her hands and giggled, while the adults exclaimed approvingly. We had decided against using candles, so it was only our reluctance to disturb the performing characters that slowed the serving of each individual slice.

Eventually, full of the overly sweet dessert, we disposed of the paper plates and plastic utensils, and I retrieved my son's gift from the SUV. A puzzled frown appeared on Derek's face as he saw the innocuous-looking package I carried. I had contrived to hide its actual shape, size and importance with an enchantment even he couldn't break: It appeared to be a cross between a tennis racket and a shovel, simple and plain. He strove to hide his feelings, though it was clear that he was disappointed. I sat down next to Emily and unobtrusively put the gift under the bench, wanting the wrapped staff to be the last package he opened. I felt my wife's hand grip my thigh as she communicated her excitement.

Ken gave him his present first, and Derek exclaimed in appreciation of his new shockproof and waterproof watch, strapping it on immediately. He was always rough on his timepieces, and due to mistreatment of the most recent watch, he had been in dire need of a new one.

"Thank you," he said warmly, with a meaningful glance at his lover. It was obvious that he wanted to kiss Ken, but felt that it wouldn't be appropriate in front of Lumina, so he reached instead for Ken's hand and gripped it tightly.

Gawain came forward next with a present from all the knights: a gift card for dinner for two at the Hillside Grill at the north end of town. Derek thanked them profusely, and both he and Ken looked extremely pleased, as that particular eating establishment was one of their favorites.

"Happy Birthday, Derek," Emily said as she handed him a small flat box.

He glanced at her affectionately and grinned as he opened the gift. "Thanks, I just happen to need one of these also," he said as he admired a handsome leather wallet with his initials on it. He immediately transferred his driver's license and credit cards from the old, beat-up one, and slid the new wallet into his back pocket.

"Okay, now it's your turn. Happy Birthday, Stepmom." He winked as he handed her a fancy pink envelope, then leaned over to kiss her cheek.

"Whoa, wait a minute, Son, you're not finished." I stood up, reached under the bench and retrieved my gift from its temporary hiding place, then handed him the awkward package with a smile. The knights exchanged glances and hid their grins behind their hands. They were well aware of the nature of my gift, having seen the staff at the shop shortly after I had finished it.

"Uh, thanks, Dad." Derek cleared his throat, ill-at-ease and embarrassed, obviously wondering what monstrosity would be revealed upon opening the package. He should have known me better than that.

He apparently decided to facilitate removing the string wrapped around it and reached for his pocket knife. Since I knew what would happen once the paper fell away, I quickly erected a shield of magical energy around our picnic space to block casual observers from the sights and sounds that would shortly be unleashed. Derek sensed the energy and paused in his efforts to unwrap the package, glancing inquiringly at me as he did so.

"Hurry, Derek!" Lumina bounced on Emily's lap and clapped her little hands together. My wife adjusted her hold on our rambunctious daughter and smoothed the wind-ruffled hair away from her face.

Encouraged to hasten the process, Derek grinned as he ripped off the outer layer of brown wrapping paper. As the last fragment of paper and bit of string fell away, and the object in his hand was revealed, a bright white light shone around us as the sorcerer's staff responded to my son's unique energy signature.

"Oh, my God," he breathed. He couldn't take his eyes from the staff as it pulsed under his hands. Instinctively, he backed away from the picnic table and held it up in the air with both hands. His straight, sandy-brown hair blew back as magic flowed through the wood, and the powerful symbols engraved upon it were activated. His eyes glowed with the distinctive gold color that was his own unique response to magical energy. My own eyes used to turn dark, almost as black as my hair, when I used magic, but recently they merely glowed more intensely green as my god powers manifested prominently in my life. Whether or not that was a permanent change remained to be seen.

I heard Ken gasp and turned to him, wondering if he would be able to deal with Derek's display of power. His face was slack with awe and hero worship, as he beheld his lover glowing like a torch, his body giving off sparks, revealing himself as the demigod that he truly was. I suspected it was the first time that Ken had actually accepted the truth, that his friend was not totally human.

"This is amazin', Merlin, thank you," Derek said, his voice thick with suppressed emotion. He lowered the staff and looked directly into my eyes. *I love you, Dad*, he expressed silently, as he walked over to me and pulled me into a brief hug.

You're welcome, Son, I know that you'll use it well. I love you, too. I returned his embrace enthusiastically. Everything I had been through recently had been worth it to receive this outpouring of my son's love and appreciation.

Finally, Derek sat back down after storing the precious staff in the SUV, and it was Em's turn to be the center of attention. She opened the intriguing pink envelope first, which contained a gift certificate for an hour-long massage and spa treatment, eliciting a squeal of feminine anticipation. The licensed massage therapist, whose services he had chosen, was a particular friend of hers.

"I love it, Derek, thank you," Em said, and leaned over to kiss his cheek.

"I thought you would," he murmured.

Ryan, speaking for all three knights, promised to wash, wax and detail her car at the earliest opportunity.

"What great presents, thank you!" she exclaimed, her face flushed with pleasure as she looked around at all of our smiling faces. As she turned expectantly to me, I handed my wife a small, black jeweler's box, with a narrow silver cord tied around it and a tiny silver bow on top.

"Happy Birthday, my love," I said softly.

She gazed into my eyes excitedly. "What is it?"

"You'll have to open it and find out."

She carefully untied the cord, lifted the lid and gasped. "Oh, it's beautiful," she breathed, as she held up a pentacle of hand-wrought silver with a polished cabochon of red carnelian in the center. "Where in the world did you get this? I've never seen anything like it in town."

"I purchased it from a silversmith in Glastonbury."

Emily looked at me in confusion. "In Glastonbury? England? When did you go there? And why didn't you take me?"

"Do you remember when the caretakers of my property contacted me in early December and I was gone for a couple of days?" She nodded, still looking puzzled. "You were quite pregnant, as I'm sure you remember, so I just teleported to the Crystal Cave for a quick visit. After we took care of our business, I decided to go to Glastonbury. I hadn't been there since 1700, and I wanted to visit the Tor again. I had hoped that I could sense a way through the portal to which I had been denied entrance so many hundreds of years ago. I should have known better; it will never be used again." I determinedly shrugged off the sense of melancholy and guilt that always surfaced when I thought of Arthur; this was neither the time nor the place to indulge in self-recrimination.

"You're right. I was feeling like a cow and looked like a blimp, so it wouldn't have been the best time to go visiting," she admitted. "I remember that I really liked Glastonbury when I was there last year, although the town was pretty touristy, the shops focused primarily on you and Arthur. Weren't you afraid someone would recognize you?"

"Honestly, I didn't even think about it. But now that you mention it, I remember receiving a lot of puzzled glances, as if people thought they ought to know me. Huh. I'm so accustomed to acting like a normal person here in Utah that it didn't even occur to me to change my appearance. After all, how many people would truly expect to find the real Merlin playing tourist in the twenty-first century?" I shrugged and grinned, then reached into my pocket and withdrew a small, tissue-wrapped packet, from which I extracted a delicate silver chain. "Here's the rest of your present, my love. Would you like me to put it on you?"

Em nodded and handed the pentacle to me. First, I threaded the chain through the loop in the top of this powerful symbol of magic. Then, I reached around in front of her so that the silver circle rested just above her breasts, and clasped the necklace at the back of her slender neck. "I love you, wife, and I don't know what I'd do without you," I whispered, kissing the top of her head.

Her eyes filled with tears as she turned around and gave me a lingering kiss full of promise. "Thank you so much, it's a wonderful gift. I love you, too, Merlin, more than I can say, and you will never *have* to do without me!"

When I heard sniffling from the knights, and both Derek and Ken cleared their throats, I remembered that we weren't alone. Lumina sat very still, staring up at us in wonder. Had we gotten out of the habit of being affectionate with each other in front of her? Perhaps so. I vowed to rectify that situation in the near future.

Looking back on that tranquil scene, I would always remember exactly when it happened, when everything went wrong.

Abruptly, our relaxing afternoon was shattered by the sudden appearance of a huge, dark shape materializing directly above us, blocking the sun. Heat and the smell of brimstone surrounded us, burning our nostrils. I was unable to move, frozen in place as I witnessed the horrific scene in slow motion.

I heard Emily and Lumina screaming in terror, and the knights shouting frantically, as the dragon reached down and grabbed both Derek and Ken in its claws, then rose ponderously into the sky before dematerializing. I couldn't move, but my thoughts roiled and fought against the imprisonment, and I knew without a doubt that this unexpected and shocking attack could only have been perpetrated by Beli. Only he could have executed this act of extreme cowardice, using a magical construct to disrupt our family gathering. It was also possible that Adrestia could somehow have escaped her hellish prison and been party to this foul deed.

With a monumental effort, using my god powers as leverage, I was finally able to break free of the force keeping me immobilized. I barked orders for the knights to take my wife and daughter home and I followed the trail of iridescent scales left behind by the beast, my god powers tracking the reek of black magic. I was to deeply regret those moments when I was incapacitated, and I was certain that the elusive scrap of bloody towel was once again instrumental in affecting my behavior.

It turned out that I had not been held back as long as I'd feared, for I flashed onto the scene just seconds after the creature had materialized above Landscape Arch and released the bodies of the two semi-conscious young men into the air. I could sense their terror, and I could hear Derek's screams in my mind. I knew I had to act quickly to prevent an unthinkable tragedy, but before I could do so, the dragon opened its mouth and spewed out a plume of fire that engulfed them both.

I screamed incoherently in horror and instantly surrounded them with healing energy, but I knew that I was too late—they were already dead as they hit the ground. I flashed down and gathered their hideously disfigured bodies into my arms, and then teleported to the apartment above my shop, where I put the remains gently on the bed.

The observer stood on the trail below the arch and watched in disbelief as a creature straight from Hell appeared out of thin air and released the bodies of two people from its claws. At the same time, what appeared to be a man materialized in the air above the dragon, just as it released a blast of flame so intense that he was blinded for a few seconds. With a gut-wrenching scream, the flying form seemed to release a brilliant white light against the flame, to no avail. Afterward, he disappeared, then suddenly reappeared above the charred remains and took them in his arms—and again disappeared. The observer looked around and realized that he had been the sole witness to a supernatural murder. The dragon, or whatever it was, had gone, and he wondered if he had hallucinated the entire event. But no, he had seen it, he thought, and he was certain that he knew the identity of the flying man. He shivered, though it was a warm afternoon, and he knew that his understanding of the nature of the universe had changed. Forever.

As I stood next to the bed, gazing in horrified disbelief at the bodies of my son and his friend, I found myself weeping uncontrollably. I knew that Derek could not truly die; already I could sense his life essence returning and knew that the process of regeneration had begun. But it was every parent's worst nightmare to witness the death of his child. Even though I was a god, I was no different; I was absolutely devastated.

And I dreaded what Derek's reaction would be to the knowledge that his friend and lover was gone forever, his life snuffed out violently. I knew that I had the power to bring Ken back to life, but did I have the right to take it upon myself to alter God's plan? If it was Ken's destiny to die today, would I be causing a major tear in the fabric of reality to change that destiny? It was also problematic for me to exercise that kind of power in this realm. However, after my recent encounter with God and the subtle changes in my being that I experienced afterwards, I thought I could get away with it. But the bottom line at the moment was entirely selfish—I couldn't bear to witness my son's anguish.

Right or wrong, I decided on my course of action, and before Derek had fully healed and regained consciousness, I had touched Ken's hideously burned and disfigured body and released the white light of the gods into him. I stepped back and watched his body regenerate itself, and I felt his spirit return, somewhat reluctantly, as if puzzled at the change of plans. His body healed rapidly and I waited for the final stage of his resurrection to occur.

Ken suddenly took a deep, ragged breath, his eyes flew open, and he sat up abruptly, staring at me in confusion and fear. "What happened?" he whispered hoarsely.

I was reluctant to tell him the truth. "You were abducted and...badly injured. I healed you." I looked deep into his being and confirmed that, at least physically, he was completely healed, and I breathed a quiet sigh of relief.

"Derek, oh, dear God, is he...?" Ken cried, as he noticed the still form on the bed next to him.

"He'll be alright—he's immortal, remember? He's still healing, but he should wake up any second now."

On cue, Derek groaned, eyes still shut, "Oh, crap, what happened, did I die? I've never felt that kind of pain; it really *sucked*! Ken? Oh, fuck, *Ken*!" His eyes flew open as he frantically sought his friend and lover.

"I'm right here, babe," Ken said softly, and reaching out, he pulled Derek into a tight embrace.

Watching their reunion, I experienced rage such as I had never felt before and I swore to avenge this assault. I was done; I'd had enough. I would go to the realm of the gods and destroy Beli. He could not hide from me, for no matter what I had to do, or what the cost to myself, I would confront him and deal with him once and for all.

CHAPTER 37

March 11

SEVERAL DAYS LATER, I had still not finalized my plans for retribution, as it had occurred to me once my ire cooled somewhat that I had Emily and Lumina to consider. I was standing at the counter in my shop gritting my teeth, still furious, my emotions in turmoil, when an elderly customer glanced at me in surprise.

"Are you okay, Mr. Reese?"

I hastily rearranged my features to a more pleasing visage, assured the man that I was quite well, and thanked him for his concern.

He didn't look convinced as I rang up the sale and bagged the tonic that he had purchased. "I can't pretend to know what's got you so upset, and it's none of my business anyhow, but I find that taking a few deep breaths and putting one foot in front of the other helps a person to get past the hard times. That, and having a little faith in the universe to look out for you." On that note, he winked at me, then turned and walked away.

As I watched the old man shuffle out the door, I wondered if this had been a message straight from the gods—or from the one God, himself. I took several deep breaths and centered myself, knowing that I had allowed my base emotions to override my common sense, and knowing also that the rage I had experienced was exactly the reaction that Beli had intended.

I was grateful that my shop was now empty of customers, and I was able to close my eyes for a moment and relive the events of the past weekend. I thought about that evening after my son and his friend had left my apartment, newly healed physically but obviously having difficulty coming to terms with their devastating experience. I had been in contact with Emily throughout that healing process, and she had been a pillar of strength when I had felt I couldn't go on. I remembered, very clearly, what she'd communicated to me telepathically.

Merlin, my love, as you have so often reminded me, there is a place inside of you that will energize and heal your spirit. Go into that Light now and let it heal you. I know that you are a god inside of that human form that I love so much, but your human emotions tend to lead you astray sometimes.

I smiled as I recalled my wife's inner voice and felt her love soothing me, and I resumed the chores I had been neglecting.

Sometime later, around four thirty in the afternoon, I received a call that caused a deep sense of foreboding; Ken asked to see me, alone. I reluctantly agreed, and suggested that he stop by The Moab Herbalist at closing time. I actually knew what was wrong, as Derek had phoned earlier in the day, afraid that Ken was about to have a nervous breakdown.

Punctually at five o'clock, Ken walked in the door and I locked it behind him, turning the sign to "Closed."

"How are you holding up?" I asked, aware that his hideous experience had affected him irreversibly and that I had not done him any favors by bringing him back to life.

He didn't answer right away and didn't seem inclined to look at me. He was distant, his thought processes scattered. He glanced incuriously around the interior of the shop as if collecting his thoughts, trying to find the right words to express himself.

I watched him closely. It had been his destiny to die, and I had altered that destiny. There were always consequences resulting from such a drastic action as I had taken, a price to be paid to bring the universe back into balance, and it appeared that Ken was the one who was paying.

Finally, he seemed about to speak, but he still hesitated to look directly into my eyes; he seemed to know what could happen if he did. I smiled thinly and asked him if he and Derek had Seen each other.

"Yeah, we did. It was the night that I first met you, knowing who you really were, the night that Derek and I, uh, made love for the first time," he admitted, looking intently at the floor, obviously uncomfortable. I should have known that they would See each other, and the information that would have been revealed to him at that time had probably created a chink in his mental armour. And then the past weekend's painful experience had drawn him inexorably closer to the edge of madness.

Derek was right: Ken was on the verge of a complete nervous breakdown. There seemed to be no other choice; I might have to selectively erase most of his recent memories—permanently. Ken's voice brought me back to full awareness.

"I…I've been having nightmares. Horrible dreams about death and graveyards and about being in Hell. Not the Hell you visited, but my own version of it. I was alone inside a giant, multistoried warehouse, running on metal catwalks in the dark, up and down stairs, searching for a way out, but I couldn't find a door, and it was so *cold*…oh, God, it was horrible, Merlin! And then sometimes, I've felt as if I was buried in the ground, suffocating; I was dead, but I wasn't." He was sweating profusely and tears were pouring down his cheeks, which had become gaunt in just a few days, his normally rich brown skin tone dull and gray.

"I can't eat and I haven't gone to work; I feel like I'm going crazy. I…I think I was supposed to *die* the other day," he finally blurted out anxiously.

I sighed with regret that the whole tragic episode had occurred, and decided that I had no choice in the matter; I would have to tell him the truth. It was obvious, however, that I would have to do as I had previously contemplated, and make him forget; clearly he was unstable and a danger to himself, and to us, to our secret. I rubbed my forehead as a tension headache suddenly throbbed. "Gods, Ken, I don't know how to tell you this, but yes, you *did* die, and then I resurrected you. I changed your destiny, and I realize now that I made a terrible mistake. I just couldn't bear for Derek to wake up, healed, and be confronted with your death. It was incredibly selfish of me, and I'm so sorry."

"You called my soul back to my body, when I was really supposed to die? Oh, my God, how could you do that to me? You're a *god*, you're not supposed to be so irresponsible. What you did was black magic; it was like saying you're more powerful than the Creator!" he cried, his eyes red with exhaustion and weeping, and his face twisted in torment. "You should have let me stay dead, because I can't live like this. Please, just *kill me,* I'm begging you!"

My heart twisted in sympathy for this young man whom I had wronged. "I deeply regret what I did, Ken, but now that you're alive again I can't just murder you. However, what I can do is enchant you, alter your memories. Unfortunately, if I do that, you won't remember the truth about Derek, about me and Emily and Lumina, about King Arthur and the knights," I said quietly. "How do you feel about that?"

Ken's eyes widened as he realized the magnitude of this decision. He had been so excited and proud to know who I was, and to be aware of the magic Derek and I possessed. He grimaced sadly and sighed. "I don't have a choice, Merlin. If you don't erase or change my memories, I swear I'll go insane. I can't bear the thought of losing Derek, but I can't go on like this." He paused, closing his eyes for a moment. "I was hoping that I could convince you to kill me, but I'll take the enchantment instead. I wrote this letter for Derek so he'll know how I feel." He handed me a thick envelope.

I nodded, taking it from him. I had considered cloaking my thoughts so that Derek couldn't sense my intent, but I didn't have to deliberate very long—I couldn't deceive my son or I would have even more feelings of guilt to contend with.

I closed my eyes, going deep inside myself to create an elaborate enchantment. I included a compulsion to leave town immediately and seek employment—and a new lover—elsewhere. And then I activated the spell, changing his thoughts and memories to create an entire back-story for him, different from what had actually occurred in the past month. Time stood still for just a moment, then resumed at its normal pace.

Ken blinked in confusion, and then said tentatively, as if he didn't know me well, "I came by to see you, Michael, because I know how close you and Derek are, and I wanted to tell you what I'm planning to do. I'm sure you must be aware how much I care for Derek, but…"

I waited for him to finish, even though I knew exactly what he was going to say, having planted the entire scenario in his mind.

"I'm leaving Moab, tomorrow, in fact. I just can't face Derek again. If he wants any of my stuff, he's welcome to it. Otherwise, my landlord can take everything to the thrift store. Well, not my red down jacket; for some reason I do want to keep that. I can't stay here wondering what's going to happen next. I feel like I've been manipulating Derek, using him, and I just can't do it anymore. I thought I could, that I would do anything to have him in my life. I'm a coward, I know." He looked so depressed that I wanted to tell him that he certainly was not a coward, that he'd been very brave to have embraced even a short-term relationship with a sorcerer. But I couldn't. He needed to believe that he had changed his mind about pursuing an intimate relationship with his friend.

"For what it's worth, I think you're doing the right thing, Ken. Good luck, and take care of yourself." I felt extremely guilty for manipulating this man's life, and the consequences of my actions would surely haunt me for some time to come, but so be it. It was done.

We clasped hands briefly, and Ken turned to walk out the door. And then he paused and looked back at me with just a glance into my eyes then away, embarrassed, and said, "I know it sounds crazy, but I feel like something just happened to me, that you did something; I just can't remember what it was. How could you though, you're not a magician, right? Well, I'd better get going. Maybe we'll see each other again sometime, huh?" He turned and walked out the door, shutting it firmly behind him.

Later that evening, I was standing at the front window looking out—and up—at the Rim, ghostly in the reflected brightness of Moab at night. We had put our daughter to bed less than an hour ago, and I had been standing in the darkened living room ever since, deep in thought. Concerned by my brooding silence, Emily walked up behind me and threaded her arms through mine, hugging me tightly. Despite my distraction, I was acutely aware of her generous breasts crushed against my back and her abdomen cradling my buttocks.

"I shall relive the past few days for a very long time," I admitted, resting my arms on top of hers.

She gave a little squeeze of acknowledgement, and to encourage me to keep talking.

"This afternoon, I enchanted Ken and sent him away."

"I know," she said softly.

"He called me at the shop and wanted to talk to me—alone. He came by around five and confessed that he'd been having nightmares about death; he suspected that he'd died, so I told him the truth about what had been done to him. And about what I had done in response. He was…incensed that I had interfered with his destiny and insisted that I kill him—which I refused to do, of course. So, I altered some of his memories and removed the ones about us. He doesn't remember who we really are, that we all have magic. He's leaving Moab, and Derek, tomorrow.

"I'm going to have to do something extreme to resolve this—'unacceptable' hardly seems like a strong enough word for it—situation with Beli," I said in a strained voice.

"True," she whispered, feeling my heightened emotions through our bond.

"If I don't, Beli will certainly come for you and Lumina next," I rasped, my throat dry as I remembered what the god had done—and in fear of what he might do next.

"Witnessing Derek and his friend die is something that I will never forget, nor will I ever forgive such an atrocity perpetrated by one of my fellow gods. If he took you and Lumina…" My voice broke. "I didn't think Beli could manipulate me from the god realm, but I was wrong. I *am* grateful that God allowed me to resurrect Ken, even though he had been destined to die that day, but I truly regret the necessity for my actions." I could feel my expression harden into a grim mask, and it was apparent that Em felt my resolve.

"Wait, what are you planning, Merlin?" she asked, pulling me around, and then placing her soft hands on each side of my face. She paled as she read the truth in my eyes and in my mind. "You're going to confront Beli in the realm of the gods, aren't you? How the hell are you going to do *that*?" Her voice escalated as her trepidation mounted, and her eyebrows made delicate brown crescents as they arched up under her bangs.

"Keep your voice down! You'll wake the baby—I mean, you're going to wake Lumina!" I admonished, my voice low but intensely angry. Then I sighed. "Em, I'm sorry…for everything…"

She frowned at my unusually short temper—and my apology—until it dawned on her what I was really planning to do. "Oh, my *God*," she hissed, and flounced away from me, running her hands distractedly through her long golden brown waves; she'd apparently picked up my occasional nervous habit sometime during the past year.

"Please don't tell me that you're going to have to leave your body to do this, this, whatever-it-is you're going to do. How are you going to get *back*? You know that doing this will be different than just connecting briefly with the god realm."

Her fear was like a physical assault, and I cringed at the strength of it. All I could think of was the hallucination I'd had, in which I had shuffled off my mortal coil, so to speak, and again abandoned my family, and the effect that abandonment had had on my poor wife.

I stepped towards her and pulled her tightly into my arms, murmuring soothing reassurances. "Let's sit down," I said softly, and led her over to the couch, where we sat close together and I held her hand firmly in mine. How was I going to tell her that I had already changed, irrevocably, during my recent tête-à-tête with God?

I looked into her eyes, wet-lashed and troubled, and paused for a moment more to consider how she might react. She grimaced and said wryly, "You might as well tell me—I know you're keeping something from me, again. You're getting rather good at keeping me out of the loop."

I sighed. "I just wasn't sure how to tell you that my spirit, my body, my god powers—all of what I am—is now a step closer to becoming the fully manifested god of magic, here on Earth." I watched the expression on her face change from one of fear and dread to the more familiar one of awe and loving devotion. As she started to get down on her knees at my feet, I held her still.

"No, not this time, my love. I understand your compulsion to bow to me, but...not this time," I said gently. "Let me explain what happened. The night that I returned from communing with God, I felt different, but I didn't know what the change was until I had fallen asleep. I thought I was dreaming that I was looking down on myself in bed, but I suddenly realized that I was in spirit form, totally outside of my body. And I understood what that meant—that I can leave my body at will now, and return to it at any time. While I am in spirit form, no matter how long I'm away, my body will remain alive without any assistance from Llyr. In fact, when we were driving out to Devil's Garden the other day, I left my body and was hovering above the vehicle."

The look of uncertainty on Emily's face surprised me; normally she trusted me implicitly.

"I intend to confront Beli in the god realm; I don't have a choice in the matter. I believe that I have been given a certain freedom of action by God to deal with him as I see fit, and, of course, Llyr will back me up. The upheaval that Beli has caused in both realms has reached a point that something must be done, as soon as possible, and I have been delegated to resolve the issue." I was convinced that I would be guided to accomplish this important task, even though, at the moment, I had no idea how that guidance would manifest.

"Merlin, you already know how I feel about this—I'm terrified that you won't be able to get back into your body." She held her hand up to forestall my defensive response. "I know you believe that you're now able to control your journey outside your body, but please respect my fear for you. I sincerely wish that someone else could handle it, but I know that you're committed to this action." Emily looked at me imploringly and tears welled in her hazel eyes. "I just want you to come back to me, in one piece if at all possible, please?"

I reached out and stroked her hair, then cradled her face in my hands. "I *will* return to you, my love; how could I not? Our marriage was destined, our lives intertwined for eternity," I whispered, feeling the strength of our bond, and the love and commitment that existed between us. Our wedding rings suddenly glowed as if confirming my statement. We were consumed in each other's gazes, until I saw the inevitable in her eyes and I nodded my assent.

As she slowly sank to the floor at my feet, I finally understood that we were two sides of the same coin: I needed to experience this evidence of her devotion as much as she needed to offer it.

CHAPTER 38

March 11 Late Night — March 12 Early Morning

I DECIDED TO LEAVE my body lying in bed and to journey to the realm of the gods that very night. I regretted that it was necessary to be away from Emily and Lumina at this time, but I knew that waiting any longer was not an option.

Just as an intersection of ley lines on the surface of the planet was a junction of energy, a focal point of powerful magic, the series of events that had occurred this past year, and particularly in the last six weeks, seemed to converge at this time and in this place. The magic went deep into the earth here in red rock country, and the power that I always felt in this place seemed to be waiting for me to connect with it. However, I knew that first I must accomplish this task.

Reluctantly, Emily finally agreed to my plan, but insisted that Derek be present to provide backup in case I was not able to return to my body as readily as I had hoped. I hesitated to bring him in on this scheme while his emotions were in turmoil over losing Ken, but he really was the only sorcerer with the power to help me if I needed it. And my wife and daughter would back *him* up, should there be a problem, since I could call upon Lumina's inner goddess from the god realm, if necessary.

It was around midnight when I summoned my son, and although he seemed tired and distracted, he claimed he hadn't yet been to bed, and assured me that of course he would be available to help if I needed him.

I haven't been very supportive lately, Dad, and I'm really sorry about that. I'll stay in your guest room if you want me to, Derek said silently, the tone of his thoughts sad and resigned.

Yes, come now; I'd to talk to you for a few minutes before I leave.

No more than ten minutes went by until Derek appeared in the kitchen with a toiletry bag in one hand. I reached out to hand him a steaming mug.

"No, thanks, I really don't want any coffee," he said as he set the bag on the counter.

"It's hot chocolate," I said mildly, taking a healthy swallow out of my own mug.

Derek grinned weakly and took the mug I offered, holding it in both hands as if he was afraid he'd drop it.

"Are you ready?"

He nodded solemnly and we headed in the living room.

As soon as we were settled on opposite ends of the couch, I looked in his direction.

"I presume you read Ken's letter." I had left the missive on Derek's kitchen table where he would see it when he got home from work.

He glanced away for a moment and surreptitiously wiped away an errant tear, then cleared his throat. "Yeah, I did. Actually, I knew it as soon as you enchanted him this afternoon; I couldn't feel his love—I mean, I couldn't sense him anymore."

"I want you to know how badly I feel about this. He accused me of using black magic, of abusing my god powers, and he was right. I crossed the line."

He looked at me so seriously that I wondered if he would be able to forgive me. He carefully put the mug down on the end table, and leaned towards me.

"Forgive you? Of course, I forgive you; you did what you did for *me*. You brought him back to life for *me!* Dad, I love you more than I've ever loved anyone, even my adoptive parents, who raised me. I worship the fuckin' ground you walk on—you have to know that! It might take me awhile to get over this thing with Ken, but I *will* get over it. I mean, he was my friend, and my partner at work, too, and now he's gone from my life—just like that!" He snapped his fingers. "But at least he's alive, even if he doesn't appreciate it." He sighed and rubbed his forehead as if to ease a burgeoning headache. "You must've thought it was kinda strange that I had an affair with him. It never felt quite right to me, emotionally. Physically, well, I liked it just fine. But what you said about havin' kids, that made me start questionin' what I really wanted. I think if this whole thing hadn't happened, with us dyin', I would have broken up with him soon anyway."

I finished my chocolate, lukewarm by now, and set the mug down. I knew he wanted me to comment on his relationship with Ken, or on the circumstances of their deaths. But what else could I say, that hadn't already been said? Truth be told, I was a little shaken by the intensity of his emotions. I knew that he loved me, and that he was devoted to my god self, but this outpouring of his feelings for me was like a flood after the dam breaks. He had better shields than I'd realized to have blocked those feelings from me for so long.

"Don't you have anythin' to say?" he asked impatiently.

"Derek, you're my son, my friend and my devotee, and I love you beyond all reason. I have always tried to support you in whatever decisions you've made in your personal life, and I always will. I felt that this relationship was not in your best interest, but it had nothing to do with the gender of your partner. Gender isn't now, nor has it ever been, an issue with me. We're attracted to the physical attributes of a person: to his or her eyes, smile, shape, movements. But the body is just a shell—it is the soul within that we truly love, and the soul has no gender. I know that better than anyone."

I caught his eye as he glanced at me and we smiled at each other, in sync once more. I felt closer to him than I had in months, but I was starting to feel restless now. I knew that we had exhausted this subject and I urgently needed to address my immediate goal.

"Not to make light of your experience, but I think we need to move on now. We need to discuss what I'm planning to do tonight. It's getting late, and I also want to spend some time with Em before I depart."

Derek nodded and leaned forward, alert and ready to help me.

I told him what I planned to do, and he agreed that there didn't seem to be any other choice. Apparently, he had already sensed my ability to leave my body, so that particular bit of information didn't surprise him. However, I think he was reluctant to see me go just as he was hoping to spend more time with me again.

I would not wait any longer to take action against Beli. I wasn't certain how long I would be gone, as time in the realm of the gods flowed differently. I might be gone from this realm for a day, a month, or a year and I wanted Derek to be available in case Emily and Lumina needed him.

"I don't expect you to stay here for more than a few days, but it will ease my mind if you would look out for them until I return."

"You know I will, Dad," he assured me. We stood up and embraced, the love and energy that we shared causing sparks to dance along our skin.

It was almost one o'clock in the morning when we concluded our discussion and Derek had retired to the guest room. I sought out my wife, who was reading in bed, patiently waiting for me. She looked up and smiled as I walked into the room, lines of fatigue and worry evident around her eyes and mouth.

I sat down next to her on the bed and she leaned forward to put her arms around me. The warmth of her soft skin enveloped me and I sighed.

"I wish you didn't have to do this. I'm going to miss you so much, magic man," she whispered and kissed my cheek.

"I know, but I may not be gone that long, and besides, my body will still be here for you to snuggle with at night," I said, suspecting that this would not reassure her in the slightest.

"Okay, that isn't helping, Merlin, because you're just going to lie there, barely breathing. It's going to be very weird. And if you never come back, how the hell am I going to explain it? What do I tell Lumina? Yeah, kid, that's your father—he just *looks* like he's sleeping." She tried to grin, but her face crumpled and she began crying softly.

I stroked her back and assured her that I would indeed be back, that she didn't have to worry about me, and that Lumina would probably be able to contact me in the god realm. We didn't talk long, as we had already discussed the details ad nauseam and I was anxious to make love.

Emily smiled through her tears and got out of bed. She stood before me and removed her nightclothes, revealing her naked form, lush and alluring. I could feel my body tighten and swell as it responded to her, as it always did. She then pulled me to my feet and encouraged me to remove my own clothing, until I was nude as well. She ran her hands down my chest, across my narrow hips and then into the thick dark hair surrounding the evidence of my desire for her. She kept her eyes on mine as she gripped my hardness and cupped my testicles, stroking and kneading until I was half crazed with wanting her. I swung her into my arms and we tumbled onto the bed. The erotic touch of our skin as our bodies slid against each other heightened our sensations. Emily became the dominant one this time and rose above me, slowly lowering herself onto my erection until I was completely sheathed within her. She looked deeply into my eyes as she began to move, and I met her stroke for stroke, thrusting and withdrawing. Finally, my male instincts to dominate made me roll over on top of her and take her with an urgency that left us both breathless. We climaxed simultaneously, almost violently, clinging tightly to each other. We lay together, our bodies still connected, until our breathing returned to normal. I looked down into her eyes and gently kissed her lips, and she grinned, flexing her inner muscles.

I chuckled softly. "I think that's all I've got for now my love, but I shall take you up on your offer when I return." My expression sobered as I realized that I had no idea how long I would be gone. For just a moment, I felt a twinge of doubt about my decision, but I brushed it off, not wanting negativity to in any way affect this mission.

We separated and just held each other close, whispering of our love and mutual devotion until my wife finally surrendered to her exhaustion.

I waited until she was deeply asleep, kissed her gently and got out of bed. I decided to prepare myself as I used to when I planned to sleep for centuries, so I headed into the bathroom, shutting the door quietly behind me. I used the toilet, completely voiding my bladder and bowels, then took a quick shower. I brushed and flossed my teeth and dried my hair, then stood staring at myself in the mirror.

"Merlin, you're procrastinating," I said quietly to myself. I sighed and flipped the bathroom light switch to the off position, and then walked naked and barefoot back into the bedroom.

I conjured a robe similar to my old Camelot attire and put it on, then teleported into Lumina's bedroom. I stood gazing at my precious daughter for a moment, and then leaned down and gently kissed her cheek. I was as ready as I'd ever be.

Back in the master bedroom, I arranged myself comfortably on the bed next to my wife—and left my body.

Emily opened her eyes and realized that she had fallen asleep, and wondered if Merlin had gone. She reached out and touched him, reassured that he was warm and breathing, but when she sought a mental connection, there was nothing but silence.

Tears welled in her eyes, but she vigorously scrubbed her face, forcing herself to contain her emotions.

"I've got to stop this—he *is* coming back!" she told herself fiercely. Knowing that she wouldn't be able to go back to sleep, she got up and put on her robe and slippers, then leaned over and kissed her husband's warm, sensuous mouth. "I love you, god man," she whispered.

She straightened up and sighed, then turned and walked out of the bedroom, intending to fix herself a mug of herb tea. However, she paused at Lumina's bedroom door, listening for any indication that her daughter was awake. She tentatively reached out mentally and sensed the little girl's unconscious mind, innocent and sweet as she dreamed her simple dreams.

Feeling a distinctly maternal urge to check on her anyway, Emily quietly turned the knob and pushed the door open. She walked over to the bed and looked down on the child's small body snuggled up under her favorite blanket—the one that had covered her in her cradle for the first few weeks of her life.

Em briefly caressed the sweet little face, slack with sleep, then turned and left the room, closing the door carefully behind her.

As she sat curled up in the overstuffed chair that she preferred, surrounded by the warm glow of a dozen candles scattered around the living room, she sipped chamomile tea sweetened with just a touch of honey.

Derek, if you're awake, could you please join me for a few minutes?

Hmm, well, I'm awake now, Em. What's wrong? Oh, hell, just let me put somethin' on and I'll be right out.

Thanks, Der.

She took a few more sips of tea and suddenly Derek was standing next to her chair in just sweatpants, his bare chest revealed in all of its muscular glory. For a moment, she stared at him, and then hurriedly reminded herself that this was her old friend—and her stepson—and she had no business admiring his body like that.

Sensing her interest, and her chagrin, he disappeared again, reappearing seconds later with a T-shirt on. "Better?"

"Yes, thanks," she said gratefully.

Then she was weeping uncontrollably and Derek reached out and pulled her into his arms, comforting her.

"He's done it then; he's gone. I thought I felt it when he left his body."

"Yes, and I'm scared to death, Derek," Emily said thickly, pulling a tissue out of her robe pocket and blotting her tears and blowing her nose.

He looked at her dear, familiar face and gently brushed a strand of hair out of her eyes. "Em, you have to trust him. He's the god of magic, not some inexperienced young wizard. I know it must be difficult to live with him as if he was an ordinary man, but he's so much more than that. Even though we have our own magic, and we've spent so much time with him, you and I still can't really comprehend what he is."

Emily was quiet for a moment, and then pulled away from his embrace. Derek dropped into the chair opposite hers and waited.

"I don't think I've ever told you what happens to me when I'm compelled to kiss his feet," she said quietly, her eyes focused inwardly.

"No, but I suspect it's similar to what happens to me," he said wryly.

"Maybe." She glanced at him, then away, knowing better than to stare into his eyes for too long. "All of a sudden, I see a brilliant light around him, like an aura, I suppose, and the truth hits me that his body is a shell containing magic itself, and love overwhelms me, drawing me to his feet. I literally can't stop myself—and don't want to—and then I get giddy and tingly all over."

They were both quiet while they examined their own experiences with the man who was the focus of their lives.

Derek cleared his throat. "Ya know, it took me a long time to acknowledge that part of him, to, uh, worship that part of him. Shit, I even have a hard time sayin' it! But when I shared that hallucination with him, and in it he manifested like Llyr does, huge and powerful, I was overwhelmed with the truth. I've seen him glowin' so brightly that his body can hardly contain it." He looked at Em and grinned. "I guess sometimes he *can't* contain it, and that's when you and I realize that he's really not human at all."

"God, don't tell him that! He's so happy to have a human life." She laughed and finished the last dregs of her tea, now gone cold.

"He'll come back to us," they said simultaneously, then reached out to clasp each other's hands.

I hovered at ceiling level as my wife and son commiserated on my absence and shared their experiences. They were so very young, and I felt such love and tenderness for them. And I was amused at their descriptions of the way they perceived me. Time was an interesting thing when one was incorporeal; it didn't exist. The hour that Emily and Derek had spent together after I had left my body was a microscopic bit of thread in the fabric of the universe.

And then the energy shifted and I was no longer in the human realm.

CHAPTER 39

The god realm

LIGHT. LOVE. HARMONY. I was consciousness, spirit and energy. I was home. I drifted contentedly, for what could have been a moment or a century.

Myrddin Emrys, you have returned. A familiar "voice" greeted me.

Llyr, my friend. I experienced the joy of being reunited with this entity that was so much a part of me.

Why not call me 'Father?'

Here the term is meaningless. And besides, you were my friend long before you became my father.

It was worth a try, bro.

He had always possessed what passed for a sense of humor here in this place that had no corporeal structure. I appreciated his "wit," but I was already tired of our game and wanted to accomplish what I came here for.

Where is Beli? The god of death must be disciplined. His enmity towards me has been increasing for a million years, and now he has gone too far—he murdered my son and his friend in the human realm.

If the term 'father' is meaningless here, than so is 'son.' And did you not kill his 'daughter'?

That was different. It was self-defense.

Hmm. Well, Beli is a troublemaker, I grant you that, my friend. I will accompany you as you seek the counsel of the one God. I believe he has been waiting for you.

Waiting...for me?

Have you forgotten already, Myrddin Emrys? You have only been gone from here for a few centuries.

Sixteen centuries, actually, not counting the short time I was here when my body died, and a few assorted short visits in between. Forgotten...what?

That you have been on a mission for God; that as the eldest spirit you were granted the privilege of being born human so that you could assist in saving humanity.

I haven't forgotten the quest, the mission, but I thought that becoming human was my idea, my request. I had *forgotten that I was the first god to be created. That changes things. Beli must submit to my chastisement whether or not I petition the one God, if I remember the hierarchy of the god realm accurately.*

Well, but you do not want to insult God, now do you? Best to go to him first, to pay your respects.

I shall do so. And you shall come with me, Llyr.

We approached God, humbly requesting an audience.

The Light and Love of the Universe swirled and sang around us as the one God spoke in the "Voice" that had created the stars—and all of the gods.

I have been waiting for you, Myrddin Emrys. I see your fellow god, Llyr, is here with you, which is as it should be, as I created him at the beginning of time itself to serve you. You have both acquitted yourselves well recently and I am proud of you, my children.

Llyr was speechless, having never expected to receive praise from our Creator, and I, in turn, felt driven to admit my failings.

I ask your pardon, Lord, for I have failed you. I have given in to anger, vindictiveness and spite while clothed in my human form, and I have many times forgotten why I was sent to Earth; hardly the responses of an enlightened soul. My energy fluctuated as I realized the possible repercussions of confessing my transgressions.

Are you questioning the role I have assigned to you, Myrddin Emrys? For I have been the one to set the stage for your experiences, so that you may become the god on Earth that I want you to be. I have assured you of my support and love only recently, and it would behoove you to heed my message. Your pain and anguish and trying times in the human plane, the mortal realm, have been a gift to you from which to learn, just as my human children have to learn. I did warn you when you began your journey, that it would not be easy, but you assured me that you could accomplish the tasks I set for you. If you are ready to give up this mission and relinquish your human life, I will not love you less, but the very existence of human beings on the planet may be threatened if you do so, and the soul of the one you call the Once and Future King could be lost for all time.

No, Lord, I could wish for no greater honor than to complete the mission you have set for me, and I will strive to reach that state of realization required for the god of magic and healing to manifest on Earth. However, I am concerned that the god Beli has become a force for evil in the human realm, despite my efforts to keep him here where he belongs. And even in this realm, he has been most disruptive. He and his 'granddaughter' continue to foil my plans and destroy lives, thwarting my efforts to move forward in the quest to resurrect Arthur Pendragon.

Ah, so the game continues. His 'granddaughter' is your 'daughter' is she not? Perhaps you need to control him through her, although it seems she is a bit tied up in the hell she has created for herself. Well, there is no need for you to confront him; I shall reprimand the god of death and direct you to the object he has kept that exerted control over you in your human form. I had hoped that Beli would use some prudence in his actions, but he has not; I must admit that he has never been a favorite of mine, but good must be balanced with evil, and he does make a fine adversary for you, does he not, Myrddin Emrys? And a sound that seemed suspiciously like a laugh resounded through the heavens.

God dismissed us and we left his presence.

Llyr and I drifted for an eternity, and then a spark of thought came to me. The one God had been aware of Beli's actions all along, could even have prompted him to take those actions. As I reviewed the events of the past year through a different perspective, I realized his greater purpose of preparing me for my true role. And if he intended to handle reprimanding Beli, there was no need for me to remain here any longer. I would keep in mind, however, his suggestion that I control Beli through Adrestia, just in case I needed a back-up plan.

Perhaps it is time I returned to my body, old friend.

Can you not stay another century or two, 'Son?'

No, I have been gone long enough, 'Father.'

You are correct, bro, those terms are just so wrong here. But I am eager to resume that role in the human realm. I find that it suits me. Give my regards to my 'grandson' Derek, and to your lovely wife, Emily.

I will do so, Llyr; they are both quite fond of you. And now, I must depart...Hmmm.

Uh, bro...you are still here.

Yes, I am. Bollocks.

Yet another thing that is lacking on this plane. No body, no bollocks.

Really, Llyr? Alright, it is apparent that I must send a message to my children...Ahh... it would seem that my strongest connection is to my daughter's inner goddess, and she will assist me ....Goodbye, my friend...

Until we meet again, Myrddin Emrys.

CHAPTER 40

May 1   Early Morning

I WAS BEING JOSTLED and shaken, but I was not ready to return completely to the physical plane. The bliss and serenity of spirit still held me captive.

"Merlin, wake up. I know you're back; you were talking in your sleep." A familiar female voice, raised slightly in irritation, called to me, forced me to acknowledge that I was back in my body. A part of me protested relinquishing the perfection of my spiritual existence. I whispered to her in Old Welsh to leave me alone, before I fully remembered where and when I was. And to whom I was speaking.

"What language is that? If I had to guess from your tone of voice, you just told me to leave you the hell alone, didn't you?" She sputtered indignantly for a moment, and then laughed briefly.

I lifted one eyelid slowly and peered at her, realizing that I had just spoken to my wife rather rudely in a language I hadn't used since I was fifteen years old. I opened the other eye and blinked a few times, then pushed myself upright. "Emily," I said hoarsely. "How long…?"

Suddenly, my arms were full of warm, fragrant woman, and kisses were being pressed wetly on every inch of my face and neck, the only parts of me not covered by the robe I still wore. And then I wasn't wearing anything as my wife disrobed me, threw off her own night attire and proceeded to ravish me. I rose to the occasion and remembered once again the advantages, and pleasures, of having a male body.

Some time later, Em purred, "Oh, my God, I needed that," as she stretched luxuriously at my side afterwards.

I got up on one elbow and gazed down at her. "Em, you probably could have used my body anytime you liked while my spirit was gone. My physical response to you is pretty automatic—you touch me, kiss me, even just look at me a certain way and I'm ready for you."

"I'm not into necrophilia, thank you very much," she murmured as she reached out and languorously stroked the silky hair around my nipples as if she were petting a cat.

I grabbed her hand and moved it down farther. "My love, I wasn't dead," I said, and then groaned as she applied herself assiduously to massaging my groin area.

She paused in her activities. "You might as well have been. You were cool to the touch, didn't move for seven weeks, and weren't breathing most of the time. I kind of got used to it, but there's no way I could have, you know, had my way with you…" Her voice broke, revealing the emotional roller coaster she had been on while I was gone. As pleasurable as it was, I immediately lost interest in my arousal as I realized the depth of her distress.

"Oh, sweetness, come here, I'm so sorry to have put you through that," I murmured as I pulled her against me and stroked her back reassuringly. "I was gone for seven weeks? It seemed that I was there for only minutes, although my interview with God could have lasted an eternity and I wouldn't have been aware of it."

I felt the awe and devotion build up inside of her and wondered what outward sign of it would manifest this time. She surprised me when she did not attempt to kiss my feet, but instead drew back slightly to gaze adoringly into my eyes. She gently brushed a lock of hair off of my forehead and smiled as she traced my eyebrows. I closed my eyes for a moment as her gentle hand caressed my face.

"Merlin, you are the most amazing, beautiful man I've ever known, and I'm so thankful you're back. I sometimes wish that I could have you all to myself, and never share you with anyone. But there are two others who would love to see you, our daughter and your son, who have missed you as much as I did. Thank God you were able to return to this realm without any problems."

I didn't answer right away, reluctant to tell her that I had almost failed to return.

"Okay, what aren't you telling me, magic man?" she asked impatiently.

"To be honest, I had help, Emily. I tried to come back, and much to my surprise was unable to do so. I was with Llyr, and if he'd been corporeal, I think he would have laughed at my predicament. I had counted on using my connection with Derek, but that was not available either. He's still here, isn't he? I can sense him. I'm pleased that he decided to stay with you and Lumina all those weeks."

"He missed you a great deal; we both did, and we were both lonesome, so we kept each other company. Obviously, he had to go to work, and I had to run the shop—I've got a lot to tell you about *that* later on—but he was usually here for dinner and stayed every night. Anyway, please finish telling me how you finally got back." She watched my face intently as I answered.

"I had to call upon Lumina's inner goddess for assistance—she was able to reach out and connect to me through my god powers, combining her strength with mine to draw me back to my body. If she hadn't been able to help me, I could only have come back here the way Llyr does, by manifesting a body that is a magical construct. It's real enough, but it's not human, and as you know, he can't stay here indefinitely. I wouldn't have been able to either."

She just stared at me, her face suddenly drained of color, and for a moment I thought she was going to faint.

"It's alright, Em, I'm here now," I said gently, reaching out to trace the contours of her cheek.

She closed her eyes and took a deep, cleansing breath, and then she seemed to come to a decision, gazing directly into my eyes. "Yes, you're here now, so that's all that matters. I had planned to work today, but screw it—I'm going to take the day off and spend it with you. Sarah can run the shop; Thursdays aren't that busy anyway."

"I would like that, Em, and…wait a minute, who?"

She just laughed and said, "A lot has happened in the past seven weeks, my love."

"I have a lot to tell you as well, wife."

We decided to wait to tell our stories until we were all up and ready to start the day. She and I had already showered and dressed and brewed our first pot of coffee when Derek appeared in the kitchen in shorts and a T-shirt, which seemed to be this family's summer look. He immediately captured me in a welcoming embrace, sporting a wide grin that revealed his straight white teeth.

"I actually woke up earlier when I sensed you'd returned, but I was gettin' some pretty strong vibes from you two, so I figured I'd better wait awhile to welcome you back," he said with a distinct smirk as we both stepped back from our embrace and went to the counter to pour coffee.

"It's a damned good thing you did, too, *Stepson*," Em said, glaring at him.

"Oh, now, there's no reason to go insultin' me first thang this mornin'," he drawled, then turned to me and winked. "Seriously, Dad, it's great to see you."

I could feel the emotion he was holding back.

"It's great to see you, too, Son," I murmured quietly and took a long, satisfying swallow of hot coffee.

A moment later, my wife gasped and cried out in anguish, "Oh, God, no!" Her coffee mug fell from her grip and shattered as it hit the floor. I sensed the change in my daughter as she entered the room and I turned to face her, already knowing the reason for Emily's distress.

"Daddy? Mommy? I grew some more," Lumina said, a look of bewilderment on her young face.

Derek stood still, his mouth open in shock, as he saw that his sister, who had been born less than four months ago, was now the size of six-year-old. Her baby blanket again wrapped around her torso, she stood in the kitchen doorway, blinking uncertainly at the three of us.

Emily could do nothing but stare helplessly at this older Lumina, so I immediately strode forward and lifted my daughter into my arms, holding her comfortingly against my chest. She whimpered a little as she buried her face in my neck, and the scent of her long dark brown hair was reminiscent of spring flowers.

"Shhh, it's alright, sweetling, Daddy's got you," I murmured, knowing that if these bodily changes were difficult for us to accept, how much harder must it be for her? As I held her, I knew instinctively that it was the magical assistance she had provided to return my spirit to my body that had triggered this additional growth spurt. I wondered if she remembered helping me.

"Come on, honey, let's find you something to wear." Emily finally came out of her trance and reached for Lumina, so I carefully handed her over to her mother. The two headed for the bedroom and I turned to Derek, who had been silent since he had seen the change in her.

As I stared into his questioning eyes, wondering what to tell him, I was suddenly aware of the truth, as if God had touched me with that single bit of knowledge. "It is her destiny, Derek, to change and grow at an accelerated pace as she assists me here in the human realm. She asked the one God for this opportunity, just as I had done so long ago, and that was the cost of his favor. I'm sure her true name will be apparent soon enough."

I paused for a moment and thought about my original plan to discuss what I had learned in the god realm with everyone at once. No, I would inform Derek now, directly. I Looked into his eyes and shared with my son everything I had experienced in the realm of the gods.

Eventually I pulled back, separating myself from the meld of our two beings, and Derek staggered. I reached out to steady him and I heard him whisper, "Oh...*God...*"

Emily brought Lumina back to the kitchen, her little girl decently, if unfashionably, clad in too-large clothing that had been set aside for the thrift store. She noticed that her husband and Derek were seated at the kitchen table, deep in an animated discussion. Her distress about the change in her daughter was temporarily muted as she admired their handsome forms.

She claimed these men—they belonged to her—and she never tired of observing how the two sorcerers interacted with each other. Over time, she had noticed small details of similarity in their appearance and behavior. A stranger might never see that they were closely related, since their coloring and builds were so different, and no one would ever guess that they were actually father and son. But she saw the same little quirks in their facial expressions and the long clean lines of their jaws, and the family resemblance was obvious—to her at least.

Just then, her husband looked up and caught her staring at him, and his thoughts revealed that he had already shared the details of his out-of-body experience with his son. Her heart started pounding as she realized that he intended to do the same with her. Never taking his gaze from hers, he asked Derek to give Lumina her breakfast and walked over to her, taking her hand in his own large elegant one and initiated the Seeing, their souls and minds merging into one.

As they came back to themselves, Emily was shaken and speechless as she tried to absorb the magnitude of Merlin's experiences. He put his arms around her and kissed her cheek, whereupon she finally blinked in awe and whispered, "Holy crap."

He chuckled. "You knew you were married to a god, my love." His slanted eyes were that brilliant green she loved, but there was something else there now, as well.

"You...you really are pure energy, the white Light you always talk about...I can see it in your eyes, and there's a glow on your skin that wasn't as evident before. I mean, you used to glow once in a while, but now it's so much more intense. Are you going to be able to control it out in public?"

He looked at her solemnly. "What if I told you that I wasn't going to? That I had decided to reveal myself?"

Both Derek and Emily were struck dumb, shocked to the core of their beings despite what they had experienced of Merlin's interview with the one God.

He took pity on them and said gently, "I'm not quite ready for that yet, don't worry. But the time is closer than you might think. Now, let's join Lumina for breakfast—a bowl of cold cereal sounds fine this morning. Em, why don't you give me an overview of what has happened at the shop since I've been away?"

She nodded, retrieved several more cereal bowls out of the cupboard, and began to speak.

CHAPTER 41

May 1 Midmorning

AS WE ATE OUR BREAKFASTS, Emily related how she had handled the running of The Moab Herbalist in my absence. She had mastered the potions and enhancement spells some time ago, so she was able to work on those prior to opening every morning and after closing every night, and Derek had come in to stock shelves, and to clean in the evenings and on his days off. The truly difficult part was trying to conduct business while watching Lumina at the same time, and in desperation, she had finally recruited the knights to baby-sit, right there in the shop. At first, she had been concerned that the little girl would take advantage of their obvious lack of magic, but Lumina proved to be extremely well-behaved and respectful of the men whom she loved, and who adored her in return. And the side benefits of having one or more of the knights in the shop became apparent as their presence drew more and more customers in. Whether it was their slightly exotic good looks, their confidence, or perhaps Percival's old world accent, people were drawn to The Moab Herbalist not only to buy, but also to relax and chat with the men in the reading area.

And finally, she had accomplished the one task that I had not: she had hired a full-time employee. The deciding factor turned out to be Derek's temporary assignment to another park for over a month, so that he could no longer assist Emily. He did return late at night to sleep at the house, but working at the shop was no longer an option.

Once she had made up her mind to hire someone, it had happened as if destined by the gods themselves. As she said this, I had to grin, as that is exactly what it was—destiny.

The young woman had come into the shop one day looking for an herbal salve to treat an abrasion on her arm, and one thing had led seamlessly to another, resulting in Em hiring her on the spot.

Sarah Gordon was in her early twenties, and had recently graduated from the University of California, Davis campus, with a degree in Horticulture. She loved plants, and through her studies had developed an intense interest in medicinal herbs. She had traveled to Moab with her foster brother ostensibly to participate in the Moab Half Marathon, which occurred annually in mid-March, and they had both loved the area so much that they had decided to stay.

It was obvious to Emily even after a short time that Sarah was an exemplary employee, working diligently and effectively at her side every day, proving that she was trustworthy and kind. The perfect employee, it seemed. Of course, I would need to meet her to determine if the most important quality was also there—a magical nature—but I suspected that she was the one we had been waiting for, so I wasn't really concerned.

It was apparent that Derek had not yet met her, as he'd had no reaction other than a polite interest as Emily related her experience in hiring Sarah.

Emily's recital of her activities for the past seven weeks finally concluded, and I praised her accomplishments highly. Although I had expected nothing less from her, knowing of her intelligence and her willingness to work hard, not to mention her desire to please me, I was still very proud of her for holding it all together while I was absent.

After she had contacted Sarah and informed her that she would be in charge for the day, Em, Derek, and I spent a great deal of time discussing the ramifications of what I had learned in the god realm. Now, it seemed that we were on some sort of a cosmic deadline not of our own making, that would affect all of us nevertheless if we did not take action, and soon.

"But I still don't understand how God himself could be so cruel as to cause you all that sufferin'," Derek exclaimed indignantly for at least the third time.

Since I understood his point of view, I tried to be patient, and to explain the situation. "The Creator can do anything he feels is necessary to attain a certain outcome, Son, and since he already knows what the future holds, it's a game he plays with us, to help us learn and grow. I can understand that on a spiritual and intellectual level, but the human mind has a hard time comprehending such machinations." Despite my perspective as a god, and having experienced firsthand the intentions of the one God, I could feel my inherent understanding beginning to fade the longer I was back in my body.

"All I am sure of at the moment is that he promised to deal with Beli so that I don't have to worry about it, and he will provide me with a clue as to the whereabouts of the bloody towel fragment." And as I said that, the truth dawned on me—it didn't matter where it was, I could call it to me as I had done with the larger piece of fabric. It had my blood on it, so therefore it was tied to me. I laughed out loud as I realized how much time I had spent wondering and worrying about this small, yet troublesome, bit of cloth. In fact, if the three of us focused our magical energy at the same time, it would take less than a second to retrieve it and give us all a sense of accomplishment, not to mention closure, on the subject.

Emily and Derek both looked at me questioningly until they read my thoughts, and then their faces lit up with smiles, and I felt their relief wash over me.

"Well, let's do it now and get it over with," Emily said, and reached out to us. We gripped each other's hands tightly, and together we focused as I intoned, "*Veniat ad me.*" Instantly, the elusive object lay at our feet, a minute scrap of dark-stained terrycloth that hardly seemed capable of causing so much heartache. We eyed it and each other for a moment then burst out laughing, effectively negating any power that it had ever had over us.

I motioned to Derek to destroy it, just to be sure. "*Ad-olebit*, ya bastard," he said, and it burst into flame, then turned quickly to ash, and it was done. He grabbed the dustpan and a broom and disposed of the tiny pile of ash, then muttered with satisfaction, "Movin' on."

Em and I nodded in agreement.

CHAPTER 42

May 2-May 10

THE DAY AFTER MY RETURN, I met Sarah Gordon for the first time, and I knew that she would be an asset to our business and more, for I confirmed that she had magic and was indeed the one who was destined to become a part of our lives. I had wanted to have someone with magic to work in the shop with us and the gods had known that. It was apparent that she was not aware of her abilities, and therefore I would have to choose a propitious time to inform her of her latent gift.

I had been back in my body for a week and a half when I became acutely aware of my need to move on with my assigned mission—the quest for Arthur Pendragon. God had assured me of his guidance and I had been awaiting a sign as to how to proceed. And I was feeling restless.

The day promised to be both warm and windy, the temperature predicted to reach the high 80s by midafternoon. Emily intended to work later in the day, so I had agreed to open the shop and work with Sarah. I dressed for the warmer weather in my usual T-shirt, cargo shorts and sandals, glad to put away my jeans until fall's cooler temperatures returned. I could adjust my body temperature and wear whatever I wished, but I found it easier to conform to the weather as everyone else did.

The morning was beautiful, so I decided to walk downtown, admiring the puffs of white clouds scudding by overhead as I strode swiftly along the sidewalk. The sandstone cliffs at each side of the valley glowed reddish-orange, which contrasted favorably with the cerulean sky, and I smiled. I loved the high desert environment of this area, in spite of—or perhaps because of—the many differences between it and my native land. I whistled a tune I had recently heard and realized that I was content for the moment to put extraneous thoughts aside in favor of mental quietude. I knew that wouldn't last, however, as my mind churned from one topic to another, especially concerning my recent visit to the realm of the gods. I continued to be surprised at the outcome of that adventure. I had gone there to commit an act of violence. I had planned to destroy Beli and had instead been assured by God that he had everything under control; in fact, that he had orchestrated every one of Beli's actions to further my growth as the god of magic and healing. As Derek would say, I was blown away by that revelation. I also felt a lingering sense of unease about the encounter, but I relegated that feeling to the back of my mind for now.

I had agreed to meet with Sarah this morning, a few minutes before opening time, as our young employee had professed a keen desire to learn more about my potions and herbal remedies. This could be an interesting discussion as I normally enhanced my potions with spells, and she was not yet aware of the power that I possessed. However, perhaps it would be appropriate to reveal not only her magical nature but mine as well. After what I had learned in the god realm, I was no longer concerned about hiding my true identity from the people who needed to know.

As I approached the shop's Main Street entrance, I could see her waiting for me, her gaze never wavering as her eyes sought mine. It was a good thing that I had control of my own gaze, or we would be Seeing each other, and that would not do—not yet anyway.

She was careful to treat me in a reserved yet friendly manner, but there was a certain...awareness on her part that seemed to radiate from her small but well-proportioned five-foot-five figure. I sensed that she was physically attracted to me, and that would be inappropriate in more ways than one. I was happily married, and she was destined for another.

"Good morning," I said cheerfully as I approached her.

"Morning, Michael, how are you?" Sarah responded, still looking intently into my face.

"I'm fine, thank you. Are you ready to learn something new this morning?" I unlocked the door and reached inside to turn the lights on.

"Yes, sir, I am," she replied respectfully as we entered the shop and I locked the door behind us.

"Alright, Sarah, have a seat while I start the coffee, and then we're going to have a little talk first of all, about a topic that you might find...enlightening."

"Okaaay," she said slowly, glancing at me appraisingly, as she sat in one of the comfortable chairs in the reading area.

I grinned to myself as I measured coffee and poured water into the reservoir of the coffee maker. I pushed the button to start the process and thought how rewarding it would be to teach her the spells I used for the potions. I had already decided just to throw caution to the wind and reveal my magic immediately; I had always enjoyed being a bit dramatic. I sat down in the chair next to her to await the finished brew.

She really is quite lovely, I thought to myself, admiring her reddish-blond hair and deep blue eyes. Her face was heart-shaped, her nose was straight and just a little bit too large for her face, and her skin was pink and glowing from being in the wind, which along with her tentative smile created an attractive package indeed. As the minutes passed she became increasingly restless, and I surreptitiously hurried the brewing process along.

"Coffee?" I asked, as the gurgling stopped.

"Yes, please, just black."

"I like it black as well." I got up and poured the hot brew in a couple of mugs, and then nonchalantly levitated them towards the low table between our chairs.

I smiled as I observed her reaction: Her eyes widened and her mouth opened in surprise. She watched the mugs until they landed on the table, then she swiveled her head to look at me in shock.

"How did you do that?" she whispered.

I walked back to my chair, then sat down and picked up my mug, taking a sip of the hot liquid before I answered her. "Magic," I said as glanced at her over the rim of the mug.

She gasped, and I could see the muscles in her throat move as she swallowed convulsively.

"Have some coffee, Sarah, it will warm and relax your vocal cords," I said gently.

Her gaze never leaving mine, she reached for her own mug and took a careful swallow, then cleared her throat. "You're a...a..."

"Sorcerer, yes," I supplied agreeably.

"I don't understand. Why did you show me this and tell me what you are? I would never have known," she said, bewildered.

"Normally, I would not reveal my abilities to a virtual stranger, but I have reasons for doing so. Can you guess what one of those reasons is?"

She slowly shook her head. "I haven't a clue."

"You have magic also. Can you not feel it within you?"

"What?" she gasped. She drew her body up straight and tensed.

I spoke quietly to her. "It is a simple matter for me to look inside you to find out who Sarah Gordon really is, to discover the extent of your abilities, if you will give me permission to do so."

"I...oh, God...I guess...uh...okay." Flustered, she clasped her small hands together convulsively.

I leaned towards her. "Just relax while I help you to See into your own being. No need to be frightened, I won't hurt you. Your magic will be quite apparent, I promise," I said softly, as I triggered the Seeing, so that both of us would experience her inner being. However, I didn't reveal myself to her, not yet.

What a simple, sweet soul she was, pure of heart and having a decent magical potential. She experienced and accepted her true self with an ease that made me proud. And I realized that I had not physically touched her, initiating the experience for both of us with a mere thought.

Sarah wept silently, tears of joy brimming in her eyes, then spilling unheeded down her cheeks. I handed her several tissues and she took them gratefully, mopping her face and blowing her nose, then tucking the used tissues into her pocket.

She cleared her throat then looked at me shyly. "I always thought there was something wrong with me. All my life I've fought to hold back my urges to create…well, magic. I didn't know that's what it was. I'm so relieved." She put out her hand and whispered, "*Lux*." She effortlessly conjured a little yellow orb of light that glowed and pulsed in her hand.

"*Volito*," she said, and it darted up to the ceiling, at first hovering, then flying to and fro above us.

"You know Latin," I said, pleased that she already had a basic command of the language and was adjusting so quickly.

"I learned it in high school, so it's pretty rudimentary," she confessed, concentrating on the orb as it glowed and circled above us.

"That's all you really need for effective spell-casting." I glanced at the clock and stood up. "We can continue lessons later; right now we need to open the shop." I flicked a hand towards the ceiling and her orb disappeared

"Thanks, Michael. I wasn't sure how to get rid of it. I'd better get to work now," she said happily, as she got out of her chair and walked over to the shelves behind the counter. She began to straighten the bottles of potions and reached for a clean rag to dust the shelves, but then paused and turned to me, her face glowing. "I can't thank you enough for showing me who I really am." She grinned widely and returned to her task.

"You are most welcome," I murmured. Then, I glanced out the front window as I heard Derek in my thoughts and knew he was outside, having sensed the magic being worked in the shop and wondering what I was doing. He had finally completed his assignment at Hovenweep National Monument, several hours drive south of Moab, and was now working at Arches National Park again. My son had made strides in getting back to normal after his traumatic experience in March, and I couldn't think of a better way to further that recovery than to introduce him to my new apprentice.

I unlocked the door with my mind and in he walked, so intent upon greeting me that he didn't see Sarah at first, nor did he seem to sense her. She apparently had a natural ability to shield herself from others. We embraced, always pleased to see each other, no matter that we spent time together on a daily basis.

"Hey, Dad, I thought I'd stop by on my way out to the park and say 'hi'...why are you grinnin' like that?" It had finally registered that I was looking over his shoulder, and he realized I was not alone. He spun around and saw Sarah.

She had stopped dusting when she'd seen the tall, handsome man in a National Park Service uniform enter the shop, and she had heard him call me "Dad." However puzzled she was by his greeting, I could see that she was intensely attracted to him, if the look of admiration and sexual awareness in her eyes was any indication. I knew that she had heard Emily talk about him, but she had not yet seen him.

"Hi, I'm Derek Colburn," he said with an interested smile, and reached out to her politely.

"I'm Sarah Gordon. It's really nice to finally meet you," she said breathlessly, offering her own hand. I smiled as I heard her thoughts: she had recognized Derek as her future mate.

And I could feel the jolt of pure magical energy race through them as they touched. Stunned, they stood staring at each other, hands clasped tightly.

"You have magic!" Derek blurted out, as he reclaimed his hand and looked in awe at his still-tingling palm.

"I…yes, I guess I do." Sarah turned to me self-consciously and smiled.

"You already showed her?" Derek asked me, surprised. *Does she know who you really are?*

Yes, I showed her, and no, I haven't told her yet. Would you care to do the honors?

Sarah looked back and forth between us as if she sensed we were communicating telepathically but could not decipher our exact words.

Sure, I'd love to. He glowed with pride as he began to speak. "Sarah, my dad has asked me to officially introduce him to you. You know him as Michael Reese, but his name is actually Merlin Ambrosius."

"At your service, my lady," I murmured, ducking my head in a slight bow.

Stunned, sensing the truth of his statement, Sarah walked over and stared up into my face, then said incredulously, "*Merlin*? *The* Merlin? *King Arthur's* Merlin?"

"Yes." I braced myself for the usual reactions: adulation, disbelief, denial or fear.

"Cool," she said with a wide grin.

I couldn't help but grin back, her reaction was so refreshing.

Derek smiled as well, and then glanced at his watch. "Look, I hate to interrupt your mutual admiration session, but I gotta take off; I'm supposed to report in at Arches any minute. See ya later, Dad; I'll stop by sometime after five. It was *great* to meet you, Sarah." He stood for another moment gazing longingly at the lovely young woman, then turned and walked out the door, closing it gently behind him.

"God, he is just gorgeous," she exclaimed. "But I don't understand why he calls you 'Dad.' He can't possibly be your son, can he?"

I gave her a wry look. "How old do you think I am?"

"Well, you look about thirty, maybe thirty-two at the most, but I guess you would have to be, uh…" her eyes widened and she sucked in a breath as she did the math, "over a thousand years old."

"I was born in AD 420, my dear, so 1,600 years old is closer to the truth," I said gently to my future daughter-in-law. "And, yes, Derek truly is my son. It's a long story that we'd best leave for another time, though, as I believe we have customers about to open the door."

The look of utter astonishment on her face was replaced a few seconds later by a welcoming smile as several clients entered together, chatting about the herbal remedies they were planning to try this day.

CHAPTER 43

May 10

SARAH FELT AS IF she was suddenly in the middle of an incredible dream. She had arrived at work that morning anticipating a simple lesson in herbal remedies from a master herbalist, and had had her entire world shift on its axis.

Her employer, Michael Reese, had turned out to be the legendary sorcerer, Merlin Ambrosius, and she had been shown that *she* also had magic. In a sense, she had gone from frog to fairy princess in the blink of an eye. *Well, not exactly 'fairy princess,'* she thought, but she had certainly not expected to be shown the magical being within her that Merlin had revealed.

When she thought about the young-looking, handsome sorcerer who was her employer, she suspected that he couldn't possibly be human, and then decided she didn't care what he was. She closed her eyes for a moment, and feeling a rush of gratitude and excitement, she knew her life had changed forever.

The two of them had been busy all morning, from the time Derek left until just before noon, when Emily and Lumina arrived. She loved Emily, and was entranced by her sweet, precocious little girl.

After a brief lunch break, in which she had run errands and then grabbed a sandwich from a nearby Internet café, they had finally been able to start on the herbal remedies. Sarah could hardly believe it. Merlin was alive and well, and standing right next to her—warm, breathing and spectacularly *real,* despite his age. He looked no older than his early thirties, and yet he exuded a sense of ancient wisdom that nearly overwhelmed her. They stood together at the workbench in the back room, with the bags and jars of bulk herbs and the empty bottles, measuring scoops and scales at hand, and Merlin cleared his throat.

"What I hadn't told you before, for obvious reasons, is that my potions are not merely herbal mixtures; they are finished with magical spells that enhance their effectiveness." He glanced at her with his remarkable slanted green cat's eyes and smiled.

Sarah returned the smile, pleased that she shared a secret with him that only a select few were aware of: The Sorcerer of Camelot resided in Moab, Utah, in the twenty-first century, masquerading as the neighborhood herbalist.

"Do Emily and Lumina have magic, too?"

"Yes, they do. My wife's magic is a little different, as it originates from her Elven heritage on her mother's side, and our daughter has inherited her magic from both of us, which has become increasingly apparent since her birth."

Sarah wasn't sure, but Lumina seemed to be about six years old, although Merlin and Emily treated her as if she was considerably younger. And she was puzzled by the fact that the couple acted as if they hadn't been together long enough to have a child that age. She shook herself free of those ruminations as Merlin addressed her once more.

"Alright, here are the herbal remedies I would like you to prepare and bottle," he said as he handed her the Old English Herbarium, conveniently bookmarked on several pages. "Make sure to read the instructions thoroughly, as each one has requirements for preparation which may include the addition of certain liquids or other ingredients. After you have finished at least six bottles of the first remedy, I'll teach you the spell for activation and enhancement, and then we'll proceed to the next one."

Sarah nodded, delighted by the old-fashioned wording contained in the small book. As she glanced through the pages of ancient recipes, or receipts, as they would undoubtedly have been called in the past, she gradually realized that the original author of this intriguing old volume was standing by her side, looking at her in amusement.

"My God, you wrote this, didn't you?"

"Well, not that particular volume, which is a reprint, but yes; I started compiling the information after I moved into the Crystal Cave, several years following Arthur's death in the fifth century." Merlin hesitated for a moment, as if expecting to feel a particularly painful jolt when he mentioned the king's name. Then he smiled, as if remembering something pleasant instead.

"I'll get started right away," she assured him, and he nodded and stepped back, apparently intending to observe as she worked.

Although it made her a little nervous to have him looking over her shoulder, her natural ability to adapt to different situations stood her in good stead, and she accomplished her assigned task quickly and accurately. Occasionally, he was called away to ring up a sale or to assist someone in choosing the correct herbal remedy, but she felt that he was aware of every move she made, even so.

The afternoon raced by in a flurry of herbal scents and learning, and by four o'clock, when she took a much deserved break in the little alcove set aside for that purpose, Sarah felt a bit overwhelmed—in a pleasant way, but still needing to rest her mind. As she settled back in the comfortable chair and closed her eyes, an intriguing image arose, of a devastatingly handsome man in a neatly-pressed uniform. She contemplated her earlier revelation that she had finally met the man she would marry, and that he was a sorcerer. Derek, Merlin's son (and wasn't it weird that they looked almost the same age?), was the most perfect specimen of manhood that she had ever seen. The instant spark of magic she felt as they shook hands had surprised the hell out of her. And it was patently obvious that Derek had felt it as well. She hoped that he would stop by the shop after work, because she was anxious to see him again. She had felt an attraction to Merlin when they first met, but now she realized that it must have been related to the magical energy that he exuded.

Her mind returned again and again to Derek, but Sarah didn't find it odd that she wanted to pursue a relationship with a man she had just met. Her intuition always proved to be accurate, and now she knew how she happened to have that particular gift—it was obviously part of her magical nature. With a start, she remembered what she had heard when Merlin and Derek had seemed to be communicating silently. The sounds that she had perceived in her mind hadn't made sense at the time, but she now realized that the two men had been speaking telepathically, and she must have at least a basic form of telepathy herself.

And she was shocked to think that Merlin could have been reading her mind all along.

"Sarah, I would never invade your privacy by entering your mind without your consent." His rich, lightly-accented voice came from the corner where he was cleaning up the remnants of the earlier potion-making session.

Startled, she opened her eyes and turned to stare at him. "But you just did!"

"No, you were broadcasting that thought so loudly that even Emily heard you." He sounded amused as he reached for a container of chamomile on a shelf above his head.

"Sorry, Sarah, but he's right," Em said from the front of the store. "Your volume was pretty high."

Fortunately, there were no clients present at the moment to hear this extraordinary conversation.

"Oh, no," she breathed, mortified. "You heard what I was thinking about Derek?"

"You were thinking about Derek? Well, no, we only heard the part about Merlin reading your mind," Em said as she walked into the back room with several empty boxes in her hands. She had been stocking the book shelves with the new arrivals.

"God, I'm so embarrassed," Sarah moaned, pressing her palms to her flaming cheeks.

"Don't be. When you're part of a family of magic-wielding telepaths, there's not much privacy." Em's voice was gentle and understanding and she grinned at Sarah as she began breaking the boxes down.

Merlin chuckled, and a pleasant sensation of warmth spread through her as she felt the truth of it. She was already a part of this unique family because of the magic they all possessed. She blinked as tears of happiness welled in her blue eyes. Even if a love relationship never developed between them, she would still be connected to Derek and these two special people for the rest of her life. That meant a great deal to her, having been orphaned at an early age and thus having been shuttled from one foster home to another.

"I don't know what to say, except, thank you, so much," she whispered.

"You're welcome, Sarah," the ancient sorcerer said.

At five o'clock we locked the doors and accomplished the closing procedures—clean-up, counting the money and preparing the deposit, and last minute paperwork and stocking—with the ease of long practice.

I could see that Sarah was anxiously waiting for Derek to come by, and I smiled to myself. Emily and I loved her already, and I knew that my son was totally smitten. Just then, he appeared in front of us, having teleported from home. It was apparent that he had just showered as he brought the masculine fragrance of his body wash with him. He looked robust and healthy, but leaner than he had been in the past year when we'd first met, and his muscular chest, arms and thighs filled out his T-shirt and jeans in a way that would certainly appeal to my young apprentice.

The look of surprise on her face was priceless, and I knew that there would be many more shocks for her in the near future, as she became a permanent addition to our family.

Em and I glanced at each other and grinned knowingly, and we left through the back door, our daughter skipping exuberantly ahead of us.

CHAPTER 44

May 10   Around 6:00 PM

SHE STOOD GAPING at him, her lovely blue eyes widened in shock, and he realized that he had surprised Sarah by suddenly appearing out of thin air.

"Hi. Sorry, I didn't mean to scare you; I forgot that you didn't know yet about the teleportin' thing." *Way to go, Colburn*, he said to himself.

"It's okay. I've had a lot of surprises today, so what's one more, right?" She was trying to take it in stride, but he could tell that she was a bit shaken.

"Uh, I realize that we really don't know each other, but I was wonderin' if you'd have dinner with me. I'm a passable cook, and I have some lasagna bakin' in the oven right now." He hoped he didn't sound too desperate, but he wanted to be near her so badly he could hardly stand it. He was careful, though, not to broadcast his thoughts or emotions, since he was pretty sure she would pick up on them, and he wasn't quite ready to share all the details of his life with her.

Her face lit up as if she had just been invited to dine at the most expensive restaurant in town. "I'd love to, Derek! Give me a few minutes to go home and change, and to tell my friend Morry that I won't be home for dinner. Where do you live?"

As he gave her his address, he wondered who the hell Morry was, and felt a sharp stab of jealousy. He quickly tamped that feeling down—he had no right to be jealous, as they hardly knew each other.

"See you in about thirty minutes, okay?" she said softly, and slipped out the front door.

Derek stood in the empty shop, thoughts and feelings running unchecked through his mind and heart. Finally, he turned off the lights and made sure the door was locked, then teleported home.

He had just finished making the salad and had taken the lasagna out of the oven when there was a tentative knock at his front door.

He wiped his hands on a kitchen towel and went to let his future wife in. *Whoa, where did that come from*, he wondered. *Kinda jumpin' the gun, aren't ya*? But all he could think of was that jolt of pure, unadulterated magical energy they had both experienced, and, if he was honest with himself, a great deal of sexual attraction, as well. He knew that she had felt both the magic and the attraction; the sensations had been intense.

Derek opened the door and stared at the woman standing on his doorstep. Sarah had taken the time to shower and change, her shoulder length hair still a little damp and curling in reddish-blonde tendrils around her beautiful face. A touch of mascara made her eyes huge, and he knew he could become lost in those azure depths. The jeans fit her like a glove, hugging her trim body, and the stretchy white top just served to accentuate her perfect breasts. She was wearing heeled sandals that added a few inches, but she was still five inches short of his height of six feet.

She gazed back at him expectantly, and he suddenly realized he was acting like an unsophisticated oaf. He cleared his throat and finally said, "Hi, Sarah, come on in, I…"

Without a word, she walked in the door, and straight into his arms. He groaned as her soft, slender, feminine body pressed against his, their magic tingling everywhere they touched. They held each other close for a few moments longer and then stepped back, grinning hugely as they acknowledged the connection between them. Despite the fact that they had just met earlier in the day, they felt that they had known each other for years. Derek wondered if this is what Merlin and Em had experienced when they met. It felt so right, so perfect; she was definitely the one.

"I've been waiting for you," they said simultaneously, and then laughed.

As his warm brown eyes gazed into her deep blue ones, Derek gently framed her heart-shaped face with his large hands and leaned down to kiss her carefully, almost chastely. She sighed and returned it the same way. They tasted each other, then opened their mouths and allowed their tongues to meet, to dance, to explore, until their kisses became fierce and demanding. As his need mounted, he yearned to gaze meaningfully into her eyes, but realized just in time that he was about to trigger the deeper connection of the Seeing and looked away.

"God, you taste so good," he moaned, his body quivering with need. He gripped her ass and drew her tightly against his body, wanting her to know what she did to him. He hadn't intended for this to happen so soon, but he couldn't seem to help himself. He was totally enthralled by her.

Sarah was overwhelmed with desire for this man, who seemed to have stepped right out of her dreams. With his chiseled features, his deep voice with its slight Southern accent, and his oh-my-God sexy body, she wanted him to make love to her. His kisses were intoxicating, and the magical energy that arced between them accelerated her arousal. It was obvious that he was trying to hold himself back, to be a gentleman, but his body had other ideas—ideas that she wholeheartedly agreed with. She wanted him inside her as soon as possible, so she boldly maneuvered him until he fell backwards onto the couch, where she threw herself down on top of him, stroking the hard bulge in his pants, fitting herself to it, riding it. She couldn't believe she was being so aggressive, but she'd never wanted anyone so badly in her life.

Derek groaned with the intensity of his arousal. "Sarah, I have to touch you." He rolled over with her until he was able to unzip her jeans. As he thrust his hand under the elastic of her lacy panties, she sucked her stomach in to give him more room, and he cupped her intimately, sinking one finger into her slick wetness.

Sarah gasped and tightened around him as she felt him caress her. She wanted to reciprocate, so she reached out and gripped his hardness through the rough denim fabric, causing him to inhale sharply and hold her close as he thrust his pelvis against her.

"We need to get naked," he breathed and she nodded her head in mute agreement. They sat up to kick off their footwear, and then stood to remove their pants. She heard Derek mumble something in Latin, and suddenly the rest of their clothing was gone and they stood before each other, resplendent in their nakedness.

"Did you just…?" Sarah asked, impressed.

Derek grinned, and acknowledged his maneuver with a shrug of his muscular shoulders.

They stood for a moment longer, enjoying the first sight of each other's bodies.

Sarah's breasts were round and high and firm, the nipples peaked, and her narrow waist transitioned to gently flaring hips. The little triangle of curls between her legs proved that her hair color truly was a natural reddish-blonde. Her face was flushed with excitement and her lips were red and slightly swollen from their passionate kisses. As she noticed Derek's appreciation of her body, Sarah was glad that she exercised diligently so that her muscles were toned and her abdomen taut.

She, in turn, admired Derek's physique. He had well-defined muscles and lean hips, evidence of long hours spent working out in the gym. His skin was a light golden brown color, and with his sun-streaked hair worn a little long, Sarah thought he looked too good to be real. His brown eyes were slightly slanted, and his nose was an aristocratic aquiline. She was glad he was clean-shaven as she didn't care for beards or moustaches. And as she looked lower, it was quite evident how much he desired her.

They came together slowly and deliberately, feeling warm skin beneath their hands as they stroked and kissed one another. Sarah fell back onto the couch, drawing him down on top of her. She sighed as his weight pushed her into the soft cushions, and his hard, hot flesh pressed against her. The feel of his body completely covering her own was so erotic that her breath came faster and her body ached with desire. Frantically, she pressed her pelvis even harder against him, encouraging him wordlessly to take her. With a groan, he drew back slightly, then thrust into her body with one long stroke until he was completely sheathed.

She inhaled sharply at the feeling of penetration, of pressure and fullness, and as he began to move inside her, her body gradually adjusted to his, and she responded by meeting him stroke for stroke.

Derek was the perfect lover, doing everything she'd ever dreamed of to satisfy her completely. She sensed that he fought to control the primitive male within him, whose only goal was to possess her, to mark her as his own. She let him know by her touch and her movements that she welcomed his possession, and intended to claim him as well.

Time seemed to slow as they gazed into each other's eyes, their bodies responding intuitively to each other, moving sinuously together, a light sheen of perspiration causing their skin to glow. When Derek finally closed his eyes she was glad of it, as the intensity of his gaze had started to feel as if he had claimed her soul as well as her body.

As they moved, breath coming faster, reaching for fulfillment, they quickly approached orgasm, instinctively drawing upon their magic, and then lifted off, soaring into their mutual climax as if each had been born to bring pleasure to the other.

Afterward, they clung to each other, murmuring of their happiness and satisfaction.

Sarah gradually became aware that something wasn't right; he felt *too* good inside of her. And then she realized what it was. "Oh, *no*," she cried out in dismay.

Alarmed, Derek responded, "What's wrong?" But as he withdrew from her, he realized just as she had, that in their undeniable haste to come together they hadn't used protection. Neither of them had thought of using a condom, and it was possible that he could have just gotten her pregnant.

After the initial shock, he realized that he wouldn't mind if he had—he knew she was already his. "Don't worry, it's up to the gods whether you're pregnant or not. And besides, we're gonna get married anyway," Derek said, secure in the knowledge that destiny had brought them together.

"What?" Surprise and confusion appeared in quick succession on her lovely face. "How could you possibly know that? And don't I have a say in the matter?"

"Merlin has known for several months that someone would come at this time to be with me. That's you, Sarah. Of course you can say no, but I don't think you will," he said with a confident grin that gradually faltered as she just stared at him reproachfully.

Disconcerted, he carefully reached out to her mind, and realized that she felt manipulated, appalled by his arrogance. But, as he began to pull back, thinking that perhaps he had made a terrible mistake, her being was suddenly flooded with the awareness that he was her destiny, and she recognized the undeniable bond between them. He let out the breath that he'd been holding and sighed in relief. The gods were with them after all.

He got up off the couch and smiled at her. "Come on, let's go." She responded with an infectious grin and surrendered her hand to him, following him down a short hallway to a large, untidy bedroom. Derek experienced a slight twinge of embarrassment at the sight of his unmade bed and dirty clothes strewn around the room, but it was obvious she didn't notice—she had eyes only for him. They threw themselves down on the mattress and made love again, slowly this time, savoring the intense attraction that existed between them, acknowledging the sexual hunger that drove them to new heights of bliss.

Several hours later, Derek's and Sarah's stomachs growled simultaneously, and they laughed, admitting that they were starved—for food this time. They cleaned up and dressed, a little shyly, and then ate the dinner that had been sitting on the counter waiting for them: the lasagna now cold and the salad a little too warm, lettuce leaves not as crisp as they had been. But the meal tasted delicious anyway.

"How were you able to get dinner done so fast, if you had to work today?" She was obviously impressed by his culinary skills; he knew that most single men his age just went out to eat after work.

"Oh, I'd fixed the lasagna weeks ago and froze it—I generally don't cook every night," he confessed rather sheepishly.

"Well, I'm still impressed. And I'll keep that in mind for when we get married," she said, teasing him.

They grinned at each other and then continued to eat in a silence.

Derek watched as she swallowed a final bite of cheese and finished her beer, and he noticed the look of uncertainty on her lovely face. "Is somethin' botherin' you, sweetheart?" He reached out and gently brushed an errant curl back from her face and then covered her delicate hand with his larger one.

"I hope you don't take this the wrong way, Derek, but I'm confused…I don't understand why Merlin, your dad, looks so young. I mean, all the legends portray him as a very old man. Is he human? Are you?" Sarah blurted out. "I mean, you make love like a human, but…"

Derek wasn't sure if he should laugh or feel insulted, but he realized that she was just trying to make sense of something that seemed impossible. He wondered whether it wouldn't be easier to just See each other.

"And how many *non*-humans have you made love with?" he asked lightly, teasing her. But seeing her anxious face, he relented and continued in a more serious tone.

"Well, Merlin was born in 420, so yeah, he's incredibly old. His mother was human, the daughter of a Welsh princess and a Roman centurion, but his father was—is—a god. His father's name is Llyr, and he's the Welsh god of the sea. In fact, Merlin himself is the god of magic and healin', and he's immortal, so that's why his body hasn't aged since he turned thirty-two." Derek figured that his father wouldn't object to him revealing this information, but he prayed that she wouldn't be scared off by it.

"Oh…God." She swallowed and looked shell-shocked for a moment. "And what about *you*?"

He scrubbed his face with his hands and sighed. Well, if she was truly meant to be his mate then she would accept him. If she didn't, it wasn't meant to be.

He took a deep breath. "Okay, here goes. I was born in the fifth century also, in 442, in Camelot. My biological mother, Cara, was human; she was King Arthur's half-sister, and she died in a fire when I was only a few months old. My grandfather Llyr brought me to California in the year 1985 and I was adopted by the Colburns, who raised me. And my dad, as I mentioned, is a god in human form. We were destined to meet again when I was an adult—last summer, as a matter of fact.

"So, I'm half human, but I'm actually a demigod and immortal also," he admitted, once again wondering how it could possibly be true. He hoped to God that she would accept his outrageous tale that sounded like it was part of a fantasy novel.

Sarah's eyes widened and she blinked. "Holy fucking shit." She just stared back at him as if trying to fit his reality into hers.

"You can say that again," he said with a grin. "But Sarah, whatever else I am, I'm your man now, and you can count on me to always be there for you."

"Somehow, I do know that, Derek. And since I've had very little in my life that I could depend on, I'm really happy to hear it. I do feel a deep connection with you in my heart, but part of me wonders how any of this can be real. I mean, seriously, how many people can say they work for the Sorcerer of Camelot, and have a lover who is not only the son of Merlin, but also the nephew of King Arthur?"

"How the hell do you think I feel *bein'* those things? A year ago, I was just some guy workin' for the National Park Service and playin' at swords and sorcery," Derek laughed ruefully. "Then my whole world changed. Do you know how weird it was findin' out that my best friend Michael was a sorcerer? That he was actually *Merlin*? And later, after he and Emily got married, Llyr finally revealed that I was actually Merlin's son. I'm still so overwhelmed by all of it—I mean, I'm immortal, for God's sake!"

"You're not complaining about it, are you?"

"Of course not," he hurried to reassure her. "It's just that I still have a difficult time believin' it." He seemed to be worried that she wouldn't believe it either.

With a sympathetic look, Sarah got up and walked behind his chair, putting her arms around his neck and leaning over to press her cheek against his hair.

"It's alright Derek, I do believe you. And I'm amazed that I'm saying this already, but…I love you," she murmured.

Derek twisted around in his chair to look into her smiling face and motioned to her to sit on his lap, where he held her against him and guided her sweet lips to his. "I love you, too," he whispered, having a flashback to a similar admission by Ken not so long ago, and wondering if he should tell her about his previous lover. He shied away from telling her about his death, which was just too gruesome a story to interject into this extraordinary evening. And maybe that was why he hesitated to have her See into his being. But then his mind jumped to the one thing that had really been gnawing at him: Why would Sarah have to report her plans to this guy, Morry? What was he to her?

He cleared his throat and decided to tell her about Ken and get it over with; she'd find out at some point anyway. Then, maybe he could bring up the topic of Morry.

"Um, I have to tell you somethin', and I hope it won't be a problem for you. A few months ago, I had a pretty intense affair with my partner from work. Our relationship seemed so perfect at the time, but now I realize that it was just because I was so lonely. It's over now, but you need to know that, uh, well…"

Sarah leaned away from him a little so that she could look into his eyes. "So what's the problem?"

"My partner was a man," he blurted out, wondering if he should just have kept his mouth shut. "I never realized that I was bisexual, and Ken…well, he showed me."

"And I had sex with my college roommate, Trish, once, so what? Oh, Derek, I don't care! It was in the past, and now there's us, right?"

"Right," he breathed, finally relaxing, not realizing until now how much that situation had confused him. Now, maybe he could mention the other thing that was bothering him.

"By the way, who's Morry? And what kind of a name is that, anyway?" He hoped he didn't sound as jealous and petty as he felt.

She seemed to read his mind, or it might be that it showed on his face. "Are you jealous, Derek? Don't be. He's my foster brother and has been my best friend for years. There's nothing else going on between us; he doesn't feel that way—"

He interrupted. “Are you sure? ‘Cause if it was me, I’d be crazy jealous.”

She continued as if she hadn’t heard him. “—about me. Oh, and his full name is kind of strange and old-fashioned—it’s Mordred. Hey, wasn’t that supposed to be the name of King Arthur’s son by his half-sister Morgana, or Morgause? I can’t remember now which one. Derek? What’s the matter?”

He couldn’t answer. He was suddenly as cold as ice, and he knew that the look on his face reflected the absolute horror he was feeling. He automatically reached out telepathically to his father. *Dad, oh God, I think we have a problem...*

CHAPTER 45

May 10   10:00 PM

EMILY HAD PUT Lumina to bed some time ago and the two of us were finishing the kitchen cleanup, when Sarah and Derek appeared at our front door. It was apparent to me that the two had already bonded, and I knew that it was only a matter of time until they made their joining official. But that was not the reason for their impromptu visit this night. Derek was concerned about the revelation, or vision, he had just experienced regarding Sarah's friend Morry—that he was his son, the child of the brief, unknowingly incestuous liaison that he'd had with his half-sister, Adrestia, while we were in Camelot. I had occasionally had a vision of an unknown child over the last few months, but I had never felt a personal connection to the child, and still wasn't convinced that it was Derek's son I was sensing. However, Derek had some talents that had been surfacing in the past few months, and it was quite possible that this vision was the result of some sort of emerging precognitive ability.

"Okay, let me get this straight," Sarah said, her forehead creased in a frown. "A few months ago, you and Merlin were transported back through time to Camelot, and not only did you meet your uncle, King Arthur, but you also had sex with your *sister*? And you think Morry is your son? Here in twenty-first-century Moab? That's not possible, that's just crazy…isn't it?" She stared at Derek in disbelief.

"That's what I thought last year when Merlin told me I was part Elf and that Derek was his descendant. And then it turned out that he was actually his son. So, I've gotten used to the impossible being real, and you will too…eventually." Emily met Sarah's gaze in complete understanding.

Sarah opened her mouth as if she were about to speak, but then just shook her head.

I turned to my son, who was sitting next to his new love on the couch, radiating fear and misery. "Derek, you can't base this theory on the man's name alone. It's true that there was a young man named Mordred in Camelot, but he was Morgana's son, Arthur's nephew, and thus your cousin. I happen to know that, contrary to some of the tales that have been written over the centuries, Mordred loved Arthur and fought at his side. He was killed more than a thousand years ago, in battle, defending the king. And I have to be perfectly honest with you. I did not share this vision of yours that someone else named Mordred is linked with you."

"It wasn't really a vision; I just had a really bad feelin' that somethin' terrible is gonna happen, and that it has to do with Sarah's friend Morry. I know that I haven't even met the guy yet, but it seems to me just too coincidental that he's here in Moab at a time that we've had trouble with Beli, and are feelin' an urgent need to continue with the quest. Not to mention the fact that at least his *name* is linked to King Arthur." Derek stared into my eyes, and I felt his conviction, if not the reason for it.

I capitulated with a sigh. "Alright, I think the first step will have to be for me to meet this person and see what I can sense from him. Sarah, since he's your friend, can you speak with him, perhaps invite him to have a meal with us in honor of your new relationship with Derek?"

"Sure, I can do that, but I think you're all being paranoid. Morry's just a nice guy I've known for years, who has been kind to me. I really don't think he has magic. I've hugged him and touched him before—no Derek, not like that—and never felt any tingling or other indication of magic. Do you think he could be Derek's uh, relative, and just never inherited the magic?"

"That's possible. Not every descendant of a sorcerer has magic. But if your friend Mordred is indeed my grandson, the son of *both* of my children, it is highly unlikely that he is without magical powers. I need to see him, as soon as possible," I said flatly.

"Well, why don't I call him right now, since it's not that late, and invite him for dinner? Is tomorrow night okay? What time would be best?" Sarah was being her usual efficient, practical self.

I deferred to Emily, and she thought about it for a moment. "How about six o'clock? I already have a pot roast defrosted that I can cook in the crock-pot, with potatoes, carrots and onions, and I can make some biscuits. And I'm pretty sure there's some ice cream in the freezer for dessert. I might have to leave the shop a little early tomorrow to put the finishing touches on dinner, but you should be able to manage without me for an hour or so. Does that sound okay?" She glanced at me questioningly.

"That sounds fine, Em. Go ahead and call him, Sarah, and we'll all Listen in," I suggested.

She nodded and pulled her phone out of her purse, touching the screen to activate it and to initiate the call. She smiled at us as she waited for him to answer.

"Hi, Morry, I hope I didn't wake you up…oh, good. You know I told you about the people I work for, and the guy I met? Well, they've invited both of us to have dinner with them tomorrow after work, and I wanted to let you know before you made any other plans…what's that? Are you at the bar? I'm having a hard time hearing you. Oh, okay, great—see you in a while. Love you, too. 'Bye." She nodded to us as she ended the call. "I guess you all heard that. Morry and I will be here at six tomorrow night."

Derek looked wearily into my eyes. "Nothin' else we can do tonight, I guess. Thanks for humorin' me. I hope it turns out to be my imagination. I do want kids someday, but, God, not this way! Ready to go?" He glanced at Sarah and she nodded.

As they stood up he gently touched her wrist and I watched the two of them disappear.

They materialized in the center of the living room and Sarah swayed slightly.

"Oh, that felt so strange," she gulped, clutching his arm. "Can all of you do that?"

"Merlin and I can, but Emily's never been able to. I guess her magic is just too different. Lumina's been teleportin' automatically since she was born, although the older she gets, the more control she has over it. You *might* be able to teleport, but it kinda depends on how strong your magic is; whether you're a wizard or a sorcerer."

"I have no idea, and I'm not sure I want to do it anyway," she muttered, holding her stomach. "'Scuse me, I'll be right back." And she walked unsteadily down the hall to the bathroom.

Concerned, Derek watched as she left the room, and wondered if she would feel well enough to make love again. He thought back to earlier this evening, before all hell had broken loose, and wished he could go back to the first time they made love—God, that was *epic.* He started to get hard just thinking about the way she'd jumped on him, as if she couldn't wait to get into his pants. And the way she had accepted him into her body—he could hardly believe it. He considered himself to be of average size when aroused, but she was a relatively small woman, so he was thrilled that she was able to accommodate him so easily. He closed his eyes and took a few deep breaths, willing his body to calm down; even if she wasn't feeling sick, she might not want to have sex again tonight.

He had to adjust the fit of his pants as he walked into the kitchen to grab a cold beer. God, he was almost thirty years old, and he was acting like a horny teenager. He started imagining himself in an ice-cold shower, which helped to put a damper on his arousal. He had a feeling Sarah would be going home—in fact, she had said as much to Morry when she talked to him. Now, there was a name that definitely made him shrivel up. What would he do if Sarah's best friend *was* his son? He broke out in a cold sweat and gulped the rest of his beer so fast that he choked.

"Are you okay?" She came up behind him and thumped him on the back, which just made him cough harder.

"Yeah, I'm alright," Derek wheezed.

"You're worried, aren't you?"

"God, yes, wouldn't you be?"

She came around and stood in front of him, looking up at his face. "Maybe so, but if he *is* your son, there's nothing you can do about it, so worrying is pointless, don't you think?"

Derek sighed and hugged her to him. "I suppose you're right."

"Of course I am." Sarah smiled. "I think I'm going to go home, honey. I'll see you tomorrow night at Merlin and Emily's. Try not to worry so much, okay?" She reached up and pulled him down to her for a goodnight kiss.

"Oh, God, you are the sexiest man I have *ever* met," she murmured as their lips touched once, then again, "but we both have to get up and go to work tomorrow, so I guess I should...hmmm..." Sarah kissed him again and ran her hand through his hair.

Derek pulled away reluctantly. "Better go, then, before I throw you down on the couch and ravish you. Again."

She grinned as she stroked his face one more time, and then turned and slipped out the front door.

He waved and smiled at her as the door closed, then immediately turned and headed for a cold shower.

After the drama of the previous few hours came to an end with the departure of Derek and Sarah, I sighed with relief.

It had been a long, eventful day and I wanted to relax. I gently drew my wife into my arms and nuzzled her neck, which made her giggle.

"Hmm, you smell good, Em. Why don't we go to bed? Seeing those two together reminds me of when we first met. Do you remember?" I gazed down at her and smiled. Gods, she was exquisite.

She held my face in her hands and kissed me thoroughly before she answered.

"Are you kidding me? Of course, I do, it wasn't *that* long ago! I remember stopping at that motel in Springville and making love with you—God, I wanted you so much. I couldn't believe that I was so attracted to a man I hardly knew. You were the sexiest guy I'd ever met, and your natural scent was so intoxicating that I just couldn't help myself. I still can't help myself—you smell like, oh, I don't know, like eternity, like the essence of maleness itself. Of course, now I know that part of the attraction is to your soul, your god self." She stared into my eyes with such yearning that I almost merged with her then and there.

We both laughed, and Em said, "Oh, and I have to confess something—it's actually pretty funny, knowing your history."

"Oh, what's that?" I murmured, as I reached out to caress her shapely derriere.

"Remember when we first left the airport and got onto the highway, the way you were staring at everything, it was like you'd never seen a car or a freeway or even a large city before. And I thought to myself, 'Where the hell has this guy been, in a cave for the past couple of centuries?'"

I laughed and hugged her even tighter. "Did you really? I was trying so hard not to read your thoughts and I must have succeeded, because I didn't sense that at all. And remember, I had seen one large city full of vehicles—London—but I was absolutely overwhelmed by my attraction to *you*. You've always been very perceptive about me—I think we had already bonded, even then."

We continued to whisper words of love to each other as we headed into the master bedroom, and our caresses were an exciting prelude to our lovemaking.

CHAPTER 46

May 11

I SPENT THE NEXT DAY deep in thought, debating whether I should look into the future and find out exactly what would happen this night, but in the long run, I chose to remain in ignorance. I understood why God placed us like pawns in these situations, when he already knew the outcome—it was to enjoy vicariously the experience of life that he had bestowed upon the beings he had created. My own burgeoning sight and dawning understanding of his intentions were perhaps the result of my imminent transformation. I was so close to manifesting on this earth as the living god of magic and healing that it was an effort to keep myself restrained. The one God would tell me when it was finally time to reveal myself, and I was convinced that it would coincide with, or occur just prior to, Arthur's resurrection. And since it appeared that his vision of Albion was still some time in the future, I would have to control my god self a bit longer.

I had sensed Derek's worry and speculation throughout the day, but I did nothing more than share my love with him, wanting him to feel my support no matter the outcome of this night's revelations.

Derek and I arrived simultaneously at my house that evening, and we immediately offered our assistance with the last-minute preparations for our hastily planned dinner party.

"Everything is under control, as long as they give us a few more minutes. I told Sarah we'd eat promptly at six o'clock and it's about ten 'til, so we can go ahead and get the food on the table." Emily indicated what still needed to be done and we set to work.

As I carved the tender roast and arranged thick slices of beef on a platter, Derek opened the wine, and Emily placed the serving dishes heaped with steaming vegetables on the table. The homemade biscuits were in a basket and a dish of butter had been placed next to them. Everything smelled enticing and my stomach rumbled with hunger. I had missed lunch as I'd been so sunk in my reverie that I hadn't noticed the time.

"I hope Morry isn't sensitive to gluten; I should have asked Sarah about that today at work," Em said, concerned that our guest wouldn't be able to eat the biscuits, which were made with wheat flour.

"Don't worry about it, love. I'm sure she would have mentioned it if he had any food allergies or restrictions." I smiled. Her thoughtfulness was just one of the many reasons that I loved her so passionately.

"Mommy, I'm hungry, can I eat now?" Lumina asked. Other than the greeting she had given me when I walked in the door, she had been unusually quiet.

"Our guests aren't here yet, but I think it would be okay if you ate now. Daddy can get a plate started for you." She reached down and caressed our daughter's upturned face, and then helped her get seated at the table. I noticed that Lumina was already tall for her age and no longer needed the child seat she had used for such a short time. I dished up small servings of potatoes and carrots, cut a thin slice of meat into manageable child-sized pieces and set the plate down in front of her.

"Daddy, I'm not three anymore. Let me do it!" she said impatiently. Emily coughed to keep from laughing. In reality, Lumina was less than six months old, and it was sometimes difficult to remember that she considered herself to be a big girl now.

As I buttered a biscuit and poured a glass of milk for her, I smiled. "I know, but you weren't three for very long, and it makes me feel good to do this for you, sweetling." As I handed the milk and the biscuit to my daughter, I found myself distracted by my son's restlessness, which had increased dramatically in the last couple of minutes.

"They'll be here any time now; I can feel Sarah's magic," Derek announced nervously, as he set out the last of the wine glasses.

The state of his nerves was palpable as a discordant note reverberating throughout the room, and I gazed at him sympathetically. "There's no need to be so anxious, Son. We don't know yet if your feelings about this young man are valid. It's possible that this is a trick on your sister's part to throw us off-guard. She could have named him Mordred for no other reason than to cause just this reaction," I suggested, forced to accept the fact that my own flesh and blood was a cold-blooded schemer who had deliberately seduced her own brother. She had to have been in league with Beli to plan such a thing, which also indicated that they'd known all along that Derek would be in Camelot with me.

As my thoughts returned to the present situation and I contemplated greeting our special guest, I knew it was time to reveal that I was one step closer to the full manifestation of my god self.

"Merlin, what is it?" Em asked perplexedly, as she noticed the look on my face and felt the resolve radiating from my being.

Derek was quiet as he gave me that look that reminded me so much of his uncle, and waited for me to explain.

"In the past, I have always had to touch someone to See into that person's being, but now, I merely think of doing it, and it happens. I experienced that with Sarah yesterday. So I will know the truth about Morry as soon as he walks through the door."

Neither of them evinced more than mild surprise at my statement, and I wondered if they suspected that I'd evolved.

While neither of them had the ability to sense my thoughts and feelings on the level of my god powers unless I allowed it, they both knew me very well in other ways.

Derek started to reply, when there was a brief knock at the door, which opened enough for Sarah to poke her head in. "Hellooo, anybody home?"

"Hi, come on in," Em called out. She walked over to the entry way as our guests stepped through the door, welcoming them to our abode.

Oh, crap, here we go, Derek thought, his forehead damp with nervous perspiration.

It'll be alright, Son, just relax. I sent him a wave of soothing energy.

"I'm tryin' to," he muttered, under his breath.

Sarah glanced over at him with loving concern as she stood beside her roommate.

"Morry, I'd like you to meet my husband, Michael Reese," Em said pleasantly as I approached them.

"It's nice to meet you, Michael." The unassuming young man with the short, straight brown hair and the large eyes behind wire-rimmed glasses reached out to me uncertainly, his voice deeper than I had expected. I grasped his proffered hand and confirmed what I had sensed when he walked in.

"I am very pleased to meet you as well," I said sincerely, gazing curiously—and cautiously—into my grandson's slanted eyes. It was obvious that he had inherited the shape of those eyes from me, which wasn't all that surprising—after all, I was his grandfather on both sides. His eyes were a striking gray, with flecks of green, brown and slate blue, and I thought he might have inherited the unusual color from my mother's father, the Roman centurion.

As we clasped hands, I wondered if he felt anything, other than the natural curiosity that anyone would feel when meeting someone new for the first time. I felt no trace of magic in his touch, but as I reached out with my inner senses to explore his aura, there was something…abnormal or artificial about it. It was like a beautiful woman trying to alter her appearance with make-up, so that her own true beauty was still there but masked; changed temporarily to make her look like someone else. How strange, I thought. And then all I was aware of was my son's response.

Oh, God, he is *my son*! Derek's inner voice cried out silently as he heard my thoughts, and felt my confirmation and acceptance of the young man's paternity.

Emily perceived everything we did, of course, and I noticed her gazing intently at Morry. Other than his slanted cat's-eyes and six-foot frame, she saw no other obvious characteristics that would label him as a relation.

I conducted my own surreptitious examination of my grandson, which lasted no more than a few moments. He was a good-looking guy; his face a little wider, his nose a bit straighter than Derek's and shorter than mine, his teeth slightly crooked, but charmingly so. He was about the same height as Derek, but a little stoop-shouldered as if he couldn't be bothered to stand up straight. He was wearing a pair of denim shorts and a T-shirt very similar to Derek's normal casual attire, although this night my son had decided to wear jeans and a short-sleeved button-down shirt instead.

I couldn't help but notice that Morry was actually a good twenty pounds overweight. I wondered how someone so out of shape had participated in the Half Marathon race.

By this time, Sarah had picked up on the tension we felt, although it was apparent that she had not been able to fully discern the reason for it. Her telepathic abilities were rudimentary, so she perceived our silent communications only sporadically. But I heard her sharp intake of breath as she looked at Morry and then at me, and recognized the distinctive shape of our eyes.

"And this is Michael's cousin, Derek Colburn," Emily said, motioning Derek to come forward, obviously hoping to get the formalities over with so we could proceed with dinner.

"Hey, how're you doing?" Morry asked a bit sullenly as he reached out and gripped Derek's ice-cold hand, flinching slightly at the contact.

"Uh, I'm doin' fine, how're you, uh...Morry?" Derek gulped, looking ill as he returned the handshake.

Morry's forehead puckered in a slight frown as he met that troubled gaze. "Are you okay, man? You look a little...pale." He glanced questioningly at Sarah, who placed her hand on her lover's arm. I could feel her effort to communicate with Derek telepathically, asking him silently if he needed to lie down.

The startled expression on his face as he turned to her indicated that her attempt had been successful, and he shook his head. She noticed me exchanging a glance of proud, though amused, approval with Emily, and realized that she had not just communicated with Derek, she had broadcast the question to all of us. She winced and whispered to me silently, *Sorry!*

I winked at her and she blushed.

Morry glanced from one of our faces to another in silent puzzlement, but obviously didn't feel comfortable enough to say anything.

"Alright, everybody, let's eat before Emily's lovely dinner gets cold," I said matter-of-factly, taking charge and directing everyone to their seats at the dining table. Lumina was still picking at her food as I sat down next to her.

"And this is our daughter, Lumina. Sweetling, can you say hello to Sarah's friend, Morry?"

"Hello," she whispered shyly as she looked down at her plate.

"Oh, er, hello, Lumina," he said uncomfortably, not realizing, of course, that she was actually his aunt.

"The food looks great, Em," Derek managed, still looking a little queasy, but trying to keep a tentative smile plastered on his face. As they settled next to each other, he reached out and squeezed Sarah's hand briefly, sending a silent, *Thanks, love, you're amazin',* to her mind.

Her face lit up with pleasure at the compliment, and she looked around the table at the group, thrilled to have all the people she cared about in one place, ready to share a meal. I nodded to Emily to begin passing the serving dishes to me, one at a time, and I adjusted the temperature of the food as it passed through my hands. Morry, who was seated directly across from me, had a speculative look on his face as he observed the parade of dishes as they made their way through my hands and were distributed to everyone.

Sarah's puzzled glances at Morry made it very clear she didn't know him as well as she thought she did. I could tell she was wondering if Morry sensed the magic being worked right in front of him.

Derek and Morry began eyeing each other like two male dogs competing for territory, and I wondered if anyone else was seeing the identical expressions on their faces. Even if I didn't know it for a fact, it would seem quite apparent to me that those two were related. Sarah was still having a hard time accepting that they were father and son, but as she glanced at me, then at the two men, then back to me again, the resigned look on her face indicated that she had finally accepted the truth.

My attention was abruptly drawn back to the conversation as I heard Morry talking about how he had acquired his name.

"My mother dropped me off at the church when I was a newborn," he said bitterly, "and she'd apparently pinned a note to the blanket, saying that my name was Mordred; no middle name, no last name, just Mordred, and that it was imperative that

I keep that name. So, I've been stuck with this stupid, meaningless name my whole life, and—"

"It's a name from the fifth century, associated with a famous king, so there's nothing wrong with it, and it's certainly not meaningless," I said bluntly.

Dad, what the hell are you doing? Derek's face had now gone from pasty white to a bright red hue.

Emily and Sarah stared at me with their mouths unflatteringly agape, both women obviously wondering if I'd lost my mind.

"Huh? What famous king?" Morry asked, perplexed, as no one had ever offered any illuminating information in regards to his name. He set the fork down on the table as if he had lost all interest in eating.

"King Arthur. Mordred was his nephew's name," I said, and to myself, *and his grandnephew's name.*

Derek had placed one hand over his eyes and was thinking rather rude thoughts.

"But…but King Arthur wasn't really, that is, uh, it's just a legend, right?" Morry asked, flustered, and I considered letting him off the hook for the sake of our dining experience.

Dad, are you sure you want to bring this up right now?

"Alright, I concede the point—who's to say what was real and what was legend. It was a very long time ago, after all. I just meant that there's nothing wrong with the name Mordred," I said mildly, taking a bite of beef.

I heard Derek release the breath he had been holding. After that, the conversation became less controversial as it varied from Derek's recent confrontation with a visitor at the park, to Em's and Sarah's interactions with the customers at The Moab Herbalist.

"Where do you work, Morry?" I inquired during a lull. I had been observing my grandson for several minutes, and was again feeling that something was terribly wrong with his aura.

"Oh, I just work at the newspaper, as a copy editor," he said self-deprecatingly.

I hoped he was going to expound on that topic, but Sarah interrupted to tell a funny story, perhaps hoping to lighten the mood. I have to give her credit—it worked. It was simple, yet effective, and we all laughed. The look on my wife's face caught my attention, and I realized that she was watching us, noticing the same grin on Derek's and Morry's faces as was on mine: three generations, and the smile was the same.

I still intended to encourage Morry to talk about himself. For some reason, that persistent sense of unreality I had about my grandson told me it could be dangerous to delve into his mind unannounced—I was afraid that there could be some kind of deep-seated enchantment at work, perhaps woven into his very DNA as he grew in his mother's womb. Gods, Adrestia was as evil as Nimue had been, and it sickened me to realize that beneath Morry's expertly crafted veneer could be an explosion just waiting to happen.

I waited until we had finished eating before I tried again. "Morry, why don't you tell us a little more about yourself?" I wasn't going to take no for an answer this time.

He complied, but with a sullen reluctance that seemed out of proportion to the benign nature of the request. And he was obviously determined not to provide any real information.

"Uh, Sarah and I came here from California for the Half Marathon in March, and we've been sharing a small place downtown for a little more than a month. But now that she's with Derek, it looks like I may have to find another roommate." He smiled, but it was a forced and unhappy expression; he obviously didn't share his friend's joy. Morry was plainly feeling jilted, and I sensed his need to go to ground like an animal who wanted to lick its wounds.

"You don't seem like a runner, Morry," I said. It was obvious that my observation made him even more uncomfortable than he already was.

"Well, no, I'm not, but Sarah wanted to do it, so I decided to enter also. I walked most of the way," he said reluctantly.

When Em asked if anyone would like dessert, he gruffly declined, thanked us briefly for our hospitality and departed abruptly, shoulders hunched; shame, anger and embarrassment radiating in powerful waves from his being.

As the front door closed behind him, Sarah, who could hardly have failed to be affected by his intense emotions, was momentarily rendered speechless. Then, she finally found her voice. "God, I'm so sorry, I can't imagine what's gotten into him! He's not usually so rude."

She was young and naïve and she truly didn't see the reality—that he had followed her here to Moab, hoping that the intimacy of a shared experience would help her to really see him, to accept him. He was in love with her, and she was now in love with someone else.

I shared a quick glance with Derek and he winced. We had both felt the overwhelming sense of loss emanating from him, and our familial connection made that emotion even more intense.

"Dad, someone brought him here, to this century, when he was a baby, like Llyr did for me, but he wasn't loved like I was. And *I* never had the chance to take care of my son and love him. Oh, God, this is all my fault…" His voice broke with emotion. Sarah put her arms around him, trying to console him.

I tried to introduce a bit of reality. "Derek, he was brought here when you were only six years old, the same age Lumina is now. You're *not* to blame; the whole situation—the trip to Camelot, your attraction to your sister, your son's conception—was a cunningly devised trap created by a twisted mind, using black magic. I believe that both Beli and Adrestia were involved in this, but that it was actually Nimue who planned it all prior to her death."

"I…thanks, Dad, I needed to hear that. I know that I was under a spell at the time, but I feel terrible that Morry had to grow up that way."

Still at Derek's side, Sarah spoke up. "Maybe it would be a good idea if I told you how I met him and what he was like when he was younger. It might help you to understand him."

Derek looked searchingly into Sarah's eyes for a moment. "Okay, that sounds like a good idea."

Emily interrupted briefly as she stood up, "Sorry, I'm going to get Lumina ready for bed; just go ahead without me."

I smiled up at her. "Alright, love. Lumina, can you give Daddy a kiss?" I leaned down and my daughter kissed my cheek. "Thank you, Lumina, I love you."

"I love you, too, Daddy." Lumina grinned at me, kissed her brother's cheek as well, and then skipped back over to Emily, who took her hand as they left the room.

"Go ahead, Sarah."

"First, I'll have to give you a little of my own background so you'll understand why he and I got so close," she said quietly. "I was very young when my parents died so I don't remember them, but I was told later that they were loving and protective of me. After the car accident in which they were killed, a distant, elderly relative took me in and I lived with her for years. We weren't that close, but she took care of me, made me do my homework, and told me stories about my family. When she became ill and wasn't able to look after me anymore—I think I was ten or eleven—I was ushered kicking and screaming into the foster care system. I lived for a short time with one couple, but that didn't work out and I ended up with the Thompson family. That's where I met Morry—he arrived at the same time I did. We were the new kids in the household, and we bonded right away. We used to spend hours hiding in the closet under the hanging clothes so we wouldn't have to go to church, reading by flashlight about King Arthur and Merlin, and the Knights of the Round Table." She smiled at the cherished memory, and I watched her eyes widen with shock as she remembered to whom she was telling her tale. Derek laughed and hugged her, and Emily and I shared a private moment of amusement through our bond.

"It's alright, Sarah, please go on," I said kindly.

She looked a little embarrassed, but continued with her story. "I wasn't shy, but Morry was, painfully so. He was nervous, and so small for his age that I was taller than he was; I stood up for him when the other kids teased him unmercifully. When we looked into each other's eyes we felt like we could see each other's souls." She closed her eyes for a moment, reflecting on the past.

Derek glanced at me. *Sounds like they were both usin' magic instinctively, and Seein' each other.*

Yes, it does, but it's unlikely, as Morry's magic has never manifested. I suspect it was just their special bonding process as two lonely orphans.

Surfacing from her dive into the turbulent waters of nostalgia, Sarah opened her eyes and continued. "We were actually lucky to be staying with Helen and Roger Thompson; they were wonderful people, kind and caring. A few years later, as teenagers, we didn't see that, of course, and very melodramatically bemoaned our fate as foster kids. Morry and I were tighter than ever in high school, and if either one of us went on a date, the other would stay up just to find out what happened: Did he kiss you? Did you touch her?

"Graduation found us at a crossroads—should we go to college or get a job? Each of us took one of those paths, and we separated for a year while we had our own experiences.

"Our foster parents, who might as well have adopted us since they really did love us like their own children, had hoped that we would stay close to home in Bakersfield, but neither of us did. I was a plant lover and particularly interested in herbs, so I enrolled in the Horticulture Program at the University of California, in Davis, which is west of Sacramento. Morry decided to forego college and went to work for the *Los Angeles Times*, starting at the bottom, in the mail room. He ended up using the last name Thompson because it sounded better than Doe, which is the name they'd given him when he was a baby. He was pretty ambitious, and began working his way up the ladder.

"I missed Morry terribly and he missed me too, so when he turned twenty he moved north and got a job at a newspaper in Sacramento.

"By the time I graduated, we were living in the same house with a couple of other roommates. I sometimes wondered why we never became lovers, but we were pretty firmly entrenched in a brother-sister relationship, and I wasn't really into having sex with my brother." Suddenly embarrassed as she remembered who Morry's parents were, she glanced guiltily at her lover, who stared at the floor and pointedly cleared his throat.

She continued, "I can look back now and see that Morry wouldn't let the Thompsons get close to him emotionally. I love him dearly, but I could never understand why he did that."

"If indeed there was an enchantment placed on him at birth, it could very well explain his inability to accept love. He wouldn't even have known what was wrong with him, and neither would anyone else," I conjectured.

Sarah fidgeted in her seat and finally said, "You know, I think I'll skip dessert also, and head home to see if he's okay. Derek, I'll call you—"

"Forget the phone. Just talk to me in your mind, Sarah, and I'll hear you," Derek said softly.

I noticed that her eyes widened in surprise. For a moment, she had forgotten the magic. "And Sarah, it's important that you do *not* tell him about us quite yet, or reveal that he is actually a part of this family. I don't think he can handle it. *I* will decide when that should happen, do you understand?"

"Yes, Merlin, I understand," she said meekly. She then gave Derek a quick kiss, grabbed her purse, and hurried out the front door.

Emily, who had returned to the kitchen in time to hear my instructions and Sarah's response, stood looking after her with a skeptical expression on her face.

I sighed. "No, she won't keep that promise; I think she's been affected by his enchantment. Having been in contact with him, and thus the black magic inside of him, for so many years, she'll do whatever it takes to sabotage his emotions.

"You may have to go over there later, Derek."

"You mean, and tell him who I *am*?"

"Use your own judgment on that, but if you do tell him, don't be surprised or hurt if he rejects you."

CHAPTER 47

May 11 8:00-10:00 PM

DESPITE THE ENERGY he'd expended in walking home, Morry felt no better than he had when he had so abruptly left the Reeses'. He should have felt guilty for taking off like that, but he didn't—he was angry and hurt and didn't care who knew it.

God, he felt like such an ass. All those years, hoping and praying that Sarah would come around, would love him the way he loved her. When he thought about the guy who had won her heart, after one lousy, stinking date, he was so furious that he wanted to kill him. Fucking Derek. That good-looking prick could have any woman, or man, he wanted—he suspected the guy could swing both ways—and yet he had chosen Sarah. His Sarah.

He sat in the ratty old chair in their tiny living room, drinking beer and scowling and grumbling, until he finally wore himself out and fell asleep.

When Sarah parked her Prius at the curb in front of the house, she noticed that the porch light was on, but it was dark inside; perhaps Morry had gone directly to Moody's Tavern. She hurried up the short walkway and unlocked the front door. As she stepped inside and flipped the light switch, she remembered how prohibitively expensive it had been renting that motel room when they first came to Moab. They had loved the town immediately and had stayed for a week after the Half Marathon was over. But they had realized very quickly that it would behoove them to rent a house if they intended to stay any longer. They had consulted a property management company who had been able to find them something suitable within a couple of days: this tiny, two-bedroom cottage a couple of blocks off Main

Street, which fortunately had been partially furnished. They had been in it for less than two months, but if she and Derek intended to live together, which would be inevitable when they got married, Morry would have to advertise for a roommate. She felt a little guilty about that, but she was giddy with the excitement of her new relationship.

She went directly to the kitchen and put her purse down on the counter. The house was so quiet, she wondered if Morry was here, but in bed, already asleep. She poked her head into his bedroom and discovered that it was empty, the bedding still rumpled from this morning. She checked in the bathroom and it, too, was empty.

"Morry? Where are—oh, there you are," Sarah said as she walked into the darkened living room. Then, she noticed that he was sleeping, in a very uncomfortable-looking position with his head at an awkward angle. One arm hung limply over the side of the chair, and there was an empty beer bottle on the floor where he had dropped it.

She reached out to caress his tousled hair, but thought better of the gesture after what had happened at their dinner party earlier. Apparently, Morry had much deeper feelings for her than a brother would normally have for a sister: the platonic relationship they'd enjoyed had been a lie—at least for him.

She felt terrible about the situation, though. She did love him, but not that way. How could she have been so blind, for so many years, that she missed seeing it? And the last few days, she had been so consumed with the joy of finding her soul mate, that she hadn't even been as attentive to him as she usually was.

What she had found out this evening had changed everything. She hadn't wanted to believe it, but she trusted Merlin implicitly, and had seen the family resemblance with her own eyes. Morry *was* Derek's son. And since Derek was the son of Merlin, then Morry was the grandson of the most famous sorcerer who had ever lived. He was also the grandnephew of King

Arthur and had been born in Camelot in the fifth century. Crap, it was just too much to take in. She had practically grown up with Morry and knew all his moods and idiosyncrasies, and this revelation of his heritage was overwhelming. The strangest realization of all was that if—or rather, when—she and Derek got married, Morry would be her *stepson.* Like Derek was Emily's stepson. And wouldn't that be freaking weird.

According to Merlin, Morry did have magic, despite the fact that there was no sign of it. The sorcerer was his grandfather on both his mother's and his father's side, so he *had* to have magical powers. And some kind of dark enchantment had deactivated them.

God, how she wanted to wake her friend up and tell him that he wasn't alone anymore, that he had family after all, people who wanted to love him—magical, wonderful, immortal people. Tell him that he had magic and was probably immortal himself. This information was just too delicious to withhold—she had to share it with him, even though she knew she shouldn't. Her conscience was squirming, warning her that it was wrong, but she couldn't help herself. "Morry, honey, wake up! I have something incredible to tell you!"

"Huh?" he responded sleepily, blinking at her through smudged glasses. He automatically took them off, cleaned them on his shirt, and then replaced them. It wasn't the first time he had fallen asleep with his glasses on. He scowled up at her, beautiful gray eyes surrounded by long dark brown lashes looking huge through his corrective lenses. "What?"

Sarah turned a light on and pulled up a stool so she could get close to him, gazing directly into his eyes. "I'm sorry it didn't go so well at the Reeses' tonight, but you really should try and get to know them."

"Why the hell should I?" His voice was rough with sleep and alcohol, his tone surly.

"Because you're related to them, they're your family. All of them have *magic*, even Emily and the little girl!" She was so excited to share this news with him that she couldn't even imagine that he would be anything but overjoyed.

It took him a moment to process what she'd said. "Magic? What are you talking about? Have you lost your *mind*? That's just stupid, Sarah!"

Before she could reply, Derek materialized in the room, right in front of Morry.

"What the *fuck*?" He leaped up out of his chair so fast that it flew back and toppled over.

"Shit, I'm really sorry I startled you." Derek gulped as he saw Morry's horrified expression. "There's something I need to tell you—God, how do I say this? I know that this is gonna seem impossible, but we're, uh, related. I'm your...your dad." Derek's face was white, and he looked like he was going to be sick any moment.

After the initial shock, Morry was furious. He had wanted a family more than *anything* when he was growing up; in fact, he considered his need for a family to be almost a sacred thing. Now this bastard, whom he hated, was making a mockery out of it. He wanted to rail at Derek, to punish him with cutting rhetoric, but he was so upset he could hardly put a coherent sentence together.

"You...*bastard*! You—you're an insane motherfucker, you know that? You're only a few years older than I am, so how can you be my father? And how the fucking *hell* did you get in here, anyway?"

"It's kinda hard to explain it, but the concept of time, well, it isn't what you think...I'll have to explain it to you later. And, uh, I teleported here from my house."

"What do you mean, time isn't what I think? Wait a minute, what did you say? You did *what?*"

"I teleported—you know, like in fantasy novels, only in this case, it's real. I can move myself from one place to another usin' magic," Derek said matter-of-factly.

Morry's eyes widened, his jaw dropped in astonishment, and then he glared with renewed hatred at the man claiming to have magical powers, who insisted that he was his father.

Derek sighed and glanced away, and Morry felt a rush of triumph as the other man seemed unable to continue the farce, for farce it must be. It couldn't possibly be real, could it? Although, how did he…?

Suddenly feeling weary and discouraged, as if it was just too much effort to deal with anymore, he closed his eyes for a moment, slowly rubbing them as if he could massage away all the ridiculous revelations of the evening.

"Mordred, look at me!" The voice unexpectedly rang out with supernatural force.

He tensed and his eyes flew open, shocked to hear his real name enunciated with such power and intent. Derek was right up in his face, eyes intense, and Morry heard him whisper something just before everything went dark.

Derek watched as the spell took effect and his son's eyes went blank. As Morry crumpled towards the floor, he caught the younger man and gently lowered him the rest of the way down to the clean but threadbare throw rug. He glanced over at Sarah, who stared, stricken, at her friend who lay unconscious on the floor.

"What did you do to him? Is he okay?" she whispered fearfully, as she realized that her lover wielded a power far beyond anything she could ever have imagined. She was merely playing at magic. He was the son of a god.

Derek couldn't bring himself to answer her at first, he was so disappointed that she had blatantly ignored Merlin's injunction not to reveal the truth to Morry.

"He's alright, he's just asleep." He frowned as he addressed his lover. "Sarah, I can't believe you did that. After Merlin specifically ordered you *not* to tell Morry the truth, you did it anyway." He paused to take a breath and get himself under control. How could he possibly marry someone he couldn't trust? Although, to be fair, Merlin had told him that she would do this, that the enchantment affecting Morry might very well be affecting her as well.

She drew herself up to her full height as she lashed out at him, furious that he would criticize her. "Well, I don't appreciate people ordering me around! And what gives you the right to scold me? *I* didn't tell him you're his father—you did!"

"No, but you might as well have! You told him we were his family and that he had magic also!" He took a deep breath and put his hands up as if in surrender, just as Sarah was about to reply caustically. "Okay, let's both just calm down, Sarah, please. I'm sorry, but Merlin gave me permission to tell him after you'd already revealed too much. You don't understand what the stakes are, sweetheart. Merlin has knowledge that we don't, and he would never ask us to do somethin' unreasonable. Morry is a walkin' time bomb with that enchantment built into his DNA. Eventually, his mom, my demented half sister, will feel that the time is right, and she'll trigger the explosion, the destruction, whatever form it comes in—and then, God help us all." Sarah didn't respond, but he could feel her resentment drain away, leaving her frozen in disbelief, horror and guilt.

Derek had to remind himself that she was young and inexperienced. He hoped that they could get past this difficult time. Finally, he knelt down beside the still form at his feet. He gently brushed the fine brown hair back from Morry's face with its smattering of late evening beard stubble, and marveled that this man was his *son*. He carefully removed the thick glasses and handed them to Sarah, then gazed at Morry's features, so different from his own, and yet so hauntingly familiar, somehow. It seemed impossible that it was only a few months ago when he and Merlin had been transported to legendary Camelot, where he had experienced an intense attraction to a beautiful woman, leading to an enchantment-induced session of unprotected sex. And the result of that unfortunate act now lay unconscious on the floor in front of him.

"I never got to see him when he was born. I never got to teach him to ride a bike, or to play ball with him," Derek said softly, regretfully. "And he had to grow up without me lovin' him, bein' there for him. That's the worst part." He looked up to see tears welling in Sarah's eyes. He would start crying himself if he didn't focus his thoughts elsewhere. As he brought his gaze back to Morry's face, he thought he saw some resemblance to Adrestia, and there was the unmistakable cat-like slant to his eyes that connected him to Merlin. Sarah had told him his own eyes had a slight slant, but he couldn't see it himself. No matter how many times he looked into the mirror, he mostly saw his resemblance to Arthur, which, to tell the truth, he didn't mind at all.

How had Morry ended up with those gray eyes that he'd stared into over the dinner table a few hours ago? He himself had the rich brown color inherited from the Pendragons, and his straight, light brown hair was only a shade darker than Arthur's own sandy-blonde. Adrestia had her mother's, and their paternal grandmother's, vivid blue eyes, and of course, Merlin had the same brilliant green eyes as his father, the god Llyr. Perhaps Morry's eyes would change color when his magic finally appeared, if he survived the transition. Derek shivered as he imagined the emergence of Morry's magic triggering doom and destruction and had to deliberately block those thoughts.

The glasses were a surprise, as sorcerers normally had perfect eyesight, but it was possible that the suppression of Morry's magic had affected that as well. When his magic was finally freed, Derek suspected that he would no longer need the corrective lenses.

As he was examining the man's body, wondering why his son had allowed himself to get so out of shape, Derek felt Morry begin to regain consciousness. He motioned to Sarah, who placed the glasses back on his face, and they stationed themselves on each side of him. Derek knew that having Sarah there to welcome him back would be marginally more acceptable then his presence alone.

When he opened his eyes, Morry was looking up into one familiar, beloved face and one face he wished he never had to see again. Derek's expression was a little wary, but exhibited a disturbingly paternal concern for his welfare, and Sarah was right there beside him, smiling encouragingly.

He immediately scrambled to sit up, as he felt at a distinct disadvantage lying in a prone position with his supposed father hovering over him. Derek reached out and gripped his arm to help him, and Morry growled, "Get your *fucking* hand off of me, or you're a dead man."

The reaction he'd expected didn't happen. Instead, he was shocked when his "father" merely chuckled mirthlessly and muttered, "Been there, done that, came back to life. So go ahead and kill me, I don't really care." As he remained motionless, taken aback at Derek's response, his nemesis cocked his head to one side and said, "No? I didn't think so." Derek got up off the floor and pulled Morry up with him, so they were standing close to each other. He ran his eyes over the younger man's form once again and shook his head in bewilderment.

"You really *don't* look like me, I mean, at all. What the hell? You've got Merlin's eyes, only they're gray instead of green, and nothin' from me except your height. You don't look much like your mom, either. Maybe you resemble Merlin's grandfather."

"What the hell are you babbling about, dude—who's Merlin? You mean your cousin Michael, *who's the same age as you*?" Morry asked sarcastically, right up in Derek's face. Derek met his thunderous gaze with one of his own.

Sarah had finally had enough of their male posturing. "Guys, I'm choking on all the testosterone here. Morry, listen up: they're sorcerers, they're immortal, and that's why Michael—who really is Merlin, by the way—looks so young. God, get over it. You're Derek's son, and you're probably immortal also, right Derek?"

"I would think so, but you'll probably age another ten years and then stop, just like Merlin did. Although, I seem to have stopped as soon as Merlin released my magic last year, when I was only twenty-eight, so, who knows?"

That did it. Morry had had enough bullshit for one day, and he just exploded, punching Derek in the gut so hard that he doubled over, retching. Sarah screamed at him to stop, but that just made him angrier. He had drawn his arm back to let Derek have it in the face, when he suddenly was caught, frozen, totally immobilized. He could see over Derek's shoulder someone he recognized from earlier in the evening: Michael Reese, and he looked pissed. His arm was extended with his hand twisted in some kind of gesture, and through the haze of his anger, Morry could have sworn the man had uttered the word, *Desino*. Latin? He tried to move, to talk, anything, but he was caught like an insect in a spider's web. It seemed like the more he tried to escape, the tighter his invisible bonds became.

Derek coughed and groaned and finally straightened up. "Thanks, Dad, he was too quick for me to raise a defensive shield, and—"

"You didn't think he would hurt you."

Derek nodded and looked at Morry dispassionately, his brown eyes narrowed and his jaw clenched. Morry stared back, channeling every bit of the hatred and anger he felt into that gaze. Surprisingly, he thought he saw a flicker of pain and disappointment on Derek's face, and for some reason that he couldn't fathom, he had to let go of that maelstrom of negative emotion. He was left with nothing but confusion and wariness, and it was at that moment that he saw Michael make another slight hand gesture. He staggered, free of the force that had bound him.

"You will refrain from any additional violence, Mordred, or I will be sorely tempted to utilize even more restrictive measures," I said in a quiet voice, that nevertheless carried such a ring of authority and a sense of veiled power that my fractious grandson could not doubt the outcome should he disobey.

I reached out to Derek telepathically and reminded him that he had my support to get through this. I recognized the heartache that he must be experiencing, being rejected by the one person who would normally welcome his attention.

As my grandson witnessed the silent but eloquent exchange between us, he looked perplexed, as if he was attempting to figure out what we were doing.

I returned my attention to Derek. *I did warn you, Son, that he would not react well to any overture on your part. I have decided to show him who he really is. I believe that it is the unbinding of his magic that will trigger the enchantment locked in his cells, and I have no intention of doing so, but I will use the utmost finesse just in case.*

"Okay, I guess showin' him the truth will have to be enough for now, won't it?" Derek asked, resigned to an unsatisfactory resolution.

As we both turned to Morry, he lashed out verbally, exuding the fear of a cornered animal. I wondered just what he had endured as a child; it was obvious that he was burdened by emotional scars.

"Don't come near me, you bastards, I *will* hurt you!" he growled as he backed away from us, pulling out a knife from a hidden sheath.

"Really, dude? Are you stupid? Maybe you aren't my son after all, 'cause I was never that dumb," Derek scoffed, and flicked his hand in a casual gesture, causing the knife to fly out of Morry's hand and across the room. Sarah let out a screech, reminding us that she was still present.

"Are you okay, Sarah?" Derek and Morry asked in unison, and then glared at each other fiercely until the younger man finally backed down.

"Alright, damn it, I give up! Just, don't kill me," Morry pleaded.

"Jesus, we're not gonna kill you, we're tryin' to help you, ya moron." Exasperated, Derek reached out and gripped his son's forearm firmly.

I stepped closer to my grandson and Looked into his eyes. I put him into a light trance, and then went deep into his inner being, searching for the enchantment that must have been placed on him even as his body developed. I discovered that every cell in Morry's body was tainted with powerful black magic, and until I found a way to counteract that enchantment, he endangered not only our family but also the population of the entire Moab valley.

It would be a challenge, but this man was my flesh and blood, my grandson, and I would figure out how to circumvent my rogue daughter's black magic. My consciousness still exploring Morry's inner being, I made him aware of my presence and my true identity, allowing him to recognize me as his kin. I then revealed to him who *he* really was, and came back to myself. I looked at him with a knowing smile and he peered at me incredulously through his thick lenses.

CHAPTER 48

May 11   Late Night

I'M...YOU'RE...OH, GOD!"

"No, I'm not God, although I am on speaking terms with him," I said, amused. "I'm Merlin, the Sorcerer of Camelot, and I'm your grandfather."

"But that's impossible!" Morry exclaimed.

I grinned. "I assure you, it is possible; you're the son and grandson of sorcerers, as well as the grandnephew of King Arthur."

"I don't believe you," came the sullen response.

I was rapidly losing patience with this irascible young man. "I just showed you irrefutable proof, inside of you, and yet you still have doubts?"

"Hell, yeah, I have doubts! There's no way..."

Without warning, I touched his forearm and we teleported to the top of the Rim. I had used this spot many times before as a proving ground. Standing in the darkness, overlooking the glow of Moab, I asked, "And what do you say now, Grandson?"

"You...this has to be an illusion. It can't be real!" He vehemently denied what his senses insisted was indeed true.

I sighed and tightened my grip. "You're more hardheaded than your father. Hold on, we're going for a little flight."

"What are you—oh, *SHIT*!" Morry shrieked as I rose straight up into the air, then soared high over Moab, city lights twinkling far below us. He started shaking and finally reached to put his arms around me, clinging like a child, his head tucked into my neck.

Well, finally, I thought. *Time to go home.*

After Merlin had departed with Morry in tow, Sarah suggested to Derek that they stretch out on her bed and talk.

Their relationship was brand-new, yet it had progressed from first date to engagement so fast that there had been no time to get to know each other, to exchange stories and to express their hopes and dreams. She had revealed some of her background at dinner, but there was so much more to tell.

And they had immediately become embroiled in a major family drama that would have no real resolution. If it had turned out that Morry was not Derek's son, their association with him could have been managed differently. But he was definitely a part of the family, at least genetically, and if he accepted his familial connection to them, he would be a part of their lives forever.

As they reclined on the bed, they occasionally touched and kissed gently, without allowing themselves to get too passionate. They needed to learn to relate to each other in other ways besides sexually, but their attraction to each other was so all-consuming that they were finding it difficult to stay focused. Sarah forced herself to ask Derek about some things that had been bothering her.

"I've got a lot of questions, but the first thing is, what in the world did you mean when you told Morry, 'Been there, done that, came back to life. So go ahead and kill me…' Did you actually *die*?"

"Uh, yeah, I did. It was horrible, and I'm not sure I should tell you about it, 'cause it would give you nightmares." Derek reached out to stroke her cheek, a serious look on his face.

"But I really need to know these things if we're going to get married," she said insistently.

He glanced away and said resolutely, "I know, but not tonight."

"Okay." She was quiet for a moment, then continued. "I'm still confused, Derek. Morry has been in the present time for most of his life, let's say twenty-two years, but he was conceived 1,554 years ago, in the year AD 460. And yet, you traveled to that year and had sex with his mother only a few months ago. God, it makes my head ache just thinking about it!" She cradled her head in her hands as if it could explode any moment.

"Time isn't a linear phenomenon, Sarah, it's more like an infinite ocean—it's difficult to explain it. Travelin' to the past really messed with my sense of how the world is supposed to work, but now I know that, even though they're not alive in *this* time, King Arthur and everyone in Camelot are still alive in the past."

"You mean that all times exist simultaneously?"

"Yeah. So the experience that I had stays alive in my heart and mind." Derek sat up and grabbed her hand, anxious to express how it had affected him.

"It was one of the most amazin' things that ever happened to me, to kneel before my uncle, the king, and pledge myself to his service. Merlin even gave me the knowledge of the language of that time so that I could talk directly to him!" Derek's eyes sparkled as he recalled that momentous occasion and he grinned from ear to ear.

She kissed his hand and smiled at his raw enthusiasm. "I'll try harder to think outside the box, okay?" She paused for a moment to figure out how to phrase her next question.

"It must have been amazing to meet a famous, legendary hero and find out you were related to him, but I still don't understand how you could have been duped into having sex with a total stranger."

"I know, right? It seems unreal when I look back on it now. At the time, Merlin kept sayin' that I was under an enchantment, and I was convinced I wasn't. I was drawn to her; I felt like I'd known and wanted her forever. It seemed totally logical to find a place to be alone, even a tumble-down shack, and to pull her skirts up and take her, right there on a pile of straw…." He felt himself merge with that recollection of intense sexual need and immediate gratification.

"Derek, Derek, hey, snap out of it!" Sarah snapped her fingers in front of his eyes, which had become glassy and unfocused.

He shook his head and blinked, then looked at her in confusion. "What happened?"

"I think while you were remembering her, you put yourself back into that enchantment," she said.

"I don't know how that could happen, but I'll mention it to Dad when he gets back with Morry."

"Um, Derek, do you notice anything…strange?"

He looked at her questioningly and realized that he was on top of her, in the process of pulling his pants down, and he was fully aroused.

"Aw, crap…" he breathed.

Morry was terrified and he clung to the man like a leech. This, this *flight* couldn't be real, but it *felt* real: the light breeze ruffling his hair and caressing his cheek as the two of them moved through the dark sky, a thousand feet above the city lights of Moab; the man's steady breathing as he soared effortlessly, now circling back to land on the Rim. Finally, Morry's feet were firmly planted on solid ground again.

"You can let go now, Grandson," a male voice with a slight accent said kindly in his ear, as a large hand patted his back, as one would do to reassure a small child. He wasn't a child, but he enjoyed the sensation of being cared for, even loved, and felt himself succumbing to the warmth of the man's affection.

He jerked and recoiled from the sense of love and belonging he felt. No, this definitely was some kind of hallucination, because there was no one in his life who loved or wanted him like that, certainly not a grandfather. Abruptly, he pulled out of the man's embrace and stepped back.

With supernaturally fast reflexes, the man grabbed him. "Whoa, careful, there's a pretty steep drop right behind you, Mordred. I wouldn't want you to fall."

"Well, I guess you could just fly down and save me then, couldn't you," he said sarcastically, although his heart was pumping wildly at the thought that he could have been falling to his death right now if the man hadn't caught him.

The man didn't respond to his taunting, but said softly, "I'm very sorry that your life has been difficult, growing up without the love and support of parents or grandparents. But we're all here now—except for your mother, my daughter Adrestia, who is still in the Hell realm—and we want you to join our family. You are our kin, after all. It will seem strange at first, since none of us are the typical family members you would expect to encounter in this human realm, but we want to love you, Mordred, and to teach you how to function as...what you are."

Morry endured his speech, trying to ignore the seductive pull of the promise of love and family. The reference to his mother being in the "Hell realm," and the other comment about the "human realm" had him stumped. What was this thing about realms, anyway? And, what the hell did he mean by that last comment?

"You don't need to fear us; we are your family, and we *will* love you. And I would be happy to explain about the realms. And about what makes you special."

"Stop reading my mind, damn you!" he yelled. "Nobody has ever loved me, so why should I believe you?"

The man's warm voice cooled and became brittle and harsh, revealing a core of mental anguish. "Do you honestly think you're the only one who has ever been alone, felt unloved, or been persecuted for being who you are? Think again. I have been alive longer than you can possibly imagine and have seen—and experienced—things that would horrify you. Your paltry couple of decades of life and your tales of woe count for very little in the grand scheme of things." He paused and took a long, deep breath, and when he spoke again, he had regained some of his calm demeanor, although it was laced with a steely resolve. "And don't imagine that I have an endless supply of patience; just ask my wife or my son about that. So, do not test me further," the man said, power manifesting in his voice, while sparks of blue flame crackled on his skin and erupted from his fingertips.

Suddenly, all the things that had occurred this evening—the dinner party he had walked away from, the things that everyone had said and done, and the extraordinary experiences he'd just had with this man claiming to be Merlin—came together for him, and he knew in his heart that it was all true. Every last outrageous and unbelievable detail was true. And it scared the piss out of him.

"Uh, I'd like to go home now," Morry said hesitantly, his voice shaking, afraid that this man, his grandfather, who was probably not human, would peremptorily decide that he was a pain in the ass and dump him over the cliff after all.

The man, who appeared to be in his early thirties but obviously wasn't, relaxed and let go of the blue fire, then nodded. "I would be happy to take you home, Grandson." He reached out and barely touched Morry's arm, and then they were standing once more in the small living room next to the over-turned chair.

I stood next to my grandson, who seemed to have finally accepted the truth, and carefully looked into his eyes as he stared back at me, wide-eyed with wonder and fear.

"I realize that I don't look old enough to be Derek's father, let alone your grandfather, but I am, trust me. And I would very much like to be your friend—can we at least start with that?" I said quietly, hoping that he would agree.

Stark emotions played over Morry's features as he made the decision to allow someone into his life. "Okay, I'll try…Grandfather." He winced. "God, I can't call you that, it's too formal, and I, well... How about Grandpa? And in public I'll just call you M—"

"Michael. You have to call him Michael in public," Derek said, as he stood in the doorway looking disheveled; his shirt unbuttoned, his hair mussed and his feet bare.

Morry spun around and gazed at the man who, like it or not, was his father, and although it was apparent that he was still jealous of Derek, at least he didn't act as if he hated him anymore. My grandson gulped and cleared his throat as he faced the man who looked like a Greek god, albeit a rather dissolute one. "Whatever you say…Dad." He groaned. "Damn, I can't *do* this. Can't I just call you Derek?"

"Yeah, you might as well. You can't call me Dad in public anyway." Derek grinned and glanced over at me. I laughed out loud, remembering how many times he had almost called *me* "Dad" while we were grocery shopping at Town Market or enjoying a meal at Moab Brews.

Then, he looked solemnly into his son's face. "But I wouldn't mind if you'd try to call me Dad when we're at home."

Morry looked uncomfortable, but he took a few steps towards Derek and said haltingly, "I…okay…*Dad.*"

Derek's face lit up and he walked over to his son and hugged him hard.

"Okay, well, umph," Morry said as he tentatively patted him on the back. "I think that's enough, man. Uh, Dad, I can't breathe, dude! Jesus, let go, will ya?"

"Sorry." Derek looked embarrassed and immediately dropped his arms and stepped back. "It's just that I have all these paternal feelin's for you that I don't know what to do with."

"Well, *I* sure as hell don't know what to do with them! Maybe we should just take it slow," Morry suggested, glancing at me, gray eyes wide with an unmistakable deer-caught-in-the-headlights look.

"Good idea," I said, coming forward and interrupting their father and son drama. "It's quite late, so let's call it a night, shall we? But we all need to gather tomorrow at my house, for brunch, say eleven o'clock? Derek, take the day off even if you have to enchant your supervisor again. I'll discuss this with Em when I get home, and I'll contact the knights as well. We have to make a plan before your sister escapes from Hell and decides to…activate… her secret weapon." And with that pronouncement, I dematerialized and went home.

As Merlin disappeared from the room, Morry took a deep breath and let it out slowly. He and Derek were still standing, facing each other, and the silence was becoming increasingly awkward. He had so many questions, and yet he feared the answers. So he just said the first thing that came to mind.

"Man, is he always so bossy?"

Derek grinned. "Usually. He's the most powerful sorcerer ever born and God's emissary on Earth, so he has a right to be, I guess. He's my dad, and I love and admire him, so I always try to do what he says."

Morry started to speak, but he was afraid his voice would break and he would sound like he did when he was a boy and his voice was changing. He swallowed hard and just stood there, staring mutely at his father.

Derek gazed back at his son with an understanding smile. "Pretty overwhelmin', isn't it? That he's…who he is, I mean. Last year, on the Fourth of July, he decided that fifteen hundred years was long enough to be alone, and he revealed himself to me, in a pretty spectacular way. I was hurt that he'd lied to me for months; that he'd led me to believe he was only a simple Welsh herbalist who'd been my friend since he'd arrived in Moab. But ya know what? I got over it."

Morry nodded to acknowledge he was listening, then walked over to chair, hefted it upright and straightened the worn-out cushions. "What did he do to convince you he was, uh, the real thing?"

"Come outside and I'll show ya." Derek turned and walked out of the living room towards the kitchen, apparently intending to go out the back door. Morry figured that Sarah had given him a quick tour earlier, or Derek had been in this house sometime in the past.

He followed, wondering if he should tell Sarah, then decided that this moment was between him and his newly discovered parent. She would have the rest of her life to witness what Derek could do. He felt hollow inside as he acknowledged that he had indeed lost the girl he loved—to his twenty-nine-year-old father. He sighed and pushed through the door into the back yard, then turned to close it quietly behind him.

The night was dark, and the vegetation was fairly thick around the perimeter of the small enclosed space. Crickets and other insects made their distinctive summer noises, and the air was warm and fragrant. He could hear the music from the club a block away, but it was sufficiently muted so it was not intrusive; in fact, it seemed to provide an interesting but incongruous background to the ancient powers his father was about to unleash. He could barely see the outline of Derek's body, but he heard him say quietly, "Just watch…"

Morry heard whispered words in Latin and saw a blue glow surround the man as he slowly raised his arms, perhaps in supplication to the god of the heavens. When his arms were fully outstretched, blue fire erupted from his fingertips and Derek slowly rose into the air until he was twenty feet above the ground. He tilted his chin and closed his eyes, a look of ecstasy appearing on his face. The iridescent flame soared up and arced over his head, lighting up the trees and bushes with an eerie glow.

Morry stared in fascination at a spectacle that he had never expected to see in real life. In a fantasy movie full of computer-generated images, sure, but in his backyard in the middle of the night? Never. And as Derek finished his demonstration and settled back to the ground again, grinning as if he had just won the lottery, it finally dawned on Morry that he might be able to do something similar. He was the offspring of magic, not an orphan with an unknown heritage.

But the inevitable doubts and questions arose in his mind, and Morry was silent for a moment as he tried to put his feelings into words. "I still don't understand any of this. What you did was totally awesome, and I would like to be able to do that myself, but there are aspects of this whole situation that seem, well, *wrong* to me. Merlin said that my mother is in Hell, and then he said that it's his daughter that's in Hell. Does that mean that my mother is your *sister*? You actually had sex with your own sister, and got her *pregnant*? That's disgusting! That's freaking incest!"

"I was under an enchantment, and I had no idea who she was; Merlin didn't even know." Derek paced back and forth, feeling uncomfortable about discussing this with his son. "Adrestia deliberately seduced me when were in Camelot at the end of January and—"

"Wait a minute, you were in Camelot? I was conceived in *Camelot*?"

Derek stared at his son in disbelief. "Morry, Merlin showed you all this when he put you into that trance and went inside your inner bein'."

"You mean *everything* he showed me was real? I was born in *460*? I get it that you're my father and Merlin is my grandfather, which is obviously weird enough, but for some reason my mind didn't connect all the dots; I assumed it was like metaphors, or something. Shit, and that means that King Arthur really was—is—my great uncle, and, oh, *fuck*, Merlin is really a g-*god*?" Morry stammered.

"You got it, kid," Derek chuckled. "Hey, I'm goin' home now. Sarah's asleep in her bedroom and I don't want to wake her up. So, I'll see you both tomorrow at Merlin and Emily's house at eleven. Don't be late…Son." Derek winked and disappeared.

Morry watched his father dematerialize and then felt himself sag, weary to the bone. Why couldn't he have found that his family was just your normal dysfunctional American family? Oh, no. *His* was a dysfunctional family with magical powers, who traveled in time, existed in legend, and would never freaking die. Great.

CHAPTER 49

May 12   Early Morning

I CRAWLED INTO BED beside my wife and fitted myself against her back, enjoying the feel of her soft skin and the fragrance of her freshly washed hair. In the summer, we sometimes slept in the nude, although with a young, inquisitive child in the house that wasn't always practical. During the short period of time while she was three years old, Lumina had teleported in her sleep several times, just as I had done as a child, and had ended up in bed with us. Fortunately, we were actually sleeping when it happened rather than making love.

Emily stirred and said sleepily, "I'm glad you're home. What time is it? Did you shower?"

"I'm glad, too; it's almost two in the morning; yes, I showered," I answered obediently, amused at how her mind worked. And pleased that she was rarely intimidated by my various personas—Michael Reese, master herbalist; Merlin, ancient sorcerer; Myrddin Emrys, even more ancient god of magic and healing; naked husband.

I could feel her in my mind, reading my plans for late morning and revising her own schedule automatically without complaint. My love for her swelled and I effortlessly merged my being with hers, reveling in the intense, ever-evolving connection that we had.

She gasped and sighed as together we experienced the pleasure of our souls dancing, and as one, we also joined our bodies, moving in concert with one another until the natural culmination of our movements became an explosion of light and joy.

We held each other as we drifted off to sleep, content and satiated.

I was in Camelot, at Arthur's side, as he reviewed maps and plans for battle maneuvers prior to the Battle at Camlann. We were excited and stimulated by the knowledge that we would finally be taking a stand against the Saxons, and against the rulers who had long opposed Arthur's plans to unite the kingdoms of Britain. We were both in the old Roman-style armour, hair bound back, Arthur's golden crown proclaiming his gods-given right to fight for all the land in his kingdom, and my silver circlet proudly worn to indicate my right to be at his side.

Guinevere promised to support her husband by organizing my physician's assistants into an efficient force to care for wounded warriors. Arthur grabbed Excalibur and I lifted up my own sword, and we mounted our horses and departed, leading Camelot's finest knights—Sir Lancelot, Sir Gawain, Sir Leon, Sir Percival and dozens of other warriors—into glorious battle...

As the dream progressed I grew more and more restless, sensing that something wasn't right, and when all of us returned to Camelot later that day, bloodied but victorious, I finally woke up, frowning. That scenario was entirely fictitious. I had been too late coming to Arthur's aid, and Arthur had been grievously wounded, then died on the way to Avalon. Sir Lancelot, Sir Gawain and many other brave men had died that day as well. We had finally been victorious over the enemy, mainly due to my increased magical efforts, but it had been at a terrible cost.

The knowledge of my failure once more washed over me and I sighed with deep regret. I forced myself to awaken fully, and I acknowledged that it had been only a dream; a realistic one, but a dream nevertheless. It was still dark, but there was a soft grayness showing around the edges of the drapes; dawn was approaching. I had been asleep less than four hours and I turned over, hoping to relax back into unconsciousness once more. As I settled myself into a comfortable position, I realized there was something caught in my hair. I reached up and felt cool metal and became instantly alert, all thoughts of returning to slumber having fled.

Emily awoke around eight o'clock, surfacing slowly from a pleasant dream of hiking in Hidden Valley with her husband, and reached out to touch him. Encountering only cool sheets, she sat up and noticed him sitting in her rocking chair staring at something he was holding in his hands. He was naked, and she smiled as she admired his muscular arms and legs and trim torso. His shoulders were broad, and he was well-proportioned, but slender. A modest amount of silky dark hair on his chest narrowed on down towards his groin. His ebony hair somehow seemed longer than it had been yesterday, shaggy and hanging in his face, and she wanted to stroke it back as she used to before she had bought him that beaded headband. She wondered what had become of it.

"Merlin, honey, what are you doing? What is that?"

He looked up at her and smiled, his green eyes more cat-like than ever. It wouldn't surprise her if one of these days he spontaneously shifted into the form of a black panther. An accomplished shapeshifter, he rarely changed form as if he could not stand to be reminded of his death the previous summer, when he and Nimue had shifted into avian form and he had killed her. Em shook off the grisly memory and returned his smile.

"I have been asking the one God the same thing, or I should say, I have been asking how it came to be here, since I am well aware of what it is." And he put the silver circlet onto his head. As if it had a life of its own, it settled snugly and comfortably against his forehead, and the band, which had to be almost an inch wide, kept the hair from falling into his eyes. It was a crown of sorts, an indicator of his exalted position as the king's sorcerer, physician and trusted advisor. It was very much like the one he would occasionally conjure along with his robes, to remind them all how he had been attired in Camelot. The difference being, this silver band had a patina of great age and looked worn and scratched from decades of use.

She was speechless as she sensed her husband's thoughts, learning about his dream and the consequent appearance of an object that had been lost long ago.

He nodded. "Yes, it's the same one Arthur had bestowed upon me when he ascended to the throne; the exact same circlet I was wearing in my dream. Apparently, my god powers were manifesting in my sleep, and somehow I brought it back from its final resting place amid the ruins of ancient Camelot. I had left it in the palace when I sought my solitude in the Crystal Cave many centuries ago. And now I wear the symbol of my allegiance once more. A sign, perhaps, of times to come?" He gestured towards the silver band resting high on his forehead. He looked regal yet very pagan sitting in her rocking chair, his bare skin glowing, with the circlet confining his unruly dark hair and his slanted eyes half-closed in contemplation.

Emily felt her reality shift as his words sounded prophetically in her ears and within her very soul. He was actually going to do it. He was going to reveal to the world that magic was real, that the gods were real—that King Arthur was real. And the god of magic and healing would walk among the human population of this planet who so badly needed someone to look up to, and give it not one but two heroes.

"Soon, Em, soon. It will happen when it's destined to occur and not before," he said softly, in his rich baritone voice. "Come, let's shower quickly and get Lumina up. We have a lot to do before our guests arrive."

"Inviting everyone over for meetings that include a meal has become a habit lately. Perhaps next time we can have an afternoon or evening meeting with drinks only?"

"You're right Em, as usual. And since our next meeting will probably be a council of war, food could be a distraction from the business at hand. I have some difficult decisions to make in the near future," Merlin stated ominously.

CHAPTER 50

May 12

EMILY HAD JUST RETURNED from a quick trip to the grocery store with several bags of provisions when Derek teleported directly into the kitchen. I felt his need to speak with me, but knew better than to interrupt when Emily was in the midst of meal preparations. She enlisted Derek's help in putting away what she didn't need at the moment, and had him plug in the electric frying pan and start heating the griddle. As she fried the sausage and assembled the ingredients for French toast, Derek got the coffee going and then turned to me, a frown creasing his normally smooth brow.

"I need to talk to you about somethin' that happened last night at Sarah's. Uh, no, scratch that, just look into my mind."

I nodded and entered his thoughts easily, immediately sensing what he was concerned about—the re-emergence of the spell that had been placed upon him while we were in Camelot. Apparently, it had existed in a dormant state until he and Sarah had inadvertently reactivated it again the previous night. I immediately allowed my god powers to surge into my son's being in such a narrow focus that they became essentially a scalpel, and I excised the dark magic from him. I considered destroying it, but decided to take it into my own being, isolating it behind a barrier of magical energy so dense that it would stay there until I chose to examine it further. I knew that I would be able to discern the spell's origin, and that such knowledge could come in handy soon enough.

Derek had gasped as I easily overpowered the darkness in his being, sighing in obvious relief as I removed the sinister spell. "Oh, God, that's much better. Thanks, Dad. I never thought I'd object to havin' an erection, but..."

"You're welcome." I gripped his shoulder affectionately and smiled briefly. "The fact that it was totally out of your control is what you objected to, I think. Now, excuse me for a few minutes while I take care of my recalcitrant daughter," I said as I realized that she was playing in the living room, still in her pajamas.

I deliberately relegated Derek's enchantment to the back of my mind as I hustled Lumina into her bedroom and attempted to get her dressed. I finally had to give up, as she adamantly refused to let me to help her. As I stepped back out into the hall and shut the door, I wondered if her insistence on being independent was caused by her growing awareness of her inner goddess, and I was more curious than ever to know just who she really was. It was frustrating to have vast amounts of power at my disposal, and the ability to see into the future if I wished, and yet I was blocked when it came to my own child.

Hearing only silence coming from her room, where there should have been the sounds of drawers opening and closing and clothes rustling, I raised my voice. "Lumina, hurry up, sweetling, our guests will be here soon."

"Ok*ay,* Daddy, I'm *coming*!" She yelled through the door. I sensed a temper tantrum coming on and hoped that she would control herself.

I grinned. Gods, what a handful she was already! And totally fearless—it was apparent that she didn't care a whit that I was the god of magic.

Just then, as I was hoping to take a few minutes to ponder the origin of the dark enchantment, I sensed an altercation outside and knew that my grandson was the instigator. I shook my head and sighed. He was a handful as well, except that Morry was much too old for such childish behavior, and the unpredictable nature of the black magic within him made it imperative that I keep him under control.

I strode purposefully down the hall and into the living room just as the front door burst open and Ryan Jones, alias Sir Lancelot, came rushing in, running his hand through his blond hair in agitation, his teeth clenched. Directly behind him was my grandson with an obstinate look on his face. Sarah glanced at me apologetically as she followed him into the house, turning to quietly close the door behind her.

When Ryan finally saw me through the red haze of his anger, he immediately got down on one knee and bowed his head, his thick locks falling forward around his ears. I realized how familiar his current appearance—blond, burly and rough-looking—had become, compared to the slender, dark-haired knight I remembered of old.

"At your service, Lord Merlin. I apologize for making a scene, but I don't understand why this troublemaker is attending our meeting this morning."

"You may rise, Sir Knight. Yes, he certainly is that, but Mordred is here today at my invitation, and you can be assured that he will behave himself." I glanced at the young man in question, who wasn't paying any attention to me at all. Well, we'd see about that. I returned my gaze to the former knight as he replied.

"I don't understand. Morgana's son Mordred is here, in this time?" Ryan looked confused.

"No, Arthur's nephew perished at Camlann, shortly after you did, and I am unaware if he has been reincarnated in this century. The young man here with us today, with the same name, is my grandson."

"Your *grandson*, my lord?" He looked profoundly shocked as his mind unwillingly processed my statement.

At that moment, Derek stalked determinedly into the room, ready to leap to Morry's defense, but I put a hand up to stop him. *Let me handle this, Son.* He nodded and immediately stepped back, but I could feel his desire to assume his parental role.

"He is *Adrestia's* son? How can that have happened?" Ryan exclaimed.

"Yes, he is Adrestia's son, and Derek's, and it happened in the usual way," I said wryly. Feeling a wave of negative emotion coming from Morry, I turned and witnessed him scowling fiercely at Ryan, clenching his fists and gritting his teeth. Rarely did I allow myself the luxury of losing my temper, but in this case, I made an exception.

Mordred, cease and desist immediately! My tone was as sharp as the edge of my dagger. *This man was once known as Sir Lancelot, one of King Arthur's Knights of the Round Table, and is now in service to me. No matter what ill-will lies between the two of you, you shall grant him the respect he deserves!*

Morry jerked as he heard my angry voice in his mind and swung towards me, his gray eyes wide with surprise. He then turned abruptly and gazed in awe at Ryan, who had gotten to his feet and was looking back at the younger man impassively. "Sir *Lancelot*?"

Ryan ignored him as he addressed me. "My lord, I am willing to come to some agreement with your…grandson…if he can discuss the issue with me later in a civil manner."

I raised an eyebrow in Morry's direction.

He kept his mouth shut, thank the gods, and merely nodded, looking slightly cowed.

Merlin, what the hell is going on in there? It's time to eat!

Hopefully nothing serious. We'll be right there, Em. "Alright, if we have that out of the way, perhaps we can enjoy our meal, which Emily has just put on the table. By the way, Ryan, where are Gary and Percival?"

"I'm sorry, my lord, I did notify them of your wishes, and they should have been here by now."

Impatiently, I reached out with my senses and found them easily. "They've just pulled up out in front." I opened the door with a glance just as the two men approached the first step.

"Come in gentleman; what kept you?" I asked in a deceptively mild voice.

"Lord Merlin, 'tis my fault entirely, and I beg your forgiveness," Percival said subserviently, practically groveling on the floor at my feet as he entered the house.

I noticed Morry watching the whole scene, especially the big knight's overly enthusiastic show of obeisance, in disbelief. He practically wrinkled up his nose in disgust.

"Arise, Sir Percival," I murmured. I recognized why these men needed to express their fealty, but Percival tended to carry the ritual to an unnecessary degree.

Gary bowed briefly, but respectfully. "I tried to get us here by eleven o'clock, my lord, but I had a hell of a time getting my friend out of bed." Known also as Sir Gawain, he had let his hair grow longer, until the wavy dark brown strands were the same length as they had been in Camelot, brushing his shoulders.

"I'll let it go this time, but we have yet another crisis to face and we cannot lose focus on our objective." I was feeling irritated, as the knights had originally been so prepared, yet recently they had succumbed to the distractions of modern life. If it weren't so frustrating it would be amusing, that the only one of them who had come here directly from the fifth century should have so fully embraced not only the bar scene, but the Internet. Sir Percival was quite addicted to the social media sites, particularly Facebook.

By this time, Emily had stalked into the living room and was standing behind me. She cleared her throat loudly. "If everyone would please sit and eat, we can discuss the situation in greater depth afterwards. I am happy to cook for all of you, but it's really annoying to have the food get cold while you debate policy." I had to give my wife a great deal of credit for keeping her temper under a tight rein. She was not always the most patient of women but had learned to do what needed to be done with very little complaining. She said she did it out of her love for me, and her devotion to my god self, but I know that she also cared deeply for those who served me.

All three knights and I apologized profusely for our lack of consideration, and I herded the entire group into the dining area where we took our accustomed places. I sat at the head of the table as was my habit, deliberately seating Morry on my right with Derek next to him, and with Emily seated on my left. Sarah sat next to Derek, and of course, Lumina, who had finally deigned to join us, sat next to Em. The knights took the chairs at the opposite end of the table. Morry seemed nervous sitting so close to me, but he was just going to have to get used to it.

We ate quickly and chatted politely, but once the table was cleared and coffee mugs refilled, I stood, patiently waiting until everyone was quiet. Emily glanced at me, inquiring silently if it would be appropriate to include Lumina in this discussion. I decided that she was much too young, although I suspected that the goddess within her was nearly as ancient as I was. I asked my wife to keep her occupied in her bedroom while I addressed everyone else. She nodded and hustled our daughter out of the room. I knew that she would hear everything that transpired through our bond.

Dad, obviously Mordred will be the main topic for discussion—do you really want him to hear what we have to say? Derek asked telepathically.

I assured him that his son needed to know the reality of the situation, however embarrassing or uncomfortable it would be for him to hear it; that unless the powerful magic within him was deactivated, he would die. Derek looked unhappy for a moment, but then nodded his head in reluctant agreement.

I slowly examined each face turned to me in rapt attention and expectation, and then began to speak. "My dear friends and family, I appreciate you joining me today, and I realize that those of you who are employed had to make arrangements to take time off—again. Thank you for accommodating me.

"We are facing a most disturbing threat. It seems that my daughter Adrestia, who has been incarcerated in Hell for some time now, had in the distant past put a diabolical plan in motion; a plan so hideously evil that I can hardly bear to tell of it, but tell the tale I must. When Derek and I were unexpectedly transported to the fifth century several months ago, he became the victim of a powerful spell; so powerful that even I was not sure of its existence. I had my suspicions, but at the time was not able to confirm it.

"The enchantment caused him to be seduced by a young woman, whom we realized too late was his half sister. Recently, we discovered that their incestuous union had resulted in a pregnancy. It seems that my grandson Mordred, Derek's son with his sister Adrestia, was born in the past and brought as an infant to the late twentieth century by his great-grandfather Beli, the god of death." I looked intently at every face and saw shock, then understanding and finally compassion in quick succession. Although I sensed that Morry was somewhat diverted to hear that he was descended from the god of death, he was obviously mortified to be the central topic of the discussion. I could hear Derek offering support as he threw an arm around his son's shoulders, and I was proud of him for assuming the mantle of fatherhood, despite the very real possibility that Morry would reject him again.

"The good news is that I was able to remove the remnants of the original spell from Derek, literally minutes ago, and I have contained it within my own being, in hopes that I can discover exactly who created it, and what the ultimate purpose is.

"The bad news is that, having explored the depths of Mordred's being, I have discovered the true purpose of his existence. His very essence, his DNA, has been infected with black magic so strong that even I may not be able to neutralize it. That powerful evil has grown in him since he was in the womb. He is a living, breathing bomb that could be activated at any time.

"I am…truly *ashamed* to call Adrestia my daughter, as I realize how completely this evil has influenced her, for she has obviously planned to sacrifice her own son to destroy me and the ones I hold dear." I paused to take a deep breath, willing my sadness and horror to abate.

"My lord, Sir Percival, Sir Gawain, and I offer our humble services to you, and to your family, in whatever way we can prove useful," Ryan offered. He had acted as the co-leader of the knights, along with Sir Leon, while in Camelot, and had willingly assumed a leadership role in the present time as well.

"Thank you, Sir Lancelot, I accept your offer of service on behalf of my family," I said, and then glanced at my grandson compassionately. "Mordred, I understand that hearing this information revealed to everyone has made you very uncomfortable, and I apologize for putting you in such a position. But, I want you to truly understand the danger you are in, and conversely, the danger that your very existence presents to the rest of us."

"Well, I *don't*!" Morry cried. "I don't understand why my own mother hates me, and all of you, so much that she is willing to kill *me* to destroy *you*." After twenty-odd years of aching for his mother, only to have it confirmed that he meant nothing to her, he was devastated.

"That is truly the crux of the issue, is it not? It all began with Nimue's hatred of me, and despite her death last summer, her cruel legacy has continued through our daughter and escalated.

"Evil has no conscience, no loyalty and no compassion. And evil is willing to use the innocent to exact revenge. Mordred, your mother does not hate you—she doesn't even know you, she is indifferent to you. I am sorry to say this, but you are merely a means to an end for her, a way to destroy me. Obviously, I am reluctant to condemn my own daughter, but I cannot forgive her for what she has done, any more than I could condone the evil acts that her mother had perpetrated. Therefore, it is my duty to remove such evil from this world, even if I have to go back to the Hell realm and somehow bring Adrestia to justice; even if I must destroy her myself." As I voiced my decision, I felt such a pain in my heart that I almost couldn't bear it, but I thrust it aside impatiently. There must be no quarter given on this, no matter whose daughter she was.

Abruptly, I realized that I would have to return to the god realm, for I suspected that Beli still had considerable influence over Adrestia. God had assured me that he would take action against Beli for his part in the recent altercations we'd experienced; however, it appeared as if nothing has been done. Despite the fact that my visit had been amazing, I had no desire to repeat such a journey so soon. If Lumina had to assist me in returning to the human realm once more, which seemed to be a foregone conclusion, she would surely age further as a consequence. Perhaps I could merely communicate mentally as I had done in the past, and not actually have to leave my body.

I was pulled from my reverie and my thoughts of possibly returning to the god realm were temporarily deflected, as everyone began discussing possible courses of action for handling this new threat.

Morry was so embarrassed that he could hardly keep from running away, as he had at that damned dinner party. He was practically hyperventilating, his face felt flushed, and he could not stop himself from fidgeting. When Derek put his arm across his shoulders and murmured encouragement, it was as if an electric current arced through his body and he practically jumped out of his skin. His emotions were perilously close to the surface and he had to bury them deep inside himself before he made things worse by crying like a baby.

He had always used anger to cover up his sensitive nature, and therefore was tempted to brusquely shrug off Derek's arm, but it actually felt kind of good to have someone comfort him. Not just any someone, but his dad. He wasn't sure he'd ever get used to his dad looking like his older brother, but at least he finally had a dad.

Morry, we'll get through this, together, I promise. He heard Derek's voice in his mind and he turned to look him in the eye, desperate to make some kind of connection. Therefore, he was disappointed and hurt when his father wouldn't meet his gaze. He hunched his shoulders defensively and started to turn away from him, but Derek sensed his distress, clamping his fingers down on his shoulder and preventing him from doing so.

You don't understand, Morry heard in his mind. *If we look directly into each other's eyes for too long, we'll initiate what Merlin calls the Seein', and this isn't the time or the place for it. I'm not as good at it as he is, and I don't want to screw it up. We'll do it soon, okay?* Derek looked apologetic as he tried to explain something that sounded rather like mystical bullshit.

Morry was somewhat mollified as he realized that the guy wasn't deliberately putting him off, so he nodded and turned his attention back to Merlin. He still fought the idea that this man was the immortal sorcerer of legend, and that he was related to him, but if he was brutally honest with himself, it felt right. As he saw how Merlin interacted with these men who were supposedly the reincarnated souls of King Arthur's knights, and he witnessed the mutual respect, even love that they had for each other, it impressed the hell out of him, but seemed too good to be true. He glanced at Sarah, who was gazing worshipfully at the man who was his grandfather, and thought, *Maybe this isn't really happening—maybe I'm dreaming.* He almost *hoped* that it was a dream.

Nope, it's real, Derek's voice again sounded clearly in his mind.

He flinched. He kept forgetting that his thoughts were no longer private.

As he was contemplating the recent, unbelievable changes in his life, Merlin's last words finally registered. He shivered involuntarily as he realized what the man had said; that he would have to go to the Hell realm and bring Adrestia back. How the fuck was he going to do that?

Apparently, Merlin had heard his silent epithet, for the sorcerer directed his intimidating gaze towards Morry, who immediately wished that he could sink through the floor. And he realized that he'd been focusing so completely on his own thoughts that he'd lost track of the conversation. He swallowed hard and waited for Merlin to admonish him for his inattention.

Relax, I'm not going to scold you; you're not a child. A moment later, Merlin turned his attention away from Morry to address a comment made by Gary Gardner—Sir Gawain—and he felt shaky with relief. God, he was really afraid of this guy; Merlin absolutely reeked of power. He had never been into the woo-woo stuff, but the aura around his grandfather was so bright that even *he* could see it. He decided to pay attention.

I noticed that Emily had rejoined us, and paused to inquire silently if everything was all right.

She looked into my eyes and smiled slightly. *Lumina is taking a nap. I decided to use a little Fae magic on her after she threw a temper tantrum about being taken to her room "like a baby." I think you're going to have to have a conversation with her inner goddess.*

I nodded. *I suspected that I would have to do that fairly soon. She is gaining strength much faster than I could have imagined.*

I turned back to gaze at the upturned faces waiting for me to continue, and suddenly reeled as I felt the telltale frisson of fear and danger that normally presaged a major vision; in this case, it was clearly a warning of impending disaster. I glanced into the living room, and it was as if the entire front of the house was gone and I viewed the sheer wall of the Rim in minute detail, each boulder and sandstone crag, each ridge and corresponding crevice, as clear as crystal. My sight seemed to be magnified a thousand-fold, and the colors and textures of the rocks were so perfect that I was mesmerized. My heartbeat slowed and time seemed irrelevant as I examined each individual pebble, and each plant eking out its existence in the sere environment was a miracle.

Finally, a sense of urgency drew my eyes slowly upward, and I sought to discover the origin of the sensation of overwhelming doom that still pulsed through me. I could hear Derek's and Emily's thoughts, which had slowed and synched with mine, and the raised voices of the three knights, competing for my attention, inquired what was wrong. The three mortals were not telepathic, but due to our shared experiences the past summer in which I had familiarized myself with their unique brain wave signatures, I was able to hear and communicate with them mentally. They all knew me well and had noticed the focus of my attention, and began moving in slow motion into the other room, peering up at the looming wall of rock.

Then, time shifted back to its normal pace, and I saw the movement and subsequent dust clouds halfway up the cliff face. Several huge boulders were preparing to abandon their ancient resting places and hurtle down the slope, directly towards us. The odds were against this kind of occurrence happening right here, right now—only occasionally did a pillar of sandstone or a mammoth boulder come loose from the bed in which it had lain for thousands of years and tumble down to the base of the cliff.

Therefore, I was convinced that dark magic had caused the disturbance.

I grimaced as I acknowledged my options. If I did nothing to stop this event, and the boulders had enough momentum, they would demolish at least the two houses across the street—one of which was Derek's and the other my congenial neighbor Rod's—before destroying the intended target, this house, with all of us in it. If I showed myself and used my magic and/or my god powers in broad daylight, I could be observed, thus losing all possibility of remaining anonymous. Waiting until later, to take care of the problem under cover of darkness, was not an option.

By the time I had determined that I really had only one choice, the boulders had started their destructive way down the hill; the sound they made as deep as distant thunder. Everyone turned to me with questioning looks, their fear vying with the confidence they had in me.

As I calmly looked at each one in turn, I allowed my god self to take over, my sorcerer's magic melding smoothly back into the deep well of power from whence it had originated. It was as if a veil had been removed from my sight and it was perfectly obvious what I must do.

I stepped out of time into a world as static as a painting; each molecule paused as if by some cosmic viewer with a remote video control device in hand. I moved effortlessly, by my thoughts alone, to the base of the incline, directly into the path of the boulders, which of course were as motionless as the rest of the world. I could see in my mind's eye an intricate pattern of energy that would be sufficient to stop their forward momentum, in such a way that it would seem quite natural within the time and space parameters of the human realm. Well, of course, it was natural. As a god manifesting as pure energy, I was nature itself. I wove a complex pattern of light and directed it to occupy the space between the houses and the base of the cliff, and it expanded until it became a giant net. Yes, that would be sufficient. I willed myself back into the stream of time and allowed it to flow once more, unimpeded.

Casually, I watched from my living room as the boulders raced down the hill and were neatly captured by the net of energy I had created. An immense cloud of dust arose and temporarily obscured the huge shapes, now motionless. Disaster averted.

I felt inordinately pleased with my accomplishment. And then, something else occurred to me as all the facts coalesced in my mind: I knew that the only way to save my grandson was to allow him—and everyone else—to die. Released from my human body, I would return to the god realm, and with Llyr's help, I would turn back time and use the knowledge I had gained to save Morry.

Suddenly, as I emerged from my self-absorption, I realized that there was dead silence in the room where there had previously been chaos. I glanced around, noting that everyone was staring at me in shock. Even my wife and son, who were accustomed to the occasional usage of my god powers, were speechless. The knights were all down on their knees, and both Sarah and Morry were awestruck.

I frowned, puzzled by their reactions. "What's going on?"

"Uh, Dad, where's your body?" Derek asked.

Stunned, I realized that I was incorporeal, a pulsing sphere of white Light.

CHAPTER 51

May 12

I HAD KNOWN the time would come when I could no longer hide my true nature from the knights. Apparently, that time was now. I had feared what their reaction would be, even though I should have known that their loyalty would withstand the test.

I stood before them, once more back in my proper body and familiar appearance.

"I apologize for deceiving you for so long, though at first it was inadvertent, since I did not know myself who and what I really was. I am actually Myrddin Emrys, the god of magic and healing." I expected any reaction from my old friends besides the one I got: Acceptance.

"I *told* you that he was a god, did I not? Pay up, my friend." Percival turned to Gary, holding his hand out. Gary pulled out his wallet and extracted fifty dollars, slapping the currency into Percival's large palm.

I must have looked nonplussed, because Ryan grinned at me at said, "My lord, we have suspected it for some time now. We have always thought that there never has been, nor ever will be, another being like you. You are unique. You glow with an otherworldly light that few are privileged to witness. No other would contemplate the task of bringing a long-dead king, as great as he was, back to life. Nor, for that matter, would anyone else seek to protect the entire human race, which doesn't even realize that it needs protection."

"Well, I don't know what to say, gentlemen. I appreciate your loyalty and, of course, your continued cooperation to keep my secret. At some point in the future, I will reveal myself to everyone, but that time has not yet come to pass. Thank you for your friendship and for your acceptance. You honor me." I felt supremely humbled.

"No, my lord—you honor us by allowing us to serve you," Gary stated matter-of-factly.

As I looked around at my friends and family, seeing all the familiar faces shining with love and conviction, I felt that my life's purpose was validated.

"Well, it has certainly been an enlightening couple of hours, but I believe we're done here for now. I will keep in touch, as usual. Mordred, meet with Ryan, that is, Sir Lancelot, before you head home, and Derek, Sarah and Emily please stay close; I have something else I need to discuss with you," I said.

I made sure that Ryan had ushered my grandson outside, and the other knights had departed, before I gestured to the other three to join me in the living room. We made ourselves comfortable: Emily sitting with me on the couch, holding hands, and Derek in one of the overstuffed armchairs with Sarah sitting on a pillow at his feet, leaning against his legs.

"Emily, do you remember what I said to you about the future, just before the battle last summer?" I turned to look inquiringly into her wide hazel eyes.

"Yes, as a matter of fact, I do. You said that there are many possible futures, and the choices we make from moment to moment determine the paths leading to each one." She looked thoughtful, wrinkling her brow as she tried to recall my exact words. "You also said that '…the actions we take and the choices we make this night will lead us to the future we long for.' It really made an impression on me."

Derek glanced at me and frowned. "Wait a minute, I thought you said you could see the future now—the actual, immutable future."

"I thought I could, too, but ever since Morry entered our lives, my visions of the future keep changing. Even when I stepped out of time to stop those boulders a few minutes ago, I was unable to see the future or the past; all I saw was the present. What Emily just said is still true: Our choices, our actions, that we make right now, especially regarding Morry, will shape the future. When we first realized who he was, and what Adrestia and Beli had done, possibly following a plan Nimue came up with long ago, I thought that I might have to go back in time to Camelot and block the enchantment, or at least, prevent you from having sex with Adrestia. But then, your son, my grandson, wouldn't exist, and I find that to be unacceptable; he is a part of our family now. It would be like premeditated murder. No, that cannot happen. But the only other thing I can think of is equally difficult to imagine."

"Provoke Adrestia into triggerin' the black magic, and allow the destruction to happen? Even if we all die?" Derek looked horrified but resolute as he read my thoughts and whispered the words. "Ah, I see. And then—"

Emily stared into my eyes, her face pale and drawn, and continued, "—and then the god of magic and healing, released from his human form, discovers how to remove the black magic from Morry's body, and turns back time to just before the explosion and, and, uh, fixes what's wrong."

I smiled and nodded. "Something like that."

"I don't understand. Why not just remove the black magic before she triggers the 'bomb,' so to speak?" Sarah asked, bewildered at what she saw as flawed logic.

"Because I cannot remove it until I learn the process by which she enchanted him to begin with. I must perceive the way the magic is released from his cells as he dies, and I can only do that in spirit form. I will try to goad Adrestia into triggering the explosion, but if she fails to take the bait, I will trigger it myself."

There was complete silence in the room as we all tried to comprehend such a drastic action.

As if acknowledging the worst-case scenario had freed his imagination, Derek, with a look of sudden comprehension, said slowly, "You know, I just thought of somethin'—what if

Nimue didn't really die last year? Obviously, her body did, but maybe her essence survived. She'd pulled some pretty amazin' stunts in the past. I mean, *you* didn't die—your soul returned to the god realm, and then you were able to bring your body back to life."

I grimaced. "Well, there were extenuating circumstances that allowed me to resurrect my body, so it's not exactly the same thing, but I understand where you're going with this. In other words, what if her essence left her body as she died in her altered form, and by prearrangement, she took up residence in someone else's body?"

He nodded. "Seems logical. I hate to say it, but I think my sister's body is now housin' Nimue's essence. I keep wantin' to say soul, but she's so damned evil that I don't see how she can actually have one."

Emily spoke up. "It would explain why Adrestia ended up sequestered in Hell—Nimue wanted to keep her out of harm's way so she'd have a convenient receptacle to use. I'll bet she—or maybe it was Beli—had come up with some kind of super-spell to automatically transfer her essence if her body should die."

"But what happened to Adrestia's consciousness when Nimue took over her body?" Derek looked distressed, and I sensed that he was remembering the sweet young woman whom we had met in Camelot, and with whom he had been intimate.

"She's probably gone, Derek," I said gently. I felt unutterably saddened at my daughter's fate, for the truth was that she had been influenced from birth; in one sense, her essence and individuality had already been consumed long before Nimue's hypothetical takeover.

Derek patiently waited until I came out of my reverie, and then said, "I think we should shelve this discussion until you've had a chance to examine that enchantment you have stored inside you. I'd be willin' to bet that there'll be a telltale energy signature that will help us decide what to do next."

"I think you're right," I said as I got up off the couch and stretched. "We're done for now."

Em and Sarah headed into the kitchen, discussing a new recipe they wanted to try using some of the sweet herbs that we had ordered a few days ago. I wondered how they could so blithely go from the disturbing topic we had just covered to something so mundane, but decided it was healthier than dwelling on the morbid truth facing us.

Derek was getting impatient—I could sense that his mind was on his son, and I knew that he wanted to bond with Morry as soon as possible. So it was no surprise to me when he abruptly asked me to show him how to block Morry from the memories and experiences that he *didn't* want him to See. He didn't particularly want to subject his son to the gruesome details of his death, nor did he want him to be privy to his experiences with Sarah. I agreed with him on both counts, and proceeded to instruct him on the finer points of Seeing, including a simple technique in which he could actually guide Morry's journey while protecting his own secrets.

As he and Sir Lancelot stepped outside together, Morry wasn't sure how he would escape unscathed from the encounter to come. He and the ex-knight were about the same height, but Ryan, despite having a good twelve to fifteen years on him, was in top shape. He undoubtedly lifted weights and watched his diet, and Morry had let himself go in the past few years. Overweight and under-muscled, he was painfully aware of his shortcomings. He hoped that this little tete-a-tete wouldn't come to actual physical conflict, because he had no doubt as to who would emerge the winner.

He needn't have worried. Ryan gazed briefly into his eyes then glanced away and said, "Look, let's just forget that our disagreement at the bar ever happened, okay? I've sworn my allegiance to Lord Merlin and his family, and now that apparently applies to you as well. But, I'll be straight with you—I won't put up with your bullshit, Mordred, even if you are the grandson of a god. I've been a knight, a warrior or a soldier in every one of my incarnations, and I can take you down without breaking a sweat, understand?"

Morry decided to accept the truce offered to him, and nodded humbly. "Yes, I understand. Thank you. Uh, by the way, you don't have to look away from me. I can't access my, uh, my magic, so…" He shrugged self-deprecatingly.

"Sorry, force of habit. I never look Merlin or Derek in the eyes for very long; they're powerful sorcerers and it's not a good idea. When Merlin showed me that I was really Lancelot, he did Look inside me, and I experienced his inner self as well. I'm not sure that he intended to share all of his secrets with me, but it was amazing, and very intense—not something to initiate lightly. I would imagine that Derek will be doing the same thing for you soon, if he hasn't already."

"No, not yet, he says he isn't that good at it and wants Merlin to help him so he gets it right."

"Are you guys talkin' about me?" Derek asked as he walked out the front door, nonchalantly flicking his hand to close it behind him.

Morry had been so focused on Ryan that his father's sudden appearance startled the hell out of him, and he practically jumped out of his skin.

Ryan cleared his throat. "Ah, Morry, I think you and I have come to an understanding, so I'm going to head home." Without waiting to hear a reply, he turned to Derek, ducked his head in a quick bow and murmured, "My lord." Then, he spun on his heel and walked swiftly out to his vehicle and drove away.

"Huh, that's strange. He's never called me that before," Derek said, confused, as he gazed down the street.

"I think he's respectful of your abilities. He said that since both you and Merlin were powerful sorcerers, he knew better than to look into your eyes. He seems kind of leery of you both. He even looked away from *me*, thinking I might be able to do what you do. I told him I couldn't access my magic, so he didn't have to worry about that." Morry's voice was filled with a combination of fear and yearning.

"I know it's hard to believe, especially since you can't actually feel the power that's inside you, but it's true." *Dad, we've gotta find a way to save him, and help him with his powers.*

I know, Derek, I'm working on it.

Morry gazed curiously at the face in front of him as Derek's eyes went unfocused for a moment. He guessed that he was communicating telepathically with Merlin.

"Are you ready?" Derek said suddenly, looking straight into his son's gray eyes. Being the same height, they could look directly at each other, and Morry realized that they were standing so close that he could practically feel his father's heart beating. He swallowed his nervousness and nodded. If this was truly going to be his life, he wanted to be able to understand, and maybe even come to...love...his new family. And for that to happen, he desperately needed to have that inner experience with his father. He'd already experienced a small part of his grandfather's reality, and even though it was overwhelming, he was glad that it had happened.

"Okay," he said with a grimace, "I'm ready." Morry stiffened, bracing himself for the imagined ordeal.

Derek grinned, revealing straight white teeth that contrasted startlingly with his tanned features. "Jesus, you look like you're about to face a firin' squad—just relax!" He held out his hands and said reassuringly, "Come on, kid, I won't bite."

Morry looked away for a moment and took a deep, quavering breath, letting it out slowly, then reached out and tightly clasped those somewhat larger, rougher hands.

He looked into Derek's eyes and felt him take control, initiating the Seeing. The sensation of sinking into a dark, infinite pool caused a moment's dread, but immediately thereafter, he experienced a warm, welcoming sensation. Morry sighed as he finally relaxed, letting go of his fear and inhibitions. This was where he belonged.

There was no sense of time passing as the darkness gradually dissolved into coherent scenes, emotions and dialog, beginning with Derek and Merlin's journey to Camelot and the experiences that they'd had there. Morry saw his mother's face for the first time as the three faced off against a phalanx of fire-breathing dragons in the streets of Old Town, and he was amazed at her beauty—and wondered how such an innocent face could have hidden such an evil core.

He knew that all of the legends were true as he witnessed his father kneeling before Arthur Pendragon, King of Camelot. The two men could have passed as brothers; it was obvious that Derek had inherited many physical traits from his mother's side of the family. And Morry was shocked when he observed that King Arthur was no older than he was.

Derek guided him through many scenes, including riding the breezes in the tops of the trees outside of Camelot, and the final departure from the castle to return home, thanks to Merlin using his god powers to travel through time. And then he was given a great gift: he was allowed to See Merlin through Derek's eyes; to experience the love, awe and devotion he felt for the god who was his father.

Then, Derek showed him his love for Sarah, and the understanding that destiny had brought them together. Morry finally recognized that he had a different role to play in Sarah's life than that of a lover; he was now and would always be, her friend, and eventually, her stepson.

And best of all, Derek revealed to him the budding parental protectiveness that was in his heart, convincing Morry beyond a shadow of a doubt that his father wanted him.

He finally felt himself returning to normal consciousness, and his first thought was that he wasn't ready—he wanted to bask in the unfamiliar feeling of love and security. As he blinked at the brightness, he noticed the sheen of tears in the eyes of the man who stood in front of him.

"Dad?" Morry whispered, the yearning in his voice tugging at Derek's heart. His son blinked his dark-lashed gray eyes rapidly behind the thick lenses of his glasses, as he tried valiantly to hold back his own tears.

Derek was overwhelmed by his love for this stubborn, moody, disturbed young man. He let go of Morry's hands then, and drew him tightly into his embrace.

"Everythin's all right now; you're home."

CHAPTER 52

May 12

MORRY WALKED INTO the newspaper office around two o'clock in the afternoon and headed for his desk. He barely noticed as his coworkers looked up from their assignments, then back down at their desks, and then instantly did a classic double-take when he walked by.

"Well, nice of you to show up today, Morry," his supervisor, Jim Singleton, drawled, not at all impressed by the unusual glow of satisfaction emanating from his employee.

"Hey, I texted you around nine o'clock this morning, saying that I wouldn't be in 'til now—not my fault if you were too hung over to read it," Morry countered, taking advantage of the fact that he and Jim were friends to get in a good-natured dig. He was feeling too good to let anything bother him right now.

"Hmmph. At least I was here *on time*." Jim scowled as he grabbed his mouse and double-clicked to open an article he needed to check.

Morry ignored the snide comment; Jim was all bark and no bite. As he sat down gingerly in the beat-up office chair, he allowed himself to imagine what it would be like to come up with a spell to transform all of his ancient office furniture into new stuff. He grinned widely as he turned on his computer, and then glanced covertly around the room. It seemed that no one was paying the slightest attention to him, which was just as well, since he was feeling so happy that he might say something he shouldn't about his unique experience—God, was it only an hour ago? To think that the man he had hated with such a passion was actually his father, a sorcerer and a demigod.

He closed his eyes briefly as he experienced a desire stronger than he had ever felt before, to use his abilities, which lay dormant and dangerous within him. Now that he had been up close and personal with Derek's magic, he could sense the power in his body struggling against the binding of black magic.

"Whatcha doin', Mor?" A taunting feminine voice practically in his ear caused him to jump.

He opened his eyes only to discover a small, pert face right up against his own. He jerked backwards, the old chair creaking ominously.

"Patty, what the hell?" he asked, scowling furiously. The tiny woman with the dreads and the huge earrings was a continual pain in the ass. Her clothes were mismatched and wrinkled, which irritated him. She was persistent, nosy and obnoxious and clung like a fucking leech. He had done everything he could to discourage her, as he wasn't attracted to her in the slightest, but nothing worked.

Maybe the truth would. He stared deliberately into her eyes in a vain attempt to See into her being, and growled menacingly, "You'd better watch out, or I'll use my magic to put a spell on you and—"

The rough sound of someone clearing his throat behind Morry caused him to swing around in a panic.

"Mordred, I would speak with you for a moment. Please." Merlin spoke quietly, but with such force that Morry immediately leaped out of his chair to follow him outside, forcing Patty to scurry back to her own work space.

Belatedly, he remembered that he should have informed his coworkers that he would return shortly, so he yanked the door open and stuck his head through the resultant space. "I'll be right back," he yelled. He didn't notice the speculative look on Jim Singleton's face.

I blamed myself for my grandson's inability to keep our family secrets, well, *secret*. I had known that he had very little common sense, and yet I had not actually insisted that he keep the information to himself. I crossed my arms over my chest and assumed a stance that I felt sure would intimidate him and just stood there, keeping my eyes averted.

"Merlin—sorry, I mean Michael—I, I just, uh…" Morry looked abashed at being caught using very poor judgment.

I sighed. He was immature and stubborn and I wanted to shake him, but of course, I didn't act on it. Instead, I had an uncontrollable urge to take him back in time to Camelot, to show him where—and when—he was born. And I definitely didn't act on that urge either.

"Mordred, I want to help you, I really do, but *you* have to be willing to accept what I have to teach you," I said quietly, gazing directly into his eyes, easily holding back the Seeing. "I have always known about my…abilities, shall we say, and was aware that I had to be judicious in sharing the truth about myself. You have just found out who you really are and what your potential is, and you want to brag to your friends that you are important, and powerful, and come from a unique background; your heritage is something to be proud of. But you need to keep that knowledge to yourself right now. Soon, the world will know who—and what—we are, but it can't happen yet. Once we bring Arthur back, however…" I must have had a distracted look on my face and paused for a moment too long, because my grandson began to look over his shoulder at the door, and to shift his weight from one foot to the other restlessly.

"Alright, I'll let you get back to work. But I would like to invite you to The Moab Herbalist for a storytelling session tomorrow night. I have something rather special planned and everyone will be there. It will begin promptly at seven."

"Okay, I'll come if you really want me to, uh, Michael. See you later," he said hastily as he turned to reenter the newspaper office.

It was then that I felt eyes upon me, and rather than reveal that I knew it, I surreptitiously sent my senses out towards the person watching me. It was Morry's supervisor, who, I suddenly realized, was the same man who had known the Old English names of the herbs he had ordered in The Moab Herbalist. And I also discovered, delving a bit deeper into his thoughts, something much more shocking: He had observed our ordeal out at Devil's Garden in March. He had been hiking and had witnessed the dragon's fiery breath engulfing Derek and Ken, and he had seen me flying. Oh, great gods.

Not bothering to hide my surprise and dismay, I turned and stared into the office through the plate glass window, and encountered the thoughtful gaze of this mortal who knew way too much about me and my family. He seemed to know that I sensed his interest. I noted that he was well-dressed in conservative yet stylish business casual attire—tailored shirt and lightweight slacks. Obviously, a meticulous and orderly mind was behind that curious gaze. I seriously considered erasing his memory of every last vestige of incriminating information, but, surprisingly, I sensed no ill-intent from the man. The immediate drawback to allowing him to keep his memories, was the fact that the man worked for a newspaper. Even though he apparently was an editor and not a reporter, he had the story of the millennium in his pocket, if he chose to reveal our existence. I made a decision that I might come to regret—I refrained from obliterating his memories. However, I would have to meet with him in the near future and determine what his motives were.

Grandson, keep still and try not to react to hearing me telepathically. You must be exceedingly careful around your supervisor, as I am sensing that he knows who I really am, and now that he knows you are somehow connected with me, he will try to gain information from you.

Morry had jerked when he heard my voice in his mind, and I could sense his struggle to keep from turning towards me. He pursed his lips and nodded imperceptibly.

Jim's mind raced as he considered the possibilities. My God, what a story this would make: OWNER OF LOCAL HERB SHOP REVEALED TO BE LEGENDARY SORCERER! But, as soon as he had expressed that thought, every fiber of his being fought against such betrayal. Damn it! He had had this unreasonable sense of honesty and fairness all of his life, and, quite frankly, it had inhibited his more ruthless tendencies to succeed in the high-powered world of news reporting. Case in point, his current dead-end job working for a small town newspaper in Utah, of all places. This had been the only job available to him when he had decided to move west the last time he was fired. And recently, ever since he had entered Michael Reese's shop for the first time, that sense had flared to an all-time high.

He didn't know how he knew the truth—he simply did. Ever since he'd ordered those herbs at The Moab Herbalist (he'd had a feeling that using the ancient names had been a red flag, but he was proud of having learned them so easily, as if he'd used Old English in some past life), the knowledge of Michael Reese's true identity had been foremost in his mind. Of course, he hadn't really believed it until the incident out at Devil's Garden, in which Michael (or should he say *Merlin*?) had swooped down and gathered up the hideously burned corpses of those two young men, then simply disappeared.

And of course, the clincher was that the man had sensed him a few minutes ago and had stared knowingly into his eyes right through the front window.

He pretended to be working as he kept one eye on Morry, who was obviously related in some way to the famous sorcerer if the shape of his eyes was any indication. Suddenly, he connected the dots and remembered the kid's real name. Jesus, was his coworker the same Mordred associated with King Arthur? It seemed utterly impossible, and yet, so was the existence of this group of people who could turn out to be immortal.

Jim, you are one lucky son of a bitch, he thought to himself with a self-satisfied smirk.

The rest of the afternoon seemed to drag on endlessly, at least in Morry's estimation. If Merlin was correct and Jim was aware of his identity, would he really use that information against him? He hated to say it, but the answer was probably yes. Jim might be his friend, but Morry knew what made the guy tick—when it came to the newspaper business, Jim was relentless. He wasn't currently a reporter, but had been one for almost a decade before coming to Moab, so he probably wouldn't hesitate to expose the whole family if it benefited him in some way.

God, he was actually starting to accept that these strange people were his family.

Morry closed his eyes for a minute and sighed. His life had become complicated overnight, and this kind of complication he really didn't need.

"Wake up, kid," a voice said from several feet above him. "It's time to grab a beer."

Startled, Morry opened his eyes and noticed his supervisor and supposed friend hovering over his desk. He peered through smudged lenses at the clock and realized that he had zoned out for a good twenty minutes. He whipped off his glasses and started cleaning the lenses on his shirt. Damn it, now he'd have to come in early in the morning to finish his assignment. He wished for the second time that afternoon that he had access to his magic—he could have that article ready in no time.

He put his eyeglasses back on and replied, "Yeah, okay, just let me shut everything down and clock out, and I'll be ready to go."

He wasn't sure he should spend any time with Jim, but it had been their habit ever since he started the job to go directly to the bar after work, suck down a few brews and maybe play a few games of pool. Besides, what the hell, he still liked the guy. He just wished that he could share his good fortune with his friend, but the consequences of doing so could be severe.

His computer having finally uttered its last gasp for the day and shut down, Morry pushed his chair back from the desk and stood up. "Alright, where do you want to go?"

"Same as always—Moody's," Jim said.

CHAPTER 53

May 12

WHAT WAS I GOING TO DO about my grandson? He was impetuous and undependable, and yet there was something so innocent about him that I found it difficult to reprimand him. His friendship with the man who had recognized me was worrisome on one level. It was clear to me that Jim Singleton was not who—or what—he appeared to be (and in that way he certainly fit right in with the rest of us!), but my subtle attempts to determine his identity had so far been futile. I suspected the one God wanted me to handle this situation a little differently.

After I had left the newspaper office, I'd headed back to The Moab Herbalist and helped Sarah stock shelves until it was time to close. Business was slow and we accomplished quite a bit. We worked in companionable silence for the most part, occasionally grinning at each other to acknowledge the connection that was forming between us. She was my newest apprentice and would soon be my daughter-in-law, and I couldn't ask for a more intelligent or lovely addition to the family. I was pleased. I just wished that everything else would go as smoothly.

Around five o'clock, I decided that it was time to go home. I asked her to prepare the deposit and lock up, knowing I was leaving everything in capable hands. I had already adjusted the wards to accept her personal magic, so I was free to leave for the day.

As I maneuvered my old black truck through the early evening traffic on Main Street, I continued my train of thought from earlier this afternoon. Perhaps Morry's friend would prove to be an ally, but in any case, because of the sensitive nature of the information he possessed, it was imperative that I meet with him. There was no doubt in my mind that he knew exactly who I was, so it was pointless to try and convince him otherwise, and I didn't feel comfortable with erasing his memories. There was something about him that seemed familiar, although that familiarity did not extend to his outward appearance. It would take Seeing inside his being to determine why that was so. I wondered whether another one of the Knights of the Round Table was going to appear just in time to get blown to hell with the rest of us. I snorted indelicately and sharply curbed that train of thought.

As I turned onto Doc Allen Drive, I could see that the house was almost bursting with energy and I easily sensed the turmoil within. I parked the truck in the driveway as usual and started up the walk.

Emily met me as I opened the front door and confirmed what I had already suspected. "Merlin, my mom is here! She's left my dad and needs to stay with us for a while, and…"

Her voice faded into the background as the vision took me. I was standing in a luxurious abode, witnessing a vicious argument between my in-laws, Rae and Jack Crandall, which had escalated to the point that he was about to become physically abusive. Rae had apparently had enough and began chanting in the Elven language, gesturing abruptly towards her husband, who promptly flew through the air, landing on his back across the room with the wind knocked out of him. Shortly thereafter, the police arrived, handcuffed my father-in-law, and took him away.

Suddenly, everything clicked into place in my mind.

I returned to normal consciousness and nodded to Emily. "Yes, of course, she must stay here. It's time."

Moody's was crowded for a work night and the two of them were lucky to have scored a table. They already had their beers and both men were looking forward to playing. Jim glanced calculatingly at Morry while he racked the balls for a standard eight ball game. His friend had been inordinately subdued since leaving the office, and Jim's curiosity was piqued.

"So, was that the guy from the herb shop who came to see you at work today?" he remarked casually, knowing damned well that it was, but he wanted to put the kid on the spot. Jim liked him, but wasn't above using Morry's gullibility to obtain the information he needed. He managed to quell the niggling sense of guilt trying to manifest in his gut. Every day of his life, a war raged between his conscience and his ambition, and he was sick of it. He waited to see Morry's reaction, which was a bit delayed due to his preoccupation.

The younger man had just taken a rather substantial swallow from his mug and proceeded to choke on it, spraying beer all over Jim.

"Hey, what the hell?" he exclaimed, as he flicked a particularly foamy drop of liquid from his left eyelid. Peering intently at Morry, he tried to gauge how much farther he could push him. "Got something to hide, my friend?"

Morry coughed a few times and then croaked, "No, not at all. Michael is my, uh, my…cousin."

"Are you sure about that? Come on, I thought you were an orphan." Jim's voice dripped with skepticism. He was so focused on getting the kid flustered that he didn't notice the rough-looking blonde guy until the man had stepped up beside Morry and clapped a protective hand on his shoulder.

"How're you doing, man? Need some backup?" The man asked in a jocular tone, underlying which was a not-so-subtle threat aimed at Morry's tormenter. Those blue eyes gazing at Jim were steely and cold, and he felt a chill run down his spine. He might not get out of this one without a few bruises.

"Whoa, I didn't mean any harm, we were just about to enjoy a friendly game of pool," Jim said hastily, surmising somehow that this man was connected with Merlin, maybe a bodyguard? It was obvious that Morry knew and trusted the guy, and by the undisguised look of relief on his face, welcomed the intervention.

Without warning, Jim's vision flickered and went dark. He gasped and staggered, then reached out to steady himself against the pool table. He felt strange—light-headed and disembodied. Instead of the familiar interior of Moody's—dim lighting, bar and accompanying stools along one side of the room and a low stage for the occasional band in the far corner—he saw a scene that he knew instinctively was in the distant past. A group of men stood in a torch-lit room, the rafters above them all but invisible in the shadows. They were speaking quietly to one another while strapping on armour that appeared to be made of stiffened leather, and arming themselves with swords and shields; in other words, preparing for battle. One man in particular stood out, as he was taller and more muscular than the rest, and his light-brown hair was short and straight. The warriors' features were indistinct, but he knew who they were: knights of Camelot. With that revelation, his senses failed him altogether, and he felt himself falling into an abyss, pitch-black and bottomless.

Suddenly, Jim inhaled sharply and blinked, his senses returning to normal. He found himself on the filthy tavern floor looking up at a number of curious male faces, several of which looked as if their owners were ready to do battle with *him*. He struggled to sit and then stand up, and a large hand reached out to assist him. He clasped the proffered appendage gratefully and lurched to his feet.

As he turned to thank the man, he happened to make eye contact with him and gasped in sheer terror—and recognition. It was the same tall man that he had seen in his vision.

"Mayhap you require a lesson in manners, sir," Percival said calmly.

Morry spoke up hastily in Jim's defense. "It's okay, I work with him. I'm sure he'll mellow out, won't you, Jim?" He scowled at his friend, who silently nodded back, a strained look on his face.

"I really appreciate the backup, but I think everything will be alright now," Morry said to Ryan and Percival. He'd seen the fear and uncertainty on Jim's face as it occurred to him that Morry had several able champions. He grinned to himself as he pictured the knights surrounding the newspaperman and exuding a great deal of menace. He was glad that he and Ryan had resolved their differences, because being on the receiving end of Ryan's glare like Jim was now, was not his idea of a good time.

A ripple of magical power washed over his senses and he turned around, seeing both his father and his grandfather coming towards him through the crowd that had gathered around the fallen wordsmith. They weren't dressed any differently than normal, in shorts and T-shirts, but both of them radiated calmness, self-confidence and authority, drawing the gaze of everyone they passed. The knights automatically nodded respectfully at the two sorcerers and stepped back into the crowd.

As if by magic, the crowd dispersed, returning blithely to their own pursuits, and Morry recognized that it was magic indeed—Merlin's, as a matter of fact. He was pleased that he was actually able to sense a greater depth to the powerful energy exuded by his famous kinsman—perhaps the black magic holding him in thrall was slipping. Then, he abruptly realized that such an occurrence could be extremely detrimental to his health, and he shuddered.

"I'm glad you're here," he said quietly, making eye contact with each man briefly.

Both Merlin and Derek acknowledged his sincerity with a quick nod and a knowing look before they focused their attention on Jim Singleton.

"You do know why we have come, do you not?" Merlin asked, his accent more pronounced than usual, and his choice of verbiage revealing the fact that his first language was not modern English.

As Morry moved to stand between Derek and Merlin, openly proclaiming his allegiance with them, he saw Jim's eyes widen as he observed an undeniable physical resemblance and connection between the three men. Jim nodded in response to Merlin's query, the constriction in his throat rendering him unable to speak.

Then, Morry felt an overwhelming sensation of power and movement, and he instinctively knew that all of them were being teleported back to Merlin's place. He wondered briefly if anyone had witnessed their disappearance from the tavern, then decided that if Merlin could accomplish such a feat, he could certainly conceal the fact from the patrons of Moody's at the same time.

I took a long breath as I released the massive amount of energy it had taken to transport all of us from the tavern to my living room, as well as to hide our disappearance from onlookers in the tavern.

I could hear the high-pitched sound of feminine voices emanating from the kitchen as Em and her mother fixed dinner, with Sarah assisting and Lumina occasionally raising her sweet child's voice to contribute to the conversation. There was a brief cessation of chatter as I communicated silently with my wife. Of course, she normally was in sync with my thoughts, but I knew that she had been focusing her attention on her mother. I gave her the option to avoid the scene in the living room, but knowing Emily, I figured that she would want to be in the midst of whatever actions would be taken in dealing with Morry's friend, Mr. Singleton.

CHAPTER 54

May 12

I STOOD SILENTLY GAZING at the man before me and knew I had to solve the mystery of his true identity before another minute passed. He was slender of frame and seemed almost feminine until one noted the obvious physical attributes of masculinity, including the faint shadow of evening beard stubble. He was not a tall man, perhaps five feet six inches in height, and he probably weighed around one hundred thirty pounds. He seemed to be in his mid-thirties, and his soft curly brown hair framed his animated features. He stared at me boldly, with a faint smile and a look of recognition that disturbed me to the point that I simply held him immobile by my will, initiated the Seeing, and entered his consciousness.

The sights and sounds of my home and family fell away as Jim's inner reality surrounded me, and I moved back in time through his past lives, feeling mildly annoyed that I did not recognize any of his previous personas. He had been reincarnated many more times than I had anticipated, and I noted that in most of his past lives he had been female, which was not unheard of, but highly unusual. As Jim experienced his soul's past, I felt his shock and disbelief give way to a feeling of delight, but I was too focused on my task to examine the man's emotions very closely.

Finally, the fabric of his past lives had unraveled to the original thread of his beginning, and I discovered the one life that I had least expected to encounter again.

Your Highness, I uttered silently and sketched a bow in acknowledgement of her status in the fifth century.

Jim's features morphed into a familiar feminine visage for a moment, as the soul of Guinevere peered out of those dark brown eyes. "Lord Merlin." My grandson was speechless. His pool-playing, beer-drinking coworker and friend had been the Queen of Camelot in a past life.

"'Tis no great wonder that I felt so guilty whenever I contemplated revealing Merlin's secret," Jim/Guinevere said in a gentle feminine voice. "He was my best friend for a long time after Arthur died; I would have done anything in the world for him."

He/She paused and ran a hand down his/her flat masculine chest, then furtively touching the slight bulge in his/her pants. "I find it most strange to have a man's body whilst remembering a woman's life." He took a deep breath and appeared to make a decision, and then he resumed his normal male voice and current personality.

He grinned wryly. "Well, knowing that I was a woman in so many past lives resolves some of the questions I've had about my sexuality. I've been experiencing flashes of feeling feminine and wondered if I was gay." He turned to Morry, who had been hovering uncertainly. "No, I'm not attracted to you, buddy, so just back off, okay?"

"What? You, you *bastard*!" Morry exclaimed, and then he tilted his head and narrowed his eyes as he looked intently at his friend. "Huh, I think you might be my great-aunt." He glanced at me.

I affirmed his observation with a brief nod.

"You're *Arthur's* great-nephew? How the hell did that happen? But in any case, I'm nobody's *aunt*, great or otherwise, at the moment." Jim looked questioningly at Morry, his eyes flickering in my direction then back to his friend. "Are you Merlin's son?"

"I'm actually his grandson. Derek is my father; *he's* Merlin's son," Morry clarified.

Jim turned his attention to Derek, who had been silent up to this point, staying in the background while the unusual circumstances played out. "So, you're a park ranger out at Arches, right? And you're the one who was burned to death by the dragon out at Landscape Arch a few months ago."

As Derek flinched and nodded, Jim realized that three women and a little girl had joined them, and he heard the tall redheaded woman gasp in shock. He glanced towards her, noticing that she and the other tall woman who must be Merlin's wife shared many physical traits; she was probably her mother.

"I'm sorry, ma'am, I didn't mean to distress you, or the little girl; I wasn't thinking. I just figured that everyone associated with Merlin knew—oh crap, I mean, *Michael*—." Jim covered his eyes with his hand and groaned. "Sorry!"

I chuckled. "It's alright. My daughter, Lumina, doesn't scare easily, and my mother-in-law, Rae, is quite aware of my true identity and has a few secrets of her own. And I believe you know Sarah, Derek's fiancée."

"Yes, I know Sarah. Nice to meet you, Rae."

Rae smiled slightly. "It's nice to meet you as well, Jim. I just didn't know that Derek had died recently, and in such a horrendous way." She looked compassionately at my son, who looked subdued, remembering what had happened later to his friend Ken.

Derek shrugged and said quietly. "I didn't stay dead and Ken, uh, was resurrected and…left town."

Jim didn't seem surprised at Derek's pronouncement but launched into reporter mode. "Well, Derek, it would seem that you're immortal like your father if you can come back from the dead. How does that feel?"

Before Derek could reply, Morry frowned in disapproval. "Really? That's just rude!"

"Once a reporter, always a reporter. What can I say, kid?" Jim smirked, and Morry looked as if he was about ready to hit him.

Before they could come to blows, Derek interjected. "Hey, it's alright, I'll just tell him and get it over with." He turned to Jim. "It was excruciatin'ly painful, okay? But I did heal up, and as you can see, I'm as good as new. Back off of this subject now; I don't want to keep relivin' it." He was practically gritting his teeth trying to keep control of his temper.

Briefly, Guinevere's compassion manifested and Jim apologized. "I'm so sorry. As I said, old habits die hard. I was going to write the article of the century, Merlin, about you and your family, but Guinevere's conscience would never allow me to do so. What a pity," he sighed. "I could have won a Pulitzer for that expose′."

He looked so depressed that I said facetiously, "Maybe you could write a novel about me coming to Moab."

Jim brightened. "Yeah, maybe I'll do that."

He thought I was serious. Ah, well, perhaps he would never get around to writing that novel. I looked searchingly into Jim's eyes, and for just a brief moment, the soul of Guinevere looked back at me.

"It's good to see you again, Gwen," I said softly.

"And you as well, Merlin, my old friend."

CHAPTER 55

May 12 Night

AFTER THE EVENING'S shocking revelations had given way to the enjoyment of a hearty meal, and thence to the camaraderie of after-dinner discussions, I quietly excused myself and sought the peaceful surroundings of my study. I closed the door behind me and breathed a sigh of relief. One would think that I would have more control over my family life, but that seemed to be one of the painful lessons that I'd had to learn—being a god in human form did not necessary give me that control.

I sat in my favorite spot for meditation, a little alcove I had created in the corner of the room with a firm cushion for my buttocks, a plush pillow at my back, and an enchantment to subdue the light to dusk, no matter what time of day it was. I had one of my favorite CDs by Daniel May, *Feng Shui-Music for Balanced Living,* playing as background music, and I closed my eyes, letting go of all extraneous memories, thoughts and impulses. It was time to examine the enchantment I'd pulled from within Derek, so that I could take the next step towards somehow removing the black magic from Morry. It surprised me how much I loved that young man. As abrasive as he could be, he had wormed his way into my heart and soul and I knew I had to save him.

"It was great meeting you, Jim," Emily said sincerely as she shook his hand.

He grinned. "Thanks. It was good to meet you, too. And I appreciate being invited to dinner; it was delicious. I love meat loaf with mashed potatoes—it's one of my favorite meals."

"You're welcome. It's not every day that I get to meet Queen Guinevere of Camelot."

He shrugged. "Well, that was long ago, and I'm not the same person as I once was. My soul is the same, true, but I live in this time now, and in this body. At least now I remember who I was, and I'm thankful for that." He paused for just a second as if pondering the vastness of time and space that he had crossed to be in this place, on this particular night. Then, he shook off the slight feeling of melancholy engendered by that inner journey, and looked into her eyes and said, "Good night, Emily, you are one lovely lady." He glanced up at his friend. "Coming, Mordred?"

"Jesus, don't call me that! I'm not even the original one!"

"Maybe not, but no matter what your name is you're Merlin's grandson. That's huge."

Morry let go of his agitation and looked thoughtful. "You're right. I just haven't really processed it yet." He looked over at Emily and grinned engagingly, his gray eyes sparkling with life and a recently acquired good humor.

It was such a change from his usual grim attitude that Em couldn't help but smile in return and pull him into a tight hug. "I'm so glad you're part of the family, Morry. Your dad was my best friend for many years before I met and fell in love with Merlin, so you're important to me, too."

That admission was too much for him, and he blushed and stammered, "Uh, thanks. I, uh, I'm still kind of confused about the whole thing, but I guess it's starting to sink in—the magic, the immortality, the link to King Arthur, even my friend having the soul of Guinevere!" He gestured at Jim. "That's pretty strange, but it shouldn't surprise me, considering everything else going on with this group." He gave a short bark of laughter and leaned over to give his step-grandmother a quick kiss on her smooth, young cheek.

"I'd better go—I've got to get up and go to work early tomorrow."

"We all do," she said dryly, "but getting together spontaneously seems to be a common occurrence with us, work night or not, so get used to it.

"And don't forget about tomorrow night!" she reminded the two men as they tramped out the door and into the warm summer night. They had to walk back to town since their vehicles were still on the street in front of Moody's Tavern, but it should take them less than fifteen minutes if they hustled.

She closed and locked the front door, then turned and walked thoughtfully back into the kitchen, where her mom and Derek and Sarah were trying to convince her daughter to go to bed.

"No, I don't *want* to go to bed yet!" Lumina exclaimed stubbornly, as she stamped her foot impatiently and folded her small arms over her chest. "I need to stay awake to help Daddy!"

Em frowned slightly. "Sweetheart, why do you need to help Daddy?" She hadn't previously sensed anything out of the ordinary from Merlin that would warrant her daughter's distress.

"Because, he's going to change *everything*," she said in her child's voice, but her face was solemn with an adult's worry.

Emily took a moment to focus more deeply on the emanations coming from the study and realized that Lumina might have a point. Her husband's thoughts had become unusually serious in the last few minutes. But she also knew that if Merlin needed, or wanted, their assistance, he would let them know.

Gently, she addressed her daughter's concerns. "Very possibly. But we need to trust him, sweetheart. He'll tell us if he needs our help."

"Are you sure, Mommy? I helped him before, when he couldn't get home after visiting God," she said, the goddess's spirit shining through her clear hazel eyes.

Recognizing that she wouldn't win this one, Em gave in. "Alright, stay up as long as you need to, but if Daddy tells you to go to b—"

Lumina interrupted hurriedly, "I know that Daddy's a god and I have to do what he says. I've always known that, even before I was born."

All four adults stared at her in shock, realizing that it was the goddess within her who had spoken.

As relaxed and supple as a large feline, I stretched as I emerged from contemplating the facts I'd gleaned analyzing the enchantment stored in my being.

Nimue. All along, it had been my old nemesis, despite the fact that her body had been destroyed at the end of the battle in July of the previous year. She and I had shapeshifted into birds and had attacked each other, eventually plummeting to our deaths. My soul had returned to the god realm and my body had been lovingly prepared for burial by my family and the knights. Nimue's soul had fled, and she had been decapitated to prevent her from returning to her body. I had come back to life and she had not, at least in her original body.

Now, it seemed apparent that prior to her death, she had set the stage for the current drama to unfold.

She had somehow manipulated her father, Beli, the Welsh god of death, into sending Derek and me back to the fifth century, to Camelot, thereby putting in motion a chain of events that would culminate in the destruction of Moab itself, along with its innocent human inhabitants.

Earth and the future of humanity would be at her mercy: Arthur would remain in limbo, unable to return as prophesied, and chaos would reign, just as she had hoped.

And she intended to accomplish this feat right under my nose, from within the body of our daughter.

Derek had suggested this hypothesis earlier and although I had denied it to myself, I'd suspected such a vile act all along. He and I had agreed that Adrestia's consciousness was most likely gone, having been supplanted by her mother's maniacal presence.

My poor daughter. Although my anger had long since been replaced by a cold determination to win this war of wills no matter the cost to myself, I vowed to avenge her.

I would go ahead with my plan to introduce my presence on earth through the story I would tell the next night, because I hoped that it would goad Nimue into reacting, but I would make one alteration to my presentation with Llyr's assistance. And I was adamant regarding my decision to have everyone present. Although my ultimate plan certainly included everyone's survival, the interim was going to be unsettling for me, and I wanted to see everyone's faces one last time.

Telepathically, I could hear Lumina rationalizing her need to stay up and help me, and I perceived the surprise and exasperation in Derek's mind when her inner goddess surfaced. I chuckled and spoke to him through our private mental connection.

Has you under her thumb, has she?

Yeah, you could say that. Her inner goddess is gettin' kinda uppity.

It's alright, Son, she's worried. I think she senses my plan and it's upsetting her.

Well, it's upsettin' me, too! I wish you didn't have to—

I interrupted his thought rather emphatically. *But I do, Derek! It can't be helped—this is the only way!*

But—

Derek, please, I beseeched him. I sighed and continued the silent communication, resigned to the magnitude of my decision. *I must. Please believe me that all will be well. No one will remember what transpires except me, and the gods, of course. I love you, more than you'll ever know.*

There was a rather long pause before his subdued reply. *I love you too, Dad.*

CHAPTER 56

May 13

THE EVENING'S SESSION started out very much like any other, except for the fact that I had insisted on the presence of my entire family and the knights, and I had persuaded numerous clients to attend who had become friends of a sort.

Sarah and Lumina sat near Derek, and Rae hovered in the back with those who had elected to stand—Emily, Morry, Jim, and the three knights of Camelot. Ryan seemed to suspect that something monumental was afoot, if his facial expression was any indication. I sent out soothing thoughts to everyone, but I wasn't fooling my wife.

Earlier in the day, when I had mentioned that we might need additional seating for our guests, she had suggested that we obtain some folding chairs from the equipment rental place in Grand Junction: I could teleport to their facility and enchant the employees, then teleport back to the shop with the number of chairs we required. According to Em, since a cataclysm would soon occur, it hardly mattered if we "borrowed" the chairs. I had sensed that she was being facetious, but was concerned about her state of mind. I had given her a long questioning look, and then turned to conjure the chairs we needed. A much more logical solution to the problem, I thought.

I remembered exactly what had happened once I'd finished setting up the chairs.

She had looked me in the eye and asked in a troubled voice, "Merlin, you're actually planning to go through with it, aren't you? We're all going to die tonight." She'd paused and rubbed her forehead as if she felt a headache coming on. "I haven't been able to read you since before you meditated last night, so I don't know the details. I hate it that you're not opening up to me." She'd been upset and angry, but I was resolute. I had to do it this way and it wouldn't help her to know the horrific details.

I had withheld my reply until the room was arranged to my satisfaction. I had taken one last look and then turned to her. She wouldn't meet my eyes until I gently cupped her face in my hands.

"Trust me, my love," I had whispered, kissing her lips gently one last time before Armageddon. She'd tasted as sweet as always and had returned my kiss enthusiastically. My body had responded predictably, and I had pressed against her, groaning with the urgency of my arousal. I'd decided we had enough time to make love before all hell broke loose, so I had teleported us to the bedroom at the top of the stairs. Impatient, I had willed our clothing gone and we'd tumbled onto the bed, clinging to one another. There had been no time for preliminaries, but she was ready, and I had entered her immediately. We had both gasped at the sensation as we frantically moved together, joined as deeply and completely as a man and woman can be. Our souls had merged and we knew we would be together for eternity, despite the very real threat of annihilation hanging over us.

I determinedly put aside my recollections of the afternoon and attempted to settle down. I was seated in one of the comfortable armchairs, in front of the attendees, who, for the most part, were silently and politely waiting, anticipating my tale. I made eye contact with a few of my favorite clients, and exchanged smiles and nods with many that I didn't know as well. There were quite a few more people here than had been invited initially, and I was pleased that I had provided extra seating.

These days I had quite the reputation for holding everyone's attention with my unusual stories of knights and feats of daring, fairies and shapeshifters, and as I closed my eyes to center myself, the murmur of voices stilled to a vibrant anticipation.

I could feel Derek's growing concern as he realized what my story would entail and how the evening would end. He tried to communicate with me but I blocked him—I would not be swayed in this, even by my son.

I took one more long deep breath and let it out slowly, then opened my eyes. I began to speak softly, telling the story I had never before revealed to anyone.

"The daughter of a Roman officer and a Welsh princess, Lilith Ambrosius was a tall, lovely girl, good-natured and friendly. She had long straight hair, black and shiny as a raven's wing, and her eyes were the brilliant blue of the sky on a clear, spring day. Her skin was as unblemished and translucent as fine porcelain, and her lips were full and soft. She had dreams of marrying the handsome son of the local chieftain and having his children, for he was everything she had ever wanted. And he felt the same way about her.

"Many times during the summer of her sixteenth year, they would sneak away down to the river and talk of their future life together. Making their plans, they would hold hands and steal a kiss or two. They yearned to explore each other's bodies but knew they must wait for the hand-fasting ceremony, for the gods frowned upon unsanctioned coupling.

"But alas, her young man was called away to fight, to battle the various tribes that threatened to overthrow his father's just rule. He promised her that he would return as soon as he was able. More than a year went by and she did not hear from him. She prayed to the gods that no harm would come to him, and as she was certain that they heard her prayers, she was content to wait. Another six months passed without a word, and then one day the chieftain returned with only a few of the brave men who had originally accompanied him. She searched among the warriors as they limped back into the city and her young man was not among them. Frantic, she sought out an acquaintance of her family who had returned with the chieftain and questioned him. Alas, she learned that the love of her life had been cruelly slain."

I paused for a dramatic moment, and heard a sympathetic murmur from many of the females in the audience, including the members of my family who had realized that I was relating a true occurrence. When it was silent once more, I continued.

"Lilith was so devastated that she turned her back on the Welsh gods, blaming them for not protecting her beloved. She then entered the convent of Jesus Christ, honoring the religion of her father's people. She was barely eighteen years old, but she knew her life out in the world was over, because the light of her life had been taken from her.

"One year after she had devoted herself to the Church, in fact, just after her nineteenth birthday, she began to have a recurring dream in which the gods visited her in her lonely cell, beseeching her to return to the Old Religion. And then, only one god came, an immensely tall, handsome god with long, wavy dark hair and kind eyes, and he would hold her in his arms and caress her, making her feel loved and wanted. Finally, one night, the god came and disrobed, revealing the most beautiful male body imaginable, sculpted and powerful, and he lay with her on her narrow bed, urging her to submit to him. She knew, even in her dream, that she would never be able wed and have children, so she removed her nightdress and thought, I want this. The god, hearing her thoughts, proceeded to caress her willing body, gently suckling her breasts and touching her intimately, until she knew great desire. He then coupled with her, claiming her virgin body, and as he moved within her she thought she would die from the pleasure he gave her. As they both climaxed, she hoped that this handsome god would plant his seed in her and that she would have a son who looked like her lover. And she knew she could ask for this since, after all, it was only a dream.

"Many nights thereafter, her god lover would come to her in her dreams, claiming her body, and she would beg the god to give her the male child she wanted so much.

"Then one night the god no longer came, and in the light of the day after, she realized that she was with child. And she knew that the god had really been in her bed and in her body, impregnating her.

"As the child grew in her belly and the other nuns saw what they considered to be a miracle, she was venerated and held in awe. And in the year AD 420, she was delivered of a healthy male child with hair as glossy black as her own and with the eyes of her god lover, and she decided to call her son Merlin."

I had originally written the story describing my own green slanted eyes, of course, but had immediately realized that as soon as I spoke the words, someone watching me might come to the conclusion that, as unlikely as it seemed, Michael Reese was Merlin. And that would not do—not *quite* yet. Although, did it really matter at his point, with destruction only minutes away? I shook off my momentary melancholy and continued.

"And of course, Lilith was no longer able, or willing, to stay in the convent and went home to her widowed mother, who immediately knew that her daughter had to have been taken by a god to produce such a child. And since everyone knew that the children of the gods were magical, they were not surprised when Merlin began to create fire from his hands and to transport himself magically from one room to the other. He could move things with his mind and was very intelligent as well, being able to read and comprehend an entire volume when still a child of five or six."

I could sense Lumina's glee as she realized that I had once been as young as she was. Telepathically, I sent her a gentle admonishment to keep her amusement to herself, which she did, with difficulty.

"As the years went by and Merlin Ambrosius grew older, the rumors of his unusual conception and birth, and the fact that he had no father, caused others to hate and fear him, and he was treated as a pariah. As always, his mother staunchly defended him, and thus she was outcast as well. The only thing that saved them from being stoned to death was the villagers' long-standing respect for Lilith's Roman antecedents.

"By the time Merlin was fifteen years of age, he had already reached a considerable height among the tallest of men, and his knowledge of the magic arts was known far and wide, many leagues beyond the village where he dwelled.

"King Vortigern himself, High King of all Britain, had heard of Merlin and bade his men to bring Lilith and her unusual son unto his presence. The king had spent many months in the north of Wales, at Dinas Brenin, trying to build the foundation for a mighty fortress, but every time the masons would complete the stonework, it would collapse. His seers declared that the gods were destroying the foundation because a proper sacrifice had not been made, and only the blood of a fatherless boy with magical abilities like Merlin would appease the gods and make the foundation of the fortress strong.

"Merlin realized he would have to convince the king that he was more important to him alive than dead, as he had no intention of being buried within the foundation of the king's new fortress. He assured the king that it was the underground springs that had heretofore caused the walls to fail, and that he could design an elaborate drainage system as well as an engineered foundation for the fortress, to ensure that the walls would stand even without a human sacrifice.

"King Vortigern agreed, and Merlin diverted the spring and designed a new foundation that would withstand any acts of nature.

"Eventually, Merlin was allowed to take his mother and return to their home, but alas, the stressful time had taxed Lilith's strength and she survived but a fortnight before her breath left her body and her spirit journeyed to the Other World.

"And at this time a king arose who recognized the skill and bravery of the young sorcerer and offered him a place in his kingdom. Merlin accepted his offer and traveled to King Uther Pendragon's land to serve him, and eventually, his son. And that is how Merlin Ambrosius came to serve the legendary King Arthur as the Sorcerer of Camelot."

As I ended the tale, I stood and took a bow as my audience clapped enthusiastically. I glanced at Derek and he looked so shocked that I reached into his mind to calm him. *It's alright, Son, I know what I'm doing. Nimue has to be completely convinced that I'm revealing myself so that she will activate the enchantment. The story is only the beginning. What happens next will convince her that I'm serious.*

Dad, I—

A bright flash of light interrupted Derek's thought, and Llyr was standing at my side as planned, regally dressed in a magnificent golden robe. He was glowing with the brilliance of the god realm, in front of everyone in the room. I could sense the crowd's shock as recognition of not only Llyr, but of myself spread through the room and the details of my story suddenly made sense.

I looked from one face to another as wonder and disbelief reflected in their eyes.

No one stirred as Llyr began to speak in his deep, resonant voice.

"Myrddin Emrys, it is time: The one God has sent me here to sanction your final step to full manifestation as the god of magic and healing." A collective gasp echoed throughout the room at his pronouncement. As he held his hand high, a lambent glow surrounded me and I felt the strength of my god powers flood through my being unchecked. My joy was a living thing, unbound, pure and intensely real. A deep blue robe of the finest weave appeared on my body, and my hair, which had become a luxuriant mane of shining ebony, was held in place by my old silver circlet. My head thrown back in ecstasy, I rose several feet in the air, and I heard a collective sigh, gasps of awe and someone whispered, "Oh my God, it's true, Michael *is* the real Merlin, and he's the god of magic!"

I could feel my body growing until I was actually larger than Llyr, taller—six feet nine inches. And this body was not a construct, it was real, so unlike Llyr, I could continue to dwell here, in this realm. Unfortunately, it was not possible, as I knew this was all for show, and that we would all be gone shortly.

I allowed myself to settle back to the floor and opened my eyes. I still felt like Merlin but I knew I was so much more. I heard a whimpering sound and glanced towards my family. Being seven inches taller changed my perspective, and it felt strange.

Emily and Derek, who were already my devotees, were kneeling, heads bowed. Sarah was on her knees but looking up at me in wide-eyed adoration, and Morry—well it was my grandson who had whimpered, apparently terrified and shaken. I beckoned to him and he stepped towards me, tears flowing freely, his glasses fogging up. He pulled them off impatiently and threw them aside.

"Mordred, look into my eyes, Grandson, and know that I love you—I would never intentionally hurt you." In my own way, I was apologizing for what was to come in the next few minutes.

As he hesitantly raised his eyes to mine, his body shook with fear, and I regretted that all the strides he had made recently in accepting me seemed to be for naught. But then he surprised me. Never taking his eyes from mine, he knelt carefully in front of me, and then gently placed his forehead on my feet. He sighed deeply, a sigh that came from his heartfelt acceptance of me as his god. And thus, my fifth devotee was created. How I wished that he could remember this…

I closed my eyes for a moment, basking in the white light and love that pervaded the scene. I smiled beatifically as silenced reigned.

Something caused me to start slightly almost as if I was awakening from a deep sleep, and I opened my eyes. I glanced around the room and realized that time had been halted, Llyr was gone and my body had returned to its normal size. A presence caught my attention: The figure of my daughter Adrestia stood still in the back of the room, a miasma of evil intent radiating from her familiar form.

"Well, there you are. I wondered when you would make an appearance," I said coldly. There was no point in further subterfuge. This was my enemy, not my daughter; had not *been* my daughter at any time since the battle at Matheson Preserve this past twelve-month. I addressed Nimue, the only being in all of my long life that I truly despised.

"What possible excuse do you have for taking our daughter's life for the sake of your own nefarious purposes? Or for making our grandson's life a living hell?"

She smiled and the magnitude of the darkness behind her expression chilled my soul.

"Why, I thought by now it would be quite obvious. Power. Once the world is rid of you and your pathetic excuse for a family, Arthur will never return and I will have control over all of humanity." She casually stalked forward, in the same revealing costume she had been wearing when I had ended up in the Hell realm months ago. Three-inch heels made her taller than her normal five feet seven inches, and her shapely body hinted at forbidden delights. I was sickened by this display, more so than the first time I had witnessed her depravity. I knew that my daughter would be horrified at this criminal misuse of her body.

"What makes you think that the one God will stand for this flagrant disrespect for his Creation?"

"What makes you think he actually cares, Merlin? He hasn't stopped my father, Beli, from his continual disruption of the god realm, as you'd hoped he would, has he? And he's made no effort to stop me. What makes you think you can?" she taunted me viciously.

I could feel her powers building within her and I knew that she had taken the bait; she was going to unleash all the destructive power of the black magic within Mordred's very DNA.

I took one last look at everyone I loved as Nimue disappeared from the room and triggered the explosion.

I experienced the blast in slow motion as The Moab Herbalist and every one of its occupants, my family and me included, were completely incinerated. With a flash of light brighter than the sun and a millisecond of the most agonizing pain I had ever felt, life was snuffed out.

As my liberated soul rose into the warm evening air above ground zero, leaving pain and the human realm behind, I sensed that the blast had completely destroyed several city blocks in each direction from the shop, leaving a gaping, smoldering crater. The resultant shock wave had leveled the rest of downtown Moab. Power was out, of course, but there was a muted red glow in the sky, evidence of the many fires burning throughout the devastated town. Sirens began wailing from peripheral fire stations far enough away to have avoided the worst of the blast, a sickly mechanical sound that couldn't begin to convey the true effect of the tragedy. Even though I was pure spirit, I experienced a jolt of emotion that everything and everyone I had loved in this town was gone.

I felt it as thousands of human souls departed this earthly plane to reunite with their Creator, and I departed for the god realm, my plan set in motion.

Myrddin Emrys, what you propose is not allowed, bro. Llyr was always a stickler for the rules until I could convince him otherwise.

I have no choice, old friend, for I must save my grandson. Nimue must not win, even if the cost is the relinquishment of my life on Earth.

At the moment, you have no life on Earth, as your body is gone, along with your entire family; including the grandson you are so anxious to save. The town you lived in is history as well.

True. But the nature of time, especially from our perspective, is rather flexible, is it not? And I believe you were able to glean the information I require at the exact moment of the blast?

Yes, to both questions. So you're planning to rewind time and repair the damage, so to speak?

Indeed, with God's assistance—and yours, Llyr.

Well, alright Myrddin Emrys, as usual you get your way, as you have for millennia. Hmm...I think you have just accomplished the impossible, considering that you have no real face here in this realm of pure spirit.

Oh? What do you mean?

You're smiling, bro.

CHAPTER 57

May 13 Redux Morning

I SLOWLY OPENED my eyes and saw the white ceiling above me, and realized that I was in our room, in bed with my wife. Time had been reset—it was again the morning before the debacle. I took a long, deep breath, appreciating the air in my lungs, and gave a silent thank you to the one God. I had succeeded. I turned my gaze to the woman next to me and smiled. Her hair was mussed and her lips were slightly parted as she sighed in her sleep. She was the most beautiful woman I had ever seen.

As if she knew I was watching her, Emily awoke. She stretched luxuriously, then turned to me with that early morning look in her hazel eyes that told me she wanted to make love, and my emotions suddenly caught up with me. I wept for joy, knowing she was alive again. All of the tears that I hadn't been able to shed previously, due to being in spirit form, now flowed in what seemed like an unending river and I sobbed uncontrollably.

"Merlin, my God, what's *wrong*, love?" Em's seductive look morphed into one of extreme consternation at my unusual display of emotion. She grabbed a tissue and gently blotted the tears from my face.

I reached out and pulled her into my arms, holding onto her so tightly that she began to squirm.

"Hey, easy, big guy, I can't breathe!"

"I'm sorry, wife, but I can't believe you're really here," I said, my voice thick with emotion. I loosened my stranglehold somewhat but continued to embrace her.

She looked puzzled. "Where else would I be?" She stroked my face lovingly, then ran her hands through my thick black hair and brought my face to hers. We kissed each other deeply and I felt as if our bodies would melt into one another. Rolling her over and then covering her lush body with my own, I reached between us and stroked her intimately until she sighed and tilted her pelvis, inviting me to enter her. As I slid into her welcoming heat, my thoughts were only of the connection that we shared; a connection that I couldn't live without. I groaned with ecstasy as the flames of our attraction to each other consumed us.

After we had finished and lay next to each other, our heartbeats slowed to normal, and everything came rushing back into my consciousness. I think I had already changed history. This morning, that is, the first time around, I remembered that we had made love, but Emily had been the instigator of our lovemaking session, with her body covering mine, and it was a gentle fulfillment compared to the inferno we had created this time. Would the change in the intensity of the loving affect the rest of this temporal do-over? And if so, would it change the outcome? Probably not. I grimaced as I thought about the task ahead of us this night.

"Okay, what's going on? Your mind is pretty much closed to me and I want to know why." She sat up and leaned towards me, concern and determination clear on her pert face.

I truly didn't want to tell her, but I knew that she needed to know the truth to help me with my plan. So I looked compassionately into her trusting eyes and opened my mind to her…

A few minutes later, I held her head as she vomited violently into the toilet bowl. Déjà vu, I thought wryly. She had done the same thing the day before the battle at Matheson Preserve, even though for an entirely different reason, and it seemed like an omen.

I had not spared her the horrendous details of our demise as I allowed her to witness everything that had happened in the original scenario—and *would* happen again, if we failed to excise the evil from my grandson at just the right moment.

Em finally pulled herself together and we showered. Refreshed bodily and in a bit calmer frame of mind, we dressed, and then sat together on the bed, neither of us quite willing to proceed with the day. We could both sense our daughter stirring in her room, and I heard the toilet flush in the hall bathroom and knew that Rae was up. And it would be only a matter of minutes before Derek joined us for morning coffee, so we needed to get going, but I was reluctant to move.

Emily sighed. "I know that Lumina is destined to grow older each time her inner goddess helps you, and what you're planning will cause another growth spurt, but I don't see that we have any choice. Even if we accepted the fact that our family was *fated* to perish, it would be unthinkable that the entire population of Moab join us in death. And we know that your true destiny is to pursue the quest for Arthur, so obviously your coming back in time to make things right, by preventing the destruction, was also destined. I presume that you did foresee this happening, in just this way?"

"Yes, love, I did, and everything has gone according to plan so far. I had to goad Nimue into releasing the black magic within Morry's cells in order to discover the details of the enchantment she used originally. Llyr assisted me by collecting the information at the instant the detonation occurred, so I should be able to effectively reverse the spell—with everyone's help. But I didn't realize how emotionally devastating this experience was going to be."

"What you showed me was terrible; I'm glad I don't actually remember it."

I reached out for our daughter's consciousness and she confirmed that she did remember going "home." She did not remember the horror of the blast, for which I was eternally grateful.

I'm alright, Dad, don't worry. I asked *to be here with you.*

Emily's eyes widened as she heard Lumina's telepathic admission. She turned to me and whispered, "Her goddess?"

I nodded briefly and tried to stifle my dismay; I sensed the real reason she seemed so much more mature than before the blast. But I intended to keep the truth from Em at least for a few more minutes.

The two of us were in the kitchen getting the coffee started when Rae appeared, yawning widely.

"Good morning, Mom, how did you sleep?" Em glanced at her mother as she reached for the coffee mugs.

"Oh, fine, but I'll be glad of the coffee." She raised an eyebrow at me and I took the hint, flicking my hand at the coffee maker, which finished filling the glass carafe rather more quickly than the manufacturer intended.

As if he had smelled the aroma from his house, Derek materialized next to me and held out a mug that had the words, "The Moab Herbalist" printed on it. I still hadn't ordered any more of them, and I was happy to see that he had one.

I filled his mug as we greeted each other, and opening my mind to him, I informed him about what had happened in the previous reality. For just a moment, he reeled from the shocking details, but he quickly adjusted and asked me what needed to be accomplished before the scheduled event this evening. I had just organized my thoughts and was preparing to answer him when I noticed Emily's stillness. She had paused in the midst of taking a sip of coffee, and despite her recent statement that she understood this might happen, her eyes widened in disbelief as Lumina stepped into the kitchen. I had a startlingly vivid flash of déjà vu as I turned and saw a girl of twelve standing in the doorway, naked except for the woefully inadequate blue and yellow baby blanket.

"Hi, Mom and Dad. I, uh, I guess I grew again," Lumina confessed sheepishly.

Rae gasped, and Em fumbled her mug, splashing hot coffee everywhere. Her hand shaking, she carefully set it down on the counter, then stood still, speechless, as our much-older daughter attempted to comfort her.

"Look at it this way, Mom, at least I'm skipping some of the difficult stages," Lumina said brightly. As she patted her mother's shoulder solicitously, she turned to gaze at me with a degree of wisdom seldom found on a twelve-year-old child's face.

I continued to stare at her, but realized how rude I was being. "Please forgive me, Daughter, but I hadn't realized that losing your body and then experiencing a time reset would trigger additional growth."

"I know, Dad. Believe me, it wasn't my idea, but Grandpa Llyr said I had no choice. I'm kind of scared, though. What if I just keep growing older? I don't want to die before I've even lived," she wailed.

"Lumina, you can't die, sis, you're immortal." Derek reassured her. He reached out and drew her into his arms, kissing her cheek and patting her back. She was going to be close to his height when she was full grown; even at this stage, she was her grandmother's height of five feet eight inches.

It was obvious to me that she was uncomfortable being held in her adult brother's arms in such a state of undress, so I encouraged her to return to her bedroom while her mother found her something to wear. She nodded and immediately disappeared.

Derek's arms fell to his sides and he whispered, "Holy shit."

Emily shook herself out of her stupor, took a deep breath, and left the room without looking back.

Rae watched her daughter leave the room, and then turned to me with a pained expression on her face. "Did you know about this, Merlin? Being who, and what you are, I mean?"

"I sensed it, yes, but I could not affect the outcome. It is Lumina's destiny; part of the bargain she made with God in order to be born into my family here in this realm."

Despite the fact that Rae was aware of my true identity, this information was so shocking that she sat down abruptly, and then stared up at me mutely.

I glanced at Derek and decided that my original plan to go out to breakfast would have to be revised. "Would you and Rae mind being in charge of breakfast preparations? I think we'd better eat here at home, in light of recent developments."

Even though he wasn't enthusiastic about cooking, Derek agreed to make a batch of pancakes and fry up some bacon, and the two of them proceeded to get the meal started.

After thanking them both for their help, I teleported into the hallway outside of Lumina's room, and carefully announced my presence telepathically.

Come in, Dad, Mom's still trying to find clothes to fit me.

I opened the door and stepped into her bedroom. "Who are you?"

She looked up at me from where she sat on her bed, and frowned in confusion. "What do you mean? I'm your daughter, Lumina."

"But which goddess are you?"

"Isn't it obvious? I'm the goddess of light; well, one of them anyway, a minor one." She looked slightly embarrassed.

"Roman?" I insisted.

Bewildered, her eyes filled with tears. I had pushed too hard, too soon.

"Never mind, love, we'll figure it out later." I sat down next to her, drawing her into my arms and kissing her forehead. "I'm sorry I upset you."

"All I've ever wanted was to be near you, Myrddin Emrys, to serve you," she whispered.

And suddenly, I remembered a spirit who had unobtrusively followed me around in the god realm for thousands of years, and I knew who my daughter's goddess was.

Emily stood in the doorway with an armful of her clothing, observing her husband holding her now-twelve-year-old daughter, and she could feel the tears welling in her eyes and trickling down her cheeks.

God, Merlin, this is awful! I thought I could handle it, but now, when I'm actually faced with the reality of it... she cried silently, on their private mental wavelength.

He gazed at her calmly over the top of Lumina's dark head and smiled. *You'll get through it, my love, and everything will be as it should be; just have faith in me.*

Em smiled tremulously as the brilliant light of Merlin's god powers encompassed Lumina, and her love for them both banished the fear and sadness inside of her. How could she ever doubt him? He was everything to her and she worshiped him with all her heart and soul.

"Breakfast is almost ready," Derek called from the kitchen. She could hear the rattle of the plates and utensils as Rae began to set the table.

Merlin got up off the bed and walked towards the door, where he paused, turned to Emily and said softly, "Take your time, sweetheart." He caressed her cheek and kissed her, and then left her to help Lumina find something to fit her, now that she was almost as tall as her mother.

"Did you know that she was gonna grow again this soon?" Derek asked curiously, as he munched on a slice of crisp bacon. The meat looked delicious and I was hungry, so I selected a piece and ate it before I answered him.

"I suspected as much, but there was nothing I could do to prevent or postpone it."

"You're actin' awfully nonchalant about this. Do you remember her from the god realm when you were both in spirit form?"

"I do now," I admitted. "She was just a minor goddess, a young spirit who kept following me. I hardly paid any attention to her—I was ancient long before God created her."

"But who is she?"

"She is a minor Roman goddess of luminaries." Derek looked at me blankly. "You know, luminous celestial bodies?" I raised my eyebrows at his lack of comprehension. "Come on, Derek, didn't you ever study the ancient Greek or Roman cultures?"

"No, Dad, I never did," he said dryly. "And I never studied the Welsh gods in depth until you came along. So, sue me." He grinned mischievously, and I shook my head in disbelief.

Then he frowned in confusion. "Wait a minute. Why would a Roman goddess be hangin' around a Welsh god? I mean, technically, wouldn't she be older than you?"

I gave him a wry look. "Derek, I was the first god to be created, before there were people on Earth. Eons later, I became a Welsh god when the early inhabitants of Wales needed a deity, and began to define my attributes to fit the structure of their lives." I laughed at the look on my son's face. "Did you assume you had me figured out?"

"I…I guess I did." He looked chagrined.

"Well, you know what they say about making assumptions." I grinned as I took another bite of bacon. Then, I heard the sound of feminine voices, and my girls walked into the kitchen.

"We're starving; what's for breakfast?" Lumina asked enthusiastically. She was wearing one of Emily's old sundresses, which fit her quite well, although the bodice was a little loose since her breasts were considerably smaller than her mother's. The sandals were a little too big—we would have to make a quick trip to the shoe store as soon as we finished our meal. She had her long hair brushed back behind her ears, which were now noticeably pointed like Emily's; evidence of her Elven heritage.

I nodded to Derek to start serving the food. "Let's eat."

The five of us sat in the kitchen for a good hour after we had finished eating, the adults drinking coffee and Lumina having her hot chocolate, while we made our plans for the evening ahead; plans that depended upon split-second timing and the blessing of the gods.

CHAPTER 58

May 13 Redux Evening

I GLANCED AT THE CLOCK and then looked around the room calmly, noting that everything and everyone seemed the same as the first time around, with one glaring exception: Lumina was now a tall, twelve-year-old young lady instead of a six-year-old child. Emily and I had tried to prepare everyone in the group, but the reality was much more disturbing than the telling of it, and several people, including Sarah and the knights, stared at her in fascination.

I knew that the timing of our actions this evening was critical, and I had briefed all of the participants as to their roles, so I was concerned that some individuals were allowing themselves to be distracted.

Wary of the visitors present who were unaware of our magic, I broadcast a terse telepathic message to everyone involved with Morry's upcoming transformation.

Please, stay alert and focused, people! Morry, as soon as the furniture is rearranged, lie down on the table and close your eyes. Everyone else, move into position as we discussed. I shouldn't have to remind you that we only have one chance to do this, and failure is not an option.

I had considered changing plans and having no one here but our group, but the closer we conformed to the original night's scenario, the better. I had the place heavily warded, but I didn't want to take a chance on alerting Nimue to our course of action.

I intended to stop time at the appropriate moment, enchant the human attendees and teleport them out of the room, then proceed with the spell, which would destroy the black magic within my grandson at the cellular level. I would have to use my god powers to create this enchantment, orchestrating everyone's magic to affect the transformation. According to Llyr, I should be able to accomplish the task alone, but I had a gut feeling that having all of us link our unique magical energies would reinforce the spell's effectiveness.

As I had the first time around, I closed my eyes to center myself, breathing slowly and deeply. I could feel myself relax physically and mentally, yet, at the same time, my god powers were honed to a razor's edge. I took one more long deep breath and let it out slowly, then opened my eyes. I began to speak softly, telling the story of my beginnings once more to a captivated audience.

This time, when I concluded my tale, I could sense that Nimue, in Adrestia's body, was within seconds of making her grand entrance, even though Llyr had not yet appeared. I decided to go with it, despite being slightly out of sync.

Instantly, I executed the prearranged signal, stopped time for everyone but my group, and teleported all the human spectators out of the shop, complete with the memory that they had enjoyed the story and had spent some time conversing with me afterwards.

In the meantime, Jim and the knights had moved the furniture as instructed, then stepped back out of the way. Morry had settled himself on the hard surface of the table we usually kept against the wall for displaying pamphlets, flyers and newspapers, and everyone capable of magic had arranged themselves around the perimeter with their hands on his body.

I quickly took my place at Morry's head and gently placed my fingertips on his temples. Sensing his fear, I sent a calming wave of love into his mind. I then gazed at each of my devotees, in turn.

Emily was first to pledge her assistance. "I offer all of my magic, my love and my devotion to you, my husband, to use as needed to save Morry's life." Our bond sang with our love as I accepted her offering.

As Derek linked his considerable sorcerer's abilities with mine, he looked into my eyes and said in a clear, relatively unaccented voice, "All of what I am, I received from you, my father and my god. Use me as you will to save my son." The link between us was stronger than it had ever been as I acknowledged his contribution.

My mother-in-law, Rae, my third devotee, was next to declare her intentions. "My purpose in life is to serve you, my lord. Please accept my devotion and my magic to heal this boy." I nodded to her and one more link was forged in the chain of power.

Sarah's offering was as simple and heartfelt as her loyalty to Derek. "My life is yours to use as you will, Merlin." I added her strength to my own.

And finally, Lumina, whose inner goddess had been devoted to me long before she was born as my daughter, said, "Please let me help, Dad; my magic has always been yours to command." I smiled as I added her abilities as a goddess to the seething cauldron of power inside of me.

As the circle was completed, a golden glow connected us all as our combined magical powers flowed into Mordred's being. As the purity and strength of our consolidated energy collided with the black magic within his cells, bright blue sparks erupted from Morry's body and he stiffened, arching his back and screaming in agony. I reached deep into my soul and called forth the power of the gods themselves as I wove the enchantment to nullify the original spell. As I finished, for just a moment Morry's adult body wavered and was replaced by a newborn baby. Then, the white Light of the gods faded and revealed once again my grandson's adult form, whole but unconscious.

Silence reigned at the conclusion of the most stunning act of sorcery ever to have been performed on the planet. As I released my hold on Morry and opened my eyes, each person who had assisted me sank to his or her knees, acknowledging the god of magic and healing. I was glowing so brightly that they could barely see me, so I adjusted my aura, then smiled and said sincerely, “Thank you. You may rise.”

Very faintly, in my mind, I heard Nimue’s scream of frustration as she realized what I had done.

CHAPTER 59

May 13 Redux Evening

MORRY FELT HIMSELF SURFACING from a nightmare in which every cell in his body had been ripped apart and reformed. He breathed shallowly, afraid that the hideous pain he had experienced would return, overwhelming him once again.

A few breaths later, he was curiously calm, and with a sense of detachment, he wondered if he was finally healed. Although, perhaps the cessation of pain was due to the fact that he had actually died of the deep wounds inflicted by the transformation he'd been forced to endure. And since he couldn't feel his body at all, he was sure that was the most likely scenario.

But as he lay suspended in that semiconscious state, his memories began to return, reminding him that he was no longer a pathetic orphan—he was a sorcerer, a man with supernatural abilities. And with that realization, his power began to fill him, now unfettered by the chains of darkness, and a bright joy blossomed in the core of his being.

A familiar voice called his name and he opened his eyes carefully, blinking in the harsh artificial light of his grandfather's shop. He guessed he was alive, after all. He pulled himself into a sitting position with the aid of numerous kind hands, and he automatically reached for his glasses as he had done for the past eighteen years. They weren't in his pocket and he glanced around for them.

"Lookin' for these?" Derek walked up to his son with the spectacles in his hand. "I don't think you're gonna need them anymore." He grinned as he handed them to Morry, who tucked them into his shirt pocket.

"I'll just keep them for now." He couldn't explain the urge to hold onto the glasses that were now obviously superfluous—he could see perfectly well without them. Perhaps he feared letting go of the past, when so much of the future was an unknown quantity?

He looked around at the expectant faces of his friends and family: Sarah, Jim, Merlin and Emily, his aunt Lumina, Ryan and the rest of the knights; they were all beaming with joy, giddy with relief. But there was only one person he truly wanted to be with right now. He looked searchingly into his father's eyes and then grinned. Derek grinned back, and that's all it took to initiate a melding of their spirits and minds. As they clasped each other's forearms tightly and touched their foreheads together, Morry sighed, completely happy for the first time in his life.

When at last they pulled away from each other, they knew that their bond would never be severed. Everyone surged forward, excitedly offering good wishes and congratulations.

I stood off to the side witnessing this moving event that would change our family dynamic forever, and I was pleased at the change in Morry. I knew that it had been inevitable that his true nature was bound to emerge as soon as Nimue's deadly influence was removed, but his immediate and complete acceptance of his new reality was extremely edifying.

I waited for everyone to have a chance to congratulate him and then drew him aside. "Grandson, I'd like to talk to you privately if I may."

He turned to me with a smile. "Sure, Merlin, whatever you need." He confidently followed me into the back room and waited for me to speak.

I casually leaned against the counter where I normally created my herbal potions. "Well, how do you feel? Are you happy?" It was a rhetorical question as it was obvious that Morry was thrilled to finally have access to his magic.

He laughed. "What do you think?" His eyes became vague as he looked inside himself. Then, as if finding what he had been searching for, he closed his eyes, and his body shimmered and changed shape. A huge brown and gray wolf stood before me, silvery eyes displaying a human intelligence. His pink tongue lolled out from between a plethora of very sharp teeth, but his mouth was drawn up in an almost human grin.

I laughed aloud. "Very good, Grandson. I suspect that this is your specialty, as it is the first act of magic you have attempted. Can you shift to other shapes without returning to your human form first?"

Effortlessly, his form shimmered and he became in quick succession, a cat, an owl and a squirrel, and then returned to his natural shape.

A wide grin transformed his normally solemn countenance. His skin glowed with health, and utilizing his magic had altered his metabolism so much that the extra weight he carried had melted off with each successive transformation. His brown hair had highlights of blond and a few streaks of black and gray which hadn't been evident before, and his unusual gray eyes shifted to green then brown then blue and back to gray again.

He laughed and tossed his useless glasses into the wastebasket. "Dad was right, I don't need these anymore."

We stood still for a moment, looking into each other's eyes and acknowledging his new life.

Morry took a deep breath and let it out slowly, as if releasing all of the fear and pain he had suffered up to this point.

"How can I ever repay you, Grandpa, for everything you've done for me?"

"Oh, I'll think of something, Mordred," I said softly. Then, I noticed the look on his face and sensed that he had questions. "What is it?"

"I was just curious about my dad. His magic is so different from mine—he can't shapeshift at all. I realized that when we merged our beings earlier."

"No," I admitted. "He never has been able to; nor can he fly. But he is a very powerful sorcerer—don't underestimate him. Within a few days of finding out about his magic, he had mastered spells that normally take months, if not years of practice to perfect. And he was able to merge with my being and save me from Beli earlier this year. I never did explore that with him—too many things have happened lately—but one of these days he and I will learn more about his secret ability."

"Yeah, I could sense his strength. Shouldn't all of us have the same magic, though, since we're related?" Morry asked with a frown wrinkling his otherwise smooth brow.

"Not necessarily. Even normal humans are different from their parents. Some traits are inherited, of course, but the children are still separate beings."

"So Derek has some of your traits and I have some of his?"

"Yes, but remember that, because I am a god, my powers are not quite the same as yours or Derek's, even though you both have some of that god energy within you. Derek is actually half human, whereas you are only a quarter human." I smiled. "You are as much a demigod as your father is, do you realize that?"

Morry looked puzzled. "But I thought that a demigod was the direct offspring of a god?"

"Since you have such a unique connection with me, you have been included in the ranks of the demigods, at my request. I'm sure you'll make me proud, Grandson."

Morry blinked. "That's...amazing, thank you, I'm honored. You know, all my life I've felt different, in a way that I didn't understand. And it really is because I'm not like anyone else; I'm barely human. I'm relieved to know there's a reason." Then a thought occurred to him. "Wait a minute, I thought my great-grandmother—your mother, Lilith—was human? Doesn't that make you half human?"

I smiled wryly. "I always thought so, and wanted it to be so, but when I finally remembered that I was a god, that changed things. I may look and act human, but I'm really not. And you're only human through Derek's mother, Cara Pendragon."

"King Arthur's half sister; God, it's hard to comprehend that." He frowned. "Nimue, my grandmother—your enemy—wasn't she part human?"

"I believe her mother was one of the Fae, which I didn't find out until recently, so no, she was not." It felt strange to be referring to her in the past tense, when her essence still "lived," in Adrestia's body.

"So I'm part Fae as well."

I nodded.

Morry didn't ask anything further, so I acted on a whim and touched his arm.

We materialized at my favorite spot up on the Rim, overlooking the city of Moab, lit up as it always was at night. He smiled, completely relaxed and undaunted by the abrupt change in location, which was certainly different from the first time I had brought him here. We stood in the darkness, gazing across the valley, and I turned towards him, only to find him staring at me intently. I grinned crookedly and asked, "What?"

"You're so amazing, it seems impossible for you to really exist." He reached out and gripped my shoulder. "Thank you again."

"You are most welcome. You're my grandson and I would do anything for you. I'm just grateful that you're here, and alive."

I hugged him affectionately and he tentatively returned the gesture. "I love you, Mordred." He didn't answer, but tightened his hold on me. I knew it was still difficult for him to express his innermost feelings, but I'd never stop sharing mine.

"Well, shall we fly?" I asked solemnly.

He pulled out of my embrace and folded his arms across his chest. "Come on, Grandpa, you know I can't," he scoffed.

"Sure you can—with me." I renewed my hold on him and we lifted off.

CHAPTER 60

May 13 Redux Night — May 14 Early Morning

THE CELEBRATION WAS still going strong at the shop despite the absence of the guest of honor, when Derek suddenly felt as if someone had thrust an ice pick through his right eye into his brain, and he collapsed. Just before he lost consciousness, he heard Merlin in his mind urgently calling his name, and then there was nothing.

As he started to come around, he heard a female voice that sounded rather familiar, and a deep voice responding that reminded him of Llyr, only, it obviously wasn't Llyr. His grandfather had some class, and this guy sounded uncouth and not particularly intelligent on top of that. The only being he could think of who fit that description was Beli, the god of death. Where in the hell was he, that Beli would be present? He tried to speak, but his tongue felt thick and dry. His throat seemed constricted.

"So, he awakens. Merlin's son with that whore Cara, the tavern wench." Her strident voice, which initially reminded him of his sister, Adrestia, now bore overtones of the one who had tried to kill his father the previous summer—Nimue, the bitch from Hell, literally.

"What…do…you…want?" he whispered, enunciating carefully, feeling as if he had the worst hangover of his life. He knew he'd only had a couple of beers, so something else had caused the pain and nausea. He tried to glance around this place where he was being kept, but it was only partially lit by torches, which did very little to hold back the dark, and did nothing to illuminate the speaker. And where was Beli, or whoever the second voice belonged to? Sounds echoed and he got the impression of a large space with a high ceiling. If the other individual was still present, wouldn't he have sensed it or heard something? He tried to determine where he was in relation to the walls of the room or cavern, but he didn't have enough information to draw a conclusion. All he knew for sure was that he lay flat on his back on a cold uneven surface, with small sharp protrusions digging into his body. Although he didn't seem to be physically restrained in any way, he couldn't move no matter how hard he tried. It had to be magic holding him down and causing the horrendous pain in his head. He knew he had to escape, so he attempted to muster his power—and failed miserably.

"Uh, uh, uh, nooo you don't. No magic for you, my boy."

"What the *fuck* do you want, Nimue?" Derek forced the words past the obstruction in his throat. He felt faint with the effort it had taken to respond to her.

"Language, Derek. No need to be crude, my boy; you're just betraying your origins."

He coughed hoarsely and then swallowed with difficulty. "I'm not *your boy*, you vicious bitch, and I—"

Suddenly a piercing white light penetrated the darkness and Derek had to close his eyes to shield them from the brightness. There was only one being who could produce light like that, and when he heard a roar that filled the space with power, he knew that it was his father shouting Nimue's name.

"Ah, and he takes the bait—so predictable." Her sarcastic tone contained a note of satisfaction that scared the crap out of him.

God, no! Dad, watch out! he called out silently, and then choked as an immense pressure on his chest forced the air from his lungs. He lost consciousness again.

When I had sensed the attack on Derek, I had swiftly brought Morry back to the shop, only to find that my son had already been taken. Frantic to find his father, Morry wanted to accompany me, but with his powers so new and untested, I couldn't take the chance that he would also be compromised.

And I couldn't spare the time to explain the situation. Hopefully, he would understand and forgive me for leaving him behind.

Following the sense of evil left by the abductor's spell, and by using our father-son bond as a homing beacon, I transported myself to this unknown place. It was immediately apparent that Nimue had intended this as a trap, using Derek as bait. What she did not realize, was that I was much more powerful than I had been when we had faced off at Matheson Preserve a year ago. Since then, the full complement of my god powers had become available for me to use, but only in a time of great need. And this situation certainly qualified.

The space in which Derek was being held appeared to be a vast underground cavern, lit ineffectively by a few torches scattered haphazardly, so that the far corners were dark, and shadows wavered grotesquely. I didn't have the patience to play this game with her and allowed the Light of the gods to escape from my body as I shouted her name with all the force at my disposal. I heard her gloating laugh and snide comment, which was immediately followed by a telepathic warning from my son, just before Nimue slammed a bolt of magical energy down onto Derek's chest to silence him.

The brilliant white Light I had released created a surrealistic tableau in front of me: Derek spread-eagled on a slab of rock and my nemesis standing over him menacingly. As she turned to face me, the sight of my daughter's features twisted into Nimue's expression of hatred merely hardened my resolve.

Her satisfaction at having outwitted me turned to anger, and then to fear, as she finally realized that the power now at my command was vastly superior to her own. She knew that I intended to kill her.

But in that split second before I released a final deadly bolt of energy, destroying her forever, I realized that there might be a chance to recover my daughter's spirit. So, I altered my plans and used my god powers to put her into a state of suspended animation, until I could somehow rid Adrestia's body of her parasitic mother.

Using the illumination provided by my god light, I found a raised area in the back of the cavern on which to lay out her body, and then created a force field around her that would remain in place until I could find a way to retrieve the remnants of my daughter's spirit. As I straightened, I glanced around the huge space and then gazed towards the cavern's ceiling, and immediately sensed where I was. The cavern was beneath Balanced Rock, that notable rock formation in Arches National Park

I remembered the time, before Derek had come into his powers and neither of us knew I was his father, when he and I had driven around the park ostensibly looking for a "special luminescence" in caves or crevices. In reality, I had been searching for the portal to Avalon. When we had visited Balanced Rock, I had inexplicably felt my own energy signature on the rock formation; an energy signature apparently created in the distant past, a past of which I had no memory. The discovery had shaken me at the time. Now I knew how it would come to be there. We were in the past now, in Nimue's own lair, and the energy I had unleashed here today would be discernable far into the future. It also occurred to me that the portal I had seen under Delicate Arch last summer could very well be a doorway into this place and time.

I turned back to Derek's unconscious form and released his preternatural bonds, then instantly transported us back to Moab, to our own time.

Unfortunately, Beli was waiting for me there, his god powers ready to challenge mine. Having already been at odds for millennia, the fact that I had recently destroyed his physical form only increased his hostility towards me.

I avoided him long enough to deliver Derek safely back to the shop, where I gently placed him on the table that only a short time before had held my grandson. Everyone converged around him, swearing that they would protect him with their lives until he could recover from the ill-effects of Nimue's treachery. They had waited all night for news and were now anxious to hear what had transpired, a cacophony of their voices drowning each other out. I raised my hand in a demand for silence.

"I understand that you are all most anxious to find out the details of the night's adventure, but I'm afraid that will have to wait until after I face Beli," I said.

Sarah, holding Derek's hand while she stroked his hair, looked up at me in consternation. "But do you think he's going to be alright? Is there anything we can do besides wait for him to wake up?"

"He'll come out of it in his own time. Nimue knocked him out with some powerful magic, and it may take a few hours for him to regain consciousness."

"Grandpa, I want to help you fight this guy," Morry said, his face set in grim lines. His eyes, however, shone with the knowledge of his sorcerer's abilities, untried though they were.

"I also want to go with you to fight this evil, Dad! Please let me help you," Lumina pleaded.

Before I could answer either of them, my wife exclaimed, "That bastard! There is something terribly wrong in the god realm for this to be happening, I just know it! Merlin, I realize that my powers won't be enough in this situation, but I just want you to remember that I will be with you, in mind and heart, during this battle." Emily radiated tension and fear, but also an unshakeable determination to back me up through our bond, no matter what transpired this morning.

The outpouring of love and offers of assistance strengthened my resolve. "I thank you all from the bottom of my heart, but I need to take care of this myself. I will stay in communication with all of you telepathically as long as I am able to do so.

Now, I need to go, or the battle between us will be observed by anyone in Moab who happens to look up above the Rim."

Just as I departed from my shop, Beli summoned me. We met at the same location where I had destroyed his body. I was sure that this reminder of his weakness only served to escalate his fury.

I was so focused on his presence that I barely noticed that the sky had lightened, with dawn only minutes away.

"Beli."

"Myrddin Emrys."

I tried to maintain an even tone of voice, while I fought to control my temper. "There needs to be a resolution to our eternal quarrel. We have been at odds from time immemorial and the strife has to end. God himself supports my mission in this, the human realm. How can you justify the misery you have caused, not to mention the demise of your own granddaughter?"

"How can *you* justify the fact that the entire god realm revolves around you and your ridiculous desire to live a human life among these primitive creatures? You are not one of them and never will be—it is a sham. What difference could it make in a million years whether the human, Arthur Pendragon, returns to this physical plane?" Beli's words dripped with venomous sarcasm.

I refused to respond, and as Beli continued to rant, it was obvious that he had no idea what had transpired in the cavern beneath Balanced Rock. He had apparently grabbed Derek, delivered him into Nimue's hands and departed before I arrived.

"Your precious daughter was weak and easily displaced by Nimue, who now resides in that luscious young body. She has used it rather skillfully to placate the demons in the Hell realm, acquiring quite the reputation for fu—" The rest was cut off as I attacked him. I knew he had been baiting me, but at this point, I simply didn't care. My anger had control of me and I gladly gave it free rein.

We both leaped up into the air, drawing on our god powers, the energy swirling between us creating a vortex of immense proportions. Black clouds billowed unnaturally fast and covered the sky over Moab, sheet lightning leaping between them. The sound of thunder echoed continuously between the cliffs on either side of the valley. Winds of hurricane strength, evidence of my uncontained fury, whipped through Moab, uprooting trees and bringing down electrical lines. Normally, I would be concerned about the repercussions of unleashing such power among the mortal population, but I was past caring.

I felt my eyes turn as black as the clouds I had generated, and without conscious thought, I threw my head back and raised my arms, causing blue fire to explode out of my body in all directions. Somewhere in the recesses of my mind, I realized that the citizens of Moab were undoubtedly witnessing this display of supernatural wrath between two gods hovering over their town. To hell with it, I thought; I'm ready to reveal myself.

Despite my pledge to maintain mental communications with everyone at the shop, I hadn't done so; therefore only Emily, Lumina and Morry were fully tuned in to my thoughts when I proclaimed my readiness to reveal my god self to the world. Faintly, I perceived their cries of protest, and in the heat of battle, I ignored them. Much later, I would come to regret that decision.

My rage surged to engulf my senses, and I channeled all of my energy towards the god of death, whom I knew wasn't powerful enough to block such an onslaught.

In the split second before my blast of energy reached Beli, the vortex that swirled around us suddenly changed shape and became some sort of funnel reaching up to the heavens, and before either of us could react, we were both sucked into its blackness and I knew nothing more.

CHAPTER 61

WHAT HAPPENED TO ME? I thought, unable to do more than gasp for air and attempt to move my leaden limbs. Even that small bit of effort exhausted me and I lay back again. While the air was fresh and cool, redolent with the rich scents of vegetation and rain, the ground beneath me was wet enough to have soaked through my thin shirt, tunic and breeches. I shivered and wished I had a cloak to pull around me. Then I blinked, and the tall trees above me came into focus; lush, green leaves of birch and alder creating a living canopy overhead. It was apparent from the occasional bit of sky showing through the tree branches, and the shadows created, that it was late afternoon. The breeze capriciously lifted the wet leaves, allowing yet more moisture to drench me.

I heard a groan nearby and wondered if there had been some sort of catastrophe. Perhaps others had been affected as well.

Being a healer and an herbalist, I was naturally drawn to help those in need, so I forced myself to sit up, thinking to help the individual who was so obviously in pain. For a moment, my head hurt abominably and I felt as if it would explode should I move too quickly. Gradually, the pain subsided enough to allow me to turn my gaze to the man lying about six feet away from me.

He was quite large, bulky with muscle and perhaps a few inches taller than I was. A sinister-looking fellow with swarthy skin, long dark hair and moustache and rough appearance, I judged that he was about my age—early thirties. I saw no outward signs of injury, but thought it prudent to do at least a cursory examination. I was not sure how I would treat the man, though, if he was wounded, as I seemed to have lost the leather pouch of healing herbs and potions that I normally carried with me. I crawled the short distance to where he was sprawled out, and started examining him, careful to avoid any contact that might cause him distress. As I gently unlaced his filthy shirt and pulled it up, I saw nothing to indicate any sort of injury. I did notice that his torso was entirely hairless, which I thought to be most unusual. I myself had less body hair than the other men in my village, but compared to the man in front of me, I had quite a respectable amount of hair on my chest.

I finished with my examination and carefully pulled his shirt back down, re-lacing it. He should not notice anything amiss.

Nevertheless, the man was startled. His eyes flew open and he tried to scuttle backwards away from my touch. He moved rather quickly for such a big man.

"What are you about? Who are you?" He uttered the words in a deep voice with a noticeable accent that I could not place.

"I am, uh…" I frowned in confusion, horrified that I could not remember my own name. Then, a faint memory came to me and I blurted out, "Emrys, my name is Emrys." I paused. I had a feeling that there was more to it than that, but my memory was faulty, perhaps having been affected by the fall.

I frowned, and wondered what made me think I had fallen. I looked around me and could not see anything that would explain why I was there, or from *what* I had fallen. There was no evidence of any manmade structures, and gazing around the small glade yielded no useful information. Nor were there any horses or any sort of cart or wagon nearby. How strange.

I clambered awkwardly to my feet and looked around, hoping to see some kind of landmark that might let me know where we were. Just then, a ray of sunlight shone weakly through the leaves in front of me, partially illuminating a rough path. I followed it, walking stiffly down a slight incline towards what appeared to be a break in the trees.

As I pushed past a large yew tree, the ground in front of me suddenly dropped away sharply, revealing a sight that made me gasp in shock. I recognized the view, but for the life of me, I had no idea how I could have arrived at this place. Below the hill upon which I was standing, a hill I somehow knew to be called Tomnahurich, the forested land stretched for several miles—to a large body of water that would someday be called the Moray Firth.

I was in northern Scotland, or rather Caledonia, as the Romans had named it. I did not know how I knew this, but I was certain of the facts. Just as I was absolutely certain that I was not supposed to be here. I looked back at the man who was struggling to his feet, and I realized that there was something about him that seemed…familiar. Also, I sensed that there was enmity between us, and had been for a very long time. As he met my eye, it was apparent that he was aware of it, but neither of us spoke to the other.

As the large man joined me, we glanced at each other warily and then turned to gaze at a view that did not make sense to me. How did we get here and why? There was just the two of us here on this hillside; where were our families, our traveling companions, our belongings? I was wearing a wedding ring; therefore, I must be married. If that was the case, where was my wife?

Answers were not forthcoming, and we watched as the light slowly faded and the stars came out.

EXCERPTS FROM JOURNAL ENTRIES

Winter 2015

It has now been almost a year and a half since Merlin disappeared. Emily asked me to write this narrative to record everything that has happened since the day he and Beli were sucked into the vortex. Having been a writer most of my adult life, it made sense for me to narrate this journal; or at least to get it started and guide others in contributing to its pages.

None of us will ever forget that summer day when Merlin and Beli battled each other in the sky above Moab, revealing to the citizens of this fair city that magic was real and that the gods did exist. We were not actually present when the wormhole swallowed the two of them, so only the telepathic impressions left in Emily's, Morry's and Lumina's minds allowed us to piece together what actually happened. After he had regained consciousness, Derek was devastated, thinking that he could somehow have altered the outcome of the event. No one blamed him for what happened, but he blamed himself—and still does.

Later, when Llyr started visiting us on a regular basis, he was able to clarify things somewhat, and each time he appeared we all hoped that he had news of Merlin. Since he was Merlin's father and was himself a god, we had assumed—hoped—that he could tell us where his son was, and how we could get him back. But Llyr continues to keep his own counsel to this day, except to say that Merlin is well, and he will eventually return when the time is right.

Needless to say, we have not been satisfied by Llyr's responses to our questions, and we are trying to find Merlin on our own. We take turns meeting at our respective homes, brainstorming into the wee hours of the morning, hoping to come up with a plan.

Morry and I now share the cottage that he and Sarah had rented when they first came to Moab, and although it's small, we have done an admirable job of making it a pleasant place to live. Both of us still work at the newspaper, and we spend many hours on the Internet searching for any sign of magical occurrences here in town and around the world that might indicate Merlin's presence.

Derek and Sarah, of course, live in Derek's house on Doc Allen Drive. They swear they won't get married until Merlin returns. Derek continues to work at Arches National

Park as a law enforcement ranger, and Sarah works long hours at The Moab Herbalist with Emily and Lumina.

Emily, Lumina and Rae continue to live in the house across the street from Derek, and they finally landscaped the yard last spring as Merlin wanted, with plants native to the area, rather than the grass and trees Em had originally desired. Rae filed for divorce but Jack Crandall refused to sign the papers, swearing that he would do anything in his power to get her back. So far, nothing has happened, but Rae is still nervous that he will someday show up without warning.

The knights decided to give up their separate abodes and currently share a house on 400 East, not far from the Ute Motel, and, coincidentally, within a few blocks of Emily's old place. They insist that we meet there as often as possible, and they have turned their large dining area into a conference room. They apparently feel that they were derelict in their duty to Lord Merlin, but as I constantly point out to them, there really wasn't anything that they could have done to change the course of events.

All of us continue to support and care for one another as Merlin would have wished, and we have not given up hope of his return.

Emily has promised that she will write a few words later on in this narrative, for which I'm grateful. Her experiences resulting from that tumultuous time will be a priceless addition to this journal. Derek also will provide some insight into the current situation by writing a few paragraphs.

And, on a more personal note, I have finally accepted that my soul is still seeking to rejoin my king, although as a heterosexual male this time around, I'm not sure how that will transpire. In any case, I have wholeheartedly dedicated myself to the quest to bring Arthur back from Avalon. And although I realize that Merlin wasn't serious when he told me I could write of his experiences in Moab, I have decided to do it anyway. It seems like the right thing to do.

Respectfully Submitted,

Jim Singleton, aka Guinevere Pendragon

~~~~~~~~~~~~~~~~~~~~~~~~~~~~
~~~~~~~~~~~~~~~~~~~~~~~~~~~~

When Em suggested that I help Jim write this narrative, I wasn't sure what the hell to say, other than the fact that I miss my dad so damn much. It's incredibly frustratin' not to be able to sense him—anywhere. And I've tried. God, I've tried. I know he's alive, but that's all.

Havin' my son Morry here has helped me get through this. He forces me to keep goin'. We've spent many late nights tryin' to figure out where—and when—Merlin could be, and we still haven't got a clue.

It still seems bizarre to have a son only a few years younger than I am, but I don't know what I'd do without him; he's become a real friend. It's been kinda excitin' helpin' him to learn how to use his powers—all except the shapeshiftin'. I've never been able to do that, so I can't really help him there, but he's a natural at it. My son the shapeshifter; how amazin' is that?

I've been thinkin' about callin' Adam Gonzalez and enlistin' his assistance—and maybe his family's—in tryin' to find Merlin. They were involved in the battle last year, and maybe I could convince them to help. But then I remember that Adam's brother Alex was killed in that battle, and I wonder if I have the right to ask them to make any more sacrifices.

My grandfather, Llyr, has spent some time with me, helpin' me fine-tune my own sorcerer's skills (includin' the use of the staff Merlin gave me), and I'm hopin' that I'll come up with some magical way to find my dad.

One day, when my curiosity got the better of me, I finally asked Llyr how he made the people in town forget what happened up on the Rim that day. Scared the hell outta me that people were gettin' an eyeful of two sorcerers—gods—gettin' down 'n dirty with some pretty impressive magic. Turns out that God gave Llyr instructions, and the temporary powers, to erase everyone's memories of that mornin'—except for everyone in our group, of course. I was kinda leery that it wouldn't work and everyone I know would be confrontin' me when they realized it was "Michael Reese" up there in the sky, throwin' energy bolts. But no one's said a thing, thank God.

My sister has been amazin'. After all the magical energy she'd expended at Morry's transformation, we all thought she'd end up an adult, but she only grew another few years older. Now she's agein' naturally, and she just got her learner's permit. We're all pretty proud of her. I mean, she's really not quite two years old, but in the eyes of the Moab community, she's almost sixteen. The fact that there's no paperwork to prove she exists has been a real problem. We've had to use magic several times to provide various government offices with "official" documents, but it's worked out okay. She wishes she could go to school like other kids, but there's no way—what if somethin' triggered her growth process and she aged right in front of a bunch of mortal kids? We'd have Llyr down here wonderin' what the hell we were thinkin'.

Recently, Em got pissed off and blew up at everyone durin' one of our meetin's. Accused us all of losin' faith. She was right. She thinks Merlin's trapped in the past somewhere, and that's as good a place to start as any. I got to thinkin' again about the nature of time, and that it wasn't linear. Maybe, just maybe, we can make that work in our favor...

Respectfully Submitted,
Derek Emrys Ambrosius Colburn

~~~~~~~~~~~~~~~~~~~~~~~

I asked Jim if I could write a few paragraphs, and he agreed that my perspective might be useful.

I haven't mentioned this to anyone but Derek, but I feel somewhat responsible for what happened to my grandfather. It seems so unfair that this should happen to him, after all the effort he's expended on my behalf. He was so angry that my grandmother Nimue, and her father, the god Beli, had conspired to use my
~~~~~~~~~~~~~~~~~~~~~~~

life to bring an end to his quest. I know that it wasn't my fault that I was born the way they had planned, as a living bomb, but...

Well, I guess it won't do any good to dwell on all that. I'm here, the darkness is gone from my being, and my magic has fully manifested. And I hereby dedicate whatever abilities that I have to finding and bringing Merlin home.

I think my dad may have a point about the shape of time—maybe we can actually, I don't know, fold it and step through? I guess we'll have to figure that out. I hope.

Respectfully Submitted,
Mordred "Morry" Colburn

~~~~~~~~~~~~~~~~~~~~~~

Jim, Derek and Morry have all worked on this journal, and now, apparently, it's my turn. I'm working at the herb shop as usual, and right now I'm on a break, so I'll grab a pen and this journal and just start writing.

I'm watching my daughter as she rings up a sale, and I still can't believe she's not even two years old yet. Of
~~~~~~~~~~~~~~~~~~~~~~

course, the clients see a pretty, teenaged girl with long wavy dark brown hair, five feet nine inches tall and slim as a reed, but I see the tiny baby I held to my breast for such a short time. I love her as she is, of course, but I miss that little baby so much.

Thank God for my mom—I don't know how I could have coped without her support. I know Derek, Sarah and Morry are here and I love them dearly, but sometimes a girl just needs her mother.

Not long after Merlin disappeared, Mom suggested, in case someone asked, that I call Lumina my niece, here visiting us until "Michael" gets back. It has worked so far; no one's questioned her presence. As long as she doesn't mention her last name, I think everything will be okay.

God knows what the regular customers make of my husband's absence. Maybe they think he's abandoned us like so many deadbeat dads do these days. That bothers me, since I know he would never do such a thing.

I miss Merlin so much that my heart aches constantly, but I still feel his presence in my mind and deep in my soul, so I know he still exists—somewhere. I feel very much like I did when he and Derek were transported back to Camelot, so I suspect that he must be stuck in the past. I wonder where he is and if he even realizes who he is. Or what he is.

I've mentioned it a time or two during our frequent meetings, that I think he's in the past somewhere, and as you can imagine, that causes quite a stir. Unfortunately, it never lasts long since none of us know exactly what to do about it...

...Sorry, it's been awhile since I wrote anything; guess I'd better get back to it! Our meetings have become increasingly sporadic recently, as if the consensus is that Merlin is probably not coming back.

The other night, I finally got fed up with the defeatist attitude, and I lost my temper. Surprised the hell out of everyone, because I've always tried to be calm and easy to get along with. Well, screw that! And for the record, I am pissed off that my father-in-law is being so reticent. I'm positive he knows way more than he's saying. I have a feeling that the whole damned god realm knows what's going on, which is fine and dandy, but they have forever, and some of us can't wait that long!

I just wish Merlin would come back...

Respectfully Submitted,

Emily Crandall Reese (Ambrosius)

P.S. I found Merlin's beaded headband today, tucked into one of the storage compartments at the shop. God knows how it got there. I gave it to Lumina to use as a hairband and she's thrilled to have something of her dad's. She promised to give it back to him when he returns...

~~~~~~~~~~~~~~~~~~~~~
~~~~~~~~~~~~~~~~~~~~~

It's almost midnight on Christmas Eve, and I had to sneak this out of Mom's room. I hate to go behind her back, but she won't let me have the journal, and I need to read it, and then add something of my own.

God, I can't stand it when she cries herself to sleep. Something has to be done, and soon, for all our sakes.

I think everyone forgets that I'm not just a teen-aged girl, I'm the daughter of the god of magic. I'm also the goddess who spent thousands of years following him around in the spirit realm, so we have a connection that no one else has. My name is Lumina for a reason—the light inside my being can illuminate the path ahead, and maybe it can guide my father back home to us. It's worth a try. Nothing else has worked and it's way past time to find him. I helped him before and I intend to help him now. Somehow.

Respectfully Submitted,
Lumina Rae Ambrosius

ABOUT THE AUTHOR

Caryl Say is a writer based in Moab, Utah. Her series, *Merlin in Moab*, which began with *The Heart of Magic*, continues Merlin's epic adventure in *God of Magic, Child of Light*. Caryl is an avid reader of several different fiction genres, including fantasy, science fiction, mystery and paranormal fiction. Among her favorite authors are Diana Gabaldon, Sherrilyn Kenyon, Keri Arthur, Sharon Shinn and Jim Butcher, just to name a few. She loves to hike in the magical red rock country of southeast Utah, and regularly visits both Arches National Park and Canyonlands National Park.

Caryl loves to travel, and has been to the British Isles several times in the past few years.

You may contact her at carylsay.author@gmail.com, or visit her on Facebook: www.facebook.com/AuthorCarylSay. If you liked her stories, please review them on Amazon.

Made in the
USA
Lexington, KY

55403567R00245